THE FOOT POST

By

William J. O'Shea

1stBooks – rev. 6/27/01

Chapter 1

Dead people and a beautiful day do not mix. Or at least they shouldn't. But in Chicago the weather is never the same for more than a day or two and people die all the time. It had just been such a nice day. And these people should not be dead.

Today had started out like any other day, slowly. No pressure to do anything other than walk up and down the street, doing whatever I felt like doing. The sun, at this time of year was as strong as in late August and I had crossed over to the east side of Clark to absorb some of the bright yellow rays. I still can't say how I got started walking up that way or what made me look in that window.

This was an old section of Chicago. Changing all the time, but not dramatically. The buildings on this north end of Clark Street were rarely over three stories, no two in a row the same. A commercial street, every establishment announcing their business with painted signs, or neon lights. These little shops and stores created a canyon of red and brown stones that wound it's way down to the Loop. I had been working on this street for over three years now. I didn't own it, not by contract or deed, but it felt like it was mine. It was as though the pavement rose up to meet my foot when I took a step, like in the old Irish blessing.

It might have been the warm breeze, coming from the south, that gently blew me northward. If so, it had been a devious zephyr, not giving me any indication that it would switch around and blow ill. Nothing had seemed to be out of place. I didn't have a feeling or a premonition that would warn me of danger. Now the danger was past.

At the moment there was something wrong with my eyes. They had defied me and were filling with tears. I couldn't see very well, the papers strewn on the floor behind the counter were unreadable. The figures printed on them were square and strange. I knew they were written in a different language, but it didn't register at the moment. I looked up and tried to focus. The photographs taped to the green, finger stained wall above the work table were just a blur. My chest tightened, I knew the people who were pictured there, smiling brightly. I tried to ask a question but the words caught in my throat.

After squeezing my eyes closed until I could see sparks inside the lids, I opened them hoping not to see the same gruesome scene. I really didn't want them to focus. I didn't want to look at the stained carpet or the bandanna, folded up, lying there next to the foot. His foot stuck out from behind the counter at an unnatural angle, there was a worn brown loafer and a stretched out blue checked argyle sock on it. Before it all became too clear, my eyes thankfully stopped seeing again.

As I lost my vision the sounds in the room became clearer. The squeak of leather came at me from every direction. The heavy sighs and muttered curses were distinct. The shuffling of feet grated on my ears. I could hear radio static, radio voices on the air, a door closing in the back and a composed voice speaking quietly somewhere in the room.

Taking several deep breaths only brought the oily smell of leather, together with the squeaking of the jackets and belts. Under that, was the musty dampness many wet feet had soaked into the tattered carpet.

The smells of humanity were the strongest. The crush of too many people in one room, the exhaled cigarette smoke, and dominating every sense, the blood. The thickening, bright red arterial stuff, greasy feeling if you got any on you. Once you had smelled enough fresh blood to recognize it at a whiff, it was always there for you.

When I blinked some sight back into my eyes I found myself leaning over the now empty display case. I hastily wiped at the drops that had run from my eyes and skied down my nose, spattering on the glass. Why was I crying? I hardly knew these people. I didn't work for them, they certainly didn't owe me anything and nobody could ever say that this was my fault. But in one little place in my mind, they were my responsibility, my people. I tried to compose myself.

"Come on, Hop," a reassuring hand rested on my shoulder. "Let's go outside and get some air."

I wanted to go, to leave without looking at anything else. But I couldn't 'not look'. I couldn't avert my eyes from the thing that I didn't want to see. As I relaxed to the hand on my shoulder, preparing to let it guide me where it wanted, my eyes defied me once more and glanced over the counter again. My eyes didn't want me to forget the thing that had happened here.

Death is undignified. Especially for someone who has led a dignified life. It's a natural function of life, but the only place that someone looks natural in death is at the funeral parlor.

The body lay in a most unnatural position, at the end of a long stripe of blood, hair, and brain matter that had run down the green wall to where it came to its final rest. Formerly life filled eyes were dark now staring vacantly, unseeing.

The hand gently guided me to the door. For some reason I didn't want to start wiping at my eyes, maybe that would be the official sign that I had lost it.

When we stepped outside, the wind now blowing down Clark Street was brisk. It smelled clean, alive. I began to feel better, the knots and nausea that were unconsciously turning my stomach eased. The wind was cold on my face as it dried my foolish tears.

"How are you doing?" the sergeant asked. Tom Davis was a new sergeant and still had some compassion left in him. He wore thick glasses. The gold checked hat came down to the top of the frame, giving him a military look.

"What? Okay, nothing, forget it!" My voice grated harshly. Compassion for my fellow man had run out of me years ago. I wasn't crying, just got a little choked up is all.

"So," his voice leveled. "Tell me what you know." It sounded like an order.

I wanted to lash out, hurt something or someone. I wanted to make somebody pay. But there would never be a way to even this score. A bit of professionalism surfaced in me and I managed to keep my pain from showing itself as sarcasm or anger.

"I don't know much." I said. "I walked by the store and didn't see anybody behind the counter, so I..."

"Hey, Sarge," Jim Geery, the evidence technician, was walking up to us from where he had double parked his squad car in the long line of vehicles that were blocking most of the street. "You want anything besides prints and photos?"

"I sure do." Tom was happy for a chance to do an easier part of his job. "I want every piece of dirt and lint collected, I want all the jewelry that's left in the cases and the few pieces on the floor inventoried, separately. I want photos, prints on all surfaces, doors, drawers, counter glass, and the phone."

"I want, I want, I want." Geery was as sarcastic as he could be without being openly hostile. "I want lunch but it doesn't look like I'm gonna get it any time soon." He didn't have a hat on and instead of a regular uniform he had taken to wearing wash and wear dark blue shirts and pants. He had Chicago Police patches sewn onto the shirt but he still looked like a gas station attendant.

Geery didn't expect or wait for a comment from Sgt. Davis and headed for the door. Tom turned to me, expecting me to pick up the conversation from where it had almost started. I still couldn't think straight. I especially didn't want to think about the two people lying dead, back in the little shop.

"You want prints!" Geery held the door open and was looking into the little jewelry store. "There's six guys rooting around in here, Becker's on the phone...Becker, get off that phone!"

Geery's voice softened, maybe from the look he'd gotten from the six individuals who were still in the building. "Come on guys you're contaminating the crime scene." He said pleadingly. He cast an innocent look over his shoulder at the sergeant.

The words 'contaminating the crime scene' had an effect like a cattle prod on the young sergeant. He realized that his first responsibility was to protect the evidence and was calling out orders even before he got around Geery and went back into the building. Leaving six coppers alone in a demolished jewelry store had the potential for a loss greater than mere evidence in a murder case.

I went for a walk. One of my favorite gin mills was just across the street. Even though I had quit drinking, it was still a place where I knew that I would find a certain kind of comfort. My feet crossed the street and the cars stopped for me, luckily, because I wasn't looking.

The bartender Georgos and a couple of my barfly buddies were standing in the doorway of the Limelight Pub. Georgos, bald and fifty pounds over weight, was one of the finest men I knew. I hardly minded when he spouted Greek philosophy. Nicko, known simply as 'the Greek', was a small and hyper man. He just sort of jittered in place. The third man was Janis. He was an Albanian. They weren't supposed to get along with Greeks, but apparently nobody had bothered to tell Janis.

They were all sure that I had taken time out from a busy murder investigation to come across the street and give them a personal update on the case.

"What happened, Hop?" Nicko and Janis were saying the same thing at the same time. I bristled at the bombardment, not realizing that I had better get used to that question.

"How the hell should I know, Nicko?" Nicky was an easy person to be mean to, and the least deserving. I caught myself, and softened my voice. "I just went in there and they were both dead, we don't know who did it yet. Okay, Nicky?" He smiled at me.

"It was them damn kids, them ganga' bangers!" Georgos always spoke in a loud voice, it was that kind of joint. To Georgos anybody who was not Greek, and under 21 years old, was a gang banger and a hoodlum. "They come in here and I throw them out! Damn Mavro." Georgos didn't know what was happening outside his doors, and no gang members, black or otherwise would ever care to go into the Limelight Pub.

They steered me to a bar stool and I just sort of sat there and soaked in the limelight. Everything in the Limelight Pub was green. The hundred year old mahogany bar and inlaid cabinetry that lined the wall was outlined with a continuous lime green neon strip.

All the bottles lining the mirrored shelves, the glasses, and bags of peanuts and chips, glowed green. For a moment I couldn't understand how I had been able to get drunk in here so many times in the past. Right now I just wanted to climb up on the bar and go to sleep, something I had also done in here many times over the years.

"Basilli, you want something?" He used the Greek pronunciation of my first name. Georgos motioned towards the rows of bottles against the wall with one of his stubby fingers, but it wasn't really a question.

The offer of a drink, medicinal or otherwise, set off images in my head. Those thoughts, in turn, increased the acid that was already gnawing a hole in my stomach. "No, Georgos. How about some soda water?"

Georgos visibly relaxed and reached under the bar for a glass. He filled it with ice and stomach soothing bubbles and placed it on a coaster in front of me. "Kalo Pedio, Basilli...Good boy." He repeated in English.

Chapter 2

My mother named me Basil. Where I grew up Basil wasn't a boy's name, it was some kind of green leaves that Italians ate. My mother told me that she named me after my father who had been killed in 'The War'. Having the same last name as my mother's family, Cassidy, and what that meant, didn't dawn on me until I went to school and found out what fathers were. It was difficult growing up without a father. To have a father, even one named Basil, was always my first wish. I had a few uncles that weren't very good role models, so I created my own.

The serial cowboy Hop-Along Cassidy became my hero. I convinced myself that he was related to me, like a grandfather. I wanted to be Hop-Along Cassidy. My last name was already Cassidy and I hated my first name so I changed it. I even made my mother call me Hop-Along. As fate would have it, I am fifty-five years old now, and have had a full head of white hair since I was thirty-five. I even look like Bill Boyd, the actor who played Hop-Along Cassidy on television.

Well the name stuck. People call me Hop, Hoppy, some call me Basil, but it doesn't matter what people call me any more, it hasn't mattered for a long time.

After I got out of high school I got into some trouble and the judge gave me the choice of the Army or the Iron Bar Hotel. I did a tour in Viet Nam, but it was before they had started the real fighting. After three years in the Army, the Chicago Police Department was hiring and I needed a job. It was just a job at first. Thirty years later it was a whole blurred life.

"There he is! I told you he'd be in here." I turned to see Bruce Sapper and Mike Pape's huge bodies silhouetted in the bit of daylight that was able to get around them into the bar.

"Davis has been banging you for five minutes, man. Aren't you listening to your radio?" Sapper and Pape were on the late wagon. I didn't know what time it was, the days were getting longer now in April.

"2496...2496." The mention of the word 'radio' brought me back to reality. I immediately recognized my call numbers coming from the speaker attached to my shoulder epaulet.

"Well answer it, man!" Sapper said. Pape leaned behind me, fingering the glass of soda water, trying to see if there was any booze in the glass. Pape was my age, taller and thirty pounds heavier, salt and pepper hair brush cut in a military style. Georgos took the glass away from him and put it back down in front of me.

"2496." I squeezed the side of the speaker and answered the page. Sgt. Davis spoke over the squad operator before he could acknowledge my transmission.

"'96, where are you?" I wasn't ready for this.

"I'm across the street interviewing prospective witnesses." At least I was thinking clearly enough to come up with a plausible excuse.

"Well finish up and get back here, the mobile crime unit is on the way and the dicks are here already..." This job wasn't more than Davis could handle, but it was a big one and he was getting flustered.

Before I could answer, the squad operator broke in as if the sergeant hadn't spoken. "Units, wait to be acknowledged." Technically the communications officer spoke for the Superintendent of Police and they made a subtle point of it frequently. He was giving me a play for not hearing my call numbers and telling Davis to relax a bit. "2496, call the Watch Commander when you get a chance."

I answered ten-four and got up from the stool. I could have used the phone in the bar, but I didn't feel like calling anybody.

"Hop, you better get a name in case Davis wants to know who you interviewed." Sapper turned to Nicko. Sapper was so fat that his stomach strained to get out of his uniform shirt. His undershirt poked through the scalloped spaces between the buttons. He was only 40 or so but he looked older than his partner. He had thinning blond hair and a tomato red face.

"Hey, Nick, what's your last name? It's not 'the Greek' is it?" Sapper and Pape were laughing at Sapper's joke. Nobody else got it.

Nicko looked puzzled for a moment and then said, "Constandropoulos."

Sapper stopped laughing in mid chuckle, then burst out hysterically. "Constan..what?...Did you get that, Mike." He was laughing so hard that he was spraying saliva out of his swollen tomato face. I wanted to punch him in it. I wanted to hurt something. Maybe it would make my pain go away so I could go back to being a cynical cop like Sapper or Pape.

Leaving them to what ever they wanted to do, I went back across the street to see what the sergeant was going to do to me for missing my call.

The big Mobile Crime Unit bus was just pulling up and I directed traffic for a while to get them into a spot, delaying the inevitable. Then there was no where else to go and nothing to keep me from going back into the store, so I followed the two mobile lab technicians up to the door.

The door buzzed after the technician banged on the glass and pressed the doorbell insistently. The wind blowing from the north was getting harder and colder. What had started out as a nice April day was changing into a cold windy night. As a foot patrol officer, I was dressed for it, but the technicians weren't.

Once inside, I stood behind them on the oriental carpet. It had rained yesterday, and snowed last week, the rug still wet from pedestrian traffic. I looked at the tattered design, wondering if there was a clue lying there waiting to disclose the killers.

Sung Park and his wife had a good business here on Clark Street, so good that it had apparently attracted the wrong kind of attention. The door buzzed again and Jim Geery came in behind me carrying some equipment, stamping his feet and rubbing his hands in an exaggerated fashion.

Sung must have buzzed the killer in, I thought. Then I remembered that when I'd climbed over the fence in back, the rear door had been open. If I could get over that gate, anybody could.

"Hey, Hop. How's the food at that little Japanese place down the street?" Geery was still thinking about lunch. When you start work in the afternoon lunch is usually what other people call supper.

"Raw." I answered. I didn't like anybody hitting up business people on my beat. If I said anything at all about Mas's restaurant, Geery would be in there telling Mas that I had recommended his place for good food, at little or no cost.

I needed to get back to work, and this was a good time to change the subject. "Jim. Can I get a set of these pictures when they're developed?"

He reached in his pocket and pulled out a plastic 35mm film case. Tossing it in his hand he said, "if black and white is good enough for you, you can have your own pictures. The big boys want me to shoot it all over again, in color." He gestured toward the three way conversation going on between the sergeant, the dicks, and the lab boys who were already behind the counter.

Getting a whiff of the blood again made it clear to me that I didn't need to have living color photos of the scene and I took the film out of Geery's hand.

"Thanks." I said, slipping the canister into my pants pocket.

"How about that Mexican joint, you know, the one on Jarvis? What's the name..." I had already turned away from him and approached the sergeant and Homicide Detectives who were standing on the inside of the horseshoe that was created by the glass display cases.

The sergeant had gotten rid of all the unnecessary personnel but the little place still had too many people in it. The space behind the counters was small and the technicians had a hard time working together. It had been big enough for Sung and his wife Sui however, they were small people.

The back wall had a doorway in the middle of it. On the left of the door was Sung's work table where he fixed watches and tightened loose gems or fixed a broken chain. The Techs ignored the table, laden with little tools and junk, moving toward the front. They wore blue jump suits. One of them stooped to examine something on the wall, probably blood, there was enough of it. I tried not to look too closely.

The doorway in the back wall was covered half way down by an Oriental curtain, split down the middle, showing a picture of a crane when both halves were together. Now the left side of the curtain was lifted up and stuffed over the rod across the top of the frame.

I could see Mrs. Park lying on the little nap couch that they had in the small back room of the shop. She had worn a flowered blue dress today. It was pushed up around her thighs where it had billowed when the death blow had thrown her onto the couch. Though she was lying on her stomach her head was turned around more than was normally possible, showing the small face that was once very beautiful. There is no dignity in death, just a return to the inanimate.

I could have seen her if the curtain had been down, because it only covered the top part of the opening. I'd had to climb over her outstretched limbs to get into the front when I had discovered the crime. I looked away. I would still have been able to see her body if there had been a full curtain there, a door, a brick wall. I didn't need color pictures.

"Cassidy." Thankfully the sergeant had something for me to do. "Tell Voltz and Dolecki what happened before the first car arrived." Great, this was just what I wanted to do.

Pretending to look at my watch with a thoughtful expression gave me a moment to take a breath. It also made me think about where I had gotten the new leather band that strapped the watch to my wrist.

"Well, I was on patrol, it was about 1545." I wanted to say 'a quarter to four', but didn't.

"Sung usually works at his table in the afternoon, so I don't bother him too much then. He closes about 7:00 p.m. and I try to come by again around that time."

"Sung. That's the male victim?" Dolecki was writing in a
dime note pad and leaned over the side counter to indicate the
dead man at the end, near the front.

"Yes, Sung Park, and the female victim is Sui Park, husband
and wife. Korean." I ran on, trying to give them some identity,
some dignity. To Homicide Detectives they were just bodies. In
Homicide their day began where your day ended.

"When was the last time you saw either of them alive?" I
couldn't see how that mattered.

"Yesterday." My watch band had broken just after I hit the
street. Putting the watch in my pocket I'd headed north, passing
up some illegally parked cars without writing tickets on them so
I could get to Park's store. Today had been such a nice day that I
had taken my time, strolling, as if I didn't have a care in the
world. If my watch band had lasted one more day I might have
been in the little shop before they had been killed. If my watch
band had broken today instead of yesterday, my presence alone
might have prevented this terrible thing from happening.

"Jewelry stores and liquor stores, that's their two favorite
businesses." Dolecki was addressing no one in particular. "No
wonder they get hit all the time."

"Is there a crime pattern working on Korean businesses?" I
wanted some information from them too.

"No more that usual. I was just saying, you know, these
gooks are always getting taken off. They get involved in
businesses that are dangerous and they don't know how to act.
They're too dumb to make it on the streets of Chicago." Dolecki
was about 5' 11", slim and smoked cigars. I'd known him for a
long time and he had never been very likeable.

'Gook'. I hated that word, I wanted to tell this jerk that
gooks were some unseen enemy that had scared us into our
foxholes at night, generations ago in Viet Nam.

The man he'd referred to as a 'gook', Sung Park, had been
so concerned about my broken watch band that it had been
almost comical. He had taken the watch gently in his hands,
cradling it carefully so he wouldn't drop the inexpensive

Japanese mechanism. Taking several watch bands from the little plastic display case, he took time to match each one with the timepiece. Finally, he decided on a dark alligator band, without asking my opinion.

He attached the new band to the old watch and insisted on fastening it to my wrist. Refusing my feigned attempt at payment, he smiled widely and thanked me, in his accented English, for coming into his store. Sung Park was not a gook.

"They have any family?" Voltz was speaking to me, partially to cover his partners ignorant comments.

"I really only know of one." I gestured at the photo's taped to the wall behind Sung's work bench. There on the left was a picture of Ah. He was Sung's cousin who owned a liquor store in the sixty-six hundred block of Clark. When I mentioned Ah's business, Dolecki grunted in an 'I told you so' fashion.

"I don't know who any of the others are." There were several other pictures on the wall, some obviously taken far from here, showing old people in kimonos, with mountains in the background. Next to them was a space where the paint was cleaner, brighter, as if an old picture had been there and fallen off when the yellowed plastic tape had finally failed to hold it any longer.

Dolecki was getting impatient. "So how did you find the bodies?" I figured that the faster I answered the questions the sooner I could get some fresh air. The kind that didn't have Dolecki stinking it up more than it already was.

"When I walked by the shop, I looked in the window and didn't see anyone. That was unusual." I didn't mention the fear that had immediately blossomed in my mind when I realized that something was wrong.

"First I rang the bell, then I started to bang on the door." I'd tried to break the glass with my fists, pounding like a mad man, thinking that if I increased the force of the blow with each strike the glass would surely give way.

"There was no sign of anyone inside, I couldn't see behind the counter, where Mr. Park is..." I realized that I'd been screaming also, demanding that the door give way, that everything inside be alright.

"So, I went around and climbed over the gate and went in from the back...and found...first her...than him." I didn't really remember running to the corner and down to where the high gate protected the rear.

"The gate was locked but the back door was open?" Voltz was asking intelligent questions at least. I seemed to remember climbing over the gate so it must have been locked.

"Yeah." I wasn't at all sure, but I got in that way so that's what must have happened.

"Do they usually leave the back door open? If you could get over the gate..." Voltz let the obvious go unsaid.

The store was in a three story apartment building that fronted on Clark Street. Everyone in the apartments upstairs had access to the rear, via a rickety wooden staircase that wound up to each floor. They all needed to be questioned, I didn't have to mention that, Voltz knew it already.

"No...I don't know. I've never gone back there before. I suppose they might have had the door open to get some air in the place." The place needed air more than anything else right now, or was it me? The sturdy back door had been wide open with a ripped and dirty screen door covering the opening, held lightly in place with a stretched out spring. Funny how I could remember some things clearly when others aren't there at all.

"We'll have to interview the tenants." Dolecki was speaking to Sgt. Davis. I know that he didn't want me to interview anyone.

"Hop, is there anything else?" Voltz' comment brought me back again.

"Not that I can think of right now." That was an honest answer.

"If we have any more questions, I'll give you a bang." Dolecki was so interested in what the technicians were collecting from the area of Mrs. Park's body that he didn't catch what Voltz had said. "If 'we' need anything, 'I'll' call you."

14

Nobody liked Dolecki, not even his partner. I didn't have much use for partners, my last one had been the worst. Voltz knew me from the years that I had been a Burglary Detective, when I'd spend my nights in the tavern while my ex-partner consoled my ex-wife behind my drunken back.

"Hop, you have to do the original case report." Sgt. Davis knew that I didn't want to do any work right now, but that wasn't his job. He was doing his job.

"Don't be too specific." That would be easy. He looked around the room and then out the front window. "Where's that wagon crew? Probably still across the street!" Davis knew where I'd been when he was calling me. I wondered if he thought that I had gone across the street to get a drink. I didn't know if he believed that I had stopped drinking and I didn't really care.

I took that as a dismissal. Davis stamped out of the shop and started walking across the now lamp lighted street. Following him outside, I turned south and started walking down Clark Street.

My foot post is the north end of Clark Street. It's so far north that it's two miles past Uptown. My beat, 2496, ends at the city limit.

Chapter 3

I decided to take my time getting to the station. I knew that if I stepped into the street, the southbound C.T.A. bus would stop for me like a big green taxi, or I could wait around and get a ride in from one of the squads that had come to the scene to satisfy their curiosity, but both of those choices involved too many people. One more was too many.

The jewelry store was on the east side of Clark, two doors from the corner of Farwell Avenue. As I stepped past the doorways that led to the upstairs apartments of both buildings, I wondered if anyone in the beauty salon next door had heard or seen anything. Someone else would interview them, I had been ordered to write a report.

Stopping on the corner in front of the salon entrance I looked east, down Farwell. This far north all the streets went down hill to Lake Michigan from Clark Street. The red bricks of the beauty shop building ran about 75 feet and ended with a metal fence which covered the rear space that they shared with Sung's building.

The gate looked high now. When I had run back here earlier I had been in such terror that I might have leaped it in one bound for all I knew. Even though I was getting back in shape now that I'd gone sober, the sight of me going over that gate couldn't have been a pretty one.

I walked down the side street toward the gate. The pavement opposite the gate was cracked and heaved up by the heavy roots of a huge oak tree growing in the parkway, next to the curb. The gigantic tree, with its odd leaves just unfurling, took up all of the space allowed by the concrete and asphalt surrounding it. This ancient behemoth, undeterred by the city around it, was calmly and inexorably pushing the cement, asphalt, and probably the buildings if given enough time, out of its way.

Sooner or later man, in the form of a city work crew, would cut down this old soldier who had been standing his post when Indians traveled this ridge that was now Clark Street.

This old red oak knew who had committed the murders, but he cared less about the affairs of man than he cared about concrete and pavement. Did 'he' have a big surprise coming. Did I? Unfortunately the answer was always yes.

I gave up wondering and headed for the barn. The wind was blowing briskly from the north, pushing me in the back, moving me along Clark street toward the Rogers Park Police Station. I didn't stop at any of my usual spots, not wanting to be asked the question. I just wanted to get to the station, four blocks down. There was one door that I couldn't avoid however.

6733 N. Clark is the little liquor store that is owned by Sung Park's cousin, Ah. I don't know if 'Ah' is his actual name, or a nickname. It may have been just a sound that I had misinterpreted as his name. If so, the man had been too humble to correct me. Whatever the case, he answered to it when I spoke to him.

The door to the 'Sun Liquor Mart' was an old wooden frame with a thick pane of glass that had wire in it, backed up by metal mesh on both sides. You had to grunt while pushing on the door or it wouldn't open. All the other windows were obscured by steel scissor bars and liquor sale posters.

Ah was behind the counter camouflaged by a jungle of cans, bottles, beef jerky and cigarette racks. I had told him a thousand times that he was setting himself up as the perfect stick-up candidate. His cash register was two feet from the door and you couldn't see in from outside.

But he was still alive and I had come here to tell him that his cousin, the one with the security buzzer on his front door, was dead. He smiled at me. In the last few years I'd learned that people around the world smiled for a great many reasons that had nothing to do with happiness.

"Hello, Ah, I have some bad news for you." This was already not going well. I felt awkward, his smile unsettling me.

I didn't know much about the Korean people, or much about the hundreds of other ethnic groups that were represented here on Clark Street. I didn't speak any of their languages. There were too many to start learning now. If Clark Street was a ship, it would be the Noah's Ark of humanity. I'd had to learn a universal language, the language of man.

He didn't say anything. I had to hold onto myself a little tighter, his smile protected him from emotion. I hadn't said anything that required him to speak, and he didn't.

"Ah...it's your cousin Sung. He's been killed." The protective smile was replaced by a plain round face, devoid of any expression. Did he already know about the murders? I couldn't tell. News travels fast on the street, it certainly wasn't a secret.

"How?" His round shoulders sagged a bit more as he looked at me through the fringe of his soup bowl hair cut.

"Shot...He was shot and Sui...She's dead too." It was hard to talk about them, it was still too vivid in my mind. For the first time, I thought about how she had been killed. I remembered that there was plenty of blood around the front of the shop, but not any on or around Mrs. Park. If her head hadn't been turned so dramatically, she might have seemed to be sleeping. Time would dull the pictures. I hoped.

"Do they have...someone?" He asked, in what had become a familiar, consonant deprived Korean accent.

"No. But they're working on it," I added quickly.

I gave him a little more information. When did it happen? Just a few hours ago, it seemed longer. Yes, it was probably a robbery. The condition of the shop was bad, and he should expect a visit from some detectives.

"I want you to clear off part of the window so I can see in when I go by." There was no way to really re-assure him or myself that he would be safe. "I'm going to have the beat cars go by and look in on you too. You be careful, until we get these guys."

I knew that he had a pistol behind the counter, but so did most of the business men on Clark Street. Park had one and it hadn't helped him. Just then I remembered the question that I had tried and failed to ask back in the shop. 'Did anyone find a gun?' I made a mental note to ask Davis if they'd found Park's gun.

"I will tell Chung," Ah said, catching me thinking about something else momentarily.

"Chung?" For a second I didn't know who he was talking about and then I realized that he was talking about the old man who ran a small martial arts school down on the next block.

"Chung is our Uncle. I must call him." He said flatly.

That was fine with me, since I didn't like to go into 'Chung's Tai Kwon Do Academy'. Chung was a little old man who had a bad leg, usually using a stick for support. The few times that I had talked to him he had only grunted at me. I had determined that if he was some kind of fighting instructor, he could take care of his own rude self and hadn't really bothered with the man or his business in the three years that I'd been on foot.

I told Ah to be sure that he called me at the station if he needed anything, and checked to see that he had one of my little Chicago Police business cards taped to his cash register. I told everyone to call me at the station, not many did. It was said more to get away from these people than as an invitation.

The rest of the walk back to the station was uneventful. When I passed by the Tai Kwon Do Academy, it was dark inside. Good. I didn't want to talk to any more family members today. And not Chung on any day.

Chapter 4

The station house was the usual ordered chaos. Ernie Perez was coming out of the men's room with a glass coffee pot, full and dripping cold water. Sergeant Andrews was at his little desk, way back from the counter, purposely not looking up, but aware of everything that went on. Smoke rose from the overflowing metal ashtray at his right hand, more smoke rising from the ever present cigarette sticking out between his yellow stained fingers.

The counter, that divided the huge room roughly in half, was about chest high and made out of the same gray brick that the Rogers Park Station was made of. Those bricks had recently stopped bullets fired in through the plate glass windows by a drive by shooter. Desk personnel were ordered to wear firearms while working now, as if that was some kind of solution.

On the near side, three people were exchanging insurance and personal information, reporting a traffic accident to the female officer sitting opposite them, on the police side of the wall.

"He's looking for you." Jane Gallagher looked up from her accident report and gestured over her shoulder towards the Captain's office.

After giving Janie a wink and a little smile, I started looking for Captain George Stokes. He wasn't in his office, the wall that faced the lobby was glass and the door was open, showing the entire room empty.

The long wide hallway, that led to the rear doors of the station, was painted in two tones, off white on the top and awful brown on the bottom. I passed the side hall that led to the lockup and went on down to the tactical office.

Tactical teams are plain clothes officers who work on specific crime patterns. They are usually the young aggressive guys, interspersed with a few veterans who can't get the rush of a drug raid out of their systems. I have never been on a drug raid and am not looking forward to ever doing so.

The door was always open and one of the young tactical officers, Doug James, was leaning up against the jamb, talking to someone in the room.

"They're dirty, Cap. I can tell just by looking at them," James said. He was wearing a denim jacket and blue jeans stuffed into biker boots, with his police star on a chain around his neck. A Glock 10 millimeter automatic poking out from under the jacket, finished off the ensemble.

"Well you better be able to substantiate any allegations, and remember that I have seen the condition of these, so called, prisoners. I will also re-examine them should you ask me to approve any charges." I had just come even with the doorway and saw the speaker was 'Chicken George'. He stood there in his spotless captains uniform, refusing to approve any charges unless there was a smoking gun and video of the crime, as usual. I knew what he was referring to though, Garcia and James spent more time answering 'brutality beefs', than making arrests.

"Here's Cassidy now. He knows these rats." Doug James turned to me with a 'give me a hand' look on his face. "Tell the captain that these Eagles are always on Clark street hassling the Oriental businessmen. These are the guys that did the killings at the jewelry store, Hop, I'm sure of it."

"Who are you talking about Doug?" I was willing to help, but the days of 'you lie and I'll swear to it', were long over, and I had no faith in gut feelings at the moment.

"In the back. Tell me these ain't the guys." James said pointing. He wanted a double negative answer, I felt that I could provide that. I walked into the Tact Office, the Captain puffed his ever present cigar, examining it closely, and not looking at me.

The tactical office has its own holding cells, with a connection to the lockup in the back wall. I looked through the little wire glass window to see three young men cuffed to rings that were cemented into the walls at three foot intervals.

They sat on a long bench that was painted the same color as the walls. I knew them. They were Gray Eagles, members of an Asian street gang. Coming from Viet Nam, Cambodia, and now even some from South Korea, this new breed of street gang specialized in terrorizing only Asians.

Alex Garcia was just coming out of the holding cell with a box that contained all the items that a thorough search of the arrestee's had produced. I wanted to get a look in that box. I didn't know what I was looking for, but the glint of gold made me want to look more closely. The main business of the Asian gangs was smuggling counterfeit designer items manufactured on the Pacific Rim, mostly jewelry. I had jewelry on my mind right now. They rarely trafficked in drugs, supplementing their income with extortion, and robbery.

They robbed restaurant owners, forced protection on other businessmen and generally did what they wanted, regardless of boundaries. Since they targeted only Asians they had a fragile truce with the other gangs who claimed only drug territory for themselves. Although they had superior firepower, they never fought with other gangs unless one of their protection contracts was violated. Most other gang bangers in Chicago would shoot at each other on sight.

"They're Eagles alright. The one in the middle is the leader of the local chapter." Even if I hadn't recognized two of them I would still have known what gang they belonged to by the way they wore their black and white colors.

Standing alone on a street corner, nobody would have realized that any of these young men were soldiers. Sitting together on the bench, their clothes gave them away to someone who understood how gangs worked. White Tee shirts with commercial baseball jackets, black pants, and black and white gym shoes that looked like they weighed fifty pounds each; that was the uniform of the Gray Eagles street gang.

Innocent people were sometimes injured or killed for wearing the wrong color clothing or making an unknown gesture that was mistaken for a gang signal. These young men were killers who defied society.

"Just because you recognize them, Cassidy, doesn't mean that they are guilty of anything." Chicken George had risen in the ranks, thanks to getting run over by a drunken Alderman, back when he was a rookie directing traffic at the St. Patrick's Day Parade. George hadn't done any work since that day. When you had a good clout there was no need to get involved in making any decisions.

"Why don't you call the dicks, they're probably still at the scene with Tom Davis." I said to Doug James. "I'll bet that they will want to talk with these lads in any case."

"You know the General Orders, I don't want these individuals detained for one minute longer than allowed." Nobody paid any attention to the orders until they had to. It took half an hour to find a typewriter around here. Captain Stokes was looking at his watch. "By the way, what was the justification for stopping them in the first place?"

"Ugh...Motor Vehicle Code violation, Captain. Broken tail light," Doug said haltingly. Stokes snorted, he wasn't approving any trumped up charges. If they wanted to hold these guys, they would have to do some fancy talking to the Assistant State's Attorney on duty.

"Cassidy, I want to see you in my office." I figured I was going to find out why I had been ordered to call the station. I didn't want to know. He only glanced at me before leaving the room.

The captain walked back down the corridor towards his office. Alex was grabbing himself obscenely and gesturing in the captain's direction while James tried to keep from laughing because he was still in the doorway where the captain could see him if he turned around.

"I'll be right there, Cap." I said, as Stokes kept walking, pretending not to hear the smirks that usually followed him from a room. Turning to the box with the personal items in it, I started to sift through the contents, looking for something that might connect the Eagles to the Park murders.

"When we tried to stop them, they slid for awhile before pulling over. If they had any dope, they must have tossed it in the block or two that it took us to stop them. I searched them good but they were all clean." Garcia watched me as I looked at a gold watch for a serial number, identifying it as counterfeit, like Sung Park had showed me. Park would never have had junk like this in his shop. "Those can't be real watches," Garcia said.

"No, but they're getting serious about prosecuting counterfeiting cases," I said, showing him the back of the phony 'Rolex' I was holding and how to tell it was a fake. "I hate to agree with the captain, Alex, but what do you have to charge these three with? A gun, anything?" He just shook his head negatively. There was nothing that looked like proceeds from the jewelry shop in the box, just cigarettes, rolling papers, a few wallets and some keys and change.

"No," James answered, then brightened. "We can charge them with the watches, can't we?"

I held up the packet of rolling papers. "If you had some marijuana, and probable cause to find it, you could hold them. But nobody is going to approve charges for possession of three fake watches. If you had a box full maybe. Let's have a talk with them, shall we?" Garcia nodded eagerly.

Two of the dark haired youths, both slim built and under twenty, turned at the sound of the door opening. The one in the middle was older. He was the one I recognized as the leader of the Gray Eagles. He didn't turn, pretending that it was beneath him to be concerned. His name was David Tso, he was about twenty three, medium built and had a thick pony tail holding his long hair back.

"Where were you when the police stopped you, David?" He didn't turn, but I could see that my question had gotten his attention as he stiffened slightly. He had some kind of special gang name, which I didn't care to know, and didn't like being called David. I didn't like the name my mother had given me either. Tough.

Alex Garcia had followed me into the room and when no one answered my question he kicked the bench they were sitting on, spilling them all to the floor with practiced violence. "Answer the question. Where were you!"

They hung from the wall rings. The smallest one, who I didn't know, righted the bench with difficulty and they resumed their places. David Tso just smiled at Garcia, then held up his fingers in such a way that it represented the sign of his gang. If you recognized the hand signal, you understood it to be an insult. Garcia advanced on the youth and I grabbed his arm as if asking him a question was more important than his disciplining the prisoner.

"What were they doing when you stopped them, Alex?" I'd steered him to the center of the room, more than striking or kicking distance away.

"Driving down Clark Street. Right past the murder scene." He raised his voice as he spoke, emphasizing the words so they could hear him. "You know, like returning to the scene of the crime."

"What kind of car were they driving? Did you run a check on it?" Hundreds of people had driven past the crime scene. I was still trying to find something to hold them on. Feelings weren't admissible in court.

"A black Hyundia. We ran it, but it wasn't on the 'Hot Sheet'." Black was the color of most of the cars that this particular gang used.

"They run a lot of cars." If you had a black foreign car in this part of the city, and didn't take some steps to protect it, the Eagles would steal it. Foreign cars were the easiest cars to steal. In countries where the walls and doors are only there to keep out the weather, locks aren't a big concern. This mentality extends to their design of automobiles. It's so easy, the Eagles sometimes steal a new car when the old one runs out of gas.

"They're number specialists. Did you check to see if the Vehicle Identification Number had been tampered with?"

Seeing a possibility of placing some real charges on his detainees, Garcia started for the door. "Good idea, Hop. We'll check the engine block to see if we can get a confidential number to run." He picked up a heavy flashlight, weighing it in his hand before smiling at me. "I've got to fix their tail light anyway."

I turned back to the three on the bench when Garcia left. "How much more help would you like me to give these guys in finding things to charge you with, David? I'm in a real creative mood. Are you going to answer my question or not?"

Tso turned to me, a little crest fallen. Or maybe it was just an act. "Look, man, we just saw all the cop cars and wanted to see what happened, that's all." He sounded truthful and sincere, so I knew it was a lie.

"I don't care what you wanted to see. I want to know what you were doing on Clark Street? On my street!" My voice had risen until it had an edge of violence clearly ringing in it.

The smallest one, who had to pick up the bench for the other two, spoke up. "You don't own the streets, man." He tried to sound tough, but it's hard when you have a squeaky voice.

"Does he speak for you, David?" I knew how their hierarchy worked. This was a junior member speaking out of turn. I decided to let the leader handle him.

"Shut up, man!" The punch that Tso gave the younger gang banger with his free hand was hard enough for me. Then he turned to me, speaking for himself.

"We're clean, Cassidy, you can't hold us. I know that we ain't supposed to be on Clark Street, but we was just cruising, man. We were partying man, not humm'in." I assumed that humm'in was bad and partying was good.

Before I could tell Tso what a liar I knew he was, Garcia and James came back into the room. Garcia looked a little disappointed that the prisoners were in good shape.

"It looks legit, Hop." James said to me, half smiling. "We even pried the tag off so we could show you." He held the little

26

I.D. tag in his hand, smiling broadly now. The Eagles wouldn't be able to get their car back from the pound without paying a heavy fine and a re-tagging fee.

The third youth, I knew him only as 'Key', hadn't said a word thus far. When I looked closely at his face, I could see by his dilated pupils that he was high on something, and it wasn't Vodka; on that subject I was an expert.

"Last chance, David. Are you going to tell me what you know about the jewelry store, or not?" I had sworn off believing in gut feelings, but mine was churning now.

"They weren't my people, I don't know what happened to them." I was pretty sure that Park hadn't been paying protection money to the Eagles. Yet there was something different about this kid. He wasn't violent enough or something. I'd had a lot of dealings with him in the last few years and he had always acted like the crazed killer that I knew him to be.

"If they had been my people, they wouldn't be dead right now," he added smiling, stinging me to the bone.

Garcia was holding the door open, James froze in mid comment. They just stood there waiting for me to explode. Unfortunately it had happened before.

Holding tightly to the rules that I now tried to live my life by, I stepped into the outer office and started looking in the box that contained their personnel possessions. More to give myself something to do than anything else. One of the items in the box was a fake leather Gucci wallet. The wallet had plastic compartments with a few pictures, and some singles in the side pocket, but was otherwise unremarkable. No ID, no drivers license. Then it dawned on me, it was a throw away.

"You know, Doug," he still stood next to Garcia in the open doorway. "One time, years ago, my kid accidently dropped something out of his wallet." I had actually searched my sons things on a regular basis.

The pictures I was looking at were the kind that came with the wallet, blond models that none of these three would ever know. Between two of the photos was a piece of graph paper, folded smaller so that it couldn't be seen. Turning the plastic compartment upside down and squeezing it, the graph paper fell out onto the desk. Hundreds of little squares with part of a red dragon faintly over printed on them.

I looked over at David Tso. I could see that I now had him by the balls. Key sat farthest away, but his eyes were like saucers as he watched me gingerly unfold the paper.

"My oldest son had a little slip of paper with squares printed on it. Just like this." I handled it with my finger tips only. "I had a friend of mine at the crime lab test it for me. It was only a few squares, not as many as this, but it was coated with L.S.D."

I smiled my most satisfactory smile at Tso, he turned away. The colorful look on Key's face faded a bit. "I wouldn't handle that very much with bare hands. If it's been soaked in 'acid' it could get into your system through your skin." James and Garcia were smiling like I'd just bought them both cotton candy at the State Fair.

I felt so clever when I left the office. My feeling that David Tso was acting suspiciously having been satisfied. I should have realized that he wouldn't be worried about an arrest for drug possession. That was a big mistake. Life is a series of mistakes. It's the constant interaction of everyone's mistakes that causes all the confusion.

Chapter 5

When I walked into the Captain's office, the door was open and I didn't knock, Sergeant Davis was with him. Davis was probably giving him a report on the double homicide that had occurred on my beat. I had washed my hands several times with the green soap that burns your skin and was still holding the wet paper towels, trying to dry them more thoroughly than was necessary.

"Did they release those prisoners?" Stokes interrupted whatever Davis had been saying.

"Well, Captain, I don't see how they can. The prisoners have about three thousand hits of L.S.D. in their possession." Davis just looked at me, not happy knowing that he would not get to finish whatever he had come in here for.

"What," Stokes' usually gray complexion tinged crimson. He bit down hard on his cigar and rushed from the room.

"I better go write my report." I wanted to smile, but didn't have it in me. Davis looked too tired to comment, he just sighed and sat down in the captain's chair. He picked up the phone and was dialing when I left, without another word being said.

When I stepped into the lobby, Ernie Perez was on the phone and motioned for me to pick up an extension. The grin on the desk man's face told me he was up to something.

"Uh. Here's Officer Cassidy now. Officer Cassidy, there's a phone call for you." Perez was setting me up for something. The looks the rest of the desk personnel gave me confirmed it. I didn't want to talk to anybody, but it was too late. I picked up the counter phone.

"Cassidy," was all I could manage to say into the receiver.

"Officer Cassidy? Oh great. You were the first person on the scene of the double murder up on Clark Street tonight, weren't you?" I could tell from her perky voice that the person on the other end of the line was very pleased that she had been able to get me on the phone. I wasn't pleased, scowling at Perez. I hated 'perky' at the moment.

"Who is this?" I asked.

"Oh, I'm sorry, I thought the other officer had told you, this is the City News Desk." City News was the local independent news service that was situated in a little office on the 29th floor of the old Jeweler's Building on Wacker Drive. City News was as old as the building, maybe older. It had been around when the UP and AP were using carrier pigeons.

"Come on," I said, "who is this really?" City News was the bottom rung on the media ladder. The reporters were all rookies, I doubt if they even got paid half the time.

"No, seriously," she said as professionally as she could, "this is the City News Desk, Ellen Brighton. I'm working on the double in the jewelry store."

She was working on the 'double'. Just another story. Just another double homicide on a Thursday night in the city with big shoulders.

"Come on, quit fooling around. Who is this really? Is that you Mary? I know that nobody down at City News would want to talk to little 'ol me'." I was technically a hill-billy so I twanged an accent without feeling like a bigot.

"Really, this is the City News Desk." She said it like she was calling from the lavish CNN News Room, instead of the little cubby hole that was City News. "What can I say that will convince you that I am sincere?" She felt that if she could just clear up this bit of confusion, she would get all the information she wanted out of me. Everybody at the desk was listening in on the conversation.

I pretended to think for a second, then had a pretend flash of inspiration. "Oh! I know. Tell me what it says over the doorway at the City News office." It's the coolest thing about the place.

"Oh, that's easy." She was relieved that she could finally end this confusion, knowing that she would be able to easily answer the question, verifying her identity.

"It reads, 'IF YOUR MOTHER SAYS SHE LOVES YOU, CHECK IT OUT!'" I could tell that she was reading it off the wall as she spoke, very proud of their famous motto. I waited for a moment before giving her the punchline, timing was everything.

"Well, Ms. Brighton, and I do believe you are a reporter, I suggest that you call your mother and tell her that you love her. If she says she loves you too, thank her for being the only person willing to tell you anything."

I hung up and smiled back at Perez. He had known just how to cheer me up. The rest of the sick humourists at the desk were in hysterics. No copper in his right mind would give an interview to a reporter. It was their job to make police officers look stupid and they usually did it well enough without my help. Ellen Brighton would find that she had chosen a difficult profession, I knew I had.

We weren't supposed to use the Juvenile Officer's typewriters, but I had a key to their office and nobody ever said anything. Most of my arrests were juveniles anyway. I had learned long ago that a police report lasts forever, in one form or another, and it takes a certain amount of thought to write one. Even a non-specific one. When I finally looked at my watch to make the 'time completed' entry next to my name, it was almost ten o'clock. Tempus fugit. It had flown for me, it had stopped for the Parks.

Stokes hadn't looked for me and I didn't look for him, hoping that he had forgotten that he had ordered me to call the station and then ordered me into his office. I dropped my report in the box and went for coffee.

The coffee didn't warm me, the north wind didn't clear my head. I didn't know what to do. Did I have to do anything? Not officially, but personally it was weighing heavily on my mind. It was after 11:30, check off time, by the time I walked back to the station. Chicken George was long gone by that time, and had probably forgotten all about demanding to see me when he'd left the Tact office.

31

I checked the arrest log and found the three Gray Eagles listed and charged with possession of narcotics. That decision alone must have driven the captain to the edge of professional sanity. There was also a sign in for an interview by Dolecki and Voltz. They knew their job.

Sapper and Pape were already in the locker room when I went to change, it was later than I'd thought. Pape's locker was a couple away from mine and I could hear Sapper's gravel pit voice lecturing someone on the best cleaner for refinishing an old desk. Sapper was a junk collector that passed himself off as some kind of antique expert.

"Did you handle the bodies tonight?" Pape, who had his back to me, was putting his street clothes in a laundry bag and hanging his gun belt in the locker.

"What? Who? Oh, the people from the jewelry store." He was in a hurry to get going and didn't understand the question at first.

"Yea, we had to take both of them, the other wagon pulled the old 'flat tire' on us and they had to wait four hours for the repair truck to come and fix it. They're always pulling that kind of stuff when there's a crappy job to do." He closed his locker and pulled on the lock to make sure it was locked, then put his jacket on, picked up his laundry and left without another word.

"See ya later, Mike." I said to him, as he left. He grunted an answer and was out the door. I was glad that he wasn't in the mood to make me look at the stack of pictures of his kids that he always carried.

"Hey, Mike, how much was that stripper we got at the warehouse outlet store?" Sapper's big voice bounced off the walls of the large cinder block and steel beamed room. I was sure that he could be heard out in the hallway, probably outside.

"He's gone, Bruce." I called out in a normal voice that I knew could be heard easily.

"Dat you, Hoppy?"

"Yea."

"You gonna stop?" he asked. 'Stop' was the official code word for cocktails after work.

"No, thanks, buddy." Sapper's voice lowered to a whispered volume as he continued his conversation. I could tell from the hushed voices that they were talking about the two people who were killed on my beat today. The killings that I should have prevented.

Not wanting to hear the question again today, I got changed quickly. Walking to the end of the row, I pushed on the first of the two doors that led out of the locker room. Coming from the opposite doorway, into the little passageway in between, was Donny Cramer.

While Pape was big, and Sapper was morbidly obese, Donny Cramer was a giant. He'd been a college football lineman. It was natural for people to call him 'Little Donny' or 'Tiny'. He filled the narrow space between the doors so completely that I held my door open in self defense.

"Hop, there you are. Didn't you hear me call you on the P.A. system?" He didn't wait for an answer. "You're on a car tomorrow. Brian White went on the medical and you're stuck with his rookie." Donny's face showed that he had bad acne when he was a kid, but I bet nobody ever kidded him about it.

"Damn. Whose idea was that?" As if I didn't have a sneaking suspicion. Chicken George hadn't forgotten about me after all. He had stabbed me in the back, with a rookie, before leaving. Field Training Officer for a day was not my idea of a good time. I wondered if White had gotten sick or maybe injured by a mistake his rookie partner had made.

"I don't mess with four to twelve shift business, strictly midnights for me, buddy. Extra pay and its nice and quiet. That is, after all you pain in the ass 'real' police leave." We had stepped out in the hallway where I didn't have to worry about getting crushed and Donny was turning toward the front of the building. He was a light duty officer and usually worked the desk. Carrying around over 300 pounds, even on a 6' 6" frame, eventually had to wear something out. Donny had knee replacements.

"Oh, Hop. I forgot this." We both turned. He had a piece of paper in his hand. "It was in the message box." If someone called for you at the station, and you weren't right there to get the call, there was a 50/50 chance that the desk person would take a message. If they bothered to write something on a scrap of paper, it went into a shoe box in the corner. That was usually as far as their efforts went. Little Donny was a good guy and did a good job, light as it was.

Taking a few steps toward each other, he slapped the little square into my hand. "Now you can't blame me for not giving you the message. Can't tell her it was Donny the desk man's fault you didn't call. Ha, Ha, Ha." His baritone voice boomed in the cavern of the hallway as he walked toward the front. I thanked him, turning in the opposite direction and heading for the parking lot, where my beater was parked.

When I got to the glass doors that were the rear exit, I paused with my hand on the metal bar that opened the right door. I wanted to read my note in the last of the bright light before I went out into the parking lot where it was darker. What was written on the torn page froze me.

It was just a quick scrawl. It read: CASSIDY, CALL SUE, 583-4986.

The person who had taken the call had written the time and the date on the note. The call had come in at 1300 hours, less than twelve hours ago. Probably taken by someone on the day shift.

I looked at it again, willing the words to change. I wouldn't be returning the call, the desk man had mis-spelled the name. It probably sounded like Sue, when she said it on the phone, but I knew it was spelled Sui. Sui Park had called me today, an hour or so before she had been murdered. Called me for help maybe. Sorry, I didn't get the message.

Couldn't blame Donny for not giving me the message, he'd already said so. What did blame accomplish anyway? Did it bring people back from the dead? It all came back in a rush. Her body lying on the couch. His head half blown off. If the words on the page changed, I wouldn't have been able to see them. Somehow I got outside and into my car.

The next thing I knew, I was cruising my old beater west on Devon Avenue. It was a miracle that I didn't stop at the tavern next to my house. It had not been an accident that I rented the converted attic apartment on this little street. The shorter the walk home, the more you could drink.

Chapter 6

I usually felt great in the mornings these days, a side effect of not drinking all night. But not today. It was cold in my little apartment, I hadn't turned the space heater up last night. Dragging myself out of a shower that didn't revitalize me, I noticed the light blinking on my answering machine.

'Hello, Dad...it's me...Johnny.' My finger was still poised over the play button.

Anger flared up in me, "Of course I know it's you, Johnny, I'm your father. Don't you think that I know the sound of my own son's voice?" I shouted at the machine, then had to rewind it to hear what he was saying. But the kid had a point, there had been times...when was the last time I'd spoken to either of them? Not since Christmas. No. I hoped not.

John was the younger of my two boys. Billy was graduating from college at the end of this year.

I was very proud of them both. They had done well, despite having a rough home life. John went on to point out that Billy was graduating, not months from now, but in a few short weeks. I had been helping them all along, especially since they had gone to college in Florida.

The boys loved their mother, but hated their step-father. I hated them both. When they had gotten old enough to go away to school, we had all been happy. Now their work was paying off. Bill was going to be an engineer. John a doctor. I didn't care if I had to work five jobs to pay for it all.

Things were great at school, he hinted that he could use a couple of bucks to get some new clothes for the graduation, which made me smile. His idea of clothes and mine were vastly different. I paid their bills, lack of a social life builds equity, but deserved none of the credit. I hadn't been there when they'd needed me often times. Paying their bills never paid those debts.

'...and you can stay with us when you come. We've got lots of room.' I could only imagine. 'You know,' he said slyly, 'it's really beautiful down here and I read in the paper that they don't have enough qualified police officers and stuff...so if you liked it when you came down...' It was a nice feeling to be invited and have your kids worry about you a little. I wrote the information down so I wouldn't forget it and put it with my other note that I couldn't forget.

The slightest things choked me up lately, my damn biorhythms must be screwed up or something. I got dressed and ate a granola bar on my way to the 'Y' where I worked out until every bone in my body was aching and every muscle was burning.

In the antique tiled shower at the YMCA, where they have the hottest water in the world, my brain started working again and reminded me that I was training a rookie today. When I moaned, anyone around me might have thought that the steamy water was easing my pains. I'd just had a new pain.

We were all lined up for roll call inspection. Chicken George called off my name without any emotion. He said the car number, 2423, as if I worked that car everyday. He said 'Cohen' after my name and I heard a little squeak of a 'here, sir', down at the other end of the row. I wanted to moan again but everybody else was smirking and laughing so I kept my moans to myself.

Benjamin Cohen. There had to have been a million Jews with that name over the last three thousand years. My partner looked exactly like all his namesakes. Just one look at this 5' 6", 125 pound kid told you that he was as Jewish as Lox and Bagels. The shiny new police hat, held up by his horned rimmed glasses and thick curly hair, didn't do anything to increase his stature. He was the most unlikely looking police officer I'd ever seen.

When I got to the radio room by the rear doors, Cohen already had two radios signed out and was holding the keys to the car. Only 'hot shots' took out two radios. Supposedly, if you got separated in a dangerous situation, the officers would be able to stay in contact. The veterans way was not to get into dangerous situations, therefore, two radios weren't necessary. I wondered if I was sick enough to go on the medical now, instead of waiting to get really hurt out on the street with this kid as my back-up. I was definitely not feeling well.

"Let me drive. Okay, Hop?" I hadn't told him my name or that he could call me Hop, in fact, I hadn't ever spoken a word to the lad before. But his effervescent enthusiasm was bubbling out all over the hallway. I didn't care to stand there and entertain the jokers waiting to check out their radios, so I just took one of the radios and walked out of the station.

The regular car was in the shop and we were stuck with a million mile pool car, probably an afterthought by Captain Stokes. Some budding art student had decorated the dash board by burning rings into it with the cigarette lighter. There were no mats and I could see the pavement through the hole in the floor board on the passenger side. The hole that must had formed on the driver's side had a metal plate welded over it.

Cohen opened the trunk and checked the spare. Unnecessary, because if we got a flat, I was going to burn the car. When he got through inspecting the vehicle he got in and tested the lights and siren. I gritted my teeth.

"There's some damage on the right rear, I better go in and make out a report." If the fender was off maybe.

"Forget it, they don't care about the pool cars." Everybody in sight was smiling at us if they could manage to catch my eye at all. I just wanted to get out of there.

"But White says that if you don't report all damage and the next crew does..." I didn't want to start off on a bad foot with this kid, but I could tell it was going to be a long night. It was getting longer by the minute.

"Look, Ben. It is Ben isn't it? This car has more miles on it than Shanghai Lil. Don't believe anything that Brian White tells you. You've been working with him for a while now, haven't you?" His head was bobbing up and down like a Cupie Doll's. "And you haven't figured out that he's an asshole yet."

His eyes opened wider. "Well, he is kind of..." He was unsure if he should share his opinion with me.

"Well," I mimicked him, "if you want to drive, get going." I pretended to look in the glove compartment to check on the supply of blank case reports. There were none. He noticed but didn't say a word, just started the car and revved the engine while it coughed blue smoke. When he put it in gear the transmission clanked.

Just as he was about to pull onto the side street, he stopped, looking at the dash board. "We only have half a tank of gas."

"If we run out we'll suck some out of a passer-by." I was not having a good time. He didn't say anything. He rolled the car onto the street.

When we got up to the corner of Clark Street, he stopped at the sign. "Is there anywhere that you want to go."

Doing personal errands was a part of the police officer's day. White had taught him something at least. Being a foot patrol officer gave me more than enough time to keep up with banking, laundry and the other necessities of life, but I was kind of hungry.

"Lets take a personal and get a bite to eat. You hungry?"

He started to say something then thought better of it, as I reached for the radio receiver snapped to my epaulet of my leather jacket.

"Any early cars out of the gas line yet?" The squad operator's voice came from the little plastic grill before I could get my request in. I wished I had listened to the kid and gotten in the gas line where we would be safe from getting a job right out of the box. Nobody volunteered, everybody was getting gas but us.

Cohen was vibrating with enthusiasm, dying to take the call. Poor choice of words. I sighed, it was going to be a long night. Did I say that before? I was getting nuts already. "2423. What'a'ya got, squad?" The radio had been poised in front of my mouth anyway.

"Got something right around the corner for you, '23. Check an injured person, 1709 Arthur. Apartment 1A, Gilford. Let me know if you need an ambulance or a wagon on that 2423."

Then in a more personal tone the dispatcher added, "that you, Hop?" After using the radio for years, you knew dozens of people by their voices alone.

"That's a big ten-four, Bob." I didn't try to cover the weariness in my voice.

"F.T.O. tonight, Hop?" I couldn't hear them smirking down at the communications center but I knew that they were.

"What...is it in the daily bulletin or something?" I was getting pissed off now.

"They issued a Special Notice," the dispatcher said. Now I could hear them smirking in the background.

"Well, you know what you can do with it."

"Ten-four, 2423. 2064..your name check came back, ready to copy?" He got back to business.

"I'm sorry." Cohen said. I felt foolish. Concerned about how unfair life was being to me, and not taking into consideration the feelings of the person who I was working with.

"Don't worry about it, Ben. Everybody has to be a rookie sometime. It's part of the job. I shouldn't let a little ribbing get to me either. The captain put me on a car tonight as a little punishment, and they all know it."

The call was just around the corner and back west a few buildings on Arthur. I made Cohen double park rather than walk from the corner. Police privilege, especially since there were never any legal parking spots available in Chicago.

The hallway door at street level had long since been converted to the locked outside door. The mail boxes and door bells were amended to the outside of the door frame. Allowing access to hallways in this neighborhood hadn't been an option for years, too many burglaries, rapes, etc.

Cohen leaned on the top bell, the names had been graffiti'd over tenants ago. Regardless of how they numbered them the floor plans of these buildings were pretty consistent. I tried to look through the sections of beveled glass in the once classic door, to the landing where I knew the first floor apartments were.

The first thing I saw was a bare leg, then another, as they came walking out of the doorway on the left side of the landing. The guy was naked. He came down the stairs like he always answered the door in the nude. The sectioned glass kept me from seeing him clearly. I wasn't trying to look too hard, I was going to get a good look shortly.

"Jesus," I began to swear under my breath.

"Christ." Cohen finished the oath for me when the man opened the door. I gave the Jewish lad a sideway's glance.

Mr. Gilford was a male white, about 60 or so. There were lacerations and blood on his penis. I don't know why it's human nature to look at the genitalia when you come upon a naked person. Even a bloody penis only held my attention for a millionth of a second however, because the guy had an ice pick sticking out of his chest.

A doctor can tell you exactly where your heart is and what size and shape it is. You can feel with your hand and locate the area of the heart by the beating. But most people have an inherent idea of where the heart is located within the body. This guy had at least four inches of the pick imbedded in the left side of his chest, directly where you knew had to be the center of his heart. Right between the nipple and the breast bone. The handle on the thin shaft of steel waved slightly, like a dart in a board, when he moved.

"Jesus Christ!" The man shouted at us. "Yes..He told me..." He grabbed the wooden handle of the ice pick with his right hand obviously intending to pull it out of his chest. Cohen was frozen by the bizarre scene. I practically jumped on the guy, grabbing for the hand that clutched the ice pick, fighting with him, trying to hold on.

"Hang on there, sir. You don't want to be pulling on that right now." I turned to look at Cohen, he hadn't moved a muscle, eyes wide.

"Uh, Ben." I said, as calmly as I could with two problems on my hands. "Call for an ambulance and mention, calmly, what we've got here." I got Mr. Gilford in sort of a hug with my other arm, trying to keep the ice pick from moving around. I spoke to him reassuringly, quietly, waiting for help to arrive.

I was talking as much nonsense as he was, but from what I understood of what he said, I gathered that the cuts on his genitals and the ice pick were self inflicted and had been inspired by some conversation with the Lord.

The EMTs were just as freaked out as we were and hurriedly went about their job. They slowly peeled Mr. Gilford's and my white knuckled hands from the ice pick. Then they packed it with whatever they could grab out of their equipment packs. When they had finished wrapping the man up and securing the shaft in it's place, Mr. Gilford looked like a mummy. They strapped him tightly to a stretcher and only then did we manage to take a breath.

"Where are you taking him?" I looked at the number on the side of the Fire Ambulance. Firemen didn't have names, not as far as I was concerned, just numbers. 41.

"Masonic." the bigger one said over his shoulder as they loaded the still jabbering Mr. Gilford into the back.

"Isn't Masonic Hospital a little far?" Cohen said to me. He was right, there were a number of hospitals closer than thirty blocks.

"Masonic is a major trauma center, if the guy had a chance of making it, Masonic is the only place where they might have been able to save him." We headed for our car. The street was blocked by us and all the pain in the ass police who wanted to come and see the guy with the ice pick in his chest. The Tact team, Garcia and James, were assigned to check out the apartment and see if there was any crime that had occurred. Other than a man's crimes against himself.

"Why are you talking about him in the past tense? You act as though the man is already dead. If Masonic is the place where they could save him..." Cohen's voice softened when he saw the look on my face. I had blood on my uniform and hands, which were numb from fighting with Mr. Gilford, trying to keep the ice pick lodged in his heart.

"Okay, rookie, you asked the question." I looked over at him trying to determine if he was ready to face reality. "I'm speaking in past tense, because the guy was dead before we even got the call. I don't care if Doctor Christian Bernard is waiting for him in the Emergency Room, with his gloves already on. When they take that ice pick out of Mr. Gilford's chest, he is going to die."

"But you said not to worry. You told him that he'd be alright when the ambulance came." I didn't exactly remember what I'd said to him while we fought over the handle. I must have been convincing because Cohen believed it too.

"Ben, let's start at the beginning. I said I was hungry, then we got a call. If the guy pulls the ice pick out while we're standing there, he drops like a rock, dead. No lunch. Two hours of doing reports and notifications. You think that the EMTs stabilized him because they thought they could save him? They didn't want him to die in the back of the ambulance while they had responsibility for the guy. Just like I didn't want him to croak on us while we had the paper." Two people dying on me yesterday were enough, was my quiet thought.

"Now I'm still hungry, and Mr. Gilford is still technically alive. Ambulance 41 is going to keep him alive until someone at Masonic, who is a professional, takes the ice pick out and he dies in the hospital where they're used to that kind of thing. Gilford will probably end up as an article in some medical journal. Now let's go." The ambulance tapped his siren to get us moving out of his way. I pointed west, the only way we could go.

"I'm sorry," he said again. "I've never seen anything like that before, and I thought, you seemed so sure that..." He pulled away from the scene. When he got to the end of the block, I signaled him with my thumb to make a right turn, tired of talking. Tired period.

"Let's go over to the restaurant on Greenleaf and Clark," I said trying to change the subject. I got on the radio and told the dispatcher that I'd gotten blood on my pants and was going to change them. There was still tension in the air, I wanted to change the subject but it wasn't going to go away without some explanation.

"Look, man, just because I tell someone that they are going to live, doesn't mean that they will. I never saw a guy with an ice pick sticking out of his chest before either, alive or dead. But that's the job. You just have to deal with what comes. Did you think he looked like he was going dancing tomorrow when he answered the door?" I wished that I could make things right just by saying that they would be. If that was the case, I had a request to make regarding the events of Thursday afternoon.

He relaxed a bit. "To tell you the truth I was so freaked out that I didn't know what to think, or what to do. I'm sorry, I wasn't much help." We were cruising north on Ravenswood, next to the elevated commuter train tracks.

"Quit saying you're sorry all the time. I was motivated by hunger, and I'm still hungry, that's all. Turn here." He put on his turn signal, which didn't work, and turned right. He looked over at me trying to contain himself from saying he was sorry for saying he was sorry all the time.

"You never stop getting freaked out, no matter how long you're on the job. You just think a little better when you get a little time behind you is all." Thirty years had gone by for me and I still didn't think that I had seen everything or would always do the right thing when I did.

Chapter 7

As soon as we turned the corner, I said, "Stop".

Cohen stopped abruptly when he saw the group hanging around the front of a red, brick, six flat on my side, about halfway between Ravenswood and Clark.

These young Americans were another of the dozens of gangs on the north side. They called themselves the New City Royals. Their colors were royal blue (real clever) and black. Their symbol was a stylized crown, which was not to be confused with the crown that the Latin Kings identified themselves by. The Royals considered themselves a 'white' gang because they had a few white guys, some blacks and Latins and most of the other gangs were strictly ethnic.

There were six of them and I wanted to feel them out about the Robbery/Homicides. I knew them all. Gilly Rodriquez, the leader was half Mexican and half Puerto Rican, which made him an outcast in both cultures. Pinchy, Flako, Danny and Toker were his back-ups. The two girls were the tall pretty blond Marie, Gilly's girlfriend, and fat Angie, everybody's girlfriend.

There were about ten other members in this little branch of the larger Royal gang. Their territory ran from Pratt north to the city limits. My beat, Clark Street, ran through their supposed turf. They knew that if I caught them on Clark Street, they went to jail. Usually they obeyed the unwritten rule. I wasn't concerned with how close they were to Clark at the moment, I wanted to have a chat with Gilly.

As I began to slowly roll down my window, Cohen jumped out of the car like it was on fire. The six people on the staircase didn't move, but all came to alert status. They looked from me to the little guy struggling to put on his hat while holding his night stick and fumbling with his radio.

I hadn't planned to get out of the car but Cohen had already changed the plan. Reaching over, I turned the car off, took the keys and opened my door, automatically grabbing my hat from the back seat with my other hand.

"Bora`cion," one of the boys said under his breath. I let it go.

"Gilly," I said, "come here." I flexed my index finger to emphasize my request. At first he pretended not to hear. Then, when an appropriate amount of seconds passed, enough for him to save face with the gang, he stepped from the porch and came towards me with his hands in his pockets. The timing was everything, he had known he was a half second from me coming to get him. I let that go too.

"What's up, Cassidy man?" He said with a cocky attitude, stepping off the curb. Gilly was a junkie and slim built, but had ropey prison muscles. His long black hair was slicked to his head and plaited in a braid that reached down between his shoulder blades. The Royal uniform was dark blue sweats and black gym shoes.

"Get your hands out of your pockets!" Cohen was supposed to be my back-up and was giving conflicting orders. I wondered again how Brian White had gone on the medical rolls, stabbed in the back when he turned to tell his rookie to shut up perhaps. I didn't move, watching everybody at once, or trying at least.

Everyone slowly slid their hands into view, showing them to Cohen, smiling, mocking him. I tried to ignore the side show and ask my question. "Did you hear what happened down by Farwell yesterday?"

The answer wasn't what I cared about, it was the eyes. Gilly and I hadn't taken our eyes off of each other since I'd come around the corner. Now Cohen had caused me to loose concentration, breaking eye contact however briefly. Cohen had given everyone permission to move and I couldn't watch them and Gilly at the same time. Did I see something in his eyes when I mentioned the murders, or was I just hoping to see something there?

"I wasn't down on Farwell yesterday." He answered, still smiling and coming to a stop just a little more than arms reach away from me.

"I didn't ask you where you were yesterday. I asked you if you knew what happened down there." We were only three blocks from Farwell, four from the end of Royal territory. Gilly knew everything that went on in his territory.

"Everybody knows. So what? I wasn't around all day yesterday, ask Marie." He turned and looked back at the tall pretty blond girl. She was so thin that the bulge of her pregnancy was all the more obvious under her stretch blue jeans and baggy sweater. She was maybe seventeen. She smiled coyly, willing to swear to whatever Gilly said.

"Everybody knows, 'what', Gilly? Like who did the killings, for instance?" There was something in his eyes for sure this time, I think.

"Sure, man, everybody knows. We ain't got no treaty with them so I don't mind telling you it was the fucking Eagles did it. They kill their own people. They have no family, man." He turned to look at his extended family. Some sort of distorted family concept was part of the gang mentality.

He looked at me with a phoney sincere expression. I knew for sure now that it wasn't the Eagles. But I had the feeling that Gilly could tell me more.

"I knew that you wouldn't be around, Gilly. You're never around when it goes down. But you always know something. I know that." I iced my voice and gave him the most menacing look that I could muster.

"I think that later, we'll all take a ride over to Area 6 Headquarters. Then we'll let the dicks ask you where you weren't and where the Eagles were, yesterday when the jewelry store got hit." That wiped the stupid expression off of his face. I could have called for a wagon and sent them over right now, but Captain Stokes would have had a fit for detaining them without charges, and I was hungry.

I turned to Cohen, dismissing Gilly. "Let's go, Ben." He looked at me incredulously, still thinking that everything that I said while working the street was going to happen. He didn't argue at least, although disappointed that we weren't going to arrest these people. I got back in the car and handed him the keys just as he realized that they were missing from the ignition.

The restaurant that I wanted to eat at was just up at the corner, on the other side of Clark Street. We could see the sign for the 'Bagel Nook' from where we sat. I directed him to cross Clark and park in the illegal spot on the corner, almost in the crosswalk.

He tried to contain himself from asking stupid questions, but couldn't. "What happened on Farwell yesterday and why didn't we lock them up, if they have information?"

Gilly and his boys were always on the street, I could grab him anytime I wanted. But that wasn't what I wanted to talk to Cohen about. I wanted to talk about things that had to do with my personal safety. I wasn't going to be taking anybody anywhere with this kid backing me up.

"Never get out of the car and leave it running. If you catch public enemy number one and the car is gone when you get back to it, they're going to hang you regardless." He was about to say something, I held up a finger stopping him. I didn't want to hear what he had to say.

"More importantly, never tell a bunch of people to move unless you're directing traffic. Telling someone to take their hands out of their pockets, even though you're mother told you it was impolite, gives them permission to pull out whatever they're hiding in there. Get it?" He was doing his cupie doll impression again, head bobbing rhythmically.

"If you want to give commands, tell them 'don't' move, which most smart gang bangers already know, then walk up to them and feel their hands through their clothes. It's hard to shoot a police officer while the gun is pointing at your own prick.

He beamed at me, looking at me like I was some grizzled old man departing the wisdom of the ages. Unfortunately that's just about what I was. He wasn't going to repeat his question, but I was feeling sorry for him so I answered it anyway. "There was a double homicide at a little jewelry store on my beat yesterday." That stung.

"Gilly or one of his boys might know something, they patrol their territory more than I do. If they do know anything, a little stewing will do them good. I can always find Gilly when I want to." When I questioned Gilly again neither Cohen, nor anybody else, was going to be around.

Whether they knew anything or not, at least they'd be hiding from me for the rest of the shift. "Hey, are we going to eat or what? I'm still starving." Cohen had already passed his limit of how much police work I was going to do with him tonight.

The Bagel Nook had been owned and operated for over thirty years by a little Jewish couple. I'd been coming here for almost that long.

"Hello, Hoppy," Cyril said from behind the cash register. He had better color and was thinner since he'd had a heart attack, and the doctor had finally convinced him to take better care of himself.

"Hi, Cyril. How'r ya feelin?" There were a few regulars in the restaurant. Also some immigrant faces that I didn't recognize.

"You driving today? You have a new partner?" He said, ignoring my question regarding the condition of his health.

"Cyril Lebowitz, this is Benjamin Cohen, one of your Landsmen." He was smiling at Ben who was already embarrassed.

"Wonderful. We need more Jews on the police. You know how much trouble we've been having lately. The police...eh...they do nothing. No offense, Hoppy. We still have Kristallnacht every November. They break the windows on the Temples..." Cyril had Cohen by the arm and was steering him to a stool at the counter where I always sat, while he filled him in on all the anti-Semitic activity in Rogers Park.

"Irene, come see the nice Jewish policeman we have now." Irene was short and on the heavy side, but looked like a million bucks. You'd think that she worked at Tiffany's instead of a deli, by all the diamonds she wore. First she smiled at Cohen then her expression turned sour.

"Oh, Hoppy, look how young he is." Cohen's face was red. "How could you? They should be ashamed of themselves, this boy is too young to be doing your job." He wasn't doing my job.

She looked out the window at the dimming daylight. "Good Shabbos," she said sincerely to Cohen. He mumbled an answer, embarrassed to the maximum now. Irene had him by the face with both hands, I thought she was going to start kissing him.

"Oh, I know you're a good Jew, I can tell just by looking at your face. We are too, but business is so hard these days, and you can't close on Friday night anymore." She looked over at the table where the two immigrant men sat and frowned. "Nobody respects the old ways any longer."

"I'm going to go in the back and take my pants off, Cyril." I said smiling and loud enough to snap Irene out of her reverie.

"Sure, you go ahead, Hoppy." Cyril smiled, not knowing what my game was but always willing to play along.

"You don't be taking anything off in my place, Mr. Cassidy. There's no panky panky in my restaurant." I had her attention now.

"I have to wash up, Irene, I've got blood on my pants." I held up my dirty hands to stop her question. "Ask Benjamin, he'll tell you all about it, and I'll have whatever the soup is and a turkey on whole wheat."

Cohen gave me a helpless look and I gave him the finger. He smiled at me sheepishly, and I heard Irene saying that I shouldn't do that in her restaurant either, as I let the swinging door to the back room close. Cyril followed me back to the old double sink.

"What's with blood, Hoppy? You are hurt, or what?" He was genuinely concerned. I filled him in on the last job while I washed, Cyril liked police stories. When he asked me about the murders of Mr and Mrs Park, I filled him in less about that, pretending to be engrossed in cleaning my pants. They were actually going to the cleaners the minute I left here, I didn't want to talk about the Parks.

"...at the Gentile church," he finished saying something to me.

"What? I'm sorry, Cyril, I didn't catch that last thing."

"Tomorrow," he repeated. "At the Korean Church on Lunt. They're going to have services. Ten o'clock."

"Oh, yea. I better see if I can make it to the service." The thought of two coffins in a church didn't do much for my state of mind.

When we finished eating, Irene gave us half priced checks and asked if I would keep the kids from the side of the building. I told her that we had taken care of that before we came in.

It reminded Cohen of something and he turned to me at the cash register. "You know, Hop, I speak a little Spanish but I never heard the word 'bora`cion' before. What's it mean?" He'd been fed, met some nice people and was feeling relaxed.

"It's slang for 'drunk'," I told him casually. Cyril, behind the high counter, shook his finger and frowned in disapproval at Cohen. It was impolite for a good Jew to mention a Gentile friends shortcomings. I laughed at Cohen's continued embarrassment, grabbed him by the arm and pushed him out the door, waving at Cyril as we left.

Chapter 8

"Go north and stop at the cleaners up by Touhy Avenue," I directed when we had started rolling again.

"I'm sorry about that, Hop. I was hoping that you might want to switch with White and be my Field Training Officer, but I guess that won't happen now that I've put my foot in my mouth." I resisted telling him to stop apologizing again.

"Ben, I'm usually the Clark Street Foot Man. I never work with a partner. Rookie or otherwise. Captain Stokes is just teaching me a little lesson tonight because he likes to play boss and he can get away with it."

"But if he took you off foot patrol..." He had a hopeful look on his face now.

"If he tries to move me permanently, there's several people that I go back further with than George Stokes. I hate burning favors, but it usually doesn't come to that with George and I. He just likes to screw around with me now and then."

Cohen had a crestfallen expression on his face now. "Why do you want a new F.T.O. anyway? What kind of problem are you having with Brian White?" I could only think of about a dozen or so possibilities.

"He says that I'm not tough enough. He says that I'm a Jew boy and I have to have a thick skin. When we were eating the other day, he threw a piece of ham on my plate and said, 'Better learn to eat it, there isn't going to be a kosher restaurant open all the time so you can have Jew food'."

Cohen knew he was violating unwritten rules complaining about this bigot that he was working with. Anybody could become an F.T.O. if they had enough seniority and took a one week course at the academy. There was a grade level pay increase that went with the job, which was the reason that White was an F.T.O. He had a number of ex-wives and children to support.

"He's right, in a way, Ben. You have to toughen yourself up a bit. You need a thick skin to keep White from getting under it." If being called a Jew boy bothered him, he was in the wrong business.

"I can take it." He appealed. "And I'm tough enough. I've got a black belt in Tae Kwon Do. He just won't give me a chance, he never lets up on me. I could teach him a lesson the next time he calls me 'little Jew', or wimp..." His voice trailed off. This kid might be a black belt or whatever, but he would never be mean enough, or was it dumb enough, to hurt someone just to prove a point. As much as White might have it coming.

"You said you were sorry about that 'bora`cion' thing, right?" He nodded. "Why, when it's the truth? They really didn't mean for us to hear it, but I know that's what they call me behind my back. So what? I was a drunk for a long time, I earned the name. Now I should go around kicking ass every time somebody calls me by it?"

"I know. It's different for you." I held up my hand to stop his apology or excuse. "Let me tell you something, the only two things you can be sure of in this life are dying and staying a Jew. You better come to terms with both of them if you want to work the street."

We pulled up to the double store front that was the Moon Cleaners. I directed Cohen into their loading zone. The boss Inon Moon was always asking me to fix tickets that he got on his vehicles when they were parked there during rush hours. I tried to tell him that I couldn't fix a ticket after the bike men had written it. I also tried to explain that his loading zone wasn't in effect between 4 and 6 pm, but he never understood.

"Finish the case report and give me a few minutes in here before you come up clear, with a Hospitalization Case Report." I dictated his words to the dispatcher. There was a knack to talking on the radio, it took time to learn. Cohen was almost finished with the report, his neat handwriting covered half of the page that was clipped to the metal beat box on his lap.

When I went into the cleaners, Moon's wife was behind the counter. I said hello nicely. She was a bitter faced black haired woman who obviously disliked me and hated to clean my clothes, because her husband never charged me for the cleaning.

She held up a tan parking ticket and waved it in my face. "We pay for loading zone, and you give ticket!"

I took it from her and looked to see that, sure enough, one of the motorcycle guys had written it yesterday at 5 o'clock. "Mrs. Moon, I told you that even though you have a loading zone for your store you can't park there during rush hours. There are signs up and down the whole street."

"I got sign too! I pay for sign! It MY sign!" She snatched the ticket from my hand and threatened me with it some more, sticking it in my face. Her husband suddenly appeared, hollering at her full blast in Korean, I thought he was going to belt her. If so, I would have to step in and break it up after an hour or so.

He took the ticket from her and pointed toward the rear of the building where a bunch of illegal Mexican immigrants slaved over the various washers and steaming machines. She didn't say another work and headed for the back room.

Moon turned to me all smiles. "No problem," he said. This was the first time he had been so nice about getting a ticket. He was never as irate as his wife, but he was never this happy either. He still cleaned my clothes for free and I gave his vehicles a play whenever I could. I kept an eye on him when he went to the bank and checked on the store when it was closed. I figured that we were even on the cleaning bills.

The wiry dark haired man, short and slender but tough looking, quickly retrieved my shirts and pants. He presented them to me waving his hand in the universal 'no charge' sign. I took a pair of pants out of one of the bags and told him that I needed to use his little office behind the counter to change into them.

He seemed upset at my using his office but I needed to get the bloody pants off. I just sort of waved his objections off and walked around the counter and into the office closing the door partially. What was he so worried about? I wasn't going to steal his money or anything. Although I could understand how the police had earned that reputation.

I left the door open enough so that he could see his desk while he hovered outside. There wasn't even any cash around. The few papers that were on the desk were all written in Korean. The square figures reminded me of the papers that were strewn around the jewelry store yesterday.

When I finished, he seemed relieved and I apologized for the bike guys who'd given him a legitimate citation, saying that I would talk to them and ask them for more special consideration for Moon's loading zone.

"You driving today?" He asked conversationally, smiling, gesturing towards the blue and white squad occupying his loading zone.

"Just for today." I knew he wasn't laughing at me like the guys at the station. "Tomorrow I'll be back on foot so don't worry." I was glad that he hadn't asked me about the Park murders. He must have known them.

One of the units was asking for a personal. The operator denied their request and was giving them an assignment when I heard our call numbers over my radio. "2423," Cohen's voice was unsure, "we're clear with a hospitalization case report, and we can take that job squad."

When I got my laundry hooked in the back window and got into the car, he looked at me and said, "we've got a job."

I just shook my head wearily at his 'who me?' expression. "Ben, you ever been in the Army, a Kibbutz or anything?" He gave me a frown and a negative head shake.

"Well, I know you've heard the expression, 'never volunteer'." His head went in the 'yes' direction now. "Well, it goes double on the police department." This kid was going to work me to death. An unfortunate choice of words.

The call was a 'disturbance' on the third floor of a building on Morse and Clark. It had been subdivided over the years until there were ten apartments on a floor. There had been no other improvements for years. From the hall ceiling a smoke detector hung by its wires, burglarized for its 9 volt battery. The stairs were covered with a worn rug and littered with trash.

We found apartment 3C halfway down the hall on the left. I knocked on the door after pushing Cohen out from in front of it. As we stood on either side of the door, we listened for some sounds of movement within the apartment.

There was a lot of lock turning and chain rattling before the door was finally opened a few inches by a white girl in her early twenties. She had a very anxious expression on her face, which was also a bit flushed. I pushed the door open a little so I could see over her shoulder and through the crack where the door hinged. She didn't seem to have any company. I sniffed a the air when she spoke to see if she had been drinking or smoking pot.

"You've got to help me," she said in a voice that bordered on hysteria.

"Yes, ma'am, that's why we're here. What can we do for you?" I smiled and spoke softly, trying to calm her.

"Those men down the hall are doing things to me." She was obviously on the edge, scratching her arms, leaving long red marks on her skin. Medium built, she had short brown hair, and except for the wild look on her face, could have been considered pretty.

"Which men?" Cohen looked over his shoulder, down the hallway where her wild eyes directed.

"Over there." She pointed at a door near the stairs.

"Just what did they do to you, ma'am?" She was wearing just a tee shirt and shorts, small breasted and quite thin. I saw no bruises or blood on her.

"They're hurting me...They're doing Voo Doo to me." I looked in her 'pits' for track marks, all that scratching had made me think she was a junkie. I could see no needle marks on her arms or legs.

Cohen was about to ask her a question, thinking that she was rational. I figured that we didn't have enough qualified mental health facilities in this city. I cut him off. "We'll go and have a talk with them. You stay in your apartment so they won't know that it was you who called the police." I gave her a friendly conspiratorial look. She wasn't completely irrational, returning my look and nodding agreement before she closed her door.

We went down to 3E, Cohen moved out from in front of the door without being pushed this time so I let him knock as a reward. After much less chain rattling the door was opened by a small Latino man. He had the round face of Indian and Spanish ancestry and I could see that he was terrified by the police coming to his door.

"Senor. Habla English?" I asked. There were over 200 hundred languages spoken in Chicago, most of them could be heard on Clark Street. Far too many for me to start learning any of them now. I usually made due with universal communication.

"Poco," he sighed, knowing that the language barrier would detract from his side of the story. Just then Cohen, who had said he spoke a little Spanish, started speaking like a native. As the words poured from his mouth, my mouth just hung open in amazement. I could see that the little man was pleased that he could communicate with us now. The last thing Cohen said as he motioned down the hall was Voo Doo. That I understood.

"No! No," the little man pleaded, looking from Cohen to me. He pushed his door open all the way and gestured into his little apartment. Against the far wall was an altar, complete with the blue and white statue of Our Lady of Guadalupe. There were fake flowers all around it. Tall vigil candles burned on both sides of the three foot statue.

Terror in his eyes again, he said to me in broken English, "we no Voo Doo Senor Polici, we Cat-toe-lick." He was the only person in sight, but 'we' could be any number of immigrants cramming into this little room to sleep at night. After they said their prayers before the altar, that is. I hated the circumstances that had made this little man so terrified of my uniform, the Central American society that he had probably fled from, and the one of false hope that he had fled to.

"Look," I said maybe a little too sternly, backing him off a bit. "This is America. Do you understand me? If you want to do Voo Doo, you do Voo Doo. This is a free country. Tell him what I said, Ben." When he finally got it, we all stood around smiling at each other. He started to say something rapidly to Cohen, pointing at the girl's door then at the floor.

"He says that she is disturbed," Cohen pointed at his head. "They pray for her," he translated. "He says that one night she put fried chicken by his door."

"What does fried chicken have to do with anything?" I didn't get it.

"The Voo Doo. Apparently she got some fried chicken to-go and arranged the pieces in a cross on the floor outside his door, here in the hallway. She must have been trying to counteract his spells."

"Let me get this straight. She couldn't find a live chicken to sacrifice so she went to 'Chicken Lickin' for spiritual guidance. Is that what you're telling me?" We were all laughing now, having a good old time. "Better tell him not to eat the chicken if she does it again. She might have a counter spell on it."

When we sobered up enough to go and talk to the girl, I found that she was on medication that she wasn't taking. We assured her that we had taken all of the Voo Doo equipment away from her neighbor and called her doctor's office leaving a message that he should check on her. She was happy, everybody was happy. Good Police work.

The radio was quiet as I came clear from the job, so I took Cohen on foot patrol. It wouldn't get busy until after dark, even on a Friday. It took awhile for everybody to get gassed up. Every team was supposed to go on foot patrol for a little while each night. I preferred all night.

Why did I have to get stuck with this rookie on a Friday, of all days? The worst night of the week. Forget Saturday for violence. Forget the stories about the full moon causing humanity to go a bit nuts, it was Friday that made people wild. Pay day.

The liquor store around the corner on Clark was already busy with people coming from the Currency Exchange across the street, where they had just paid to have their checks cashed.

"Watch out for this guy, Cohen," I emphasized the Jewish name loudly when I walked through the door, "he's an Arab."

Abby, the olive skinned man behind the counter, was busy ringing sales while his brother John, bagged the bottles and ran the lottery machine. On payday the little blue box popped tickets out of itself practically nonstop.

The poorer the people, the more lottery they bought. The Mexican Bolita and the Afro-American Policy Wheels had been put out of business on the first day of the Illinois Lottery. More precisely the State had taken over the long running vices themselves. Now the State exploited people with the hope of winning a new life for a small investment, a piece of their present life.

"Don't listen to him, I'm not that kind of Arab." Abbey didn't miss a thing that went on around him, no matter how busy it got in the little store.

"He looks just like the ones you see on television, don't he, Ben? I mean look at that schnoz. Abby, you sure you aren't related to King Faisal?" Cohen was staying out of this one, trying to keep from smiling.

"Just like your grandfather is Hop Along Cassidy?" He was trying not to smile, but he had come back with a good shot, I had to crack a grin. Abby automatically reached up to the cigarette rack, pulling down several different brands for a customer without looking.

"Uh, oh. He gets mad when I make fun of his bugle, Ben," I continued our little routine. "Besides, Abby, I found out long ago that my father was some guy named UNK not Cassidy. I just look like Hop Along Cassidy." I took off my hat and posed a bit before stuffing my too long hair back under it.

"I never seen him, but he must be ugly," Abby shot back.

"Just think of Lawrence of Arabia with a big black hat, and riding a white horse named Topper."

"I never saw him either. You know," he looked down his nose at me, "that a large nose is a sign of intelligence in my country." Abby rang up another sale, bagging the booze himself as lottery tickets popped out of the machine John was running. John was a carbon copy of his brother, except he had no hair on top of his head. Two lines were forming.

"You want something?" He said to us. "Get a pop." He said to Cohen, gesturing toward the cooler behind us, that was filled with a variety of sodas.

"No," we said in unison.

"Hoppy, they give you a partner because of last night?" I didn't take a negative meaning from his question. He didn't hold me responsible for the crime committed on my beat, I did. Abby was just rightfully worried about the escalating crime and the possibility of becoming a victim himself.

"No, I'm on a car tonight. They're short of manpower," I gave him the same story that the desk personnel had given me.

"That's how these things happen," he said disgustedly, referring to the murders, "there's not enough police." He shook his head.

"Don't worry, I'll be around, Abby." I wondered if I sounded convincing to him, I wasn't all that confident in our ability to save anyone.

Abby was another business man that I knew had a gun behind the counter, the chances of it helping him were slim. But it was a chance, like the lottery. "We've got to go, Abby, I'm going to introduce Cohen around."

"See you later. Nice to meet you, Ben. Stop by when you don't have Cassidy of Arabia with you," Abby threw another shot as we headed for the door. The whole idea of foot patrol was to let the customers and possible bad guys know that you were around, there was no rule against making friends and having fun while doing it.

"You know, Abby, I heard that 'long ears' are the sign of intelligence. A long nose is a sign of a 'long' something else," I said from the doorway. We both laughed when he shook his head and showed me his thumb and fore finger held about an inch apart.

"What did he mean when he said that he wasn't that kind of Arab?" Cohen asked as we walked down Clark.

"Abby's a Palestinian Christian. You never hear about them because the Israelis and the Moslem Palestinians were able to agree on one thing early in the game. The Christians were expendable, and they kicked them out of the Holy Land." I smiled at him.

"Those are your landsmen, Benjamin Cohen." I said, still smiling.

"No, they're not," he smiled back. "I'm not that kind of Jew."

Two doors down was a little Mexican place that serves the hottest food in the world. Nobody but Mexicans ever ate there. Jose, the rotund little cook, was standing just on the other side of the plate glass. He was busy carving chunks from a gob of pork skins and herbs that was skewered and racked in front of a Greek style gyros machine.

The burners on the back of the machine flared as the fat spattered onto them. Jose waved to us and motioned toward the three foot high, two foot wide, heartburn he was working on, emphasizing his gesture with a knife that looked like a sword.

It was topped with a Bermuda onion the size of a softball and he laughed when I did my usual stomach grabbing pantomime mouthing the words 'no thanks, too hot!'. The grin stayed on his sweaty face as he cheerfully returned to slicing the brown bubbling strips from his creation.

"You like hot food, Ben?" I asked as we walked.

"Love it. My wife and I eat it all the time," he answered.

"The guy's name is Jose, just tell him that I sent you in there and he'll take care of you." We came to the door of the Public Library that was in the middle of the block.

"I couldn't do that...I mean make him give me free food." Cohen had to learn the difference between a bribe and favor.

"Sure you could. He'll give you what he wants, you won't make him do anything. And he'll ask you for a favor in return. He'd love to have a policeman come into his store occasionally, it's good for business. With my stomach I can't even smell the air in that place without getting indigestion."

Stopping between the doors of the Rodgers Park Branch Library, I turned to him so he would understand the importance of what I was saying. "I'm telling you to go in there and do police work. It might not happen right away, but if a chance arises you'll help that man. Do you think he cares about giving you a couple of tacos? He'll think of a way for you to do something for him, believe me."

"You won't catch me telling any free loaders," I thought of Jim Geery, "to go in there and use my name. You're the real police now, and you want to do police work. It's not all running around putting hand cuffs on people." I was screwing up, the kid was looking at me like I was a professor.

He was hopefully only going to be with me for one day, so I decided to cut short the unorthodox training session.

"Look, do what you want. Just stop in there sometime with your wife and talk some of that fluent Spanish for him. I guarantee that in five minutes he'll be stuffing chilis down your throat and you'll be explaining a tax bill for him or making phone calls to his Jewish suppliers who never seem to understand him, probably on purpose."

I wanted to give him a long speech on the importance of contact with the community, and didn't. Young coppers wanted to break doors down and chase bad guys, community service was dull and not immediately rewarding. I was just learning the importance of it myself after thirty years.

When we stepped into the library, the manager was behind the counter. "Hi, Fran. What's up?" She was a tall woman, gray haired but youthful, well educated and looked the part of a librarian.

"Everything's quiet tonight, Hoppy," She emphasized the word 'tonight', referring to the incident yesterday. Two doors down from the library was the Park Jewelry Store. We had been coincidently moving toward the murder scene, for the last half hour.

"Yeah, it was a terrible thing. You didn't happen to hear anything or see anyone run by around three o'clock did you?" Terrible wasn't word enough to describe the scene, but I wasn't going into further detail. I don't know why I asked the question. I told myself that I was just making conversation. A little investigation on my part wouldn't hurt anything. If I learned anything, I'd call Voltz at Area 6 Homicide. I had a few questions that I wanted to ask him anyway.

"No, I'm sorry, Hop. We didn't know anything even happened until we saw all the squad cars and one of the guys came in and told us that the Parks had been..." She didn't want to say it; neither did I. "Sorry."

"Heck, it was worth a try." There were several other people who worked at the Branch, but I could tell from her answer that they had all discussed the matter and none of them knew anything about the murders.

"School tonight?" I referred to the tables pushed together over on one side. There were a dozen or so people sitting around studying, each one looking like they were from a different corner of the globe.

"Yes, it's an E.S.L. class. They weren't here last night." She added the last comment probably thinking that I would disturb the class with questions about the murders. Now that I thought about it, what could it hurt? The librarian gave me a familiar look.

"English as a Second Language?" Cohen spoke up, preventing me from getting disciplined by the librarian for disturbing the peace. It wouldn't have been the first time.

"Is it in conjunction with citizenship or a G.E.D. program?" I left them to discuss higher education while I looked through the newspaper racks. This was part of my daily routine, though today maybe one of the papers would tell me something about the murders that I already didn't know.

Ben and Fran were deep in quiet conversation when I finished reading what little there was in the papers and walked back over to the desk. There were murders in Chicago every day, and even the most spectacular didn't command much space.

"Cassidy, they shouldn't be wasting this young man's education giving out parking tickets." I didn't know what they had been talking about. I'd made it through high school and had just completed an associate degree from the community college. I didn't feel that they were wasting my education on writing parking tickets. We said our good-bye's and headed out.

If we continued in the direction we had been going, the next stop was murder. I grabbed Ben's arm and stepped between the parked cars, 'jay walking' across the street. I didn't want to look into the jewelry store, so why was I fifty feet away from it? The murders were affecting me, negatively. I was acting strangely. The librarian had treated me as though she perceived it. As though I was going to start threatening innocent people, demanding that they tell me things that they didn't know.

On the west side of Clark, across from the library, was the V.F.W. Hall. I stuck my head in the door and gave them a wave. There were a number of my buddies sitting in their usual places along the bar. All veterans of one war or another.

I could tell by the looks they gave me that they all had the 'question' on their minds, and I declined their friendly gestures and smiling faces. "If we go in there, they'll never let us leave," I said, walking Cohen away from the Hall. I didn't tell him the reason for my statement, I was having eye trouble again. It would have been easy to turn back toward where we had parked the car, we should have been getting back up on the air. Instead I led Cohen toward the Limelight Pub, my eyes flicking across the street.

Someone had locked the scissor gate across the front door. It was hard to see into the darkened space behind the large plate glass windows. My eyes tried to focus, the inside of the store was lighted only by what light came in from the street lamps. Before I could make out any of the gruesome things that were pictured in my mind, I got a hold of myself, shaking like a cold breeze had blown up my back. Cohen looked at me questioningly. I didn't explain. We reached the Limelight and stepped up to the door.

Pushing open the heavy wooden door, we were bathed in the sickly soothing glow of limelight. "Basilli!" Georgos was keeping an ever vigilant watch on his front door from behind the bar.

"Hello, Georgos." I said. There were no customers in the place. At this time Nicko would be in back preparing the ingredients for the limited menu they served. "This is Ben Cohen, I'm showing him all the dives that I used to get drunk in."

"Dives!" The insulted look on his face vanished, replaced with a frown for me and a smile for Cohen. "He don't drink no more." Georgos poked a fat finger at me.

"You think your funny?" His smile faded. "Instead of embracing the wonders of civilization we gave you, you want to be a comedian!"

"Komoidos!" He shouted at me. "The singer. That's where the word comes from. Do you think we created these beautiful words without thinking. 'Think' about it. You can't see the humor in life until you can sing." He pointed to his head with a stubby finger, the same one he had been threatening me with a moment earlier. As usual I didn't understand what he was talking about.

"You must learn to sing, Basilli. Learn to sing in your heart." He raised one eyebrow and fixed me with a stare meant to telepathically transplant knowledge into my head.

Holding his hands dramatically over his heart, Georgos began to sing and stroll down the aisle behind the bar. Picking up a towel and wiping at imaginary dirt as if it was a scene from an opera, he crooned something in Greek that sounded like a love song.

You wouldn't know it from looking at the balding pate and spare tire around his middle, but Georgos had a sweet voice and he knew it. Later tonight he'd allow himself to be dragged up on stage and sing with the Greek band, that was mostly Armenians.

"What language is that?" Cohen asked quietly.

Before I could answer, Georgos, more than happy to spew more philosophy, pointed toward the ceiling. "Pedeo!" He said to Cohen.

"It is 'THE' language. When you want to speak words of love to your sweetheart, you speak French. When you want to discuss a beautiful work of art, you speak Italian."

He screwed his finger towards heaven for more emphasis. "But when you want to speak to the god's you speak GREEK!" He rolled the word around in his mouth for a moment, savoring it.

Cohen smiled widely, taking the hand that Georgos extended, wincing just a bit from the crushing strength in the grip of the vigorous Greek.

"Georgos Kastanas," he said to Cohen. "This barbarian doesn't appreciate civilization as the Greeks have given to the world, but I can tell that you do."

"Ben. Ben Cohen. Glad to meet you, Georgos Kastanas." I could tell that he wanted to say something in my favor and just barely understood that it wasn't necessary. Georgos had been partly responsible for saving me from drinking myself to death. I owed a part of my life to this little man, the part that wanted to live. I guess that it showed.

"You want a pop?" Georgos asked us both. You could get popped to death on Clark Street if you weren't careful.

"No." We answered in unison again, then I added, "I just wanted him to meet the great philosopher and singing star."

"It was my pleasure," he said sincerely, taking no cynicism from my comment. Then he smiled broadly, the gold backing on his European dental work glowing greenly.

"Basilli, you catch him yet?" Georgos looked at the corner of the room. His line of sight, if the wall hadn't been there, would have crossed the street and focused right on the jewelry store.

"No. Not yet, Georgos." I was anxious to leave suddenly, wanting to avoid further questions that had no answers.

"I'll remember him when you show him to me. He had the tail all the way down the back..." I turned back to him confused.

"What are you talking about, Georgos?" I said directly. "Who are you going to remember?"

"The one I told you about yesterday. The Mavro. He was in here just before all the police cars come out in the front. I throw him out when he say 'to use the phone'. I can tell that he did something, but I didn't know what at the time. You remember, I told you yesterday."

How could I be so stupid? Of course he did tell me yesterday, or tried to tell me. Instead of acting like a professional I was feeling sorry for myself when I should have been paying attention. They wanted me to train a rookie, I was acting like one myself.

"Please, Georgos. You said that he was 'Mavro', a black man. But he wasn't black was he? Tell me again about him," I asked, trying not to say I was sorry for not listening when it had been important.

"Not black, but dark skin. He come in yesterday, very nervous he was acting. Looking out the window. I say to him, 'Get out, you lousy punk'. He say, 'please to use the phone'. I tell him it's my phone and he better get out or I call police. I don't really call, Basilli, you know I'm not scared of these punks, but I pick up the phone here behind the bar and he run out." He pointed west up Farwell Avenue.

"Describe him to me, will you, Georgos?" I had a feeling that I already knew who he would describe. I thought of the black and blue bandanna that I'd seen on the floor next to Sung Park's body. Black and blue were the colors of the New City Royals street gang.

"You know them, Basilli. The ones that are by Greenleaf Street all the time. He's the tall skinny one with the braid down his back." Georgos gave me everything but his name, and I knew that. I'd just talked to him. Gilly Rodriquez.

Chapter 9

When we stepped out of the pub, onto the corner of Farwell and Clark, the squad operator called us and gave us a job at 1620 Jarvis, several blocks away. "Tell him we're on our way back to the car and ten-four the job, Ben."

As Cohen fumbled with his radio, writing the address down on a paper in his hat, my eyes wandered across the street. It was a little darker now and the street lamps seemed to cast more light into the shop. Enough for me to visualize blood spatters that were probably shadows. I could see the doorway in the rear, the left half of the crane curtain still stuffed up over the rod.

I'd bragged to Cohen that I could put my hands on Gilly any time I wanted. It was serious put up or shut up time now. I debated calling Voltz and telling him what I'd learned.

I had Cohen zig-zag around to the usual spots where the Royals hung out, while we headed to the job. Not a Royal in sight. I'd done a fine job of making them stay off the street.

We were a few minutes late getting to the job and I felt worse when I realized that this woman had gotten more beating while I was on a personal wild goose chase. We were on the third floor of an average apartment building. One of the children, there were four, had answered the door. She was about seven and had blue eyes, swollen from crying, and thick brown hair. It was obvious that the children were of mixed race.

Cohen was freaked out by the condition of the victim. He had every right to be. The woman sat on the battered green sofa, holding her damaged arm, unable to do anything about the side of her face that was swelling and turning from red to purple.

She looked European. I found out later that they had met and been married in Germany, when he was stationed over there in the Army. What had looked like a beautiful future in Germany, had turned into a tough reality, four children later, here in America.

"Ma'am," I tried to consol her. "Who did this to you?"

"I'll tell you who did it, mother fucker." A huge Afro-American man in his thirties came out of what must have been the bedroom. He was wearing only red shorts and had a look of fury in his eyes.

His hands were empty and there was nowhere he could hide a weapon, being almost naked. Lucky for us because if he'd come out of that room blasting, our Kevlar vests would have been the only things that could have saved us, and they didn't cover certain areas that were very important.

I could feel Cohen tense next to me and move into sort of a fighting stance. He had his night stick in his hand. We were not going to display the latest hand-to-hand techniques taught at the police academy. I was much too old to be fighting with any of these people. I stepped toward the irate man, moving between him and both the victim and the rookie.

"Ben, you talk with Mrs...? What's your last name?" I said to the onrushing bull, trying to de-escalate the situation a bit.

"What the fuck do you care?" He bellowed, stopping just inches from my face. I was looking up into his bloodshot eyes. "You want some of me too?" He screamed in my face. My movement might have been a little too threatening, I decided, but not as threatening as what I thought Cohen had in mind. Cohen was ready to fight and so was this giant. I couldn't think of a worse combination.

"Phew...Man." I said, waving my hand in front of our faces. "You've got some bad breath. "Phew. What-ta-ya been eatin anyway, onions or what?" I could see the brain behind the eyes switch to another channel.

He thought for a second, then stammered, "Well, I just brushed my teeth."

"Try that blue Listerine that they have now. It really works for me." He just stood there breathing heavily and trying not to get any on me. Everyone was silent and still, even the children.

"Now, I get paid to let people call me a mother fucker," I laughed, "but you don't. That's why I asked you what your name was. The radio guy said it was Brookfield, is that right?"

"Yeah, that's right." The steam was going out of him gradually.

"Okay, now we're getting somewhere," I said rubbing my hands together in feigned exuberance. "Mr. Brookfield, why don't you and I go into the kitchen and get an ice bag for your woman and we can talk about what happened". I started toward the lighted kitchen, drawing him behind me with continued conversation.

I glanced back at Cohen who was still frozen in a fighting stance and mouthed the word 'wagon', then I said loudly, "Ben, you talk with Mrs. Brookfield. We'll be in the kitchen talking." I lowered the volume on my radio so the giant wouldn't hear Cohen call for help.

The kitchen was a mess of dirty dishes, baby bottles and garbage. There were a few food encrusted chairs, but I'd already dirtied one pair of pants today, so I didn't sit down. "So tell me what happened, man. There's always two sides to every story." I had to keep him talking until the wagon got here.

"I just can't take it anymore man, I work my ass off and then if I stop and have a few drinks on payday, she starts on me first thing. I ain't drunk." He started crying. That was a bad sign, especially when the crier was 6 foot 3 and 250 pounds. I'd been much drunker than he was many times, but I never beat my wife, drunk or sober.

"Look, man, I can understand that with four kids, you might need a little liquid support before you come home to face the music." I laughed and he smiled a bit, slowing the water works.

"But you can't have a few cocktails then come home and beat on the old lady. It just isn't done anymore, man. This domestic abuse is a serious thing nowadays. I'm going to have to take her for medical treatment," I held my breath for a moment, "and your going to have to go to the station."

His eyes flared up again and I turned to a little boy who was standing in the doorway to misdirect the conversation again. He was wearing only briefs, his eyes red from crying and nose running a gush.

70

"What's your name, buddy?" I asked. Keep talking, it was better than the alternative.

"Dwight." He said sniffing up his runny nose, which immediately ran back down.

"Dwight, can you go and get your daddy's pants and shirt for me?" I looked at Mr. Brookfield to see how he was going to handle that request.

I held up my hand to stop his protest and put a little seriousness in my voice. "Look, man, these kids are your blood, you see how upset they are. You want to hurt them worse? You want them to see you fighting with the police? If he's outside and needs help, you want him to not ask a policeman for help because he saw the police beating his daddy up?" As though I could actually stand up to this guy for one second.

He nodded to the kid who left to get the clothing, but he wasn't resigned to going to jail, not yet. "Hey, man, you don't have to take me anywhere, it's cool now. I can take care of her." I could imagine just how that would go. I may have been late getting here, but Mrs. Brookfield wasn't getting any more beatings tonight, no matter what I had to do.

I opened the freezer looking for ice cubes and not looking at Brookfield. One package of frozen spinach. It was still in a plastic grocery bag. I took it out and gave it to another little face that was peering around the doorway, instructing the little girl to have her mother put it on her eye.

"Sure, I can tell that your cool now. But I've got a job to do man, just like you do. This is more serious than you think, you've got to go to the station with us." I should have asked him if he thought the Cubs would win the World Series this year.

"And if I say I ain't going to jail." He seemed to swell up a bit, tensing. I held up my hand in feigned resignation, actually a split second from a quick left to his jaw and a right to that rippled mid-section. His hands were at his sides, fists clenching. Doubting that I could actually hurt this guy, I hoped I could keep him off me long enough for Cohen to get in here and try to save me.

"Well then, let me tell you how that will work. That little guy that I'm working with loves to beat people. That's why they put him with an old guy like me. They thought it would calm him down." I was about to get pounded down to the second floor by this monster and I was threatening him. I vowed to get even with Captain Stokes for putting me on this car tonight.

"He's got about ten black belts and a stack of brutality complaints against him. They say he uses that stick like one of them samurai swords. Cracked more skulls than Internal Affairs can keep up with. You saw how he almost attacked you when we first got here? You don't want me to tell him that you're resisting arrest, do you?" He sort of shook his head, but I hadn't convinced him totally yet. When I glanced into the living room and saw Cohen holding the frozen spinach up to the side of the wife's head, I wasn't convinced either.

"And that isn't all. The wagon crew are just as bad. The rest of the cars in the area will all be trying to get up here to get a piece of you. If there's anything left. You won't be getting home any time soon." There was confusion in his eyes.

"Listen to me." This was the moment. "If you'll go along with me, I'll give you my personal guarantee that nothing will happen to you. Nobody will lay a finger on you and I'll get you a private cell. You have my word on that." That, or I'm going to stomp on your bare foot with my size twelve oxfords and hit you over the head with this kitchen.

The doorbell rang. Thoughts of reinforcements having desired effects on both of us he said, "you promise?" I crossed my heart in kindergarten style and he started to get dressed.

The wagon crew was Leo Prange and another recruit, Gloria (something Spanish). I couldn't remember her name. Leo drank a gallon of coffee and smoked five packs of cigarettes per shift. The Latino rookie was less than 5 feet tall, much less. There wasn't enough meat on the two of them to make a good sandwich. Mr. Brookfield went quietly and I kept my promise, not letting my partner or the vicious wagon crew beat him up.

When we walked into the station Jane Gallagher informed me that Captain Chicken George was out at his favorite Chinese restaurant. The wagon crew had already finished processing the prisoner and he was in back, in a cell by himself. We had taken Mrs. Brookfield to the hospital and made all the proper calls to make sure that she got additional help. She could have signed complaints herself, but she refused and we had to sign them.

The story was old. She feared it would get worse when he got out of jail if she signed complaints. There were more safe guards to prevent women from recurrent abuse, but there was never enough. It often took years before a woman could escape an abusive relationship, if she wanted to escape at all.

Luckily, we had gotten a neighbor to watch the children. Four less headaches. If I could get Felony charges placed against the husband, Mrs. Brookfield would have a little more time to recover from her fractured jaw and dislocated arm.

Without the Captain there, I called the States Attorney's office myself and spoke to an Assistant States Attorney named Colleen MacCarthy. I smoozed her a little, asking her if she had red hair. With a name like that chances were better than even. I suggested Aggravated Criminal Domestic Battery, a Felony, and she approved the charge. I could tell she was smiling when I finally finished chatting with her and hung up. I was smiling too.

Banging out the case report, I signed Captain George Stokes' name to the charges and faxed them all over the place. His egg foo young was going to come out his nose when he realized that I'd slapped a major crime on his watch and forged his signature, approving it all. The desk personnel, who all hated him as well, had gone along with the whole idea. I was feeling much better when we left the station. Job well done.

Chapter 10

"What a stroke of luck for you to notice the onions on that guy's breath and comment about it." Cohen was feeling like the real police now. "His bad breath saved us from having to fight with him I'm sure." I doubted that he was sorry we didn't have to fight the guy. "We sure were lucky," he repeated annoyingly.

"Luck has nothing to do with it. I've used that bad breath routine a dozen times." He might as well understand what happened. "If they're both irate, I sit down and start watching television. When they get tired of arguing and curious enough about why I don't jump into the fray I tell them that I'm not getting involved until they become civil. Never escalate, Ben."

"You made up all that stuff to keep me from getting hurt? That's why you stepped in front of me. To protect me. I can take care of myself." Famous last words. I hated to stick a pin in his bubble but as a training officer, that was my job. Thinking back to when I'd been a rookie, thirty years ago, I remembered when everybody that went to jail got a beating. Personally, I got tired early on of proving who had the bigger balls every time I made an arrest.

"I don't care if you can take care of yourself or not, Ben." I said, none to kindly. "I wasn't protecting you, I was protecting myself. You took one look at that woman and then at the offender and wanted to pay the guy back on the spot. They found out that doesn't work a long time ago. You may be able to take care of yourself, but I'm fifty-five years old and I've been too old to fight with irate husbands for...how old are you? Twenty-five? For longer than you've been around."

"But this isn't the first time he's done that to her..." There was real emotion in his voice. "She said he beats her all the time..."

"Listen to what you're saying, rookie." I said it in a derogatory manner. "' He beats her all the time', that's right, all the time. Which means that she goes back into a relationship where she knows she will be abused, all the time. Does that make her nuts? I guess it does a little bit. He knows what he's doing is wrong, but he does it again and again. He probably justifies it in his own crazy way. If you ask her why she goes back, she'll probably tell you that she knows he really loves her, deep down. And if you ask him if he loves his wife and children, he'll say, 'absolutely'."

I softened my voice a little. "There is no right and wrong, kid, it's just a point of view, remember that. Even if the whole world thinks something is wrong, the person committing the crime has his reasons, and they make sense to him."

"Our job was to stop the beatings, put the bad guy in jail and get her some help. That's what we did. But our job is just part of the process that needs to take place. Our job is not to kick his butt and punish him for what he's done, while working out our own aggressions at the same time."

"I'm sorr...well, Brain White handles domestic disturbances a little differently." I was glad he didn't apologize at least.

"Yeah, I know how Brain handles jobs. He thinks that the old 'street justice' is still the best kind. Let me tell you something about White, he's tough and likes to hurt people, but he's really a wimp."

"That's what he'd like you to think you are, but you're not. So quit trying to prove yourself, you'll get your chances." He cracked a small smile.

"The whole point is to use your head not your fists. There's an old unwritten rule on the job, if you get sweated up, the day is a total loss." I thought about a comment that Fran, the librarian, made.

"Your supposed to be well educated. Start using your head. How many degree's do you have anyway?"

I looked at my watch after noticing the surprised look on Cohen's face. I'd hit a nerve. "Drive up to Howard Street, I try to be around when they close the Currency Exchange."

We headed north to the last street in Chicago. When we passed Mama Lea's West Indian Restaurant another forgotten responsibility came to mind. Call Claire. Cohen concentrated on his driving and we made it to the neon lighted currency exchange before they closed, parking out in front.

"I figure, a Social Science degree at least, or maybe Political Science." I said it casually, hitting the nerve again. Claire was just finishing her Masters in Poly Sci at Northwestern. I thought of how angry, or maybe hurt, she must be that I hadn't called her. Our last date had been something very special, and I was screwing up another relationship before it had hardly gotten started.

"You're scarey. But you were right about the 'battered woman syndrome'. On average the victim of abuse goes back into the situation seven times before getting away for good." He was trying to change the subject.

"You've got a Master's degree, don't you?" I pointed at him, surprised.

"You are scarey." Then he resigned himself. "Two," he said, confessing.

"Two? Two what?" I was more that a little flabbergasted by what I'd heard. "You have two Master's degrees and you want to be a cop?"

"I know I can trust you not to say anything." He tried to whip my own game on me.

"Trust this! What the hell are you doing out here, you should be downtown making policy, or at least teaching somewhere. Not driving a blue and white around the north side, wearing a bullet proof vest and shining like a new penny." Why was I angry with this kid? His life was his own. If he wanted to risk it, that was his choice. Maybe I felt a little like I was part of an experiment instead of a partner.

He looked at me pleadingly until I relented. "Oh, alright," I said. "Your secret, that you're the most highly educated idiot on the job, is safe with me." I waved at the Pakistani, Mostar, who had turned out the lights and was locking the exchange. We watched him until he got into his car and then I told Cohen to drive around and try to find Gilly.

Gilly's girlfriend, Marie, lived with her mother in a little run down apartment building on the same street where the gang hung out. When the mother was working one of her two jobs, her apartment usually became the hang out. I had Cohen stop on Greenleaf, just east of Clark. I could see from the street that nobody was there, all the lights were out in the upstairs apartment.

The game room on Jarvis, which was another of their hang outs, was empty. The slimy pig that owned the place wasn't even there, just a scared little teenage girl behind the counter. The redneck tavern that served them alcohol, even the underage gang members, was also devoid of black and royal blue clad soldiers. I'd closed the place four times for serving minors, and each time it reopened under a new name, with the same old customers. They didn't like me at the game room or the Shamrock Bar and the feeling was mutual. Not everybody on Clark Street valued the foot patrolman.

We cruised our beat for another hour. Cohen gave a guy a ticket for not using his turn signal. I wouldn't have even noticed the violation. I pointed out to him that he was driving a car that didn't even have working signals and suggested that he give himself a ticket. He looked at me to see if I was kidding and I did my best to keep a straight face.

"That guy was from Cambodia. I've never met anyone from Southeast Asia before," he said, trying to make conversation. I was a little cranky.

"You haven't met one now either, just gave him a bullshit ticket, is all." I had suggested that he let the guy off with a warning, but he was worried about checking off without any moving violations. I told him that a felony arrest for domestic battery was activity enough for one team.

I didn't really care. One more hour to kill and I'd be through for the night, and hopefully through being a field training officer. When we were at the station, I'd checked with Ernie Perez and found that Brian White had just had a tooth pulled and would be back tomorrow.

We were facing west on Rogers Avenue, stopped at the light where it intersected Clark. The silence had been a little too deafening since I'd made that crack about the Cambodian guy, so I started talking to break it up. "You see that plaque over there on that building?" It was dark but we could just make out the foot square brass plate on the building. I couldn't read any of the words from where we sat twenty feet away, but I knew what it said.

"Yeah," he sounded like he was also looking forward to the shift being over soon. It had been a long night, the radio being constantly busy since sundown.

"It marks the Indian Boundary Line, honoring George Rogers Clark, who with his brother William and two other guys, negotiated a treaty with the Indians here in 1816."

He looked up at the huge red brick building that had a florist on the first level and a bunch of apartments on the three floors above. It didn't look, even remotely, like an historical site.

"You mean Clark, like in the Lewis and Clark Expedition? That Clark?" He squinted at the unreadable plaque.

"Well, I see that history wasn't one of your minor, or best subjects." He smiled agreement. "William, the baby brother, was the Lewis and Clark explorer. He's the more well known brother, but not the most accomplished. Hell, the whole family was famous for one thing or another. No, George, a Revolutionary War hero, bought all this land from the Indians. This street marks where the boundary used to be. The land he got from the Indians went from here south to Lake Calumet.

I had his attention now, the light had changed and he hadn't noticed. "George Rogers Clark got all that land, which is now Chicago and most of its connecting suburbs, from the local Indians. And they think Manhattan Island was a good deal!" We laughed and I motioned for him to obey the light when it turned green again. He turned and we went down Clark, slowly heading for the barn.

"If they could see it now," he said. "Millions of people living here, in just a few hundred years."

"There's over 200 languages spoken in Chicago," I said. "And I'll bet that you can hear them all on Clark Street."

"Two hundred?" It sounded like a lot.

"More. Not only languages and nationalities, but religions. All of the ones that your boy Abraham started 4,000 years ago, and all the rest, more than I can name. Buddhism, Hinduism, Shinto, and up north just a few miles is the Bahai Temple of all faiths. There are only seven Bahai Temples in the world, one on each continent. The one in North America is just up the road. Pretty interesting, if you ask me."

"How do you know all this stuff, Hop?" He asked, looking like I'd imagine a little boy would look up at his father. I didn't know what not having a father had caused me to miss out on in life. It was tough answering the questions for yourself all the time. Usually I had to make all the mistakes and take the losses before I figured it out. It had never been an very efficient method.

"You aren't the only guy to take a class, Cohen. But even before that, I've always been interested in people." I looked down the lighted tunnel of Clark Street. It ran it's own course, askew of the rest of the well ordered streets in Chicago, following an ancient ridge that must have been a trail for hundreds of years.

"Take Clark Street, for instance. It has to be the most unusual street in the world. But of course, I'm partial when it comes to this street. Arab next to Jew." I pointed at two stores that we passed, then at a little pub. "Irish Catholics drinking with Orangemen. All the restaurants and businesses, Philippine, Japanese, Scandinavian, African, South American. I can't even begin to count all the variations, but they all co-exist on Clark Street. Most of the time," I was forced to amend.

"Sometimes it reminds me of a toy that I bought for my kids one Christmas. You filled a bowl with water and dripped all these different colors of paint into the water. The paint floated on the top, swirling together. Then you took a pencil or something, and stuck it into the bowl. When you pulled it out all the different colors of paint would stick to the pencil. Thousands of little rings, all different colors."

"The colors didn't mix though. They were all there, each one separate and vivid, crammed in next to its neighbors. Sometimes I think that's how Clark Street is. The street is the pencil, coated with all of it's rings of different colors, nationalities, and religions."

"And you called Georgos a philosopher," he laughed. I'd asked for it, waxing philosophic. "And what is Basil Cassidy? The lead in the pencil?"

"I only let women call me Basil, Benjamin, or discuss the lead in my pencil." I kidded so that I wouldn't have to think about what my relationship to this street really was. I had enough friends in high places to get myself a desk job somewhere. Just what was I doing walking a foot post on Clark Street, five years after I could have retired? One more question that I didn't have an answer to.

Cohen gave me a reprieve from my thoughts, coming out of left field with his statement. "I can't take working with White any longer. You wouldn't consider having a new partner, would you?" There wasn't enough money in the world to make me trust a partner again, and I wouldn't be a Field Training Officer for twice that much. I didn't have to say it, he could see it in my face.

"If you haven't already heard the story, when you feel like hearing a real life soap opera remind me to tell you why I don't work with a partner." I took the moment his confused look gave me to start talking about someone other than myself.

"Okay, so you know White is an asshole. That's common knowledge on the job. Right?" He nodded. "He says things that are rude and he does things that make you want to punch him out. Right?" More cupie doll impressions.

"If you want to play the game the way he does, you have to be ruder than he is. I could tell you a story about him that will shut his mouth once and for all. Want to hear it?" I could tell that he would never deliberately hurt anyone's feelings, but was willing to hear the story. It was about the second most notorious story on the job.

"One time, years ago, when I was a detective, my partner and I were on the same radio zone as the Task Force. Those guys were the 'real police'. Real tough and real wild. Their parties, at a bar that used to be called 'The Slammer', are legendary."

"A Task Force car came over the air and announced that they had a party girl down by the lake and she was taking all comers. My partner and I were pigs like the rest, so we headed east. There was a line outside the car by the time we got there. The girl was a police freak, just like rock groupies are nuts for musicians. Well this girl was really going, doing one guy after another, she was practically supernatural. The line was getting shorter, but Brain White was ahead of us, next before me. When the last happy customer got out of the back, and White got in, you'd have thought that a bomb went off in the car. The party girl was his wife, instant grounds for divorce. We had to disarm and handcuff him to keep him from killing her or himself."

Cohen was flabbergasted. It was a hell of a story. "Now all you have to do when White says something you don't like, is ask him if he knows any party girls or make a comment about his sexual ability. Say it with a look in your eye that lets him know you know the story. If you want to punch him in the nose as well, that's when you'll probably get your chance."

He'd stopped at a green light again and looked over at me, shocked. "No, I don't believe that you would hurt someone's feelings intentionally. The point is that you have to consider the source when someone tries to hurt your feelings. People usually hurt others because of their own inferior feelings. The ones who deserve your respect usually act like it."

I don't believe in E.S.P., the Greek's telepathy, or anything like that, but sometimes you could swear that some people can hear it when you think about them. I felt haunted when the dispatcher called our number.

"2423." I repeated the number, acknowledging the call.

William J. O'Shea

"23. They want to see you in the station, and would you check on a man down at the Morse 'L' for me on your way in?" It was a new voice on the radio, they had changed shifts already.

Before I could say anything in return, the captain's voice came over my radio. He must have been listening to make sure I got the call. I wasn't surprised to hear it, he was the person I'd been thinking about, after all. "This is 2401, give that job to someone else and have 2423 come directly into the station."

I immediately regretted thinking I was so clever, signing his name to felony charges. I'd wanted to get even with Stokes then. Now I just wanted to go home.

"You heard the man 2423," dispatchers would sometimes argue with sergeants, but a captain was a different story altogether. I tuned out the rest of what was coming out of the radio.

We were halfway to the station just passing Farwell. The signs from the Limelight mixed green in with the street lamp's yellow light. I could hear Bazuki music coming from the pub, but my eyes were looking into the jewelry shop. I couldn't help it.

"Ben," I didn't think that there was any stress in my voice, but Cohen stopped the squad in the middle of the intersection.

"I want to take a look in the jewelry store," I pointed back to our left. "Make a 'U' turn." I don't know why I wanted to look in that window again, I thought it might be just to delay going in to face the captain's music.

Cohen made the 360 and stopped in front of the jewelry store. The scissors gate looked secure and now that it was on my side of the car I could see into the empty store clearly. There were no visible signs of the carnage that had taken place in there yesterday. The shadows were just shadows. For a second I doubted the instinct that had caused me to suspect something was wrong.

"The curtain's down." I automatically grabbed for my hat as I started to get out of the car. Cohen grabbed my arm from where he sat, holding me back.

"What curtain? What's the matter, Hop." He was right, I was rushing. He was my partner and needed to know what was going on.

"That's the place where the double homicide occurred yesterday. When we passed by here earlier, the curtain in back was up over the rod, now it's down. That scene is supposed to be secured with Coroner's Seals."

"What are we going to do?" Another good question.

"You go around the corner, down Farwell. I pointed. "There's a chain link fence and gate in back. That's the rear entrance for this building. It should be locked. Keep an eye on it until we can get a back-up unit over here." We got out of the car. He remembered to take the keys but not his hat. Rookies didn't like to wear their hats, you couldn't be cool with a dumb looking checkered hat perched on top of your head. It took a long time to figure out, that for some reason, the hat made your job easier.

"2423. We may have someone in a building that was the scene of a homicide yesterday. Get me another car over at Clark and Farwell to assist in a search." The dispatcher was sharp and put the call on the city wide zone, to improve our chances of faster response. I heard Chicken George's voice questioning the operator and tuned him out. I knew he wasn't coming to help me.

Cohen disappeared around the corner, and I approached the windows that I was afraid to look into. Cohen and I were officially separated now, good thing we each carried a radio, like the hot shots. I hoped we wouldn't need them, I didn't feel too hot at the moment.

When I peeked around the edge of the glass from the bottom corner, I was relieved. There was no one inside, everything looked normal. Just a false alarm. The curtain panel must have come down by sheer weight after hanging up there, precariously, for so long. I stood boldly in front of the windows now, cupping my hands around my eyes to block out the street light and get a better look at the inside of the shop.

Just when everything in the shop came clearly into view, the curtain moved. Not a lot, just a flutter as if a slight draft had stirred it. As though someone had opened a door. It all happened so quickly after that. Why didn't I react quickly? I've asked myself that question a thousand times.

A figure came crashing through the doorway from the back room, tearing the crane curtain from the jamb. It hit the counter and rolled backwards, effortlessly, flipping over the counter and landing in a crouch. Then another figure came out of the back. It was Cohen. I pounded on the glass.

"Son of a bitch!" I screamed. Knowing that my pounding was futile, I started to run for the back.

Just as I started to turn, I saw another figure rise from the floor next to Cohen. A karate kick to the chest blind sided the rookie, stunning him. I took out my gun, thinking that I could shoot through the window. Cohen fell back into Park's old work bench. Before he could straighten up, the figure who'd flipped over the counter, was in the air, feet first. He was flying straight for Cohen's head.

There was a blur of hands and feet. Cohen miraculously recovered and countered the flying kick with his night stick, which I'd swear he didn't have in his hand when he came out of the back. With the same blow he whipped the other advancing figure with the billy club. Cohen went wild, it looked like a Kung Fu movie in the little shop. Spinning kicks, fists flashing and the night stick whirring like a samurai sword. Just as I'd lied that he could.

I couldn't believe it. The two offenders were fighting for their lives. I finally unfroze and ran for the corner, turning it and heading for the back gate. "2423!...TEN ONE! TEN ONE!" I ran.

When I got to the gate, my gun was still in my hand. I realized that I'd have to put it away before I'd be able to climb over the gate again. I hoped that whatever had gotten me over it yesterday was still in me.

My Colt back in it's holster, I stretched for the highest place I could reach on the metal links. When my hands were up in the air, the gate exploded outward, hitting me square in the face. My hat absorbed some of the blow as it flew off my head, but the stars came out by the millions and I found myself sitting on the sidewalk. Just as I was starting to focus on the figure who'd pushed open the gate, he kicked me in the chest, knocking me flat. He ran over me, turning east down Farwell.

I struggled to my feet and looked at the fleeing figure. It was only a split second's thought of going after him, but he was out of my reach and my partner was still inside with the other one. The gate was wide open now. A gaping black hole. Foot patrolmen didn't need flashlights, not until tonight. I drew my Colt again and stepped into the darkness.

It was about thirty feet to the back door of the shop. As my eyes adjusted to the dimness, I saw a figure move in the area where I knew the rear door was. There were no sounds.

Shoot. No. It could be Cohen or the rookie could come out of the shop and step into the line of fire. The figure moved.

"STOP OR I'LL SHOOT!" That was about the dumbest thing anyone could say. It only makes the bad guys run faster. I crouched a little more, to reduce my back lighted silhouette and make my combat stance look more menacing.

I thought that he had nowhere to go, but he turned away from me and ran up the rickety wooden stairs. I couldn't see who the figure was, he was dressed in dark clothing like a ninja. He took the stairs three at a time and disappeared around the turn of the first landing.

"Ben! Ben!" I called frantically as I pounded toward the doorway which was a gray square in the wall to my left. Before I was halfway there, someone came running out of the doorway, my eyes must have adjusted somewhat, because I could see that it was Cohen.

"Where?" Was all he said. His voice sounded winded and strained but he didn't sound like he was hurt, thank God.

"Up the stairs." I should have waited until I got to where he was standing before answering. Before I could take another step Cohen leapt up the staircase and disappeared after the fleeing black figure. "Wait!" I shouted. He didn't.

When I reached the stairs, I took them two at a time, but I wasn't closing the distance between us. At the second landing I stopped and listened for footsteps. Were they still going up, or away down the hallway of the second floor?

Just as I figured out the location of the footsteps and started running down the hallway, I heard a crash come from that direction. I ran past the apartment doors as fast as I could, mouth hanging open, sucking air like a bellows.

Cohen was standing at the end of the long hallway. He was looking out of an opening in the wall that a moment before had been a window on the front of the building. When he turned to me with a look of horror on his face, I panicked.

"Are you hurt? What's wrong? Are you alright?" I grabbed his arms, searching him for wounds.

"I'm okay," he whispered, "look." He pointed out of the window. The pained look returned to his face as he looked down into the street. I was so happy that he wasn't hurt that I'd forgotten all about what we were doing.

Stepping up next to him and looking out the window, I saw a light show of flashing lights and heard the sirens for the first time. Cars were pulling up from all directions. I looked down to where our squad car was double parked in front of the building. There was a figure lying on the hood of our car. It wasn't moving. It was shaped like a man, and he was wearing black ninja clothing. I started to laugh.

It was sort of a maniacal laugh, tinged with relief. "Stop or I'll shoot!" I hollered down at the inert figure. He just laid there, face down, unmoving. There were people milling around in the street now, some coming from the doorway of the Limelight Pub.

"Well, whata'ya know, it worked." When I didn't stop laughing, Cohen looked at me like I was losing it. Which was not far from the truth. I got a hold of myself and looked down into the street again. Good thing I'd stopped laughing, there were a lot of faces turned in our direction.

"Come on, kid. Let's go see who that mope is. You didn't toss him out the window, did you?" I said it jokingly, but he didn't look like he thought it was funny.

"By the way," I said, pushing him roughly in the back, "what were you doing in there in the first place? You asshole! I'm responsible for you and you're doing a Bruce Lee impression with two bad guys. Are you crazy?"

"But I thought...I heard...well, you didn't say what I should do if the gate was open." I hit him again, not too hard, and read him the riot act all the way downstairs, dismissing all his excuses like a mother who disciplines her child after a near accident, to alleviate her own fears.

"If Brian White ever saw you fight, he wouldn't be calling you names any longer. By the way, where did you learn to fight like that? Not at the police academy, I'm sure."

He avoided the question shyly. "You look like you've been fighting yourself," he pointed at my shirt and face when we stepped out into the lighted side street. I felt under my nose and smelled blood at the same time, not surprised to feel the sticky greasy wetness between my fingers.

"Looks like your day was a total loss, Hop," he said smiling, remembering my comment about the day being a loser if you got hurt or even sweated up. I was the only one sweating and bleeding.

"I knew it was going to be a loser the minute I saw your skinny ass, Cohen." I laughed and he caught it, laughing with me. Partners, if only for a little while.

*   *   *

"Nice job, Hoppy," Mike Pape was standing near the front of our car where the figure lay on the hood. There were people milling around all over the place now. Police and civilians.

87

Squad cars blocked the street in every direction. I could hear the dispatcher giving repeated 'disregards' and telling everybody not involved to clear the street and leave the scene. It looked like it was going to take more than a voice on the radio to get that job done.

I went up to the car somewhat hesitantly, as if the guy was going to get up and go into his ninja act again. Mike Pape was standing next to the fender on the driver's side. When I approached, he handed me a handkerchief. Pape stepped aside so I could see the body. Cohen stood watching from the other side of the car, next to a parked car that was covered with glass and debris.

The way the figure's head was twisted in death reminded me of the way Sui Park had looked, unnatural. The head had hit the windshield, not going through, but putting a curved dent in the shattered safety glass.

Pape was wearing latex gloves. He was a true wagon man, dead bodies never fazed them. There was nothing that was too gory for a wagon man. He grabbed the head by the sopping wet hair and pulled it back. It was evident from the way it lolled that the neck was broken. There was blood everywhere, must have severed an artery.

"You know this guy, Hop?" He pointed to the face with his gloved finger, as if he needed to focus my attention on the face that I stared at. I put the handkerchief up to my face, suddenly very tired.

The windshield had smashed the face, and it was stained red with blood, but there was no mistaking the who it was. "Yea, I know him. He's one of the Gray Eagles. His name is David Tso." I thought about the last time I'd seen him alive, yesterday, when Garcia and James had him in custody.

"It 'was' David Tso you mean." Sapper had come up behind us carrying a stretcher. "Now he's nothing but an organ donor." Sapper and Pape thought that was real funny.

Chapter 11

Sergeant Davis approached the little hood party that we were having. He was wearing his gold checked hat and although it was hard for him to do, he had managed a scowl. He was on the nerdy side, tall, slim, and usually had a difficult time asserting his authority. Not tonight.

"Sapper. Did I tell you to bring a stretcher over here? Since you want to help speed up the process so much, you take charge of the scene." Davis waved at the civilians who were gaping at the bizarre scene. "And put your damn hats on!"

He lowered his voice when it was evident that he had the attention of everyone in sight. "Clear all these people out of here. Get the evidence technician over here, and don't move the body until Geery takes pictures of it." He said the last thing to Pape, who still held Tso's head up by the hair, animating it like a bloody puppet.

Pape bounced the head contemptuously on the hood, the body had already slipped down from where it had hit the windshield. "I was just checking to see if he was still alive, Sarge. You know, like we were gonna give him CPR for awhile, you know, to make it look good for the crowd." He gestured toward the civilians lining the street, turning so he could stifle his laugh. Sapper was going into convulsions behind the sergeant, his jowls and huge belly shaking like Santa's.

"Shut up, Pape. Sapper, I'm going in back and when I come out here again, there better be some crowd control going on or you're going to be writing reports until dawn." Davis was madder than I'd ever seen him.

There were different kinds of personalities on the job, but every cop had that certain spark. It came with the star. Davis was fired up. Sapper stopped laughing abruptly when the sergeant turned and Sapper saw his face.

"Cohen, come with me, I want you to show me what happened, and where." Cohen almost jumped out of his skin, running after the sergeant who had already started for the corner. He didn't ask me to come along and I didn't volunteer. I just stood there with David Tso staring vacantly up at me.

"What's his problem? These new sergeants are a pain in the ass," Sapper said, when Davis was out of earshot around the corner. He went to the truck, got his hat and started waving it at the crowd, telling them to break it up.

"No big deal, we just slide this scum bag into a ziplock and wash the car. We don't need all this other bullshit." Pape was a very practical guy. He leaned over to me conspiratorially. "Anyway, I'm sure you had a good reason to toss this garbage out the window, Hop." He stripped off his bloody latex gloves and threw them into the street to mix with the rest of the garbage.

I looked at him as hard as I could. "Mike, we didn't toss him out the window. We just chased him and he jumped through the glass."

Pape thought that was real funny. "Sure, Hop, your recruit scared him so much he decided that taking a header off the second floor was better than facing the rookie. Ha ha." I wasn't sure how close he had come to the truth.

Pape stifled his laughter long enough to call for an Evidence Technician. "2423," he used my call numbers, "we need some flicks and picks over here, pronto. Make whatever notifications for us will ya? 2472 will be transporting the body." He added.

"What do you have over there, 2423?" I could tell from the dispatcher's voice that he knew it wasn't Cohen or me he was talking to. I could understand Pape using my call numbers though. Nobody wanted to get involved when there was a chance of collateral liability.

"Accident." Pape winked at me, speaking into the microphone and smiling. "Some guy jumped out of a window. He's DOA."

Sapper's voice was growing louder as he tried to disburse the growing crowd. There were squad cars blocking the street in both directions, which only gave the civilians more room to mill around.

Pape, seeing a problem about to start, headed in the direction of his partner. Sapper was bellowing like a wounded moose now and waving his night stick in people's faces. I looked more closely at the crowd, and I immediately saw Georgos. He had his telepathic eye on me, trying to get my attention.

I could only imagine what I looked like and what my facial expression must have been for him to have a look of such concern on his face. He must have been watching me since I came out of the back.

His telepathic stare grabbed me and asked me if I was alright. Feeling a small guilt pang for not realizing that he would have been worried about me, I smiled at him as broadly as I could. His worried look didn't change however, the blood on the handkerchief in my hand explained that.

Sapper was about ready to start beating people for not listening to him. He was just a huge mound of fat and couldn't have done much damage, but Pape was an ex-marine and although he was a large person, he wasn't fat. If Pape had to back up his partner's foolishness someone would get hurt.

I gave Georgos another 'okay' signal, gesturing for him to get everybody off the street. He immediately went into action, relieved that everything was alright, and having something to do besides stare at me and worry.

The crowd started to thin. Sark, the Armenian bazuki player, was outside with the rest of the band and he waved his little guitar at me. I gave everybody a big smile and a wave. They all waved back, thinking that I was gesturing to each one personally. That got everybody moving up and down Clark, or back into the bar. Sapper was happy to see that he'd finally gotten his point across by reaching the optimum level of threatened violence.

The car party had also thinned. It was just David and me now. I was leaning against the driver's door, my legs were hurting. David's head was laying on the fender, at an unlifelike angle to his body. I looked down at him, as he looked through me.

"Well, David," I said to the former gang leader, "now would you like to tell me about the Park murders?" I got the same answer as the last time I'd asked that question.

"Or maybe you'd like to tell me just what the fuck you were looking for in there that would make you jump out a window for it?" Still no answer, this guy was a tough nut to crack. I looked around suspiciously, to see if anyone was listening to my one sided conversation, just like crazy people do.

"Okay, if you don't want to answer that question, tell me what my laundry man was doing in there with you." I couldn't believe it. That gate must have rattled my brains. I was so confused that I was standing here talking to a corpse. I looked around again and found that everybody was busy doing something else, besides paying attention to my ravings.

Could I believe my eyes? When my vision had cleared, for only a moment before he kicked me, I was sure that I saw Inon Moon. The owner of the cleaners. Looking down at my now filthy pants, I remembered going in there earlier today and his acting a little strangely. Did I really see the man who complained about parking tickets and starched my shirts too much? It was sure a long jump from sewing on collar buttons to donning ninja clothing and doing night insertions.

I still couldn't be sure, the idea was ridiculous. Maybe it was somebody who looked just like the guy. I looked down at David Tso again, blood was running from his nose and mouth down the side of the fender. He was laying on his stomach, although his face was turned up. Something drew my eye to his neck area and I caught a glimpse of white inside his collar.

The little flash of whiteness reminded me that it was the first time that I'd seen David Tso not wearing his black and white gang colors. For a gang member to die violently without his colors was like a cowboy dying with his boots off. The lights were on in the jewelry shop now. Nobody was watching me through the window as I tugged on the corner of the piece of paper that was inside the dead man's collar.

As I pulled on the triangle, I realized that is was just the top sheet of a number of papers that David had secreted inside his jacket. I looked at the pieces of glass and window frame strewn all over the sidewalk and the parked cars, then up at the second floor window.

It was only about 25 feet to the ground, not necessarily a suicidal jump. The placement of our squad car must have thrown his landing off. Or maybe he had seen one Kung Fu movie too many. I could almost understand someone jumping from a window to escape with their jacket stuffed with papers, green papers, bunches of them, with numbers and President's pictures on them. This stuff looked like a third graders homework. Nobody took a chance like that for answers to the math quiz.

I hunkered down over the body, lifting the left shoulder with my other hand while I pulled the folded over stack of typing paper out of his jacket. They were 8 ½ X 11 size, folded lengthwise, and looked to number about thirty or forty pages. To this day, I don't know why I hid my actions, but that's what I did.

I don't know what possessed me when I stuffed the bloody papers into my own jacket, snapping the buttons over them as I straightened, looking around guiltily. I hoped it wasn't temporary insanity, because that was only a defense on television.

I felt like a kid stealing candy, looking around to see if anyone had seen what I'd done. Why was I doing this? Was it a need to find out before anyone else, or was I letting personal feelings cloud my professional judgement? That sounded about right. The questions were staggering, and so was I. I was just real tired, probably. It was hard to get my legs moving toward the back of the shop to see what I could sort out with the sergeant and the rookie. I especially needed to get Cohen alone and ask him a few questions.

I found my hat next to the big tree on Farwell. The beak and silver shield were smashed. I was glad that I always grabbed for my hat. It had saved me a larger headache than I already had, a new hat was no problem. A new head was a different matter. I thought about the laundry man again.

Davis and Cohen were just coming out of the gate, which was fine with me because I didn't want to go in there. I especially didn't want to go into the little shop with the lights all burning brightly. There would be no visions of blood and death to easily dismiss as shadows. The fluorescents would bring yesterday's horror pictures back with vivid clarity.

"Why does this stuff always happen at the end of the shift?" Davis said to no one in particular.

"It's Friday night, Tom, worst damn night of the week," I said agreeing with him completely and adding my own complaint.

"Oh yea, it's Friday. I promised the old lady that I'd be home on time tonight." He had more on his mind than just the problems here on the street. "The kids are overnighting with friends, we were going to play horsey tonight."

I couldn't help him there. This job was hard on wives, and husbands too. When we got back to the front, both Sapper and Pape had their hats on and the E.T.'s car had just run one of the blockades. Geery double parked behind our car. It wasn't going anywhere for awhile.

Davis told an always reluctant Jim Geery he wanted pictures of the body and prints on all surfaces that would take them. "...and search the body to see if we can find out why they were in there in the first place," he said to Sapper and Pape. Then he made the wagon men more unhappy by making them responsible for the bloody squad car and affixing new coroner's seals on the rear door.

"Are you going to get the other wagon to transport the body?" Sapper had to ask a dumb question.

"After the pictures are taken, you put the body on that stretcher you were carrying around and put him in your wagon. I want the body stripped and every stitch inventoried. Then you drive the car back to the station while your partner drives the wagon. Is that clear enough, Sapper, or do I have to write it down for you." Davis was still fuming.

"How am I supposed to see to drive this thing? The window is broken and covered with blood. There must be some rule against driving a police vehicle when it's is an unsafe condition." Sapper was admiring his logic, thinking that the sergeant wouldn't be able to figure a way out of his clever reference to regulations.

"Fine, you have your choice. Either drive it, roll down the window and stick your head out to see where you're going, or wait for a tow truck. You're still in charge of this scene, Sapper, regardless of whose call numbers you're using." Steam was coming out of Davis' ears. He looked at Pape, who had used our number. Mike looked down at the street, not wanting to prolonge the sergeant's tirade. He wasn't going to argue for Sapper, especially when his partner was wrong, as usual.

Davis wasn't through though. "...And if you screw up this crime scene, or don't do exactly what I told you to do, I'm going to stick the rule book up your fat ass!" Davis caught himself before he lost it completely. He turned and walked toward his car, motioning for Cohen and me to follow.

"He ain't got no right to be calling me 'fat ass'," I heard Sapper say sheepishly to his partner.

"No, you're right about that, Bruce," Pape said. "He should have called you 'fat head'. Nobody could say he didn't have the right to say that." This was not the first time that Sapper's mouth had gotten Pape into some extra duty.

We got into the sergeant's car, Davis had to move all of his papers and junk off of the passenger's seat before I could get in. The sergeant drove and Cohen sat in back, behind him. I just sat there and hugged my hidden papers to my chest, wondering how the rule book was going to feel when it was up my ass.

Chapter 12

"Tom, drop me off at the cousin's liquor store, will ya? I want to make sure he's alright." A glimpse of the writing on the papers in my jacket told me that I couldn't read them. Ah was the only person I felt I could trust, who could also read Korean. "I'll walk back and meet you at the station afterwards."

"It's past midnight, Hop. He's closed already, look." Davis pointed at the darkened store as we drove past. "Besides, the captain is long gone by now, so you don't have to worry about going into the station." I hadn't thought about it, but the captain was going to be another problem.

"Valdez will be the watch commander by now, and we can talk to him." He continued talking while he headed south. "The only problem we might have is that Cohen was the only person to see the guy jump. I don't know how we're going to explain that."

The street was back to its normal busy Friday mode. The street lamps overhead lighted the way down Clark, seeming to come together in the distance. The long ridge of Clark Street looked like a canyon, lined with buildings, no two alike.

"I saw the whole thing, Sarge. Cohen didn't look around so he didn't know that I was there. I was running down the hall after them when the kid jumped right through the glass. Damndest thing I ever saw. Cohen was nowhere near the guy when he jumped." Davis looked at me uncertainly, until the last comment, then his expression changed to one of relief.

I put my arm on the back of the seat, cringing when my jacket crinkled. Cohen was about to say something that would blow the lie I'd just told. I speared him with a pointed finger hidden behind the sergeant's back, freezing the kid's comment before he could get it out. Davis didn't believe that Cohen would throw a man out of a window, neither did I. The problem was that believing wasn't going to keep this kid out of trouble. Cohen needed a witness, without one they'd hang him out to dry.

96

He was a probationary patrolman, they could fire him for not having his shoes shined.

I wanted to keep Davis' mind off of Cohen. "Tom, this is all still the same case. My case. It started yesterday when I looked into that window."

"You're not an investigator any longer, Hop. You're just the foot man who discovered the crime. It's not your job to find out who committed it." It was a harsh statement, but it was true.

He was right. I almost told him about the papers in my jacket. I should have. But I'd already lied about seeing what happened in the hallway, and I told myself that I was the only person who could find Gilly Rodriquez. I was willing to tell myself anything, apparently, to satisfy this drive to find out who killed Sung and Sui Park. I had to find out. Me.

"Why don't you take off when we get to the station, Tom. I'll do a report on what happened tonight, then I'll call Voltz and Dolecki and they can decide whether it's tied in with the murders or not." Once you start lying, it gets easier.

"Oh no you don't," he said. "I heard about what you pulled on that Aggravated Battery. Stokes is furious. I don't want to come to work tomorrow and be surprised at all the reports that I supposedly signed." He laughed. That wasn't the reason that I wanted to get rid of him, I needed to get these papers off my chest, they were pressing heavily on me.

Just then I saw another way. I was also getting desperate. "Stop here for a second, will ya Tom?" I'd seen a light burning in the back of the Tai Kwon Do Academy.

"What now Cassidy?" Davis said, exasperated, but he stopped.

"That's the Uncle's place. Chung. It's pretty late and there's a light on. Maybe we should check it out?" What was I doing? Was I so desperate that I would seek help from a man that I not only didn't trust, but one who scared the hell out of me. I changed my mind when I thought of the old man. Forget it. These papers could be a laundry list for all I knew. They'd wait until I could get Ah alone.

William J. O'Shea

The inside of the school was quiet. After looking in for a few moments and seeing no movement, I agreed with Davis when he said we should have another car check it out. As we started to pull away from the school, Cohen made a little whispered confession.

"You asked me where I learned Tai Kwon Do?" I'd asked him where he'd learned to fight like a whirlwind, I didn't know it had a name. If he called it Tai Kwon Do, and he'd learned it in this school, that was fine. It only made me more sure that I didn't want to have anything to do with Chung and less sure about everything else.

Davis didn't say anything, but he was all ears. He must have also been wondering how Cohen had managed to fight off two offenders by himself. "You know this Chung?" I asked. I should have waited until I had Cohen alone, but his statement startled me into asking.

"I've studied with him. He's trained a lot of recruits. Master Chung offered everybody a special deal, it was posted on the bulletin board at the academy." I bit my lip. Master Chung? Who the hell is Master Chung? ...and don't tell me that he taught you to fight like a mad man in the six weeks that you've been in rookie school. The list of questions that I wanted to ask this kid scrolled by in my mind. It was attached to another long list of unanswered questions.

*　　　　*　　　　*

As we walked up to the rear doors of the station, I looked at my reflection in the plate glass windows. There was blood on my forehead, in my hair, on my face, and down my shirt into my jacket where it met the bloody papers that I had hidden there. There were no white corners sticking out of the leather jacket on the bloody figure that I examined in the window.

I don't know whether it was my wretched reflection that startled me more, or the forbidding Captain 'Chicken George' Stokes, standing inside the doors, waiting for us. He had his little, powder blue, civilian 'members' jacket on over his white captain's shirt and a murderous scowl on his face.

Stokes and I used to be drinking buddies. Stopping for cocktails regularly when I'd first gotten dumped back into the Patrol Division. We weren't getting along very well lately, though. I could tell from his blood shot eyes and puffy face that he was still drinking heavily. We'd had a strange understanding when we used to stop after work, maybe a kind of friendship on a molecular level. I'd hoped that it would still be there when I stopped drinking.

"You're getting a number on you Cassidy!" He shouted at us in the cavernous hallway. The usually busy police station was deserted. Stokes had scared away all the little fish, but where ever they were hiding, they heard every word he said.

"And you, Mister Cohen. You notice I said 'Mister' and not officer? You're finished with your probation. I'm recommending you for immediate separation. The Deputy Superintendent will be here any minute to determine what charges will be placed against you both!" He had foam in the corners of his mouth and was spraying it around when he shouted. I wondered if I could shoot him and claim that he was rabid. I was a little mad myself.

"What, no 'you look hurt, Cassidy'? Are you okay, Cassidy? I thought you waited up for us because you were worried about us, captain," I said, trying to keep my fists unclenched.

"If you'd obeyed my direct order and come into the station, you wouldn't be hurt. And I wouldn't have a dead kid on my hands. That's three in two days." He was right, except they were all on my hands, not his. We walked down the long hall, the captain shouting all the way. Not surprisingly, no one at the desk seemed to notice us when we reached the front.

"If you hadn't been playing detective, this wouldn't have happened!" He was raging. "You aren't a dick anymore, Cassidy. Remember, you got dumped for the same shit that you're trying to pull on me...you...signed..my name on..." He looked like he was going to choke on his foam. His face had turned from gray to a shiny red, with the purple veins on his nose and cheeks pulsating.

"I didn't get dumped for the same shit that I'm pulling on you, George. They're a lot smarter in the Detective Division." I thought that would push him over the edge nicely. I hoped he would jump on me, I needed to release some tension.

The Patrol Division always hated the Detective Division. Dicks got more pay for what Patrol considered less work. Dicks were suit wearing prima donnas and were hated by uniform officers. That is unless you passed the test and became a dick yourself, then you were glad you were out of Patrol. All the 'real police' enjoyed seeing a prima donna detective get dumped back onto the street, in uniform.

All of a sudden I was nose to nose with the captain. I must have been losing my mind. Stokes was basically harmless, why was I antagonizing him? Thank God Davis jumped in between us, giving us both a moment to recover sanity. Police Captains were like Senators, they stayed in office until they died. It never paid to be on the wrong side of them. Davis took the Captain by the arm and steered him into the Watch Commander's office. It was long after our shift and the midnight Captain and his crew had already taken over the office, but it soon vacated except for Davis and Stokes.

Davis had many qualities, I had to hand it to him. He talked slowly and calmly and had the Captain doing the same. Davis took control of the situation. The sergeant is the workhorse of the department. They only make it if they can do more than one trick, however.

When the redness cleared from my brain, I realized that I needed to be someplace else. Preferably hiding the evidence that I'd removed from the crime scene. I told Cohen go to find a typewriter and get some blank case reports while I went to the bathroom to wash the blood off my face. His forlorn expression reminded me that he had more to worry about than I did. His career as police officer had just been declared over. I had to do something about that too, when I got a chance. Right now the papers felt like a ticking bomb in my jacket.

Nobody at the desk paid the slightest attention to what had just happened. I'm sure that not a word had been missed though. Nobody looked at me, collateral liability was heavy in the air. Collateral liability was a term we used when other people got dragged into your mess just because they were in the wrong place at the right time. A good example was when an officer got sued for something. The subpoena always had your name on it and the letters, 'et. al.' Which was Latin legalese for everybody who had knowledge of the incident, before, during, or after it occurred. The last thing anybody wanted, was to get named an 'et. al.', that meant that they shared in the liability.

It looked to them like I'd gotten the short end and was going to keep getting it. Davis only saving me temporarily. Nobody wanted any part of the mess that I'd gotten myself into. When I sulked off to the locker room to hide my secret, it fit with their impression of how I must have felt and was not far from the truth.

I checked each bay of lockers to see that I was alone before I went to mine. After I spun the combination and opened the lock, I hid behind the little door and slipped the stack of folded papers out of my jacket. Blood covered most of the outside page, I wondered how much of it was mine and how much was David Tso's. I looked through them, they were just square figures running up and down each page in regular sequences. There seemed to be a little blood on every page. There also wasn't a word of English anywhere.

After each series of the geometric calligraphy of Korean writing, there were numbers. Those were the only figures I could understand. All I could tell from the stack of papers was that they were some kind of lists. They weren't laundry lists though, the numbers were 6 and 7 figures and looked to be dollar amounts. Most were written in blue ink, with what looked like an old time fountain pen. They all seemed to have been written by the same person. A hand writing analyst might have described the writer as an educated person with a gentle, artist's touch.

Out of the stack of thirty or so pages, four were different from the rest. They were very old, brittle yellow and creased from repeated folding. Covered with official looking stamps and engravings, they looked like they were diplomas or important documents. It still told me nothing, only deepening my confusion.

The bottom third of my locker was full of used up ticket books. You were only supposed to keep the onion skin copies for one year, but I wrote a lot of parking tickets, and was just too lazy to throw out the old ones on the bottom. I dug down a couple of years worth and stuffed the bloody papers under the old ticket books.

Almost leaving without washing the blood off of my face, I went into the adjacent bathroom. One look in the mirror deepened whatever it was that was making me feel like shit. It took me another five wincing minutes to inspect the cuts on my forehead and wash the off the blood. My nose didn't feel broken, but I felt like I'd been punched by Muhammed Ali. I dried my face in the hand dryer, and fingered my white mop of wet hair into place. One more glance in the mirror (not as bad as when I'd come in), and out to face the music.

The music turned out to be one of my favorite tunes. The Deputy had arrived and he was in the office talking with Stokes. The Deputy was an old friend of mine and Stokes knew it. It had been a long time since I'd been in the academy with Brett Calder. Thirty years ago all we cared about was whether we were going to the Jewish Deli for lunch or getting a greasy Polish with kraut from the corner stand. Since then, Brett had studied and taken his chances, worked hard and risen steadily in the ranks. Thirty years, family, and friends, had gone by for me in a drunken blur.

The door to the office was closed but the wall facing the lobby was glass, with mini blinds covering them from floor to ceiling. The blinds were partially open and I could see Brett standing in front of the captain's desk, behind it Stokes stood rather than sat in the blue cloth chair. I wished that I could hear what was being said in that room.

The only way to hear what was being said in the office was to stand near the door and surreptitiously listen while pretending to do something else, which was exactly what Tom Davis was doing. I walked over to him and pretended to be interested in the report box that he wasn't really looking in.

"What's going on, Tom?" I asked, trying not to move my lips to much or gesture at all.

"It looks like it's going to be alright," he said, answering my next question. "When Calder came in, the first thing he did was sign the log book." I had my back to the office door, Davis didn't look up as he spoke softly.

"Stokes saw Calder standing out here by the desk and he came running out of his office and started screaming at the Deputy. I couldn't believe my eyes. I don't think he likes Calder very much," he said, knowing that Calder was my friend.

"Calder told Stokes to get a hold of himself, and walked past him into the office. Stokes had no choice but to follow. I closed the door on my way out, almost closed it, that is." I could hear muffled voices coming from behind me. He couldn't smile, but I could.

"Stokes started shouting again about you signing his name to Aggravated Battery charges, and demanding that the Deputy get a Complaint Number on you. Calder calmly asked the captain where he was when all this was happening and Stokes said, 'out to lunch'." Davis glanced into the office behind me to make sure they were still busy, not paying attention to us.

"Calder said that he had just signed the log book and hadn't noticed Stokes' name in the book signed out for lunch. Then he came out here and checked it again. According to the official log, the captain never left the station. Then Calder read the case report you wrote on the domestic battery." I didn't move, though I knew that I should get my butt out of there. Davis held me there with his recounting of the confrontation.

"When he went back into the office, Calder left the door ajar again. I think so I could listen. Then he asked the captain what charges he thought should have been placed against a man who breaks a woman's jaw and dislocates her arm? When Stokes stuttered and couldn't answer, Calder threatened to get a number on Stokes and have him 're-evaluated', as the Deputy put it." Davis snickered a little, but didn't show a smile.

He picked a case report out of the metal box, to continue the facade. "After that, Stokes calmed down and Calder pretty much..."

Just then Davis looked up and I heard the door open behind me. I tried to shrink myself down to unnoticeable size, though I could feel Stokes' eyes burning on my back. Afraid to move, I just stood there.

"Don't worry, George, I'll call you tomorrow and tell you how it works out." I could tell from Brett's voice that they weren't approaching Davis and I.

"This whole thing actually happened after your watch was over anyway..." The voices faded as Calder walked Stokes down the hallway toward the parking lot. I risked a glance over my shoulder and saw Calder reach up and pat Stokes on the back and then rest his hand on the captain's shoulder as he spoke softly to him. Once that problem headed for the rear exit, my mind cleared for a moment and a question surfaced.

"Tom, did anyone find a gun in the jewelry store last night? I've been meaning to ask you but with all this other stuff going on..." He looked at me like he was going to tell me not to investigate, but then had a change of mind.

"No. Should we have?" Answer a question and ask one in return. Davis wasn't a bad investigator himself.

"Well, yes, I think," I said, not knowing if I was the one being interrogated.

"You think?" I was being interrogated. "Did he have a gun or not?"

"Yes, he had a gun. If you could call it that." The puzzled look I got from him forced me to explain myself. "He showed it to me a couple of times. I don't know what make it was, never saw anything like it before. The thing was huge, like an old army six shooter. It broke down at the breech and had a long barrel that looked like a cannon. Must have been forty or fifty caliber, I don't know much about guns."

He didn't ask me if I'd ever checked to see if Park had registered the weapon. He knew as well as I that many businessmen had guns. He didn't know that some of them were ninjas however.

"Well, we didn't find a gun last night, big or small. And they didn't find any gun tonight either. Maybe the one who got away had it?" Calder came back before we could discuss the one that got away anymore. I thanked Brett for helping me, and we got down to serious report writing. Not completely truthful, but serious. Everybody went along with my story of what happened.

I even let the issue become more clouded when Davis suggested that Tso might have been high on L.S.D. when he jumped through the window, being that he had been arrested for possessing the drug last night.

There was never any discussion of throwing people out of windows and Cohen was so grateful for not losing his bullshit job that he was pathetic. Calder told him that he should have learned a good lesson, and should always wait for backup when going into a situation like this. Cohen just grinned and bobbed his head a lot. I agreed with Calder that we should have waited for a backup and wondered who my backup was going to be on the situation that I'd gotten myself into.

Captain Valdez also helped, approving all the reports and Davis stayed with us until the very end, signing the final case report. Burglary, committed by two offenders, one died when he tried to jump out of a window to escape. The other, unknown offender, got away with any possible proceeds from the crime. Davis was a big help with the narrative section on the reports also, they looked so good that I thought we might get an Honorable Mention Citation. I thanked him as sincerely as I could, knowing he given up a horsey ride for his men tonight.

I never got a chance to get Cohen alone and ask him some questions, the sergeant let him go a little while before we finished. Just as well, it was 3:00 am by the time I left the station, dog tired, head hurting just a bit more than every muscle in my body.

I thought about an early morning steam bath at the 'Y', but vetoed the idea when I remembered I had a funeral to go to tomorrow. My beater made it home without needing a fan belt, oil, or any other repair. I was going to hit the bed with all my clothes on when I saw the light blinking on the answering machine.

I wished that I had missed it until morning, like I had last night. What the hell, it was morning. Besides, I knew that I would have to listen to the messages or it would keep me awake, wondering. There was only one message on the tape.

"BEEP...Cassidy, you better know who this is!" She sounded as though she was teasing, I hoped. It was Claire, I looked at my bloody shirt in the mirror and decided to take my clothes off before hitting the sack. Her voice was like French Vanilla ice cream, with just enough colonial English to make it smooth and eloquent. I would have known it at a whisper.

"Sorry to have to call so late at night. However, I need to speak with you regarding something that is disturbing me greatly." Claire is from St. Croix, in the Caribbean U.S. Virgin Islands.

'I've been hoping that you would call me or stop by. If you could come by the restaurant tomorrow, I would appreciate it. Thank you, and good night, Basil.' She had every right to be sore at me. We'd had four dates, two of them serious ones. They had been so wonderful that I had started thinking about having a relationship again. 'I love you,' were words that I hadn't used or heard in a long time.

It didn't take me twenty years to screw up a relationship these days. Just four dates. I promised myself that I would go over to Mama Lea's restaurant tomorrow and try to patch things up. My bed was in the corner of the room, where you couldn't put a chair because the roof angle cut the wall off in the little attic apartment. I jumped into bed, only just remembering to set the alarm.

Chapter 13

Nine o'clock came around within moments. The first thing I thought about when the radio went off, was why Claire was upset. That would continue to disturb me until I got over to the restaurant later. I wished I'd missed the message all together. I dragged my aching body into the shower, sorry that I hadn't gone for a steamer last night. My nose was a little blue on the sides and I treated it gently, surprised by how much blood I washed out of it. The scratches on my forehead looked non-lethal, but obvious. I dabbed them with alcohol, the kind you can't drink.

I dressed in slacks, a white shirt over starched at the Moon cleaners, and a blue sport coat. I found a clean black uniform tie, even though the bloody one might have been perfect for the occasion. I didn't have to wear my uniform, I was off today and tomorrow. Having weekends off, instead of working six days in a row like the regular patrol personnel, was one of the benefits of having a foot post.

The sun was promising a nice day. The Korean church where the funeral was being held was on Lunt Street, a half block east of Clark. It was a little after ten by the time I got there. There was a sign on the front lawn that read 'FIRST PRESBYTERIAN CHURCH', I wondered how high the numbers went, second, third, ninety-ninth?

Under the English lettering was the same square pictography of the Korean language that I wished I could decipher. Comparing the figures with the words I could read, even though I knew they said the same thing, still told me absolutely nothing.

There were two hearses in front of the church and I hoped I wasn't too late to catch the services. Rushing up the wide staircase that skirted the towering brown stone building, I yanked hard on the right handle of the huge wooden doors, expecting them to be heavy.

It opened easier than the door on my old Chevy. The door came open with a whoosh and I catapulted myself into the sanctuary, preparing to rush up the side aisle to the front where I expected a few people would be gathering.

Boy, was I surprised. The church was packed. The sun coming through the facets of the huge pie shaped windows over my head, cast a rainbow of colors onto the multitude who had gathered for the service.

There were no ceremonial costumes in evidence or foreign looking services going on. If it wasn't for all the almond shaped eyes that turned to look at me after my abrupt entrance, it would have looked like any American Christian congregation attending the funeral of important friends.

Thoughts of moving over to the side aisle vanishing, I did sort of a bowing curtsy, looking down and squeezing into the end of the first pew on my right. I felt that I'd disturbed the service enough already. Most people stopped staring at me as I tried to shrink down to an unnoticeable size, which was difficult, because I was the biggest person in the church.

The minister wore simple clerical clothing and spoke loudly in Korean. Everyone wore their finest clothing, all western styles. Children were being disciplined by mothers who were embarrassed by their misbehavior. There were many old people. It looked like it could have been a Sunday service, except for the caskets.

I started looking for familiar faces, especially Inon Moon's. It was difficult, because I'd never seen so many Koreans in one place before. Although I knew that there were over a hundred thousand Koreans living in Chicago, I had never thought about how many people that really was. It looked like half of them were packed in the huge church.

After searching row by row with my eyes, I found Moon's pinched faced wife sitting in one of the side pews, close to the front. She was wearing an ugly black hat that matched her personality. The only reason I spotted her, was that she had been staring straight at me with one of her patented scowls. Maybe she was looking for her husband too?

Seeing no one else that I recognized, I gave up searching and looked up to the nave of the church. The caskets were side by side, the one on the left was sky blue metal. The other had a flag covering it. I figured it was the Korean flag, but I could only see the white part from where I sat.

There was movement on the altar and I realized that the service was over. I looked down and said a serious prayer for my friends, I wasn't a Presbyterian, but it didn't matter. Church was church. The Big Guy would get the message.

The caskets were rolling slowly down the aisle now, led by the altar boys and followed by the minister who prayed out loud. Next came a gob of pall bearers, both male and female, all wearing gray gloves and subdued clothing. I saw Ah, he was walking with an old woman, they both looked very sad.

I moved a bit to get Ah's attention when he was about to pass be. He looked up and I nodded. Then I pointed to myself, pantomiming that I wanted to speak to him. He nodded in the affirmative and went back to concentrating on helping the grieving woman out of the church.

The pews emptied from the front, one after another, creating a procession of friends and mourners flowing down the center aisle. I looked over to where Moon's wife had been sitting and couldn't locate the ugliest hat in the church. I wanted to cut through the steady flow of people to get across the aisle and look for her, but that would have been the height of impropriety.

Thinking about being rude anyway and leaving out of turn to find Mrs. Moon, I was stopped in mid thought by the sight of Benjamin Cohen helping the old man Chung, down the aisle. On a closer inspection it looked like Chung was in deep conversation with Cohen and wasn't being helped at all. I knew that the old man always walked with a cane or stick for support, but there was none in evidence.

Cohen looked up and, seeing me, smiled. Chung noticed me but just looked through me with watery eyes. Most of the mourners were elderly, but he was obviously the oldest, the grief only added years to his countenance. They walked past, the old man lightly holding Cohen's elbow.

By the time it was my turn to leave the pew, I was one of the last to leave the church. Outside, a line of cars stretched westward up and over Clark Street, then out of sight. I only remembered seeing the hearses when I'd arrived.

Now, behind the hearses were several black limousines, the rear door on the first one was open and Ah stood there by it patiently waiting. I hurried down the steps of the church to where the little man with the soup bowl haircut held up the funeral procession for me.

"Ah," I said catching myself before rushing into my own business. "Please accept my condolences on your loss and extend them to the family." I bowed awkwardly, then extended my hand which he took. East meets west.

"Thank you," was all he said. What did I expect him to say, 'don't worry it wasn't your fault'?

"Do you know what happened last night?" He gave me a sort of nod, as if he knew but didn't care.

"Will you be at your store later? I need to talk to you." The funeral director was folding what I now saw as the red centered and black barred Korean flag, but I could tell he was waiting on me. He was just about to come over and say something when Ah spoke.

"No. I will not open today. Later I will be at my uncles's school." There was a harsh word from the darkened interior of the limo, must have been Chung. Ah looked to the approaching funeral director and turned him around with an unseen gesture. The man went back to the lead hearse and got into the passenger seat. Ah turned and got into the limo without another word and closed the door, leaving me standing there watching the procession begin.

The brown stone church towering behind me suddenly came alive and I turned too quickly, only to see Cohen's smiling face right behind me. "What the...heck, are you doing here?" I looked uneasily up at the cross topped spire, biting off a curse.

"Well, yesterday when you pointed out Master Chung's place and said that his nephew had been killed, I called him and asked if I could come to the service." The answer seemed simple enough.

"You weren't just at the service, you were with the family." I wasn't satisfied with his answer.

"The old man doesn't want to show weakness to the other, younger, old people," Cohen said, smiling at his own comment. "So he invited me to come along and be his 'stick' for the day, as he called it."

Wondering about Chung and his stick, and still not satisfied, I asked, "How old is he anyway?"

"Oh, I don't know really, older than all the others, probably late eighties or ninety." Chung looked old but not that old, which reminded me of another question I'd wanted to ask.

"How long have you known this Master Chung?" The pieces of the puzzle were not coming together.

"Since he came to this country." I could see in Cohen's eyes that I had asked a good question.

"And that was a little while before you started at the Police Academy. You didn't just meet him when he posted a flyer on the bulletin board?" He didn't answer, but it was obvious. I stood there trying to drag information out of him, while the cars continued to pass us slowly by. I felt like I was directing traffic.

"Well...yes. I've known him longer than that. I've been training with him since I was a kid." He still was a kid, that didn't mean anything to me.

He continued on, anticipating my next question. "This used to be a Jewish neighborhood, remember? Master Chung came here when I was around 13 and I started in one of his classes. You know the story. 'Wimpy little Jew goes to martial arts school to learn how to defend himself against his Anti-Semitic tormentors'." He smiled at me. I didn't smile back.

What I saw this kid doing in the jewelry shop last night had nothing to do with defending himself. What I saw was two ninjas defending themselves, and desperately trying to get away from Cohen's ferocious onslaught. I was confused, though it seemed he was being completely honest with me. I knew there was another question I wanted to ask him but the end of the procession had reached the church.

"I gotta go, Hop. The old man will need me for his 'stick' when they get to the cemetery." He started across the street for his little foreign car before I could stop him.

"Are you working today?" I called out to him.

He turned, the smile gone from his face. "Yes, 2423 with Brian White. He's back."

"It's only for a few more weeks. You can handle it, Rookie." Trying to give him encouragement, I was diverted from asking him another question, or even remembering what it was.

*   *   *

Rearranging the chenille bed spread that covered the front seat of my old Chevy, I started the gas guzzler and headed north on Paulina Avenue. It paralleled Clark for a few blocks and was faster than waiting for a light every other block on the busy street. I couldn't get my priorities straight. The side issue stuff was building up instead of solving itself like it was supposed to. The message from Claire had never been far from my mind, only giving me more things to speculate on and worry about.

Driving past a different church every two blocks made me wonder whether there was a chance that some help could come from a higher power. I was willing to stand out in the rain and catch a bolt of lightening, if it would tell me what I wanted to know. Seeing the 'GE' of the Gray Eagles painted on a wall, and the word ROYALS with it's familiar stylized crown painted over the 'GE', told me that there were other people competing for the lives and souls of the people in Rogers Park. I faced reality. The chances of finding out the truth were slim, and of getting any help, were none.

The news that waited for me at Mama Lea's worried me on a personal level and subconsciously, I tried to put it off a little while longer by taking the film Geery had given me to be developed. My friend Leo, the druggist, was busy in the back so I didn't have to answer the question. I just gave the plastic canister to the girl working the front counter and told her to put my name on it.

Then I rode around for awhile searching up and down Clark Street, and its tributaries, for Gilly Rodriquez or any of his Royal underlings. The streets were devoid of gang-bangers. On any other day this would have delighted me. I told myself that they weren't hiding from me, it was too early for any of them to be about, and headed back up Clark.

Someone else who wasn't around was Inon Moon. The cleaners was closed on a Saturday for the first time I could remember. I went around the back, trying every door in the single storied building without any luck. I spotted one of the Mexicans who worked for Moon sitting in a parked car in front, and started asking him questions, which he hardly understood. Scaring him more than anything else, I found out only that he had come to work and found the place locked.

Finally giving up worrying about other problems, I went to see how badly my personal life was going. Mama Lea's West Indian Restaurant was far north on Clark Street, near Rogers Ave.. It was just a storefront in a long line of similar buildings on the west side of the street. Her sign had been hand painted by Claire. It showed a beach scene with palm trees and had 'Mama Lea's" painted colorfully on it.

There was a city ordinance against having heavy wooden signs hanging over the sidewalk. I didn't know that until I had to toss a building inspector out Lea's front door on his bribe seeking ass. I whispered a few threats in his ear and he hasn't tried to extort money from anyone on my beat since. I liked Mama Lea and her sign too. That was how I'd met Claire,

Mama Lea's niece. Besides, when I'd started this foot post I'd made a personal rule, nobody shook down businesses on my beat, city inspector, gang-banger or copper.

I found a parking spot on a meter, and had no change. I tried to secure my mop of white hair but it wanted to play in the light breeze. I had lost weight since I'd been running and working out, and my clothes hung on me. With the addition of the cuts on my face, I must have cut a sorry looking, penniless, figure when I stepped into the restaurant.

It was after noon and there were a few customers sitting at the clean little red tables. One of them was a Jamaican named Ozzie. He had long thick dread locks, dark brown tinged with gold in an island style. Ozzie had one of the yard long strands tied around the rest holding them up, on top of his head, and out of his breakfast. He was a striking figure, like a living Medusa with snakes writhing on his head.

Ozzie was a singer in a Reggae Band. He had a clear strong voice that sounded like Bob Marley's, which always assured him of work. He spoke to me in patois, heavily accented, offering me greetings and the blessings of Jah.

From what I could gather, their religion stemmed from a visit by Haile Selassie after Jamaica won its freedom from slavery and Great Britain. They called it Rastafarian. It seemed to me to be based on Zionism. Whatever it was, he practiced it, and that was okay with me. They ate no pork, right now he was eating salt fish and aki for breakfast, with fried plantain on the side. It wasn't my favorite dish, by a long shot, but my stomach told me that it was time to eat something, soon.

You couldn't tell by looking at Ozzie, or by talking to him for that matter, that he'd done two tours in Viet Nam and could speak perfect English. It was little known that U.S. citizenship could be obtained by doing a stretch in the Army. The government usually only made it known when they were having a war and needed cannon fodder. Ozzie was a U.S. citizen and had done more than most to become one.

I smiled back at Ozzie's gold trimmed dental work and said, "Irie, mon," which was the only patois I knew.

"Well, I was going to send the police for you." I turned at the melodious voice. Claire came out of the kitchen with another plate of the scrambled eggs-looking 'aki' and placed the Jamaican national dish in front of a young girl having lunch with her mother.

"Hi, Claire, I'm sorry about not calling you," I said, feeling like Cohen, apologizing all the time. She was so beautiful that my tongue immediately tied. I wanted to say other things, but I just stared at that lovely mouth full of pearly teeth. She smiled at me and her laughing green eyes told me that she was happy to see me and I wasn't in that much trouble. I was greatly relieved and started to relax.

"It's no problem, mon," she said in her island accent, from across the room where she was getting something for another customer. I could tell that there was a problem, now that I heard her voice again. When she spoke with an accent, it meant that she was covering something up, trying to be humorous.

The table nearest the kitchen was the unofficial family table, used by the cooks and staff for sitting around when there was no business. I slid into one of the chairs as I waited for Claire to finish with her customers.

Through the louvered swinging door I could see Mama Lea, her familiar flowered dress billowing around her tremendous frame. She was the best advertisement of her wonderful cooking ability.

"Good morning, Mama Lea," I said, expecting a torrent of beautifully accented words to come flowing out of the kitchen. I was sure she'd ask me about the sport coat and tie that I was uncharacteristically wearing on a Saturday morning.

"Good mar'nin, Cassidy," was her only cool comment. The way she said it told me that something was wrong, and I was the only one who didn't know what it was. She went about busying herself, chopping up a helpless chicken with a big cleaver. I put a finger in my collar and stretched it unconsciously.

116

When Claire came and sat down, I had my face turned strategically so she couldn't see the bruises. That didn't last long. Taking my dry bone white hand in her soft tawny one, she turned me around and looked at me severely. "Oh, Basil, what happened to your face?"

"Actually, I walked into a door," I said, trying to sound light hearted. She looked worried, but seemed to accept a reason that nobody else would.

"I have received some disturbing news, and it concerns you, Basil. It concerns us both." The subject changed quickly, but her worried look stayed the same. I could see what she was leading up to. We had made love like wild teenagers, careless of the world around us, or its consequences. And just like a teenager, I was going to be a father at the wrong time in my life. How stupid could I be?

"Claire honey, whatever happens, I want you to know that I'll support you and any decision you make." There were a lot of things to consider these days, especially for a woman forty years old.

"You don't understand, Basil, it's not as though we have a choice in the matter. Let me explain." I interrupted her, feeling badly, as though I had already said the wrong thing, trying to correct it.

"It doesn't matter, whatever happens, don't worry." I was saying a bunch of rambling nonsense.

"Basil, please be quiet for a moment and listen to me." Her expression shut me up.

"It's about my grandmother." That was it, her grandmother had died and she was going back to the island. I could see how that was disturbing news, but it was better than her being pregnant.

"She had a dream about us. A very powerful dream." So the grandmother was alive and we were back to babies.

"And she saw us having a baby," I finished for her, trying to ease the stress she was putting herself through. If she wanted to tell me about it in a round about way, that was fine.

117

"I asked you to be quiet and listen to me, Basil, and you haven't done either one." She was getting angry, but I still loved the way she pronounced either as 'eye-there'.

"What are you talkin' about babies, man? My grandmother might make me marry you, but she can't make me have any more children." I knew she had a grown daughter going to school in Florida and could understand her not wanting any more kids. But I still wasn't hearing right.

"Aren't you pregnant? I thought that's what you were trying to tell me." She laughed, shaking her head negatively. What a relief. Finding out that you weren't going to become a father at fifty-five has to be in the top five of, 'the best news I've ever heard'. The other four things could fluctuate but, 'the test was negative', was always near the top.

"You foolish man, I can't have any more children no matter what my grandmother dreams." She patted my sweaty hand, smiling. Then my mind registered something else she had said about the dream.

"Did you say 'she can make you marry me'?" I must have heard her wrong.

He smile faded and she looked down at the red table cloth. "My grandmother had a dream that I was married to a man with white hair," she confessed, with a look of dread on her face.

"I'm sorry Claire, but I don't understand what I've done wrong." If I hadn't gotten her pregnant, everything else was great as far as I was concerned. Who cared about her granny's insomnia?

"It isn't what you've done, it's what you are going to do." She couldn't look me in the eye, it was so terrible. I wanted to see those greenish brown eyes smile at me again.

"I don't care what your grandmother dreams, Claire, nothing can ever make me do anything to hurt you, nothing." I really believed that.

"Oh, I know that, and so does she. She knows everything. It was a good dream. She's very happy for us." She glanced up at me, trying to see how I was taking this incomprehensible news.

"Okay, so you told her about us and she had a good dream. So what? I don't see anything wrong with that." I was finally getting rational.

"I've never told her anything about you. She saw you in her dream." She was almost in tears now as the words poured out. "And it does mean something. My grandmother is an Oba-woman. When she has a dream it comes true. Not sometimes, all the time. You're going to marry me, you have no choice." She sighed heavily. It was like she had finally gotten it out, the worst thing in the world. I tried not to laugh.

"She's an Oba-woman? Is that some kind of Voodoo or something?" I said, thinking about the Voodoo girl on Morse Street.

"It's not a joke, Basil. This is serious. She would not have gone to the trouble of contacting Aunt Lea all the way from the Caribbean if it wasn't really going to happen." She gave me a stern look. This was the wrong time to smile, I didn't.

"I'm sure it is serious. To her," I said. "But we don't have to get married if we don't want to. There must be something else we can do?" I tried to discuss her problem objectively.

"You can try throwing yourself off of a cliff, but you'd probably survive until the wedding." She acted like she was in a hopeless situation.

She squeezed my hand, surprising me with her strength. "I'm telling you my grandmother has the 'gift'. People come from all over the world to seek her advice. Years ago, she stopped telling people if she had seen their imminent death because several people dropped dead on the spot." She believed every word she was saying.

"What kind of gift does she have? Is it E.S.P. or does she see the future or what?" I had to act like I was willing to believe it if I was ever going to understand what was going on.

"There is no way to describe what it is, Basil, but don't make light of it." I didn't think I was. Actually, maybe I was being a bit insincere, and not hiding it well enough.

119

"In my family we just call it the gift. My grandmother says that the gift skips a generation and that I have it, though I don't listen to it." She stared at the wall for a second as if she had brought up an unpleasant thought.

"But she listens to it, and she's never wrong. If my grandmother tells someone who's never been anywhere in their life that she saw them going on a long trip, they start packing." She wasn't kidding.

"Okay. So she had a dream and it might come true." I still felt that I controlled my own destiny. I couldn't say that I'd get married just because an old lady living in a mahogany forest on St. Croix said I'd do it.

"Why are you so upset? It wasn't a dream about seeing us both dead or something."

She looked away again. What else could be wrong? Finally, after a long pause, she turned to me and said. "Basil, don't take this the wrong way, but I don't want to get married. Not to you or anyone. I've been on my own for so long now that I'm not sure that I want to give that up."

For a moment I felt like I had been spurned. As though I had proposed marriage and been turned down. I examined myself. I wasn't that old. I was in the best shape I could remember. I wasn't that bad a catch. What was wrong with me really?

I caught myself before I could bring up that lengthy list. "I can understand that, honey," I said finally, lamely.

"See how nice you are, Basil." I couldn't see it at all. She had tears in her eyes again now, but they were smiling. I didn't feel too nice.

"I understand," I didn't, "we enjoy each other's company and it doesn't matter to us, but I guess we're not exactly the typical couple." Claire wasn't very dark skinned but I was so fair that if I went into the sun without sun block, I blistered in minutes. There was a dramatic difference.

"Oh Basil, you're so considerate. But that's not what concerns me." She looked over her shoulder into the kitchen, the sounds of food preparation having ceased. Mama Lea looked down and started concentrating on her work when she realized that her eavesdropping had been discovered.

"It's not a racial thing, Basil. It's cultural, and it does concern my family in that way." She took my hand in both of hers, smiling at me warmly. "Even though I am an American, I'm from a different country. Our culture is entirely different than yours here in America. The women keep the history in my family and have done so for over four hundred years."

My family tree was a stick with one branch. My mother had come out of the 'holler' in the West Virginian mountains, some sixty years ago. I have some uncles and cousins around somewhere, but I don't have four hundred years of history. There was a part of me that knew what I was, and that my life could be looked at as barbaric, but it wasn't usually pointed out to me so clearly.

"I know that I'm a mutt. The only places that I've ever been are Florida, Vegas, and Viet Nam. I told you about my past, my drinking and about my divorce and all...and about being a cop." I ran on trying to excuse my past by owning up to it.

"No, darling. That's not it at all. You are perfect just the way you are." Surprised the hell out of me. "I considered all those things before I decided to go out with you." We had been friends for a year before I asked her out. Looking at my bruises, she took my face in her hands like Irene had done to Cohen.

"One thing I don't understand though, is your job. This foot patrol. Isn't that a job for a younger man?" Hit the nail on the head why don't you. "You should be a lieutenant behind a desk, not walking up and down the street in all kinds of weather." I didn't feel like telling her that I couldn't even become a sergeant in the few years I had left before mandatory retirement. And I didn't want to face the fact that my job could probably be done better by a younger man.

"Well, I do have enough time and age to retire. The boys are on their own now and I don't really have any debts to work off." I wasn't really thinking about it. I think. And I didn't know why

I was giving her the impression that I would quit my job because she thought it was too hard for me.

"Even if you went in the office," she said, taking a different track altogether, "I still couldn't live in Chicago. I only came here to finish my Masters and help my aunt start her business. I can't take another winter in this city." She shivered involuntarily.

I'd never thought about it much but fifty five winters in Chicago was more than enough. Suddenly I wanted to slap myself a few times to wake myself up. "Wait a second, honey," I said, covering her little hands with my dinner plate ones.

"Let's take this a little slower. We have the whole summer ahead of us before the winter, you can't stand, will be here," I said, smiling with her. My mouth, or was it my heart, had been running way ahead of my brain.

"How about dinner? We can talk some more about it later. You get off at nine tonight, don't you?" She nodded eagerly to all my suggestions.

"Good, I'll come by and pick you up then. I have a lot of things that I have to look into, so I'll probably be busy until then." I thought about some of them.

"I wish I had 'the gift' right now. It might help me get something off my mind that's really bothering me. Then maybe I would have more time to think about personal matters." I winked at her happy face.

"What is it, Basil?" She asked. I didn't really want to talk about it all and was sorry I'd made the comment.

"The jewelry store murders the other night." She nodded solemnly.

"There's nothing but questions, no answers. If I could just figure out one piece of the puzzle. Find a place to start." I sighed involuntarily.

"The best way to solve a puzzle is to take the facts that you have, and examine them one at a time, from every angle. Let me help you. Tell me one of your questions." She was eager to help, I was sorry I'd said anything.

If I could have the correct answer to any question, which one would it be? How many questions did I have? Who killed my friends, was one? The answer to that question was too much to ask for. I'd be happy if just one of the little ones were answered. Time was already passing, the facts were beginning to cloud together. I thought out loud for a second to try to refresh my memory.

"Okay," She smiled, thinking I had relented and would make my wish. "I can't understand how a guy who runs a laundry could be involved in all this. I can't believe that he murdered the Parks, but I'm almost positive that I saw him coming out of their shop last night." I left out the part about Tso going jumping through the window, that was another question.

"Well, what do you know about him?" She was trying to help. I humored her a bit, even more sorry that I started this whole conversation.

"I don't know very much, now that I think about it." I had a lot of thinking to do. "All I can say for sure is that's he is Korean and..."

"North or South?" She asked, interrupting me, but it didn't matter, because I couldn't remember the next thing I was going to say anyway. I just sat there with my mouth hanging open.

"North or South Korea?" She repeated, as though I hadn't heard her the first time. I was still stunned, but I was beginning to believe in the gift.

"I don't know, but I had better go and find out," I stammered. My seeming return to normalcy brought the smile back to her serious face. "I've got to go, but I'll be back tonight. You've really been a big help, I think." She smiled pearly white teeth at me and glowed happily. Then she noticed that one of her customers was trying to get her attention and got up to do her job.

I got up to leave and Mama Lea stuck her bright turban out of the kitchen. "Cassidy, don't you want to eat some'ting?" The smile on her face told me that I was back in her good graces.

Her brightly colored dress was 'V' cut, and it strained to hold her ample breasts within the confines of the material, as she leaned out the door. Mama Lea didn't have regular breasts, this woman had bosoms. Enough bosom to comfort any number of children, or men for that matter. I wondered if God was an enormous black woman.

"I wish I could, but I have to go." My stomach groaned at the news of no food. Even the salt fish sounded good. She smiled brightly at me. I could see the family resemblance. "I'll see you later, Aunt Lea," she beamed even more when I called her 'aunt'.

As I walked by Ozzie's table, he was just cleaning his plate and he looked up at me with a golden smile. "Con-gratulations, mon!" He said jovially. The husband was always the last to know.

Claire was across the room, I smiled and waved good-bye to her. Then, just as I had the door handle in my hand, I remembered something else she had said. "When did 'you' decide to go out with me, Claire?" I was the one who had done the asking out.

"A long time before you ever thought about it, Cassidy!" She said smiling slyly, and went back to her work. I left the restaurant with thoughts that were relieved, confused, and wondering just what gifts were left in the world.

Chapter 14

The beater didn't have a parking ticket on the cracked windshield, the bike men who gave Moon parking tickets wouldn't be working on Saturday either. The weekends were basically free parking on Clark Street. Driving down Clark, the sun was so bright that I had to fish a pair of sunglasses out of the glove compartment. I looked for Gilly, or any Royal as I drove.

Nobody was around. I went over to Marie's mother's house on Greenleaf, left my car double parked like a squad car and walked up to the third floor. I pounded on the door for awhile without an answer.

Finally giving up on the Royals for a moment, I drove south, passing Pratt Avenue. Pratt was the middle of my beat and the beginning of Disciple territory. There wouldn't be any Royals south of Pratt. There were lights on in Chung's place so I hurried on to the station to get the papers out of my locker.

I tried to get in and out of the station without being seen, but Mike Pape was at his locker when I came around the corner of the door. "I thought you were off today, Hop? You didn't have to go to court on Saturday did you?" He said, referring to my coat and tie. I peeled off my sport coat and started to get my gym clothes out of the locker.

"No, I went to the funeral for those people who were killed the other night. I thought I might as well work out for awhile as long as I was up this way." I didn't know what else to say, half a truth and half a lie. Unfortunately I was getting good at that.

He finished whatever he was doing at his locker and started to walk past me. "I know you're trying to work off some stress, Hop, but don't go at it so hard. You have to build it back slowly. Strength and stamina, that's the secret." He slapped me on the back for emphasis, so hard that he almost knocked me into the locker, and went out the door.

The papers made an obvious bulge in the front of the thin blue serge of my coat. I snuck out of the locker room and made it to my car without seeing anyone else. The school was only a block away, but I took my car, squeezing it onto the corner in an illegal spot. I walked the few doors up to the school, looking around suspiciously.

The door was open and a little bell tinkled when I entered the storefront. It took my eyes a few seconds to adjust from the sunlight. The room was spacious, with thick woven mats everywhere. The posts that supported the room were thickly wound with the same material. The wall on my left was lined with mirrors. I headed toward the rear where I knew the little office was.

Against the back wall on the left, what I thought to be only a pile of rags, moved. I froze halfway to the rear. He wore an elaborate hat that swooped up into peaks on the sides. The costume, and I could only think of it as that, looked like it had come from the 12th century. It was the old man.

The dark blue silk was embroidered with figures in swirling, muted colors. I couldn't see, from where I stood, whether the figures told a story or had other significant meaning. I would never know, because I wasn't going near the guy.

Chung's infinitely wrinkled face, surrounded by the hat and ornate Kimono was the living definition of inscrutable and mysterious. He sat stiffly cross legged on the floor. He must have moved only to get my attention, because I felt that he could sit there, unmoving, forever, bad leg or not.

In front of him was a little incense burner from which tiny blue trails of smoke rose to the ceiling. I could smell the sweet woody scent now that the initial shock of seeing him was beginning to wear off. On his right hand was a small bowl of rice with a pair of red chop sticks sticking out of the top of the little ball of white grains.

"Ah," I called out softly, not wanting to disturb or address the scary little man directly.

From the office door that was on my right, I heard a rustling. Ah stuck his head around the edge of the doorway, he had a telephone in his hand, the cord going back into the office. He waved me to him.

I walked slowly, reverently, trying not to disturb the ceremony that Chung was conducting. Watching him closely out of the corner of my eye, I prepared to bow or genuflect or whatever, if he looked my way. His small watery eyes, looked away to a place that only he could see.

As I approached I saw the small cup, that usually contained rice wine, in his left hand. That part of the ceremony I could understand. Ah was just hanging up the phone when I came level with the office doorway. He bowed, which I returned awkwardly, and then offered his hand, which I accepted. East meets west again.

The cluttered office had only one chair which he offered and I declined. There was a lot of preliminary procedure prior to getting down to business with people from the Pacific Rim. In more than one culture it was considered the height of rudeness to come right to the point when doing business.

I asked him about the funeral and offered my condolences again. Then I complimented the church services and reflected on how well respected the Parks were to have so many people attend. I was dying to ask him a question about that too, but I kept my place and waited for him to ask me why I had requested to see him at such a difficult time.

"Last night, something happened?" He asked, finally opening the door for our real conversation to start.

"Yes. Two men broke into Park's shop. One is dead." He was watching me closely and I knew that it was not an accident that Chung could probably hear the conversation from where he meditated.

"You know him?" He prompted me to continue.

"Yes, his name is David Tso. He was the leader of one of the Asian gangs that hang around Argyle street, in Little Viet Nam." That was an area about a mile south of here and east along the lake. I wasn't sure that I should ask him about Moon, but I didn't have any other ideas.

127

"The other one was Inon Moon. Do you know him, Ah? He owns the cleaners up by Touhy Avenue." Now it was my turn to watch him. His reaction, or lack or one, told me nothing.

"I know him." He said casually. He wasn't exactly a babbling brook of information.

I reached inside my bulging coat and pulled out the bloody stack of papers. That got a reaction out of him. He recognized them immediately. He tried to act as though nothing had happened, but he couldn't take his eyes off of them. For a second I thought that he was going to jump on me and try to take them away from me. He kept still, but I could feel his tension.

Then his eyes looked behind me and I thought that the old man was creeping up on me. I stepped to the side and looked back at him. Chung hadn't moved, but a slight move of his head told me that he hade been looking our way.

"Do you know what these papers are, Ah?" I asked him, as if I hadn't noticed a thing.

"I don't know." Ask a dumb question. They were still folded in half, why should he know what they were. I took out the center page and held it out to him, afraid to let him hold them all for some reason.

He looked at it for a second, and then handed it back to me. "It is names of Korean people, I don't know them." We were moving right along.

"Ah, look, you know me. You know that I wouldn't do anything to hurt you or the Parks. I need to know what's happening though. What are these papers and why did Moon want them?" He opened his mouth to plead ignorance again and I stopped him with another question.

"Is Moon from North Korea?" Ah just looked at me blankly. "Tell me, Ah, is he a North Korean?" I raised my voice, the old man just sat there and contemplated the mysteries of the universe.

"He come from Taiwan, I don't know." He didn't want to tell me but I wasn't going to give up.

"Yea, so he came here from Taiwan. But he's not Chinese, he's Korean, right?" Ah nodded. "And if I meet someone from Alabama, I can tell from the way he talks or acts that he's not from Wisconsin."

"Is there any chance that this guy is from North Korea?" He just looked at me, but it was an answer.

"And these papers, what makes them so important that a North Korean would risk his life for them?" A price that had been paid already.

He just stared at me blankly. Then I thought about the four yellowed old documents that were mixed up with the others. I thought about the flag that had been draped over one of the coffins and about the old army style gun that Park kept behind the counter.

Leafing through the stack I took one of the yellow sheets out and held it up for Ah to see, but not to hold. I could see a sadness in his eyes. "Ah, what did Park do before he came to America?"

No answer again. "Was he in the Army or with the Government, or something? Look, Ah, if you won't help me, I'm going to have to start asking other people what all this is about." A look of resignation came over his face, he glanced over to where the old man sat. I didn't move, but I was ready to.

"Yes. Park was a colonel in the Army." That was all I get? I wanted to grab him and shake him a little, but after seeing Cohen in action, I didn't think I was the toughest guy in the place.

I put the document back in the stack and took out the hand written sheet that I had first showed him. "Ah, could you translate this page for me?"

He looked at it and started to speak. "No, I want you to write it down for me." I offered him the chair and he sat down. Taking a clean sheet of paper from a drawer, he began to transcribe the names and numbers, translating from Korean to English.

All the names looked Korean and each had an address and a dollar figure under them. The addresses were from all over the globe. The dollar figures were all over a million.

When he finished, I took both pages from the desk without waiting for him to offer them. "Now tell me, Ah, what was Park doing with these names and how did he get them?" I waved the stack in his face for emphasis. I wasn't leaving without some answers. Even if the old man had to beat me up to get them.

He hung his head looking down at the desk top for a moment, the old man didn't rise from the floor and attack me. Finally, Ah looked up at me with great sadness in his eyes.

"During the war, when we were in Korea, it was very hard. Everyone wanted to come to America. You do not understand how bad it was. People would pay anything, but Park never took their money," he said, attempting to soften whatever bad thing Park had done forty years earlier. It was my turn to wait and look inscrutable. I just looked at him expressionless.

"Park was in charge of Immigration. All requests for passports were approved by him. He never ask for payment but he know how much money they take with them when they leave. He make sure he know who they are and where they go." He gestured toward the papers that I still held.

His look became a pleading one. I didn't move a muscle, he was on the hook, not me. "Park told them that someday he might need a favor and that they would have to do it."

He went on quickly. "But that was long ago, it was war then. No one knew what would happen after it was over. Park never asked anyone for anything. He could have but he didn't. He was a great hero to his country. He never disgrace his country or hurt his people. That paper is an honoring from the government."

First the guy wouldn't talk, now he wouldn't shut up, but he wasn't saying much. So Park had brought some insurance of a good life with him to America. People who had sneaked out of Korea during or after the war, taking large amounts of cash with them had to get Park's approval before they could escape. He had exacted future promises from them as payment.

From the way the Parks lived, they were comfortable but certainly not millionaires, I could see that Ah was telling some of the truth. I remembered the stretched out argyle socks and worn out shoes that Park had been wearing when he died. Even one of the names on these lists might be worth a lot more than the price of new shoes and socks.

"Who are all these people, Ah? Are they spies? Or corrupt officials, criminals, or what?" I still didn't know what to do with this information.

"Not bad people." He said, hesitantly. "Good people." He sounded as though he was trying to convince himself as well an me.

"Some maybe not so good," he hurried on. "But not spy or criminal, just...you give papers to police?" he asked.

So most of the people on the list were good people, now at least. How did I separate them from the bad ones. If these names got into the wrong hands people would be hurt. I could tell that much from what he said. The million dollar figures told me that they might still be rich or powerful people, and why David Tso and Moon wanted these names badly enough to risk their lives to get them.

Each would have their own uses for the names. Moon, a North Korean. Possibly a spy or whatever the hell they called them these days and Tso the extortionist. There were hundreds of names on these pages, people who had been in this country for generations, who had come here with millions of dollars and the influence that it bought.

"I 'am' the Police, Ah," I said trying to cover my own unprofessional activities. He just looked at me, not believing it anymore than I did.

"I don't know what I'm going to do with them," I said finally, truthfully. "If these papers can help me find out who killed Sung and his wife, then I'm going to do whatever I have to do with them. They were Park's insurance policy, maybe they'll pay off for him in a different way."

I didn't wait to hear his objections. I thanked him, stuffed the papers in my coat and headed for the door. Chung never moved, but I wanted to get away from him as fast as I could, far away.

Chapter 15

The bundle in my coat felt like a ticking bomb next to my heart. What was I getting myself into? North Korean spies and secret lists, people with mysterious pasts. My job was writing parking tickets. Why did I suspect the system, of which I was a part, of not being able to find out the truth about the murders? Why did I think that I was the only one who could serve justice?

One thing for sure, I needed help. Pulling the bed spread off of my front seat, I took the stack and stuffed the papers, (worth who knows what?) into a hole in the seat of my old beater. Years of driving with my gun belt on had torn the fabric and foam under it. I replaced my chenille seat cover, hiding the bundle, and drove to a payphone.

The Chevy's rear end was blocking the crosswalk. I was standing right next to it where two payphones were connected to a light pole. Phone booths were a thing of the past in Chicago. Trying to get behind the little phone shelter, I turned the collar up on my jacket in an effort to keep out of the wind that had come up.

When I asked the person who answered the phone at the Area Homicide desk for Voltz, he put me on hold. It was clouding over now and my pant legs flapped in the chilly north breeze while I waited. The changing spring weather in Chicago looked like it was brewing up a storm.

Looking at my watch, I noticed that it was still early afternoon, an hour before Voltz would be at work. I realized that I was being overanxious and was prepared to leave a message with the desk man, hoping that Voltz would get it when he came in.

When Dolecki came onto the line it surprised me. I had been thinking about the phone message from Sui Park. It was in my pocket. I hoped that I could find out who wrote it and ask that person some questions. "Dolecki." He sounded as though the call had disturbed something important.

"This is Cassidy, from Rogers Park." I said, not wanting to give him a chance to say 'Cassidy who?'. I've known the bastard for twenty years now, and I knew what he thought was humorous.

"Cassidy who?" I could tell he was smiling.

I didn't say anything. He gave up first. "What do you want, Cassidy?" I could tell that he still thought his twenty year old joke was funny.

"Where's Voltz?" I knew that would irritate him, everybody asked for Voltz because Dolecki was such a jerk.

"You think that he would come in two hours early," he said, like he was such a dedicated public servant. Dolecki was an overtime cheater. Some of his overtime checks were bigger than my regular pay.

"When you guys hit the street, I'd appreciate it if you'd meet me up here in 24." If I didn't ask nice, Dolecki would blow me off and I'd be looking for Voltz all night.

"What'a ya got, Cassidy?" He would love to get a jump on his partner if he could. Another sign of a jerk.

"I've got something to show you, is what I've got. So meet me up here around 4. Okay?" Why was I telling this slime that I had something for him? I must be getting desperate.

"Sure, sure. We'll meet you at the station when we get out of roll call." They must have been stuck for a clue on the murders. I had a few.

"One more thing." I said authoritatively. "Why are you there two hours early?" I knew he was beating the company for overtime.

"I had to finish some...what the fuck do you care why I'm here, Cassidy." He got mad at himself for telling me that he was collecting time and a'half for doing work that he should have finished while on his regular shift.

I laughed. "Just wondered how the taxes were being wasted. See ya at 4." I hung up before he could curse me out again.

I shivered at the cold wind that was blowing stiffly south, taking all the dirt and garbage downtown. The cold wind saved me, though. Instead of walking around the car to the drivers door, I ducked quickly into the passenger door. When I lowered my head to scoot over to the steering wheel, the windows went. I kept my head down as the glass shattered all around me and the bullets bounced around the car. I sounded like the Fourth of July.

I don't know how many shots they fired at me, they were coming so fast that it was impossible to count them. I wasn't thinking about counting anyway because I was cowering on the filthy floor of my Chevy. The shooting stopped and I heard a car speed away.

My keys were in my hand and I started the beater from a kneeling position, while trying to brush glass shards off the seat with the sleeve of my coat. I peeked around carefully. Looking east bound on Morse, I saw the brake lights of a car come on brightly at the next corner. Then I heard tires screech and saw that they almost collided with another car in the next intersection east.

It was foolish to go after them, glass shards poking me in tender places, but that's what I did. I climbed behind the wheel and made a 'U' turn, burning rubber. When I sped past St. Jerome's Church I wished I could stop and remove the glass from my butt like he had done with the lion's paw. The car I was chasing was black, which told me nothing because all three gangs in the area had black as one of their colors.

It looked like a little foreign car, but not a cheap one. I came thundering down the little hill and skidded to a stop at Paulina, right where they had. The glass dug into me even more but I managed to avoid an accident.

When the car, that I had almost hit, passed, the black car was already turning south on Ashland. I punched the gas pedal and the old four barreled carburetor opened up, sucking in air and gas with a deep funneling roar. That little sporty foreign car might have a high performance four cylinder engine in it, but I had a souped up old Chevy short block under my rusty hood.

I rode the four hundred horses around the corner and closed the distance between us quickly. They turned east again at the next block, Pratt, and had to slow a little to avoid traffic. I laid on the horn and blew right through the intersection, in true police chase fashion. Without consideration for myself, or the unwary public.

They picked up speed going down Pratt. When they got to the C.T.A. elevated train viaduct they made a hard right and slammed into the long concrete wall that ran north and south. The driver of the black car must have been momentarily stunned because they just slid along the wall for forty feet or so and stopped.

Seeing what happened to them, I slammed on my brakes to slow my speed and slid around the corner, wheeling onto the street behind them. The driver recovered, and the car, a Honda, pulled away from the wall at foot to the floor speed, but not before I saw the terrified face of Key in the back window of the black car.

He didn't look 'high', like he had when Garcia and James had him under arrest with David Tso the other night. Now his face had the look of a frightened rabbit about to be pounced upon by a tiger. And that was exactly how I felt about it too. When we made eye contact I smiled, he started shouting something to the people in the front seat.

I had them now. There were only two car lengths between us. I was going to punch this baby and jump right through their back window at 80 m.p.h. I could see Key's wild eyes, his mouth open in a scream that I couldn't hear.

They shot past the viaduct on the next block just as a young couple was about to step into the street. Just one more step and those people would have been dead. I hit the brakes, managing to stop before the viaduct. The Latino boy and girl crossed the now quiet street looking at me strangely, as they had every right to do. Fool, I thought, you don't risk killing people because you're more pissed off than scared.

My heart was pounding and my ears were ringing as the adrenalin coursed through my body. I was shaking. I got out of the car and started brushing the glass from my clothing. The seat covers came out easily. A good shake and a little grooming with the snow brush had me back in service. There were a number of burning sensations coming from my posterior, but I didn't feel any wetness so I figured I wasn't bleeding badly. My hands had little cuts all over them. Just a few more scratches I thought. Soon my body would be all cuts and bruises. I was running out of unaffected areas. At least there were no bullet holes.

So the Gray Eagles had snuck up on me while I was chatting on the phone, oblivious, standing there exposed to the world. Why? Because I was on my street and had gotten too comfortable, letting my guard down. The biggest fool in town.

Like a rookie, I just let those punks wait for me to get off the phone, double parked on the other side of my car. They knew they had me cold, they had played it like a game. And the luck had been with me this time. I didn't deserve it. What did I think I was doing by chasing after them? They had automatic weapons and I had a five shot snub nose pistol in my belt. A gun that you couldn't hit anything with, unless it was close enough to spit on.

I thought about how lucky I was that they didn't turn around and shoot the shit out of me. I considered going to the station and admitting that I had been the victim of a botched drive by shooting. A call of shots fired must have come out after all the shooting. What the hell I thought, deciding against it, just one more violation of department directives to add to my list. I pounded on the steering wheel in frustration until I realized how much that hurt my hands.

There were no side windows in my car now. Bullet holes in the body and doors. The windshield was a spider web, but I didn't have another car. Luckily, the condition of the body, before the new holes had been added, was so bad that the new damage was hardly noticeable.

What was noticeable was a person driving a windowless car on a cold windy day. I shivered as I limped back up toward Clark Street. I parked my car behind the Legion Hall and sneaked into the back of the Limelight Pub, making sure that nobody saw me, or the bulge in my coat.

Georgos was making hamburgers and I ordered two. I gave him the papers, silenced him with one of his telepathic 'don't ask' looks, and told him to hide them while I tried to dab some peroxide on my butt in the bathroom mirror.

I was worried that Georgos might be in danger if he knew what the papers were. I also didn't tell him what he should do with them if anything happened to me. Probably because I didn't know what to do with them myself.

Maybe the Eagles had tried to kill me over Tso's swan dive out the window last night? I shivered. There had been several times in the last thirty years, when I had almost bought the farm, but there was no time like the present.

After I came out of the bathroom, and sat down to eat, Georgos gave me a good lecture on the philosophy of life, death, truth and deception. To change the subject, I told him about Claire and her grandmother the Oba-woman. He believed it immediately and was all for it. Citing several examples in Greek mythology, which he hardly believed were myths, Georgos happily pointed out the fact that soothsayers really existed.

When I was released from the alcoholic ward, Georgos came and took care of me everyday. He forcibly kept me from starting to drink again, until I had the strength to do it myself. He was only five years older than me, but he treated me like a son so I just grinned and bore his philosophy and his joy in my impending marriage.

Chapter 16

At 3:30 I headed for the station. It hadn't started to rain, but you could smell it in the air. The wind whipping through the gaping windows of the Chevy, felt cold enough for it to snow. I wondered if the cost of new windows would be more than the car was worth? She'd been a good horse. Now her white paint was peeling around rust spots and she'd taken enough slugs to kill any car. Almost any car.

Parking in the rear of the station, I went directly into the locker room and put on a clean pair of uniform pants. Gratefully, there was no one around to ask me why there was blood on my briefs. I didn't have a change of underwear but luckily, the Moon Cleaners had provided me with several pairs of uniform pants before their abrupt closing. My slacks were shredded on the seat, I threw them in the trash.

My backside was stinging in a dozen places and though I was still a little shaky from the failed drive-by, I didn't feel like sitting down. I started to put my star case and other junk back into my pockets. I had placed my snub nose on the bench that ran down the center of this bay of lockers. I looked down at the little hand gun and then into my locker.

Hanging on an unused back hook was my .44 magnum. A modified Model 28-2, Smith and Wesson, nickel plated, with rubber grips. It only had a regular 4 inch barrel, but I still had to buy a special shoulder holster for it because the size of the rounds made the weapon so wide. I used to carry it when we had solved a burglary pattern and were staked out at the criminal's next job waiting in ambush for them to arrive. I'd only fired it at the range a couple of times but it looked like it could protect me better than the snub nose.

Snapping the silver and black blunderbuss out of the leather braces, I checked the load. Six, dime sized brass buttons, with smooth primers looked up at me. At least the bullets weren't green with mold. It wasn't a fully automatic pistol like the

Eagles had used, but this gun had a different kind of power. If I shot their car with it, there would be one dead Honda. I felt better when it was snugged up warmly under my arm pit, with the jacket nicely covering it.

Then I thought about another thing that I didn't want to do but had to. After looking at myself in the bathroom mirror for five minutes, and not seeing anything because my mind was a popcorn machine, I steadied myself and headed for the Watch Commander's office.

George Stokes was in there with Sergeant Andrews, who never missed an 'AA' meeting and was never without a cigarette in his hand. George was behind his desk and was obviously startled when he looked up at my knock on his open door.

"Captain, can I speak to you for a minute?" What could he say? I hoped only one thing, my butt was burning as it was and I didn't feel like begging.

"Sure, Cassidy. Bob..." he said to Andrews who would have been content to sit there with a long cigarette between his lips. The smoke curled up over his face. I could never understand how he could breathe, or see. Andrews got up and walked past me without a word, an inch long ash clinging tenaciously to the burning butt.

I didn't close the door or even wait until Andrews was out of the room, "I'd like to apologize for any misunderstanding that might have occurred and for not waiting for your signature on charges. I was completely out of line." He was so flabbergasted that he stuttered but couldn't get any words out. I was 100% wrong. Continuing to feud with him was stupid, especially considering everything else that was happening to me.

It was evident that I might need as many friends as I could get. Even though we weren't drinking buddies any longer, George was still a captain and deserved the respect that went with the rank. Stokes hadn't been a bad boss until life and years had caught up with him. His family was scattered, like mine was and he was staring mandatory retirement in the face, as I would soon be. That door had nothing on the other side for some. I feared it too.

"Well, I guess your buddy Calder took care of everything for you." He wasn't being very gracious about this at all. I bit down on the first three things I was going to say.

"That's not fair, George. Everything went alright because we handled it correctly. Has their been any heat from Downtown?" I hoped the answer was 'no'.

"Your friend must have taken care of that too." I know he was happy about that but wouldn't admit it. "...told me to go home and have a stiff drink. What does he think I am, an alcoholic?"

There was not doubt about what I was, apparently. Where was this guy coming from? Was he talking to me or about me, or about himself? "Captain, nobody has said that you're an alcoholic."

"You're an alcoholic. You didn't quit drinking." So there it was. George Stokes sitting alone with a bottle, thinking that everybody considered him a drunk. That could actually help, if you stopped drinking because of it.

"You know that I haven't had a drink in over three years." I was indignant. If he wanted to get personal, I wasn't going to compromise my few remaining principles for anybody.

"Andrews says that you don't go to meetings and you can't stop if you don't go to the damn meetings." He was talking about himself. When you went to an AA meeting, you had to eventually stand up and admit that you were an alcoholic. You had to do that, no matter which course of treatment you chose. I softened my voice and he realized that he had been almost shouting.

"Look, George, I don't go to meetings and I don't drink anymore. It's not the meetings, it's you. I still think about it almost every day, but I had a doctor convince me that I would definitely die if I didn't quit drinking. I also had friends that helped. Andrews is right, it's hard to do without support," I admitted finally.

He just looked at me helplessly. Not speaking. I thought seriously about what I said next, because it couldn't be taken lightly.

"George, knowing that you have a problem is the first step. Talk to people, there's a lot of help out there." Then I added, "I'll help you. Call me anytime, day or night and I'll come."

He didn't say anything, just looked at me with grateful eyes. I thought he was going to start crying so I turned and left the office. There are crying drunks, violent drunks, and happy drunks. I'd been the happy kind, and never cared much for the other two, but I had offered to help and I would if he asked.

The desk was busy with Saturday afternoon shift change. The phones were ringing and people were bustling about. Ernie Perez was making coffee, as usual, and Jane Gallagher answering two phones at once.

Andrews sat at his little desk, smoke clouding around him, other people were milling all around. The usual see, hear, and smell no evil, condition of the desk personal. It was also evident from the normal chaos around the desk area that there had been no big deal about some shots that were fired up on Clark Street earlier. Just an 'Unfounded' incident. Apparently no innocent passers-by had been caught in the crossfire. I was grateful for that.

On the far side of the desk, Brian White, just back from the medical roll, was giving a young girl a ticket. She looked like a student and was probably Thai, a Siamese beauty. She wrung her little brown hands, as White filled in the spaces on her ticket. She didn't look like a DUI, that was Brian's speciality.

White's brother had been killed by a drunk driver years ago. After that, he'd attended the Northwestern Traffic Institute and became a traffic vigilante. If he had a mother, I'm sure he gave her tickets regularly, just to keep his attitude sour. He wrote five to ten movers a night, with several 'Driving Under the Influence' arrests thrown in.

That was fine, except that while he was down in the station giving little girls tickets, making them post bond and name checking them, the rest of the street crews were doing all the police work. The other guys would have to handle disturbances on White's beat, write up burglaries, robberies and shootings while he played traffic cop.. That was one of the reasons that nobody would work with Brian White. He was practically forced to be a field training officer, the rookies had no choice as to who they worked with.

Cohen, standing a few feet from White and the nervous teenager, was just hanging up the desk phone when I approached him. He smiled broadly. "Hi, Hop," he said brightly.

"Hi, Ben," I said, waiting for White to notice me so I could say hello or acknowledge him with a nod at least. He ignored me, engrossed in giving the girl her first ticket.

"Listen, do you have a minute? I'd like to ask you something." He said sure, and when he turned to follow me, White spoke up.

"Hey, Rookie! Get over here and learn something. And stay away from that guy." Cohen hesitated, I gave him a look and then looked over to White.

"I know you're joking, Brian," I said. "But you've always had a poor sense of humor. So you can stop now." Nobody liked this guy, especially me.

"I'm not fooling around, get over here!" He was pressing it.

"You better finish abusing your prisoner first, if you want us we'll be back here." I turned to walk away. "Come on, kid."

Cohen tensed and turned with me. For a second I hoped that White would come over and get physical with us. I'd love to turn this Jewish chain saw loose on him. We headed for the vacant Tact Office without another word being said.

"I've just come from Chung's place. He's sitting in there dressed like the Emperor, doing some ancient ritual, incense burning, the whole bit. Tell me about him. Did he come from Taiwan, or did Ah, the nephew?" I could see that Cohen felt that he was possibly betraying a confidence. I didn't care.

"He never said anything about Taiwan and I don't know the nephew, but I think he came here directly from Korea." That didn't tell me a lot, but it was a start.

"Yea, that's what I thought. What I really want to know about is their past, do you know anything about when he was in Korea? What he did there?" I figured that I was going to need a better source of information than Cohen.

"I don't know very much." He stated flatly.

"And that is?" I prompted.

"You said that you were over at the school? Did you see the trophies and awards?" I hadn't really looked closely at anything except the old man, but I remembered that the walls of the office had been lined with shelves and the walls had been covered with junk.

"I did notice, but I didn't have time to look at any of it closely." I'd been too busy watching my back.

"Master Chung is a very famous martial artist and teacher. For many years he was the greatest fighter in the world." There was that 'master' stuff again. These karate guys were a dime a dozen. In Chicago there was a school on every other corner. How Cohen could state that Chung was the best in the world, must be just student/teacher admiration. I said as much.

"He was the greatest fighter in the world, because he never refused to fight, and he never lost," Cohen staunchly defended his master.

"Sure, kid, you win a few and you lose a few. If the referees on your side, maybe you win more than the other guys, but it's just a sport. A game." I was trying to chase away some of the primal fear that I had for this unlikely little old man.

"There was no help form any referee, nor was there anything sporting about the way they fought in Korea," he said, as if he wished he were there. "When Master Chung fought, years ago in Asia, those matches were all to the death."

"Wait a minute. Are you telling me that wrinkled up old man fought with someone until he killed the person?" I couldn't believe my ears.

"Fifty-eight," he said flatly. I was shocked. And I was never going near Chung again. Master Chung, that is.

"It's not what we would call a sport today, but they considered it one. Two men on a raised platform surrounded by spikes. Either you killed the other guy on the platform, or you threw him onto the spikes. Either way..."

"Some sport, good thing we taught them baseball." I tried to joke about it to cover my revulsion. "How long ago was this? Did they fight like that here in America?" I was ready to believe anything.

"Oh, it was before World War II." He said it like it was hundreds of years ago. "Long before he came here. He hurt his leg in the last fight and had to retire, undefeated." Obviously.

"So he couldn't kill people with his karate any longer, because he hurt his leg the last time he'd done it." I was getting cynical.

"It's not karate." I didn't care what the hell they called it.

"Whatever," I waved it away. "What I want to know, is this guy some kind of deadly weapon or what? Come on, Ben." Could he have killed his niece and nephew, was my unsaid question. "Does he still have the capability to kill people?"

"Well, when he first came here, he was about sixty five or seventy years old I think, he got jumped in Grant Park by two guys. They each outweighed him by 50 pounds and he couldn't run away from them because of his bad leg...so he had to fight them." He looked around the room, expecting ears to start growing on the walls.

"Don't tell me a seventy year old cripple killed two muggers." I had the feeling that I wasn't going to get that wish.

"Well, one of them had a gun and the other a knife..." He didn't want to say it, and I didn't want to hear it.

"Okay, so what happened? They let him off with a self defense plea or got a sharp lawyer to pay off a judge or something. That's what's bothering you, isn't it?" I could tell there was a big secret here. It had to be that, otherwise the old man would still be in jail.

"They didn't believe him. He tried to tell the police what happened, he couldn't speak English at the time...And the condition of the bodies...They couldn't believe that one person could have done...They just saw a crippled old man, so..." He didn't have to say anymore, that old snake was going to be deadly until he drew his last breath.

"So there's an open murder case, from fifteen or twenty years ago on two dead assholes. Is that what you're so worried about?" He nodded solemnly.

"There's no statute of limitations on Homicide, Hop," he whispered lamely. Torn between his heart and some bullshit that they taught him at the police academy.

"Hello. Mister two master's degrees. Nobody gave a shit twenty years ago and if they didn't believe he did it when he was willing to confess to the crime, they sure aren't going to believe him now." We had enough murders, on a daily basis, to keep every cop in the country busy with current events. Who cared about twenty years ago? Just a rookie with a warped sense of justice.

"But what about the new forensic techniques. They're using computer fingerprint scanning to solve old homicides...do you think that they..." He had a grave look of concern on his face. He worried a great deal about his old teacher, but seemed to have adjusted well to David Tso jack-knifing onto the hood of our cruiser.

"You're making a mountain out of a mole hill Ben. There's no way that any of your nightmares are ever going to come true, so just forget about it." I slapped him on the back for emphasis and to snap him out of his worst case scenario depression. Just then Dolecki appeared in the doorway.

"Teachin' the kid how to beat a confession out of a prisoner, Cassidy?" He smiled.

Cohen almost jumped out of his skin at the sight of the Homicide Detective behind him. I covered his alarm. "Believe me, Polack, he doesn't need any teaching, where's Voltz?" I said, trying to piss him off twice in one sentence.

I said, "see ya later," to Cohen. Giving him the high sign and receiving one of gratitude in return. He slid from the room without meeting Dolecki's eye, so smoothly that the Homicide dick didn't notice that we had ended our conversation abruptly.

Chapter 17

"Is that the kid who tossed the gook out of the window last night?" Dolecki said, looking after Cohen. There were always at least two versions of any story, the official one and the scuttlebutt version. I only had control over one. I had tried to answer that question when Pape asked it, and now realized the futility of trying.

Coppers never believed the official story. That was one of the signs of becoming a veteran. Denying that Cohen had flipped that kid out of the window was useless. Nobody was going to believe it. I wasn't sure myself. Cohen and White passed by the doorway on their way to the parking lot.

"Read the report, Polack. You do read, don't you? Or does your partner have to do that for you too?" I thought that starting an argument with him was preferable to discussing something that neither of us had seen, not officially anyway.

"Fuck you, hill-billy." He said in return.

"If that's the best you can do, I'm going to stop calling you names. I guess that all those Polish jokes have a basis in fact." I stung him good with that one and got in the next word while he bit down on his cigar, searching for a retort.

"Good, here comes your better half, now we can get down to business."

Voltz came into the room, Dolecki was still standing just inside the doorway. Voltz slid around him like Cohen had, and sat on the desk that was between us. I sat on a chair behind the desk.

"So what's up, Hop?" Regular detectives wore an assortment of cheap sport jackets, like the one I was wearing. Homicide detectives wore suits, and looked like bankers or politicians. Even Dolecki wore an expensive looking gray wool blend with a light stripe running through it, a camel's hair top coat and Italian shoes. His outfit cost more than my car.

Voltz never had a hair out of place and always had a manicure. His suit had a sheen that looked like silk with a beautiful blue checked pattern to the fabric. When I'd worked in the Detective Division, Homicide's wardrobe was always a topic of discussion for the lower classes, who all dressed like used car salesmen.

"I want to know what you guys have come up with on the Park murders." I said.

"What!" Dolecki shouted, then stuttered. "But...but you said you had something to show us!" He looked pleadingly at Voltz, who was probably fed up with Dolecki's mistakes.

Voltz realized that I was playing with his partner and went along smoothly, not looking back at Dolecki. "We got a quicky from the medical examiner. The woman's neck was broken. Fourth and fifth cervical vertebrae were shattered. Besides a bruise on her cheek there were no other marks on her body. No other broken cranial bones. If someone had used a baseball bat or a pipe on her it would have done more damage. But someone hit her hard, that's for sure. The coroner said that it could have been a fist, but he'd never seen anything like it before. Maybe it was a lucky punch." I was sorry I'd asked. A lucky punch. I wanted to punch myself.

"Come on, Cassidy. You said you had something to show us, didn't you?" There was a pleading note in Dolecki's voice. I just sat there.

Voltz went on smoothly, as if his partner hadn't spoken, still playing along with my little joke. I didn't want to play anymore. "And the male...uh...Sung Park, that was his first name, wasn't it?" He looked in his notebook and smiled at me.

I just stared back, speechless, the perfect straight man. "That was strange, too. He was shot with a huge caliber bullet. Not a .41 or a .45 even, but a fifty caliber, low muzzle velocity. Took off the whole left side of his head. They had never seen a bullet like that before either. There was nothing to match it with in the files."

Finding my voice, I said, "He had a big gun that he kept under the counter. I saw it once or twice, the bullets were really big but I don't know what caliber they were." I rambled, still in shock from the autopsy report.

"You could have told us that over the phone, Cassidy. You think that all we have to do is come all the way up north..." Voltz held up his hand silencing Dolecki. He was as sharp as they came and had realized that I wasn't playing the game any longer.

"What else, Hop?" He coaxed quietly.

"I don't know. I don't even know what kind of gun it was. It had a metal ring on the butt, you know, like an Army gun, where they put a cord through the loop." I was just talking, I wanted to help but didn't know what questions I wanted to ask or what I should tell them.

"Was it blue steel?" He asked.

I nodded, saying, "it had a breech opening." I made a twig breaking gesture with my hands.

"Well, the killer might have shot him with his own gun. It's happened before. Maybe he pulled it out and the killer wrestled it away from him." Voltz said, putting forth a possible scenario.

"That could have happened, I guess." What did I know?

"Hop, did you ever have any knowledge of Park or his wife fencing any stolen jewelry?" This guy was a master of interrogation. He knew how and when to ask a question. I was stunned by it.

"No. I'd never heard of them buying gold or anything." Voltz was looking at me closely, a human lie detector. Did he think I was lying? He'd caught me off guard. Hell, he'd put me off guard, then dropped a bomb on me.

I couldn't blame him though. Having the police in on illegal activities had always been good for business. The foot man was one of the best guys to pay off. Either him or the Captain, stopping trouble at either end of the chain of command.

Apparently satisfied, (although I'm sure Dolecki wasn't), that I was telling the truth, Voltz gave me the scoop. "We got some information from Gang Crimes, and the guys in the Pawn Shop Unit, that Park was willing to buy hot jewelry." He knew that I had liked those people and was sorry to be telling me that they weren't exactly kosher.

"I can't believe it. You saw how they lived. Their little apartment upstairs. They couldn't have been making much from any fencing operation," I said, sticking up for my dead friends.

"He made a lot of his own jewelry, we found the molds and equipment. They have almost fifty grand in securities and they owned that building." Dolecki was glad that these 'gooks' were not the wonderful people that I'd believed them to be. He was glad that it bothered me too.

"That's not a lot of money," I said thinking about the dollar figures on the lists and how much they could have had. "Were there any papers that were collected as evidence?" I asked Voltz.

"There was no money found, I'll tell you that for sure, Cassidy. Not after all the beat men that you let root around in that crime scene!" Dolecki was asking for it.

Voltz waved his partner's stupidity away again, signaling me not to pay attention to Dolecki. "Papers? What kind of papers are you referring to, Hop? There was no gun but there were a lot of papers strewn around. They were all written in Korean, so we didn't bother with them. We sealed up the building, but we hadn't thought to send any technicians back to collect anything else yet."

"I think that's what the break in last night was all about." They were both looking closely at me now.

"Tell me about last night, Hop." Voltz said hypnotically.

"It happened just like the report says," I said, staring Dolecki in the eye. "But at the time I wasn't sure who the one that got away was. Now I'm pretty sure I know who it was."

"Who was it, Cassidy?" Dolecki said, as if I wasn't going to tell them and needed the information beaten out of me. Voltz frowned at him and then looked back at me, gently urging me with his soft brown eyes, to continue.

"I think it was the guy who owns the Moon Cleaners up on Touhy Avenue. His name is Inon Moon, 5'7", 150, dark hair." Voltz just looked at me waiting for more information, that he knew from experience, was forthcoming.

I took a deep breath. "This might sound strange, but I've checked around and this guy might be from 'North' Korea." Dolecki let go with a disbelieving grunt and snorted disgust.

"That's it? Spies from the Red Hoard? You could have told me this bullshit over the phone and I'd be eating my dinner right now instead of standing here up to my ankles in it." Dolecki held up one of his alligator shoes to show me the imaginary 'caca de toro'.

Voltz just kept watching me closely, waiting patiently for the real reason that I had called this meeting. I took out the piece of paper that Ah had transcribed for me and handed it to Voltz. He smiled satisfactorily.

"That's what I think they were after, names and addresses of Koreans. See, if you can find out who they are, will ya, Voltz?" I said, trying to end the interview without Voltz getting any more information out of me. Like where the rest of the papers were.

"Where'd you get this, Hop?" Voltz asked quietly, ready to let me keep the secret for a while longer if I wanted to, but unable to keep himself from asking. He hadn't asked who I checked with for the information about Moon, which relieved me a for the moment.

"Off the dead guy," I said. It was partly the truth and Voltz didn't comment. Dolecki was a little stunned by my revelation, but recovered quickly.

"Yeah, the gang leader, Tso. We knew they were in on it when we found one of their bandannas at the scene." I thought about it for a moment, Voltz just watched me, waiting patiently. The classic pair, 'dumb cop—smart cop'. Neither one was acting.

"If I remember correctly the color of the bandanna in the shop was black and blue?" I had to say something, I was supposed to know what colors the gangs used, the gangs on me beat at least. If I hadn't said anything, and if Voltz already knew, then he would have caught me lying. Omission was considered a lie in homicide.

"So?" Dolecki agreed. Not seeing where I was going.

"The gang banger that died last night was a Gray Eagle." I wondered where the rest of the Eagles were, especially Key. "Their colors are black and white. Gray, get it, Dolecki? The New City Royals have black and blue as their colors."

"Hell, they're all the same. Punks." Dolecki said, dismissing anything that I had to say. Voltz waited for me to finish, his Monte Blanc pen poised over the paper he was taking notes on. He wasn't letting me go yet.

"The leader of the Royals in the neighborhood is a guy named 'Gilly Rodriquez." Voltz looked up at me while writing. "Guillermo is the first name." I spelled it for him and gave him some details on Gilly. "I've been looking for him for a few days now, he might know something." That seemed to satisfy him. He closed the leather cover on his notebook and was prepared to leave when I had another thought. He perceived it and paused, waiting for whatever it was I had to say. If you were a criminal, you didn't want this guy after you, he was supernatural at his job.

"You know, I went to the funeral this morning." I thought about the information they had gotten from the Medical Examiner. An autopsy had been performed, the bodies had to have been prepared for burial, the crime hadn't been solved, and yet...

"How did they get the bodies released so quickly for burial? I don't think it was because of a religious reasons, they were Christian." Voltz shrugged and then thought for a moment.

It was his turn to be unsure. He looked at me with a thoughtful gaze. "That's a good question, Hop. Somebody made a phone call, I guess." He was going to do more than guess, he was going to find out. I thought about all the people packing the church, wondering how many 'phone calls' were in the bunch.

We were out in the hall, Dolecki was already heading for the rear exit, and dinner, but Voltz held back for a moment. "Did you find him?"

"Who?" I said, thinking of a few 'hims' that I'd like to find.

"Moon, at the church." I shouldn't have been so surprised that he was so smart. I answered as quickly as I could recover so he wouldn't tag me with another 'omission'.

"No, but his pinched face wife was there. She got away before I could talk to her and the cleaners was closed today for the first time I can remember. Employees showed up, expecting to work." He nodded, that giving him something more to think about. I said I'd keep in touch and he agreed to do the same.

Chapter 18

Voltz followed his partner, who was already going through the double doors. I went into the bathroom and tried to see if any of the burning cuts on my butt were bleeding as much as I envisioned.

When I had dabbed at a few, my briefs weren't in very good shape, I thought about going home and changing them, then I thought about the note in my pocket. I continued to amaze myself at how stupid I could be. I had been around all day and didn't think to show it to any of the daytime desk people.

There were only two words on the paper, my name and hers. The rest of it was all numbers, but it was still handwriting. The person who wrote it would recognize it, even if nobody else did. What the hell, I thought, I had time to kill. I went up to the front.

George was in his office with the door closed and the blinds drawn, which was fine with me. I didn't feel like a crying jag right now. Behind the desk, Pape had Jane Gallagher cornered and was making her look at pictures of his kids.

Standing at the front of the desk, were White and Cohen. They already had another traffic pinch. I could tell, from the yellow form that White had in his hand, that it was a drunk driving arrest. The guy that stood between them, had obviously gotten an early start on the evening. They'd be down for two hours at least, with the breath analysis and all the paperwork. Meanwhile, the rest of the street crews would be handling the jobs on their beat.

"This is Karen's new costume. She's gonna wear it at the National Skating Competition in St. Paul, next month." Pape was narrating each photo. Jane tried to flip through them quickly, but Pape slowed her down with each explanation.

Pape and his wife couldn't have children of their own. After they'd been married for a number of years, they tried to adopt a child, but they'd waited too long. There were no babies for an older couple. If they wanted to adopt an American child it would have to be an older one. There was a whole story that went with the pictures, I'd heard it more than once.

Pape's wife wanted a baby, an infant. So they went overseas and adopted. Now they had three children and everyone was happy. Two girls, Chinese and Korean and a little Romanian boy. The kids were their life, ballet, figure skating and the boy played the violin.

The Papes spent all their time, and all their money on the children. Pape worked all the overtime he could get. Once he showed me a picture of a little tutu outfit, that he bought for one of the girls, that cost him $1,200. I stopped complaining when my boys wrote for money after that. I decided to save Gallagher.

"Jane. Oh, sorry to interrupt you, Mike, but I need to ask Jane about this before I forget again, it could be very important." Pape looked around for anyone who had not seen the pictures of his kids a hundred times. Finding no takers, he put the photos back into his jacket.

He didn't offer them to me or make me agree to look at them later, thank God. They looked like they might be new ones, ones that I hadn't seen already. I took Janie by the arm and taking the note from my pocket, acted like it was vitally important that she and I discuss it and not look at pictures. I'd heard that Pape also had hundreds of hours of video tape on the kids to look at if he could get you over to the house.

"Can you tell whose handwriting this is?" I asked her. She thought that it was a dumb question but went along with the implied vital importance of anything that would take her away from Pape. She'd seen enough tutus to last her awhile.

"Well, Hop, I don't know. But it looks familiar. I don't think it's Ernie's, or the Sarge's." Ernie was coming out of the bathroom with a coffee pot in his hand, as usual, and Jane moved across the desk area to intercept Ernie at the other side of the room. A tactical strategy designed to put distance between her and Pape. I moved with her.

Ernie Perez was 120 pounds soaking wet. Probably had to do with all the coffee he drank. He looked closely at the note and decided that he didn't know who'd written it. Sergeant Andrews looked at it through a thin line of smoke and said he knew who wrote it, but couldn't think of who it was at the moment.

"Let me see that." Brian White said from the other side of the counter. The drunk swayed while Cohen tried to ask him a question, in Spanish. Gallagher handed White the note.

He looked at it for only a second and handed it back to her. "I wrote it. I took that call the other day when I stopped by the station after court. The phones were ringing off the hook and everybody else was busy. So I took the message." Sergeant Andrews commented that he knew it had been White's handwriting. Nobody paid him any attention.

White's comment sure got my attention though. My heart soared and sunk in half a second. Was he serious? He'd said it so casually. It dawned on me that the note only had significance for me, at the moment.

"Brian, the woman who called, Sui. That was the woman who was killed in the jewelry store on Thursday. About an hour after you took this call." Cohen stopped talking to the drunk. Everybody stopped talking.

White just looked at me, the fringe of his curly red hair circled his bald pate like a tonsure. He was as Irish as Paddy's pig and looked it. Strong square jaw, wide chest, and smart as a rock.

"Did she say why she wanted me to call her? Or did she sound excited or anything?" I didn't know if he could even remember back that far.

He just looked off into the distance, like he was trying to think back for a second. After he stared into space for a moment, he looked at me and said, "no, she didn't say nuttin. Just left the number." I wanted to stick the note down his throat.

"You sure are a big help, White. How'd you ever become an F.T.O. anyway. You can't even 'F'!" Sapper sprayed saliva into the air, bursting out laughing at his own joke, which nobody else got. He was the only one laughing, as usual.

"Sit on this, fat ass!" White said with a considerable amount of vehemence, following it up with a nice descriptive gesture. Sapper stopped laughing abruptly, he was apparently getting fed up with people calling him 'fat ass'.

"Yea, you'd like my fat ass, too. You always were a butt man weren't you, White?" He said seriously, leading up to something. White just stood there staring at him with deadly intent. Sapper turned to Pape, an unwilling straight man.

"You know, Mike, when I used to work with White, all he wanted to talk about was butts. Regular guys would see a nice looking girl and say, 'Wow, did you see the tits on that one?", but not Brian. He'd say 'Look at the ass on her'." Jane Gallagher found a reason to leave the desk.

"At least I'm not a big fat slob who couldn't get laid if he paid for it," White said, not countering well. Although I couldn't see anyone having sex with Bruce Sapper for love or money.

Sapper was going for the jugular. "But since we got 'AIDS' now, you never hear him talking about his favorite thing anymore. You know, Mike, I bet he's got it. 8 to 5 White's got the H.I.V. You better watch it if that guy starts to bleed around you, kid." He said to the flabbergasted Cohen. White didn't say anything or even move, but from the look on his face I thought he was going to pull his gun and shoot Sapper.

So did Pape, who took the huge wagon man by the arm and pulled him down the hall. "Come on Bruce. That's enough goofing around." The drunk picked that moment to start protesting his arrest in drooling Spanish-accented English. I got the hell out of there before it got around to my turn. I had enough to worry about.

Chapter 19

In thirty plus years, I'd never been shot at, much less having several automatic weapons emptied at me, at close range. There was a freezing rain when I left the station. Once in the parking lot I shivered involuntarily when I looked at my holey, windowless, car. It had taken awhile to hit me. Life sort of came into a different kind of focus then. I just stood there freezing, unable to get into the car.

Suddenly the janitor, Jose, was standing next to me asking me if anything was wrong. I recovered somewhat and pointed out the obvious. No windows. The brawny little man ran into the station and in less than a minute returned with clear plastic bags. Cutting them up, he deftly taped them to the window openings and covered the wet seat in my old chevy.

I thanked him and shook his hand with one that was already shaking. Freezing cold, with the heater barely making a dent in my uncontrollable shivering, I headed for home and a hot shower, with my windows flapping loudly in the wind.

There were still a couple of hours to kill before my date, so after a hot shower, I cleaned house. I hoped that Claire would agree to be invited back to my apartment after dinner. It's surprising how vacuuming and scrubbing the toilet clears your mind and gives you a different perspective on things. At first I had been angry, then when the realization that I had almost been assassinated hit me, I had been afraid. Now I was a little of both, I figured that would be best. I was also going to have to get used to the fact that things were taking a turn in my life. Whether left, right, or God forbid, a 'U' turn, I wasn't sure.

After tending all my wounds, which were minor but numerous, I changed into clean clothes. The pile of dirty clothes was growing, but I didn't want to think about laundry. Not sure if I was thinking correctly about anything, I put the .44 magnum back under my arm pit before I left.

It had stopped raining and was just cold now, but the duct tape wasn't sticking very well. I tried to fix it but it was hopeless. So, flapping in the breeze, I headed for Clark Street, hoping that Claire would have her car, or agree to go on a public transportation date.

"Do you mind if we use your car? Mine is..." My arrival had been greeted by a big smile from Mama Lea and a hand squeeze from Claire.

"No problem." Claire agreed too quickly, offering her little foreign car. She'd ridden in my car before. I almost felt hurt, but then I realized that I had been saved from explaining the new damage that I was sporting.

"Are you ready?" I asked her. It was a little before nine and there were still customers at many of the tables.

"Do I look ready?" She did a small pirouette and I noticed how nice she looked. Mama Lea looked at her approvingly, then she looked at me, speaking volumes.

"That's a trick question," I said smiling broadly.

Claire had gone home and changed since this afternoon. Now, instead of her blue jeans and blouse, she wore an gathered printed skirt with a white scoop neck sweater that did nothing to hide her statuesque body.

Her short hair was auburn and fell in soft curls, like a Leonardo Angel. Her features were oriental, and her skin, her soft tawny skin just seemed to radiate...When I realized that I was floating away, I cleared my throat and stammered like a prom date.

"You look beautiful." Three words were all I could get out. From the light in her eyes, it seemed to be enough. Mama Lea shooed us out the door.

Once I had squeezed myself behind the wheel of her economy car, I started it, and let it warm up for a minute. I couldn't tell if it was one of those foreign car shoe boxes that was made in America, or a model of an American car that was made overseas. It didn't matter really, I was just grumbling because I had to sit in a fetal position. After an eternity, some heat started to come from the little vents. "I asked you to dinner, but didn't think about where we might go. Do you have any ideas, honey?"

She said she had a taste for fish and I suggested sushi. Claire eagerly agreed, telling me about an island dish, called Escovich Fish, in which the acids of a marinade of lime juice and onions cooks slices of raw fish. My stomach growled. Well, I'd learned to like sushi, but I was glad that I'd taken a stomach pill before leaving the house.

When we walked into 'Taboki', Mas, the owner and sushi chef, gave us the traditional Japanese greeting. Which I could tell, from the smile on his face, that he really meant.

"Konbanwa, Mas-San." I said good evening the way he had taught me. He answered me in Japanese, and I said domo-arigato. Claire gave me a sideways glance.

"See how easily I cross cultural lines?" I said slyly.

"I'm beginning to." She grinned up at me, squeezing my arm excitedly. I was glad she didn't want to hear any more Japanese from me, because I had used up my vocabulary.

The restaurant was small and uncrowded, and Mas frowned momentarily when I indicated that I wanted to sit at a table instead of my usual spot at the sushi bar. Then, realizing that I had a 'special date', he spoke a word to the waitress and she showed us to the table I wanted.

Claire was seated across from me, her back to a wall. I sat where I could see her, the door, and the street, through the plate glass windows, without turning my head. The huge six shooter under my arm felt ridiculous and I knew I was being over paranoid about watching everything. I tried to relax.

"Do you want some saki or plum wine, Claire?" I asked when the waitress brought us hot towels and waited for our order.

She hesitated a moment, probably thinking about not wanting to drink alcohol in front of me, tempting me. I told the girl to bring me some green tea and a glass of plum wine for Claire. She shrugged. If I could take it so could she. I was never going to be able to drink alcohol again, there was no reason for others to suffer the same fate.

"I always do better with women if they're a little crocked." I said trying to smooth over any awkwardness with a little comedy. She relaxed, slapping my hand and smiling.

The only thing bad about Mas's restaurant is that he never lets me order any food. As soon as I sit down, food starts appearing in front of me. Whenever I ask what this or that is, he growls at me and says, 'just eat it'. That's how I learned to like sushi.

I knew the girls brought the little wooden plates and ornate bowls and took them away, but I never seemed to notice them doing it. My only request is that he not make anything too spicy, but I knew that Claire liked hot food, so I told Mas to do his worst, hoping my stomach pill could fight off the hot horseradish. He hadn't poisoned me yet.

"So tell me why they call you Hop?" Claire asked as she worked on a crab and cucumber salad with her chopsticks.

I never liked to talk about the real reason. It was like trying to tell someone why you'd gotten a tattoo forty years ago, but Claire was different and she thought she was just making dinner conversation, instead of asking a deeply personal question. I took a deep breath and started.

"Well, when I was a kid, my favorite television character was Hop-along Cassidy. Other kids wanted to be Superman or Robin Hood. But I was a cowboy and I convinced myself that I was the grand son of Hop-along Cassidy. You know, same last name and all. I never had a father and did a little more role playing than was probably normal for a kid."

"At the time you could be the happiest kid in the world, but if you didn't have a father, society considered you illegitimate. It was even on my school records." I thought about those first hard years at school. "I wanted everybody to call me Hop. I even made my mother call me Hop."

I remembered being adamant about not answering to the name Basil. "When I started school and found out that Basil was considered a 'sissy' name, Hop became my name. When I figured out how the pecking order worked, anybody that called me Basil got punched in the nose. If I couldn't beat the person up, I stayed away from them until I could. But nobody called me Basil, not if I could help it."

It all sounded so stupid now as the confession poured out. "Then when I grew up the name stuck. My hair turned white when I was fairly young..." I looked out the window at nothing for a second, thinking about years gone by.

"What does white hair have to do with it?" She brought me back to the conversation.

"Well, now I look just like the guy." I explained poorly.

"What guy?"

"Bill Boyd." I said not telling her anything.

"Who is Bill Boyce?" She asked again, hearing me wrong.

"I'm sorry, he's the actor who played Hop-along Cassidy on TV, like George Reeves played Superman." She looked more confused, and I could understand why. I wasn't telling this very well. *Christopher*

"Back up to the dock, Cassidy," she said seriously. "I never had a television until I came to the states when I was twenty, and I wasn't even alive when you were a child. Tell me about this Hop- along superman character."

"You never had a television? And I thought that I grew up poor." I said.

"We weren't poor. My grandmother owns half of the mountain and has given houses to all her children for wedding presents. Being an Oba-woman pays well. We never had a television because we didn't need one." She explained proudly.

"Besides, there were no television shows transmitted to the islands in those days." She smiled. In America having a television had become a symbol of making it to the middle class. "So there wouldn't have been anything 'on', even if we did have a TV set."

We laughed together at the American cliche, digging into some of the colorful and delicious things that had appeared on our table.

After eating a bite or two and thinking about the man with the black hat and white horse, Topper, I tried to explain my childhood philosophy again. "Hop-along Cassidy was the ideal American pioneer, cowboy and lawman. He would always fight for the underdog. In the end, he would shoot the guns out of the bad guys' hands, there were always five or six of them, and they'd ultimately surrender. Then, he would accept gratitude only from the people he had saved, and ride off into the sunset." I could picture it clearly.

"What did he do with all those bad guys?" She said feigning intrigue.

I smiled, remembering. "They would all get on their horses and the bad guys would hold the reins with one hand and hold the other hand up in the air as they rode away. Totally resigned to their fate." I said, flourishing my chopsticks.

It was cold and people hurried up and down the street outside the window. Two men passed the restaurant, looked in, and then after going on by, came back and entered the sushi bar.

Mas gave them a half hearted greeting, he was cleaning up for the night already, but couldn't turn down the business. We were the only people in the place now. The two guys sat at the table behind me and I thought about just how much I'd exposed my back in my eagerness to sit where I could look out the window.

They must have been bar hopping, I could tell that they'd had a few drinks. They ordered whiskey and had to settle for beer, Mas didn't have a hard liquor license. When they looked at the menus they both expressed disgust at some of the items, asking the waitress some questions that were decidedly rude.

They were both Afro-Americans. Well dressed, from what I'd been able to see when they walked in. Probably enjoying decent jobs and the ability to move about in a class of society that was not the highest, but not the lowest anymore either.

I was trying to see with eyes in the back of my head so hard that the ones in front of my head didn't register what I was looking at. Two people hurried past the restaurant, down Clark Street. It was Gilly Rodriquez and his girlfriend Marie.

She was blond and a head taller that him. He had his coat pulled up around his wiry body, trying to hide his face, but he couldn't hide that blond. They didn't see me, and I'd almost missed them trying to pay attention to the two goofs behind me.

"Honey, will you be alright for a second?" I didn't wait for her to answer. "I just saw the guy I've been looking for." I put my napkin on the table, got up and rushed through the door.

The wind was freezing when I stepped out onto Clark Street. The thin material of my coat didn't stop it from blowing through. I turned south, the way they had gone, and saw Gilly and Marie at the corner, hurrying at the same pace as when they had passed the restaurant. The wind was at my back when I started to run after them.

Chapter 20

What makes a rabbit sense danger from behind? The shoes I was wearing were soft soled, but Gilly turned and looked around when he got to the corner, spotting me trying to sneak up silently behind him. He was gone in a shot. I breezed past Marie before she even knew anything was going on.

I ran awkwardly, holding my arm down to keep the heavy gun in the shoulder holster from bludgeoning me to death. After Gilly's quick initial burst of speed we settled down to a foot race. The pavement was wet and we pounded down Clark with the street lights glaring off of every surface. By the time we got to the next block, he had used up a lot of his energy and looked back to see me gaining on him.

His face had several kinds of fear on it, I had a sardonic smile on mine. He tried to slow me down by running into the street. Even though it was late, Clark Street was always busy until the wee hours of the morning. He dodged several cars, so did I. I was glad I had been working out steadily, now it was paying off. My heart was pounding and my mouth gaped open, but I was closing the distance between us as we ran down the double yellow line that divided the street.

We were at the next block now, Morse, where the Eagles had shot at me, and the stoplight was just changing to green. Good, I wouldn't have to worry about cross traffic. There was a C.T.A. bus pulling away from the bus stop, merging into the flow of traffic, a thick cloud of black diesel smoke pouring out the back as it accelerated.

Gilly jumped for the back of the bus and managed to find hand holds where there was only smooth metal. His feet found purchase on the edge of the thin bumper. He'd hitched a ride. I tried to make a last effort. I lunged like a defensive back trying to make a touch down saving tackle.

My fingers brushed his clothing and I fell head long onto the street, fortunate that the oncoming car stopped in the middle of the intersection and didn't run over me as I lay sprawled on my face. When I realized that the car had stopped a few feet from going over me, I looked at the departing bus.

There was an ad for something that covered the whole back end of the bus, window and all. It was a man and a woman, relaxing with a cold beer. Gilly was hanging on to the woman. I know he would have waved at me if he wasn't holding on so tightly. I knew because of the smile he had on his face now. He said something that I was glad I couldn't hear.

Horns were honking at me when I picked myself up and waved a 'thank you' at the driver who hadn't run me over. He looked back at me strangely, I was getting used to that. I started for the curb only to run back into the street again. Waving my arms wildly, I flagged down a car that was a few down in the line, it was Cohen and White in 2423.

White was driving, but I was on the passenger side when they stopped and spoke to Cohen, gasping for air between words. "I was chasing Gilly Rodriquez." I stammered.

"He jumped on that bus." The bus was several blocks away now, but the bright tail lights marked it clearly.

"Catch him for me and I'm buying dinner. I'll be down at Taboki eating, if you catch him." I was still gasping but the offer of free lunch had the desired effect on Brian White, he popped the lights on and went up the oncoming lane after the bus.

My hands were dirty and scratched, but my cloths were to, so I wiped them on my pants. I headed back to the restaurant, sweat freezing on my skin as the cold wind blew in my face.

I took me a few minutes to walk back, I might have been walking slowly but it still seemed far. When I walked into the restaurant, the two black guys were sitting at my table with Claire. I didn't like the look on her face.

I hesitated to call these men, 'black'. After Claire told me how many Caucasian ancestors she had, most of them un-consensual, I understood the term African American decent. Other blacks around the world were more or less black

167

depending upon how history had treated them. Claire had even had a great-grandfather who was an escaped Panama Canal digger. He had been Chinese. I wanted to think of these men in a politically correct manner, but I wasn't in a democratic mood at the moment.

"Excuse me, gentlemen, but I'm having a private dinner with this young lady." I said, finding polite words somewhere in my vocabulary.

"You were, you mean. You ran out on her. Now she's having dinner with us." The smarter one said. He was wearing a brown suede jacket, had a nice mustache and short hair, with a line cut around the bottom in the current fashion.

I was standing with my back to the window now. Claire looked up at me from my right, I was standing in front of the only empty chair at the table. The smart one was across from me, the dumb one on my left. He had longer hair that was done in greasy looking curls. I don't know why they struck me as one looking smart and the other dumb, but those were the kinds of weird things that go through your mind when you're about to snap.

"Claire," I said, watching the two men closely. The dumb one with the leather coat had his left hand in the pocket of the coat. "Do you want to have dinner with these two gentlemen?"

"No Basil, I do not. In fact I asked them to leave me alone and they've continued to bother me." I could hear the frustration in her voice that she hadn't been able to take care of this herself. She also sounded a little scared.

I looked up at Mas who had been watching closely, he had a huge cleaver in one hand and the phone in the other. I didn't want him to come around the counter with that hatchet, it would only complicate things. I wasn't sure what I wanted to do.

"Basil. Ha, ha, ha." The dumb one on my left said, laughing. He was just about to say something else, but I had already taken my cue. It was snapping time. I popped the 44 out of the leather braces, simultaneously grabbing hold of a hand full of greasy curls with my left hand. The barrel of the magnum looked like a sewer pipe when you stared down the business end of it.

I cocked the hammer back, rotating the cylinder as I stuck the end of the barrel in the dumb ones right eye. I turned his head with the hand full of hair so that the gun was pointing at the other one. With the dummy's head in between.

"Don't move," I said to everyone, looking across at the smart one. "This cannon is cocked and pointed right at your head. If you piss me off just one more little bit, I'm gonna blow your head off." I twisted the barrel in the dummy's eye and he groaned. "With his head!"

They had both been drunk, but they were sobering up quickly. He stayed, so did the one with the gun in his eye. "Mas, call 911 and get me a car over here." I said without looking up.

The one I was holding, moved his hand slightly, the one he had in his pocket. I twisted the silver magnum, his head and body going with the motion, pressing his left arm against the table. "You must be the dumb one." I said to him.

"I told you not to move. I've been watching that hand since you came in here. Now do you doubt that you are going to be headless if you move again?" He whimpered.

The smart one sat frozen with his hands flat on the table. I was glad he didn't move. Because I had obviously snapped a while ago and, if I was right about what this guy had in his pocket, was ready to shoot a man for the first time in my life. Two men.

"Hey, man...We're police, just like you." He had interpreted my statement to Mas correctly. That didn't mean anything to me at the moment though, it was too late to stop now.

"You moving your lips, man?" I screamed like a maniac. "That's fucking moving! I told you not to move!" The natural thing to do when someone tells you that they are fellow police, is to let them reach into their pocket for their I.D. I wasn't going to allow that, not with the day I was having.

169

I leaned over the whimpering man in front of me. I released his hair. He didn't move, but looked up at me with his other eye bulging wildly. I smiled at him and he whimpered louder.

With my left hand, I reached over him giving him a little hug, and felt along his left arm feeling for any flex of his muscles. Sliding my hand into his pocket, on top of his, I felt the pistol he was holding tightly. When I took hold of the little gun, he released it easily and I slowly stood up with the little 'Saturday night special' in my hand. It had been pointed right at Claire all the time.

Policemen, 'just like me', didn't carry ten dollar guns. I wasn't relinquishing control of this situation until I saw some uniforms. I didn't care if these guys said they were Saints Peter and Paul. Also the other one might have a real gun. I tried to calm myself while we waited for help.

It seemed like a long time, but within a minute or two Cohen and White walked casually into the restaurant. When they looked at the scene they both registered alarm. I relaxed and took the gun out of the dumb ones eye, and uncocked it, nobody had noticed that my finger hadn't been near the trigger.

The dumb one just sighed and laid his head down on the table. I kept the 44 pointed in the general direction of the smart one, who released the breath he had been holding. He seemed to think that I might have considered breathing movement. I think that everybody was glad to see the police arrive, I know I was. I relaxed a little more.

"Did you get a call to come over here?" I asked Cohen and White.

"No. Gilly wasn't on the bus and..." Cohen was saying, when the call started to come out. I'd told them that Gilly was on the bus, I didn't tell them that he was hanging on the side, not riding as a passenger. My fault.

"Units in 24, units on the City-wide..." The dispatcher was calling out the armed forces.

"Disregard that ten-one. This is 2423, if that's a call up at 7100 on Clark, squad, give a disregard. We're here and the situation is under control." Brian White said into his radio, they both had radios, hot shots.

"Ten-four, 2423. All units disregard the ten-one. What do you have over there, '23?" the operator said coolly. I hoped that would keep a bunch of curiosity seeking coppers from stopping by.

I waved a negative at him. "Just a disturbance, squad. We'll call you on the land line." White said to the dispatcher, then he saw the little silver automatic in my hand.

"What's that, Cassidy?" White said looking first at my left hand then at my right. "Your gun have a baby?"

"It's a cigarette lighter, our friend was going to give me a light with it. He says that they are police officers. Just like us." I handed White the little gun and he pointed it in a neutral direction, deftly checked and unloaded it.

Cohen did a good job of searching the other one before letting him get up and searching him again. They were security guards. I didn't want to arrest them, they might lose their jobs, but White insisted, and I couldn't argue with him. He was right. Security guard or not, he was carrying an un-registerable gun, what we call a 'drop gun'. I couldn't give these guys a break, not in front of a field training officer and his recruit.

"Hey, man, you don't have to do all of this? We didn't mean no harm." The dumb one's hands were cuffed behind his back, but he had heard me downplay the charges so he was getting brave.

White slapped him across the face with a leather gloved hand. It wasn't a padded glove to keep his hands warm, it was kid leather, designed to protect the knuckles and leave no marks. The crack almost knocked the dumb one to the floor and he wasn't a little guy.

"Shut the fuck up, asshole!" White shouted in his face. This was a field training officer? I had almost killed this man, but that didn't give anyone the right to beat him when he was cuffed. I could feel everyone in the room wince with the blow.

"You want to be on the paper, Hop," he asked me as though nothing had happened.

"Not if you're going to be lacing him up." I looked at him hardly, passing a private message between us. Then I turned to Cohen. "Sign my name to the complaints and put it on the same court date as the arrest we had yesterday, Ben."

I looked at the man who had just been abused again. Even though I hadn't done anything wrong, rule wise, I still felt that I had overreacted. "The answer to your question is, yes, I did what I had to do. You two have had a little to much to drink, but that doesn't give you the right to force yourself on anyone and then excuse it by saying you meant no harm." I looked over at Claire, who hadn't escaped the notice of the two other policemen in the room.

"I'll do what I can for you in court. Bring a letter from your boss that says you're both excellent workers and I'll talk to the State's Attorney." I could tell that Brian White would like to handle this differently. I didn't care, I'd warned him to stay out of my business.

Sapper and Pape showed up with their wagon. Even a 'disregard' on the job couldn't stop a few lookie-loo's from showing up. Once they were gone, I got a towel from the frightened waitress and tried to finish my dinner. It was a good thing that sushi is served cold.

"Did you catch the one who you chased after?" She was looking at my torn and muddy clothes. I just shook my head wearily.

"Is this the way Hop-along Cassidy would have handled the situation, Basil?" she asked teasing me into relaxation. Mas was smiling too, White had made the two pay for their uneaten dinner before being carted off to jail. Mas sent us fresh cold food.

"No, I don't think he would have. I'm sorry about all this Claire, I guess that I didn't act very professionally." I didn't tell her that much of the motivation was fear for her.

"Maybe not, but you acted gallantly." I hadn't thought of it that way.

"Would you really have shot that man, Basil, did you ever shoot anyone?" I couldn't tell how she felt about the question, but my answer had to be real anyway. I had to face the answer and live with her reaction to what I was.

"If I told you that I knew he had a gun in his pocket, you might believe me, but there would be a part of you that wasn't sure. I thought he had a gun and I had to act like he had one. I had to trust what I thought. I had to be prepared to shoot him. I was prepared to shoot them both. And if he didn't have a gun in his pocket, then I would have..." What? Gone to jail these days.

"That said, no, I've never shot anyone and I'm glad that I can still say that," I answered truthfully to her brightening smile.

"I'm glad too. Taking a life, even justifiably, must be hard on the soul." She had wisdom at a young age. "But I was so frightened. Weren't you afraid, Basil?"

"No," I lied obviously, "I have an Oba-woman who saw me happily married, so I have nothing to be afraid of until then." She slapped my hand laughing.

"I believe in my grandmother's dreams, Basil, but I wouldn't consider it a guarantee against danger. Don't try dodging any bullets, okay?" I forced a smile, not wanting to think about the ones that I'd dodged already, and started eating the food that had appeared in front of me.

173

Chapter 21

I must have looked really pitiful. Luckily for me, because Claire agreed to take me home and give me a hot bath. She nursed my apparently ill tended wounds and gave me a wonderful massage that almost put me to sleep.

"What's this, Basil?" She had her finger in a little puckered scar in the back of my thigh.

"Ask me tomorrow," I said, pulling her down onto the bed with me. I had had about all the pampering I could stand. We made love in colors, all of them. We were comfortable with each other now and my mind was able to go places that I didn't know existed, or didn't remember existed.

In the morning Claire made breakfast, there was enough hot sauce, peppers and onions in the eggs to burn holes in steel plate. I popped a stomach pill, I carried them around with me now, in a little aspirin tin, but it did little good. I could feel the cultural difference burning in my stomach.

We lounged around all day Sunday, talked about our kids and just sort of got more acquainted with each other's lives. It was real nice. I hadn't had a friend for a long time, especially one that I could have sex with.

"When is the graduation?" she asked.

"It's in May. The fifteenth, I think." I had better get the date right, because I couldn't miss this one. I'd missed too many of the boy's accomplishments when they were growing up. Besides I'd paid for this one.

"What airline are you taking?" I had thought about driving, but that was out of the question now. The beater probably wouldn't have made it anyway.

"I hadn't thought about it really." Her expression told me that something was wrong.

"You say that it is in May like that's months from now, Basil, instead of just a few weeks. I can tell that you don't travel much. Or were you thinking about driving?" She didn't know the half of it.

"No. I wasn't going to drive." I said, feigning indignance. I got up and headed to the kitchen to refill my glass, the never ending breakfast needed more water on the fire.

"You might not be able to get a flight at this late date. You should call your travel agent..." My laugh stopped her comment.

"If I ever had a travel agent he would surely have died of starvation from lack of business by this time."

"I'll call Dorman. I'm sure he can do something." Who was Dorman? I turned to go into the kitchen and finish getting my water. "Hey, Hop-along, you were going to tell me how you got that hole in your leg. Did the bad guys get you when you missed shooting the guns out of their hands?" She twanged a cowboy accent. She really thought she was being comical, I felt like taking her over to Georgos' and letting him give her some philosophy on comedy.

"You really don't want to know." I tried to blow it off, but her expression turned serious.

"Is it, 'I don't want to know', or you don't want to tell me?" She was psychic. I didn't want to talk about it. Bringing up bad memories right now didn't appeal to me. Thinking about my ex-partner and ex-wife didn't appeal to me at any time.

"My partner shot me when I came home early to catch him having sex with my wife. He saw me coming and was hiding in the bushes outside my house when I snuck up to the front door." I didn't wait to see how long it would take her to find her voice and lose the stunned expression on her face. Smiling, I went to the sink.

She finally said something that I couldn't hear. I was running the water so it would get cold. When I had put some of the fire out, I filled the glass again and went back into the living room. She was still sitting on the ornate couch with the bright batik cover.

"You were right, I'm sorry I asked. But now I have to hear the rest of the story." She said, accepting the dripping glass that

I had brought for her. She took a long drink, apparently not immune to her own cooking.

"I told you what happened." I said, giving her a hard time.

"Well, tell me again. Only stretch it out more so I can enjoy the full impact of the story." She was smiling, I gave in.

"When I was a Burglary Detective I used to drink, everyday. A lot. My kids grew up not seeing me. I was either working or drinking or both." I sat down on the couch next to her. The pillows engulfed me with their colorful softness.

"I also wasn't a very good husband. The only person that I spent time with was my partner. We both drank, but he didn't drink like I did. I never paid any attention to where he went when he wasn't with me. He was my partner and I trusted him in every way. We knew everything about each other, things that could have cost us our jobs. Our families went to Union picnics together, we shared our personal lives." I took a drink from the tall glass to give myself a breather.

I tried not to let my emotions get into my explanation, I was supposed to have gotten over these feelings when I had faced my problems. Sure. "And then I found out that when my partner had not been with me, sometimes taking off early and leaving me to finish reports, he had been with my wife. I would have never known if my bartender hadn't told me. Apparently I was the only one who didn't know what was going on. So I got good and drunk and went home to catch him in bed with my wife. I must have made enough noise to wake the whole neighborhood, trying to sneak up on my own house. Well, he went out the back and around the house and shot me in the ass when I was tip toeing in the front door." She was covering her mouth now, trying to choke back her hysterics, but her eyes were laughing wildly.

Then she burst out laughing, unable to control herself any longer. Thinking about what I had said, she asked giggling, "you said you were shot in the...the scar is on the back of your thigh." She was laughing so hard that she could hardly get the words out.

"Ask any police officer you see, it's about the most famous story on the job. Ask him where Cassidy got shot when he tried to catch his partner in bed with his wife. I don't care if it's a copper from the south side. He'll know the story and he'll say, 'oh you mean the guy whose partner shot him in the ass?', it just makes a better story that way. On this job there's always the true story and the one that everybody likes to tell."

"Where is he now? Did they put him in jail?" She asked wiping her eyes.

"Jail? There were no charges. All they did was dump us back into uniform. You don't understand how the police department works. It's a unique brotherhood. The most unlikely people become fraternal siblings. One time, two black officers got into a fight with a couple of white bikers over on Devon Ave. I got the call. They had all taken their lumps and the only way it had ended was when one of the officers had shot his gun in the air a few times. They had been drinking and could have lost their jobs for what they did. They were a long way from their home district, but the sergeant and I helped them out. We did the paperwork is such a way that they were justified in their actions, nobody got hurt. The bikers went to jail and got cut loose in court the next morning. We take care of each other on this job, at least we used to...as far as that bum partner of mine, I hope my ex-wife is still torturing him daily."

"Daily? They're still together?" She asked, incredulous.

"Who'd have them. They had to get married to each other." I laughed, feeling lighter.

"He fought for her, and he won her. The classic Sir Lancelot and Queen Guenevere scenario." She laughed more, but I couldn't brush it off as nothing.

"It was serious at the time. I was kind of a dangerous guy. He didn't sneak up and shoot me for no reason, he knew me better than anyone else. He knew I wasn't going to flip on the light and say 'Olly Olly Ocean Free'."

177

"Tell me 'bout it, mon?" She said comically, relaxing me again. "I can't believe that they didn't do a thing about it though."

"Well, they did do something. They made me go for counseling. But not him. Apparently what he was doing was considered normal. But I went, for myself. Although, I think that some of the counselors went into different lines of work after trying to solve my problems. I still can't figure out which person I was more hurt about losing, my wife or my partner."

"But that was a long time ago." She said, trying to give me some support.

"It's not the time so much as what I did with it. I stopped drinking, and after a long struggle, I ended up a new man. I've been working on making that man a better person ever since." She took my hand.

"Well, I'm glad that it all happened. Otherwise I would never have met that person, and I'm very fond of him." She smiled at me beautifully.

"I'm happy that you are. Do you want to go to Florida with me for the graduation?" The question couldn't have caught her more off guard. But she recovered quickly, saying that her daughter was in school near where the boys went and we could all get together. The plans were flowing out of her within minutes. I wished that I had a better car, I really didn't like the idea of flying, or was it the travel agent that I didn't feel comfortable with?

She picked up the phone. "I'll call 'D' and he'll take care of all the reservations. He owns Vacation Headquarters." Like I was supposed to know what that was. So was Dorman another boyfriend or just her travel agent? Who she calls on Sunday? I hesitated to ask what their relationship was. She called him at home, he apparently has a business that works twenty fours a day from anywhere, and he took care of everything. He also took my credit card number. After she hung up, she used the movement to sneak a kiss and I forgot all my trepidations about Dorman and flying and all the rest.

Claire wanted to go in to the restaurant and help Mama Lea for a while, so we took another shower and got dressed. I hated to put on the same clothes I wore yesterday, but didn't have much choice. It didn't take long to get over to Mama Lea's, Claire lives only a few blocks north of the restaurant, in Evanston.

Mama Lea welcomed me with a knowing smile. She also announced that she had made Escovich Fish. Claire smiled and winked at me. I tried not to wonder about how her aunt had known we were talking about that very same dish just last night. The whole family was probably haunted.

I looked at the tray of thin sliced, translucent fish. It had been marinated in lime juice, onions and who knows what else. My stomach, which had just stopped burning about an hour ago, notified me how it felt about more raw fish.

I couldn't hurt Mama Lea's feelings and refuse to try the dish that she had made specially for me. So I tried a little, surreptitiously scraping the onions off the smallest piece I could find on the platter. It was cold and tasted strongly of the Carribean. The juice ran down my fingers, so I took a little piece of bread to soak it up.

It would be polite, I knew, to have another small piece, it was pretty good. When I found myself ripping pieces of bread from the loaf and scooping up the onions and juice with it, I took another stomach pill. As if that was going to have any effect.

*   *   *

My car was parked at a free weekend meter a little way down from Mama Lea's. I looked across the street at the game arcade where I knew the Royals sometimes hung out. The owner was a pig who I hated and he hated me in return, his Cadillac was parked in the bus stop. I almost went across to see if Gilly was in there, or if I could find someone who I could twist the information out of, but I was chewing happily on a toothpick and in too good of a mood to go looking for trouble.

My joy faded when I saw the plastic windows of my car had mostly blown out of place. Furthermore, some friendly passer-by had rifled through the glove compartment and torn my seat covers off, throwing them in the back. While the beater warmed up, I managed to get a piece of plastic to stick to the drivers window and did a quick re-upholstery job on the seats.

When I went by Moon's cleaners it looked locked up tight, there were no lights on in the double store front. People were just getting out of the movie theater on the next block, moving quickly, having dressed for a warm day and getting caught out on a cold night.

The taco place and Nicky's Hamburger Stand would pick up a little late night business, then close up at around ten-thirty. When I went by the station, it looked deserted and my heater wasn't blowing very hot yet, so I pulled my car up on the side street, leaving it running and double parked. Then I ran in to see what Captain Stokes had planned for my day tomorrow. He probably had me assigned as a battering ram for a drug raid.

The last thing I expected was to be on my foot post, but there was my name next to the space labeled '2496' on the work sheet. Apologizing to George had already paid off. I was glad that the war was over, even if I had been the one who had surrendered.

I could still see my car over on the dark side street, running, but I didn't dare hope that someone would steal it. I shot the breeze with Janie Gallagher for awhile, to give any prospective thieves ample opportunity, it was still there when I left the station. Later, I had a hard time blaming myself for leaving it unattended, hell there weren't any windows. It's not as if locking the doors would have helped. But I should have been more careful.

The heater was blowing hotly, but I knew that as soon as I got moving, the 30 degree air temperature would quickly displace my little zone of warmth. Paulina Street was just a half block of residences between the station and the busy street, Devon. I headed south on Paulina, going home.

Quiet and dark, I couldn't have created better conditions. I'd even left the car running so he could warm up when he hid in there. I smelled him before I realized that he was in the back seat. That's why they call them senses, they're supposed to alert you to danger, so you can react. I guess the smell of fire causes a quicker reaction than body odor.

When I stopped at the sign on Devon, the cross traffic on the usually busy street was light but steady. His left hand snaked around the headrest behind me and grabbed me by the collar. In his right hand he had something sharp that I felt when he pulled me back against the seat. I knew it was sharp because of the burning sensation at the base of my neck when it broke through the skin. One of the last unscathed spots on my body.

"Do not move, Cassidy." he whispered fiercely. I didn't need to be told that, I knew the blade was only a fraction of an inch from my spinal cord. A hacker who cuts someone's throat, just cuts through enough tissue until he hits the jugular vein or carotid artery, spraying blood all over himself and everything else around. A professional finds the soft disc between the second and third cervical vertebra. Push a sharp object in about an inch, at that point, and the person dies, immediately. It hardly bleeds at all if it's done by a pro. This guy was a professional. He was also Inon Moon, master tailor and laundry man.

"Listen, Moon, if it's about the parking tickets I..." He tensed, pulling on my collar and twisting whatever he had stuck in my neck just a bit. It was foolish to resist, but if I got the chance I was going to shoot this guy, for sure.

"Please," he said, his voice pleading. I could smell his foul breath, and it was obvious from the days old sweat that he had been hiding out since Friday night. I didn't say anything, having learned another lesson about comedy. After a moment he relaxed, I felt the pressure on the blade ease and I let out a breath that I didn't realize I had been holding.

The busy cross street was devoid of cars now, not a witness in sight. Then a car turned onto Paulina, the way I had come from the station. Within a few seconds it was behind us at the stop sign, it's headlights shining brightly through my broken rear window.

I hoped it was a policeman just leaving the station. Without moving a muscle, I sensed Moon turn and look back at the car waiting behind us. My senses were working wonderfully now. "Turn left," he ordered.

"Please, I do not want to hurt you, Cassidy." His voice pleaded with me. He sounded sincere, but my neck was telling me different. "Drive to lake." I didn't move.

"Drive." His voice leveled. He didn't want to hurt me, but he was going to do what he had to do. So was I. I made a left.

The knife, or whatever it was, was just resting against my skin now, but I could feel a coolness going down my back. As I slowly made the turn I thought about what would happen if it was a copper behind us and he tried to so something. I'd be dead before he got any results.

I didn't have to think about it for long though, a glance from the corner of my eye told me that the car behind us was a black Honda with damage along the drivers side. Moon still had the Gray Eagles working for him. I sighed resignation, it had been such a nice day.

"I am sorry, Cassidy," Moon apologized. It didn't help.

"Moon. What's this all about? Why are you doing this? I've always been your friend. Please, let me go." I figured a little bullshit and begging couldn't hurt. We passed the traffic signal where Devon crosses Clark and started down the gentle slope, about a mile to the lake. At that point we could turn left onto Sheridan Road, or right to Lake Shore Drive. There were only two choices.

"Please, Cassidy. Please," he hesitated, unable to say what he wanted. I couldn't see a reason for him to be begging me for anything. He had the upper hand, it had me by the throat.

"Moon, what is it?" I asked again trying to get something out of him or at least buy time. "Come back to the station with me, I'll help you. I promise." I wasn't so sure I wanted to keep that one.

The streets were quiet for this time on a Sunday night. The traffic light at Glenwood kindly changed to green for our little two car funeral procession. I didn't know if I was more angry with myself than I was at these nuts that I had gotten involved with. But what pissed me off the most was that I was being taken for a ride, and they were even making me do the driving.

"No...I cannot go there...I cannot go anywhere without the lists of names. I must have them." He'd started out unsure, then became crystal clear.

"What are you talking about?" I tried to play dumb, not usually difficult for me.

His hand twisted in my collar, but he didn't re-apply the knife. I could feel the cool wetness spreading down my back. And, now that I thought about it, I could smell blood. Knowing that it was mine made me feel a little faint. My heart was pounding, I could feel the adrenalin coursing through me. I squeezed the wheel, and tried to focus on the street. Breathe.

"I saw you take them from the body." He wasn't begging or pleading now. He was deadly serious, I could hear it in his voice. And feel it.

"You saw me take them?" How could I doubt him? It would be foolish to act like I didn't know what he was talking about. "What was so important that you took a chance of getting caught, circling back to the jewelry store, to see me take them?" Now that I knew what he wanted, I got a little braver. I figured that he wouldn't kill me until he got his hands on those papers. And he was never going to get his hands on those papers.

"Where are they?" He screamed into my ear, it was practically a torture in itself. The sharp object jabbed into my neck again and I could feel it grate on the bone, looking for a way in. Almost my last thought was that I had figured wrong about how this maniac was thinking.

"Okay! Okay, take it easy. You can have them. I couldn't even read any of it." The pressure on my neck eased as I bargained for my life. He also may have let up because I was swerving all over the street.

"I hide under a car, I see you take paper and put in jacket. You not give them to police." I couldn't understand how he knew that I had not turned the lists in as evidence.

"You give them to the old man?" Chung? This guy had been keeping close tabs on me. We passed by the turn to go north on Sheridan, just a few more blocks to the turn south and Lake Shore Drive. I guessed that question had been answered. I glanced in the mirror and didn't see the follow car, different headlights were behind us now. Maybe the light on Sheridan had been kind to me?

"I didn't give Chung anything. Why did you kill those people? Were those papers that important?" I was getting tired of all this, especially being forced down this street with no hope of escape.

He tensed but didn't answer me. Did he kill them or not? That's the question that I was entitled to know the answer to before I died. There were several cars ahead of us now, stopped at the red light at Kenmore. I had to stop, the last stop before the lake. The light changed and I was going to take my foot off the brake when I had one of my snapping episodes.

When I was a rookie policeman I used to get dumped on the wagon all the time. The old timers showed me how they 'softened up' an unruly prisoner or a police fighter. We even had a name for it, we called it the 'the train crash'. I stamped down hard on the brake and the gas at the same time, then popped the brake when the engine sounded like it was going to explode. We shot off the street as I spun the wheel, and pulled into the oncoming lane.

Moon let go of my collar as he was slammed back into the seat and then into the far corner when I cut across the oncoming lane and hit the curb on the north side of the street. I rode the curb up and down bouncing Moon around like a ping-pong ball as I struggled to hang on and keep my foot to the floor. I thought about pulling my gun, but I'd have to stop, or slow down, which might give Moon a chance to slash me with that blade. He was better off bouncing in the corner, out of reach.

Suddenly, I looked up and there was nowhere to go. There was oncoming traffic and cars on my right, blocking the street in both directions. There was a little space though, between an oncoming car, and a tree in the parkway on the north side of the street. The driver of the car sat there, stopped, facing me. I was going about sixty m.p.h. And just went for it.

I could see the terror in his white eyes as they bugged out at the charging beast. He frantically fumbled with the gearshift for a moment, finally covering his face with his hands, resigned to his fate. I knew that I would fit. It would be a little close. I made room.

Sideswiping the tree on my left and the car on my right simultaneously, the old beater shot through the hole, sparks flying. I still had Moon bouncing. Where to go now? Now there was really nowhere to go. Ahead was a small park and a millions tons of huge boulders stacked up on the shore of the lake to break winter storm waves. Those stones would also stop any maniacs from driving into the lake. I wasn't a maniac, but I found a way. I swerved up onto the narrow sidewalk that went up into the park, just missing the boulders. I stood on the brake but I was unable to stop.

At the shore, the sidewalk turns left becoming a little broad walk that runs along the top of the breakwater. A metal pole fence keeps people off of the rocks below. The Chevy launched itself off the end of the sidewalk, over the bank and out over the black water. The rail fence snapped like a twig, my brakes squealed until they left the pavement.

It felt like we were airborne for awhile, but it had to be only a split second before the heavy front end came crashing down and we were in the water. Icy, cold black water rushed into the open windows. The first stupid thing I did was shut off the engine. The water rushed in from both sides. I finally thought to take a deep breath.

It didn't matter what Moon was doing, the lake was trying to kill me now. I remembered all the young healthy bodies I had taken from these unforgiving waters over the years. One young man had gone after a lost fishing pole and gotten caught by an undertow. I remembered that he had been bigger and stronger looking than I was, even twenty years ago. I grabbed the window frame, I had to peel my fingers from the steering wheel, when the pressure of the water eased. I was already shaking uncontrollably in the 40 degree water.

I managed to pull myself out of the drivers window. The freezing water was stiffening my muscles and my brain was shutting down, succumbing to hypothermia. I had only seconds left before I would be unable to move. Which way was up? Where was the shoreline? I tried to relax, that's what you're supposed to do when being swept out to sea by an undertow. It was just a thought. Suddenly my head was above the water and I took an gasping breath of wet air. Then I stood up.

The car hadn't sailed out over the waves to sink hundreds of feet beneath the choppy waters of the killer lake, the rear end was still on the shore. The waves were beating me around and I had to hold onto the roof. I'd forgotten to turn off the headlights, they glowed eerily. Greenly showing me the depths that I had envisioned myself sinking to. I still had to get myself out of the water however, I was freezing.

Moon was nowhere around, though I was back to worrying about him. I climbed up the side of the car and flopped myself onto the rear window. Reaching for the bumper that was sticking up in the air, I stood up on the rear window and looked over the trunk at the shoreline. I could just see a wet and dripping figure run across the confusion of traffic on the Drive and jump into the black Honda which sped off.

Climbing up the rest of the way onto the sidewalk, I sat on the edge and tried to curl up as small as I could, shaking like a leaf. I told myself that it was the cold. I wondered if I could squeeze myself smaller and smaller until I just disappeared. I heard the sirens and saw the blue and red lights reflecting off of the buildings. Somebody came and got me and put a blanket around me.

I had the streets all blocked again. There were squad cars all around, but nobody came up to me at first. The paramedics walked me to the back of the ambulance and checked me out, only a scratch on my neck. No big deal. They thought I was drunk. Probably so did everyone else.

Suddenly a finger was in my face. I recognized the white eye balls bulging out of the pointers head. He was an East Indian man. His car was still there, where I had struck it. He was jumping up and down saying something to Bruce Sapper who looked like he wanted to thump the crazy little man on the head to calm him down a little.

"That is him, Officer! The reckless driver." He pointed at me as though he'd seen the devil himself.

"I was sitting there, minding my own business, waiting for the light to change." The whole terrible moment was coming back to him. "Then I see him coming on. He mounted the curb several times, up and down. Up and down! He is coming straight to me."

The guy was starting to hyperventilate, flapping his arms wildly, as he dramatized each statement. "He flies at me. I see he will collide with me and I put my car in 'Retreat'...but he got me anyway." He let out a huge sigh, coming to the end of reliving a very scary time for him, and me."

I had to smile. This man thought that the 'R' of the steering column, stood for 'retreat'. Sapper was hysterical and took the man over to where Pape was directing traffic, so he could tell his frighteningly funny story again.

When I finally got back to the station and into some dry clothes, I called for a breath analysis. It was negative. Janie Gallagher backed me up saying that I had been at the station minutes before the accident, and I was sober. It was terrible that I had to defend myself before accusations had even been made, but I knew the ropes and wanted to be ahead of them. Especially when I was asked how my car got into the lake if I hadn't been driving drunk.

Two guys, who I didn't know very well, handled the job. I found out later that Brian White and Cohen had come on the scene and asked to be assigned, but the dispatcher had already given the job to 2432 and refused to reassign it. The two guys on 2432 were named Skinner and Taylor.

John Skinner was a young, good looking police officer, with ten years under his belt. He and his partner looked like they could be brothers. Aggressive types in the prime of their careers, these two would soon be on a Tactical team or in the Gang Crimes Unit. They could definitely be considered veterans on this young job these days. Luckily, they listened to some of my suggestions and the paperwork went the way I wanted.

Captain Stokes wasn't around to quote regulations and I got them to call a Cuban friend of mine, Balarto, who had a tow truck, to pull my car out of the drink. They appeased the Indian man, who I'd admittedly attacked, with my insurance information. Skinner and Taylor acted like they believed my story about an unknown car cutting me off and my gas pedal getting stuck. Especially after the evidence technician verified that there was no alcohol in my body, and everyone knew what kind of car I drove.

So that was that. Just another accident, although a bizarre one. Sergeant Davis didn't even wait around to see the final report. Of course the final report wasn't very final, leaving out all the important information. What could I have said? It would have to come out that the Eagles and the laundry man had been following me around, and trying to kill me. The next question after a statement like that is 'why?'. I was digging my grave nicely, it was practically six by six already.

It was after midnight now, the new crews were already on the street. Things were just starting to get real quiet when the shot rang out. There was no mistaking it for anything else. I was coming from the desk, heading for the locker room to get my heavy wool reefer coat, hair all disarrayed, still damp. Wearing half uniform and half workout clothing, I ran for the locker room, gym shoe laces trying to trip me with each step.

Guys were coming from the back, around the corner, and rushing into the rear doors of the large room that ran half the length of the building. When I went through the first door, someone was right behind me and he caught the door for the next guy. We ran past the water fountain and shower room. Taylor ran down one side of the lockers, not knowing where he was going or what he was looking for. I was running toward an overhead light, that had a thin cloud of blue smoke hovering around it, down at the other end of the long aisle.

When I got to the bay of lockers, that was under the lamp with the smoke, I could smell the burnt gun powder. There were men, in various forms of uniform, standing across the opening of the locker bay. They seemed to be held there by an invisible force. Big Donny Cramer came up behind me in such a rush that before he could stop, he pushed me into the back of the crowd.

I bumped into Doug James and Alex Garcia, in their bluejean street clothes. The others, Sapper, Pape, and Cohen were still in their uniforms. They parted easily, allowing me to pass the invisible barrier which had held them.

The wooden plank of the bench ran about fifteen feet down to the back wall, separating one side of the lockers from the other. It was just a finished 2" X 10" pine board with smooth edges. He was sitting facing us, one leg on either side of the plank, with his back up against the wall. His locker, the last one on the right, stood open.

It was Brian White, his blue eyes were open and his head was back against the wall. There was a sunburst of blood on the green cinder blocks behind his head, his service revolver was on the floor under his right hand, which hung lifelessly. His mouth hung open in a horrible 'O'. Blood had run over his lower lip, fanning out down his neck onto his white undershirt.

I approached the body, careful not to trip over his outstretched feet. He was wearing uniform pants and his usual combat jump boots. As I got closer I noticed another smell, not of blood which should have been the strongest, his anal sphincter had released when the bullet had penetrated his brain. The sides of his neck looked red, not from blood, and I bent over him to get a closer look.

"Jesus Christ Almighty!" The exclamation from behind me calling down all the powers with it's force froze me in my tracks.

"Cassidy. Get away from there!" It was Sergeant Ciccio. Tony Ciccio was the son of a former police big shot who had gotten his son up to the rank of sergeant and then died. Tony Ciccio had been on the midnights ever since his 'clout' died and he was never getting off midnights. Everybody had liked his powerful father, nobody cared for his playboy son.

"Sure. Sure, Tony. I just wanted to see if he was dead," I said, borrowing a line from Mike Pape. I stepped back across the invisible line and then looked back at the grotesque scene with the rest. The room was full of people now. Jose` the little janitor who had helped me with my car, was standing on his mop bucket so he could see over the taller policemen.

"He took the pipe." Donny Cramer broke the silence that was created by Ciccio's hysterics and inability to make a decision. 'Taking the pipe', is an old police phrase which is used to denote a coppers favorite method of suicide. The pipe being the barrel of your service revolver and the method of taking it was to put it in your mouth and pull the trigger. A fatal dose of medicine.

We all looked at the body, heads craned over shoulders to view a police officer's biggest fear. 'Will I totally lose it someday and take the pipe?' Police Officers were always in the top five of profession based suicides, year after year, right up there with psychiatrists and dentists.

Personal relationships were so hard to maintain and the job was basically dealing with a part of society that nobody else could deal with, or wanted to bother with. People never called the police to tell them that everything was just fine and that they were having a nice day.

Sapper finally broke the trance by grunting his disregard for someone who would shoot themselves. It seemed like he thought that White was better off dead. For some reason, the comment struck Donny Cramer the wrong way.

"I heard about what you said to him today, Sapper. You pushed him over." News travels fast around the station. Could Sapper's earlier comments about White cause the man to blow his brains out? Did Sapper push him over the edge?

"Shut the fuck up you big stupid, pizza faced moth..." That was all Sapper was able to say before he managed to push Donny Cramer over the edge, because right then 300 pounds of ex-football player slammed into the mountain of flesh that was Bruce Sapper.

Donny's momentum slammed Sapper into the wall. I swear the building shook. They crashed to the floor and everybody dodged the rolling giants, trying to keep from being crushed under their thrashing bodies.

Donny was knocking the crap out of Sapper, but when he rolled on top of him and raised a fist the size of a ham to give him a full force punch, I had to step in. Everybody else was content to let Donny blow off a little steam for us all, and fix Sapper at the same time. Ciccio was shouting orders, which nobody paid any attention to.

I grabbed Donny's huge fist with both hands and he flung me into the wall trying to wind up and give Sapper the 'coup de grace'. "Donny! That's enough, man!" I shouted into his ear while he was whipping me around like a rag doll, trying to free his hand and pound Sapper's face into the concrete.

Finally, I felt him relax, some of the others had stepped in to help me. Now I knew for sure that nobody ever kidded Donny Cramer about his acne when he was a kid. Nobody that was still alive at any rate.

Sapper couldn't even get up off the floor by himself, although he wasn't hurt, so three or four guys helped him onto a bench. He cursed Cramer and threatened him a little, but Donny shrugged it off and went back up to the desk after straightening his uniform. The incident forgotten. There were more important things to do. I tried to get Tony Ciccio to do some of them.

I suggested that he get some yellow tape and block off the area and get some technicians over here to start processing the scene. Somebody had called the Paramedics and I waved them off when they came running into the locker room, followed by Jim Geery who had a shocked look on his face. My neck was burning and I asked one of the EMT's, a tall blond woman, to take a look at it. They sure couldn't do anything for Brian White.

"Nice clean cut. You just popped the steri-strips, is all. How'd you do that?" She was a big boned woman with a deep voice. I just grunted in answer to her question.

"You know, if this had been a little deeper..." she speculated more to herself, "...but it's not bad, you'll be alright."

"That's a bad bet." I said, thinking of something else altogether. I could still smell Brian down at the other end of the room, at least Cohen's problem had been solved.

"What?" She dabbed at my neck with a pad and opened a new package of strips.

"Nothing. You 'bout done...thanks, honey." She frowned. She apparently didn't like people calling her sweet names. That was her right. And I didn't give a damn.

Thinking about Cohen made me notice the time. It was going on one a.m., Cohen and White should have been on their way home over an hour ago. I wondered what had happened to make them work overtime. It wasn't my 'accident', they had asked to be assigned to it and been refused.

I wondered about a lot of things. The maintenance man Jose`, usually left the station long before now. I know, because I usually see him waiting for the bus around ten at night. I looked for Cohen, he was nowhere around, but I was sure that I'd seen him in the locker room.

Sergeant Ciccio got White's home phone number from the roll-a-dex file behind the desk. Brian's wife told the sergeant that he didn't live there any longer. When he explained what had happened, Ciccio said that she didn't sound like she was very upset about it, or surprised either. She didn't care to come to the station or know anything about arrangements for the body. It was his third wife, I had only met the first one, briefly.

"Browne, I want the names of everybody that was in the locker room tonight." What a stupid order. Ciccio had given the job to Berny Browne, one of the midnight guys who hadn't even been in the station when it all went down. Browne was working steady midnights while he went to mortician school during the day and he liked to get jobs that involved dead bodies. He always had a book with him that showed the various stages of embalming. When most of the guys cleared out I stayed behind, pretending to get my coat. Browne was looking at the body while Geery went for more film.

"Sure has been a weird day." I made a ridiculous comment, just to say something.

"Yeah, I heard about your car ending up in the lake." He looked at my damp hair and odd clothing. "What was that all about?"

"Well, you know that car of mine." He smiled and nodded. "Some kids, joy riding, cut me off and the gas pedal got stuck at the same time. I couldn't stop the damn thing. It went right up the sidewalk and into the water. It was no big loss however." I laughed to cover the feeble story and he joined me.

"What do you think about this?" I motioned toward the yellow tapes, sounding as if I wanted his professional opinion. Two of the midnight wagon men, Thurman and Lisk, came up behind us as we were going under the tape. Thurman was one of the 'token blacks' that they forced to work way up here on the north side. He was carrying a stretcher and Lisk had a plastic body bag folded under his arm.

A Deputy Superintendent, one that I didn't know, had come and gone already. Only briefly looking at the body, seeing a possible future for himself, he turned the whole thing over to Sergeant Ciccio. Much to his chagrin. It was two a.m. now, I had been putting off leaving for a reason, besides not having a ride home.

William J. O'Shea

Geery and someone had moved the body from it's seat against the wall. Brian White now lay on the floor, in a more composed position. The sunburst on the wall now revealed itself as the top of a mushroom of blood, tissue, and brain matter that ran down the wall to the bench and onto the floor. It was sadly and sickeningly familiar.

"They didn't even close the eyes." Browne reached down with an ungloved hand and used his middle and index finger to slide Brian's eyelids over the staring blue orbs.

"You know that if you leave them open too long its real hard for the embalmer to get them closed properly. Sometimes they have to drain the fluid from the eyeballs, then sew the eyelids together before..." What was I doing standing here getting a lesson in eyeball draining?

"Did you notice any redness on the side of his neck?" I didn't want to bend over the body. It was all catching up with me, and I thought that I might fall over.

"That stuff is called blood, Hop." Thurman forced a cynical chuckle at Browne's joke. You had to laugh about gory stuff on this job or you ended up like White. Thurman and Lisk were anxious to get a dirty job over with. The sight of a person you know in this kind of shape affected anyone, even the most hardened veteran, in one way or another. I'd been feeling it for awhile now. Browne acquiesced and looked closer at White's neck.

"There is a light abrasion, though it could have been caused in a number or ways. His bullet proof vest could have rubbed on it for instance. His head is going to be the problem though. If they can build up the back of his head enough, they might be able to have an open coffin. But I doubt it." He clicked his tongue, tsk, tsk. The mortician was always displeased when his artwork couldn't be appreciated by grieving mourners. It was time for me to get the hell out of there.

The mobile repair truck was in the back of the station, probably changing a headlight or something. I bummed a ride with the 'R' man, as we called him. When he asked me where I

194

wanted to go, I told him to drop me off at the Y.M.C.A., about a mile from my house.

The gym and steam room is usually open 24 hours. I let the steam try to boil out some of my aches and pains, but it wouldn't clear my head. After I almost fell asleep in the foggy room, I showered and got a cab to take me home. When the driver told me what the fare was for the five minute ride, I tipped him well, it was 4 am., and resigned to take the bus to work tomorrow. I could buy a new beater car for the cost of a few cab rides.

My legs hurt, especially where I had scraped my knees. My head hurt and most of my cuts had re-opened, from one thing or another, and were oozing again. I ached all over. Every laceration on my body announced itself. My butt and neck were burning, throbbing. Thank God I was so tired that I collapsed on the bed, asleep in three seconds. Pain, and pressure on my bladder, woke me up at 9 am. Barely managing to drag myself to the bathroom, I swallowed a handful of over the counter pain pills with a huge glass of water, and went back to bed.

Around noon, the angle of the sun coming through my attic window burned me awake and forced me from the bed. Surprisingly, I felt much better than I had three hours ago. Another shower, half a box of Band-Aids, and some oatmeal, had me in reasonable shape. Oatmeal is one of my secret weapons.

I was out of clean clothes, and there were no other cleaners on my beat. The horns of a dilemma. Moon had done such a good job with his cleaning business that he had put most of his area competition out of business. Now I'd have to start paying to have me clothes cleaned, that bothered me as much as anything else. I wondered what was going on with that little man, wishing he'd stayed in the laundry game.

I thought about Moon while I was waiting at the bus stop, it was a warm, sunny day and I was wearing my cleanest dirty uniform under a light windbreaker. What motivated that man with the soup bowl hair cut? Duty? Patriotism? Fear? Fear was the unpredictable one, it could make you do anything. There were also different kinds of fear, I knew because I had tasted some of them in the last few days. The taste was bitter and it made me angry.

The bus pulled up to the curb before I even realized it was coming. When I got on, I opened my star case and 'popped the button' on the uniformed driver. Chicago Police rode public transportation for free. We were obliged to assist in an emergency and didn't have any excuses for not being able to get to work. It wasn't as convenient as a cab, but you could still buy dinner when you arrived at your destination, if you took the bus.

Actually, it took me two busses to get to work. When I transferred at Ashland, it was a straight run to the station from there, I showed the driver my star again. He waved me by, with a smile as if he was really glad to see me. It was 2:30 and the bus quickly filled up with teenagers on their way home from the area high schools.

I was sitting in the second bench from the rear. A kid with greasy blond hair and baggy blue jeans, hurried onto the bus and ran for the rear. As the bus pulled away, he pulled his pants down and pressed his ass up against the rear window, to the jeers of the other students still waiting at the bus stop.

Everybody but me and a little Philippino woman thought that it was hysterical. I made a mental note to check with Balarto, my Cuban mechanic, and prayed that my car could be fixed, or maybe he could get me another junk to drive. Anything was better than a free bus ride.

At the next stop, we picked up a few gang members, Latin Disciples. I could tell from the bits of black and red colors that they wore, and just by the way that they carried themselves. What surprised me though were the school books that they had under their arms. I thought that gangs considered education stupid. Maybe there was a chance for some of these young men who rode the fence, school during the day and gang banging at night.

There were several girls on the bus, and the boys were doing all sorts of childish stuff to get their attention. Block after block, they played the oldest game in the world, with an urban flair. Words and jests turned into pencil throwing and paper wading. Finally a book sailed past my ear, missed a ducking dark haired boy, and struck the Philippino woman in the back of the head with such force that she almost hit her forehead on the seat in front of her.

"That's it!" I shouted, jumping to my feet. "That's all I can stand, the party is over!" It was snapping time in the city again.

I turned to the guy who had dropped his pants, knowing who had thrown the book, and eyed him fiercely. "Go and get that book and apologize to that woman!" The little woman was so frightened that she didn't turn around or even act like anything had happened.

"You gonna make me," he said sarcastically, and jumped up onto the rear seat in sort of a fighting stance. Here I was in a pissing contest with a sixteen year old kid. How pathetic could I get?

I was doing the wrong thing. The driver had an emergency phone on the bus and I should have gone to the front and used it to call for a car. Instead I'd gone down to the level of a child, challenging this punk. Of course he had no other choice than to fight back in front of his peers.

He glanced around, most of the rest of the seats in back were occupied by his buddies. The signals he got from them told him to go for it, they were going to back him up. I was going for his throat, past caring.

"Hey, man," I heard from behind me, "ain't you Cassidy?"

I turned my head just enough to see that it was one of the Disciples, sitting peacefully a few rows toward the front. My hand stopped in mid air, everything stopped but the bus.

"Yeah, I'm Cassidy." I took my old felt hat off and held it up, showing the bush of white hair that had become my trademark and identified me to most of the gang members.

I held the cap in my left hand, just about even with my intended target's head. Now that I had a moment to think, I thought about how to really destroy this kid that had set me off.

Anything can be a weapon, a nice whack with the cap to distract him, followed by a short right to the abdomen, should do nicely if I got my shoulder into it well. That should make short work of this ignorant young man. He had only one chance.

"Cassidy?...You mean...Cassidy...the cop?" The kid standing on the seat asked a few stammering questions. He looked around, realizing that his support had suddenly dissolved.

"I'm...uh...sorry, Officer Cassidy. I didn't..." he started to speak very politely when he realized that the answer to his question was yes.

"Don't tell me. Tell her!" I pointed at the little dark woman, she didn't turn, my attitude hadn't changed.

He got down off the seat gingerly, eased around me, went over to the woman and got his book from the floor. "I'm real sorry, ma'am," he said, sincerely enough for me. Suddenly I was tired again.

"Now sit down and read the damn thing and be quiet. I've got a headache." I felt like the hall monitor. Reputation is an important part of life in the concrete jungle. It's a weird concept, one that's dictated by your actions, not your words. My reputation not only preceded me, it grew of it's own accord. Today was the first time I hadn't needed to live it down. We rode the rest of the way in peaceful silence. When I got off the bus at Devon, the driver's smile looked like a toothpaste commercial.

Chapter 22

The flags lowered to half staff out in front of the station told everyone who passed by on Clark Street that a police officer had died. One pole flew the US flag and the other, the four red stars and two blue bars of the Chicago flag. Under the city flag was the black and purple mourning flag that flew too often these days.

What was most unusual for me though, was the amount of suits in the station lobby. It was like looking in the window at Brooks Brothers. I went around the back to the 'Authorized Personnel Only' door. It was quiet in the hallway and I headed for the locker room. Where the yellow 'Crime Scene' tape had defined an imaginary barrier to a real tragedy, there was just another bank of lockers. The wall was clean now, only a nick in the green paint was evident on the cinder block above the bench.

A little chip in the block, it could have been caused by anything. You wouldn't know a bullet had chipped the cement there unless someone told you. Or you had seen it for yourself. Every station had bullet holes in the walls or ceilings, not usually caused by suicides though. When everybody carried a gun, shit happened.

There were a few people in the locker room, changing for work or whatever, but there was a somber air. No one spoke, except to acknowledge a co-worker with a soft word. There was sort of a library atmosphere in the spacious room, or was it more like a church, or a shrine? I tried not to think about it. I hadn't liked Brian White very much, but he didn't deserve the cards that he had been dealt.

Hurrying to get out of there as fast as I could, I stopped just before I closed my locker and reached for the belt holster that fit my 44. I took the big silver gun out of the shoulder holster, snapped it in the holster, and threaded it onto my gun belt.

I knew that I was acting paranoid. Only hot shots wore two guns, the second one usually a high velocity automatic, but I had an itching sensation in the back of my neck. There was tape over it and I couldn't scratch it. I put my long wool uniform coat over it, it hid my trepidation nicely.

Curiosity got the better of me, I hadn't done anything stupid for at least an hour now. I strolled up to the desk to see who all the suits were. They had moved into the Commander's office in front. Everybody at the desk acted like nothing unusual was going on. A bad sign. I walked around to the front of the desk and stood by the counter phone, as though I was expecting or going to make a call. From there I could see the doorway of the front office, where the executive types had gathered.

The light finally went on in my brain and I decided to get my lowly ass out of there, but of course my eye couldn't be prevented from taking a last glance toward the Commander's door. The sight of Ben Cohen coming out of the door, with his head lowered, stopped me in mid flight. He came up to me and stopped, looking up at me. He had to stop, because I was apparently blocking his way.

"What were you doing in there, Ben?" I asked, not caring who else was around or listening.

"They asked me a bunch of questions. I don't know," he said, with worry and confusion in his voice.

"Roll call! Roll call!" Ernie Perez's voice boomed over the PA system. The captain came out of his office, opposite us behind the desk, picked up the CO book and headed for the back, only briefly looking our way.

"Is that him?" The man who asked that question made it obvious that he was speaking about me. He was standing in the doorway of the district commander's office, speaking to someone who was out of sight, behind the wall. He spoke loudly so I could hear his question. I didn't hear any answer, if he received one.

But it wasn't really a question, he was addressing me, looking directly at me. Dark blue suit, about six foot, 180, well built. Early thirties. His hair, so blond that I knew that he must have blue eyes, was cut short in a military style. We looked at each other across the twenty or so feet of lobby, playing a brief game.

He took a step into the hallway, which led to the lobby where I stood with Cohen. I took Cohen by the arm and we turned in the direction of the roll call room. I didn't feel like playing right now. Especially not with a new kid.

As we walked down the south hallway, I asked Cohen what questions they had asked him. "I don't know. A lot. They kept asking me about some Korean guy. I think it was the one that was in the cleaners the other day when you went to change your pants. But the name they kept saying wasn't Moon. They showed me a picture..." Cohen was a sharp kid.

"And they wanted to know all about last night...about White and what he..." That's what I wanted to know too.

"What happened to you last night, Ben? Where'd you go?" I didn't care if he was upset, or scared or anything. I only cared about his answer.

"Outside. I told them I had to go outside." He thought that I was discussing his interview. I was conducting my own investigation.

"Outside for what? You just left?" He looked at me, for the first time realizing that I was questioning him and his movements.

"The smell, I couldn't stand it...and the way he just sat there...I'd said that I hated him so many times...but when I saw him that way...they made me show them the vomit." He said the last thing just as we were cutting through the sergeant's office into the roll call room.

"What?" I held his arm for a moment. "Who made you show them vomit? What vomit?"

"Those F.B.I. guys. When I told them that I got sick out side and went home afterward, because I couldn't stand to go back in there, they took me out to the parking lot and made me show them where I threw up." He had the door open, the early crew was milling around trying to obey Sergeant Davis' command to fall in for roll call. Captain Stokes was standing on the dias, behind the podium, with the work sheet for the day's assignments in his hand.

F.B.I. guys? My nose wasn't working again. I should have smelled those scum bags through the window, from across the street.

Stokes looked over and frowned a 'hurry up' at us, stopping my next question to Cohen. He waited until we ran down to the end of the line and dressed right, before he started calling names.

The captain called out all the assignments. Cohen was put on the wagon with Leo Prang, that meant three packs of second hand cigarette smoke, and a gallon of coffee, for him tonight. I was still on my foot post, despite the loss of a man. After the captain inspected us, we fell out, into the chairs arranged around the room. He started to read some crime patterns and hot car plates out of the CO book.

The side door, the one that I had just come through, opened and Ernie Perez leaned in, a note in his bony hand. The captain noticed him on his left, but waited until he finished what he was reading before he acknowledged Perez. Ernie came into the room, approached the captain and handed the note up to him.

Stokes read it frowning. "Leo," he said to Prang, who sat in the rear, surrounded by a cloud of smoke. "Go over to Saint Francis' Hospital and relieve the other wagon. They're guarding a prisoner."

It was a regular thing. The wagons had to take sick or injured prisoners to be treated and when the shifts changed the crews had to be relieved. Stokes was frowning because he didn't like to have his roll calls interrupted. He didn't have any important information to impart to his troops. Roll call was the only time of day that George Stokes could get twenty or more people to pay attention to him. Roll call was 'his' time, and he got pissed if anybody disturbed it.

Cohen picked up his copious notes, ticket books, scarves, hat, gloves, and what else I couldn't imagine, and followed Prang out of the room. I wished that I'd had another five minutes with him before it was my turn in the front office. And I knew that my turn was coming, I could smell it. Now that I couldn't get away, my nose was working just fine.

Stokes had just found his place in the CO book when the side door opened again. Dolecki stuck his head in and said, "excuse me, Captain, but..." Behind him I could see the blond hair of my 'eye game' friend. George Stokes was off the platform and over to the door in a flash, I'd never seen him move so fast. I could tell he was fuming. I was smiling, on the inside only.

Dolecki said something to him in a low voice and George went off on him. "I'm conducting roll call here. Nothing is more important than that!" The force of the captains voice backed Dolecki up a step, he hid behind the door for defense now.

"Tell them that they can either sit and wait until I'm through, goddamn it...or they can get the hell out of the goddamn station. You hear me, Dolecki? Goddamn it!!!' I never saw lightning come out of anyone's eyes when they cursed before, but it sure seemed like it. Dolecki was practically burned to a cinder by the flames that came out of the captain's mouth. It was obvious that some of it was meant to splash on the tall blond that was hiding behind Dolecki also.

When Stokes turned around with a satisfied look on his face I tried to turn away but he caught my eye. It was me that they had requested. My turn had come more quickly than I could have imagined, they must want me pretty badly. They couldn't even wait the few minutes until roll call would be over to start frying me.

The anger in the captain's voice wasn't directed toward me or any of the other guys. In fact I felt a spark, or a thread of support come from him, something that was only shared by police officers. He looked at me and I nodded, message understood. He read some more nonsense from the book, keeping us five minutes longer than usual.

When he dismissed the men, he motioned to me and I approached the dias. "They want to see you in the CO's office.

Government assholes. You want the union steward in there with you?" A friend in need.

"No, thanks, George. I'll handle it myself." He smiled just a little. He seemed to be glad that I was going to handle it my way. I wished I had his confidence, that I could come out on top.

*   *   *

They were expecting me. The secretary, Joe DiSanto, one of the most powerful men in the station because all assignments went through him, just gave me the 'dead man walking' look and thumbed me over his shoulder into the commander's conference room.

Six men occupied the spacious room behind the commander's office. The big oval table had eight comfortable chairs around it. I took one of the two remaining seats, unasked.

"Commander." I acknowledged Joe Mulligan, who was the top man in our district, one of only 25 District Commander's in the city. His only problem was that the brass downtown had given him a district to command 200 blocks from his house, where he lived on the far South Side. Commuting five hours a day was wearing on this short stocky man.

"Cassidy." I knew he would get right to the point, one of the reasons that I liked this man with the egg shaped head. "These gentlemen are here to ask you some questions about this Korean business." He left a lot unsaid, on purpose.

"Why so formal, Sir?" I gestured around the table and looked at the door which DiSanto had silently closed behind me.

"Merely a convenience, nothing formal about it." He seemed calm enough. My neck was itching and my nose was twitching.

"We just have a few questions, Officer Cassidy." The blond in the blue suit, was first on my right. He'd spoken out of turn as far as I was concerned, not waiting for the commander to finish what he was going to say. Next to him was a slender lawyer

204

type, in a brown suit, thin brown hair, fiftyish. Dolecki and Voltz were on my left. The last guy in the room, the one between the lawyer type and the commander, was the one to watch though.

"And you are...?" I said to the blue suited Aryan who'd interrupted the commander.

"Agent Vandeveer." He said, as if I should have accepted his glorious presence as his license to ask me questions. His first name was apparently 'Agent'.

"And you are from where...?' I asked, leaving this question hang with the last half answered one.

"We are with the F.B.I." He said, beginning to become frustrated. Now he had included the others in an attempt to strengthen his authority.

"I'd like to see your identification please." I asked nicely. The commander smiled, he loved it. Dolecki started as if I'd accused God of not being himself. Agent tried not to show his annoyance and slowly reached into his inside jacket pocket and brought out the familiar, thin leather case. He opened it and flashed the interior at me. I recognized the flat gold badge and official looking F.B.I. photo ID. His first name was James.

"Do you know this man?" Vandeveer slid an 8 X 10 photo of a youthful Inon Moon over to me, after snapping his ID shut and replacing it in his coat. I didn't answer him.

"And these other gentlemen, who I have not been introduced to are...?" The one next to Mulligan smiled. He was hulking, had pitch black, bushy hair, and a beard line that probably started to show five minutes after he shaved. I guessed a Russian ancestor or two.

"This is intolerable!" Vandeveer had a thin skin. The brown suit next to him paid no attention to 'agent' and reached inside his coat taking out a similar ID. He stood up, opened it and slid it over toward me, then leaned over the fuming Vandeveer and extended his hand.

"Leonard Pace." He said properly. I shook his hand and answered, 'Basil Cassidy, nice to meet you.'

I glanced at his ID. He reached for it, putting it back in his jacket before sitting back down. The third man, the one that I really wanted to know, the one that couldn't help making an impression on anyone he met, took his wallet out of his inside pocket. He slid it across the table, with enough force so that it stopped right between my hands.

"Stanley Jerk-O" He pronounced it clearly and waved to me, across the distance that was too far to reach to shake hands. "The 'V' is silent." He added with a grin.

I opened the wallet, it wasn't a government ID case, it was just a regular fold over wallet. It had little slots in it for credit cards and they were all full of a variety of plastic. I could feel a stack of bills on the left side under the soft leather. The bottom slot had a clear cover and his drivers license showed through.

It was issued in Virginia and the picture showed the same disturbing grin. His last name was Jurkov, it could have been pronounced many ways, but this guy liked to pronounce it in a way that was provocative.

His grin turned into a broad smile when I got his little joke. I tossed him back his wallet. "With a name like Basil, who am I to make fun of anyone?" I said laughing with him a bit.

"My friends call me Stan. I'm with the NSA." He gave me permission to do something that I could tell 'agent' couldn't do. National Security Agency, you couldn't get any bigger than that.

"My friends call me 'Hop'." I said giving him similar permission.

"Well, now that we have all the pleasantries out of the way..." Agent started to say, when Dolecki interrupted him.

"Come on. Come on, Cassidy. Are you going to cooperate or not? We already know that's your buddy from the cleaners, Moon." He said, pointing at Moon's picture. He was next to me and I wanted to give him the eye poke and face slap that Moe Howard used to give my favorite Stooge, Curly.

"It just dawned on me who the puke inspector must have been." His face reddened. "So you're the genius that bullied that rookie and made him show you where he got sick last night, eh, Dolecki?"

Voltz kept his lips together but a grunted laugh escaped through his nose. The three on my right didn't react. The commander smiled openly, even south side guys didn't like Dolecki. Agent came to his rescue.

"Is this the man who operated the Moon Cleaners at 7145 North Clark?" He interrogated.

I ignored his question and spoke to Voltz. "Ken, I asked you to find out a couple of things for me and now we're taking vomit samples in the parking lot?"

He smiled shyly and shrugged. "A lot of stuff is happening, Hop. When I ran some of those names through the computer..." He opened his palm and passed it across the three opposite him, "this is what I got."

Vandeveer was insulted by the comment. "Officer Cassidy, I've had just about as much of this posturing as I'm going to stand. If you refuse to cooperate with this investigation, certain leverage can be brought to bear..."

"Listen, Agent!" I said, much too loudly to speak to someone right next to me. "I've already been in one pissing contest with a juvenile today, that's my limit. So unless you want to go out in the playground and try to whip my ass, you better start behaving yourself."

His partner, in true partner fashion, tried to step in and save the situation. "Officer Cassidy. Please. This is a matter of National Security. We'd appreciate your help. I know you fought for your country in Viet Nam and will not let your country down now that..." I held up his patriotic speech with a hand.

"Leonard, excuse me for interrupting. But I was a clerk in Nam, never fought, never fired a shot, never even saw a dead body. Now I'm a cop, here on Clark Street. I just do my job. I'm not in the world peace business. I'm in the parking ticket business." He just looked at me, disappointed that his 'good agent, bad agent' technique wasn't working.

He wasn't giving up that easily though. "Come on, Hop." This guy was my buddy. "We're all on the same side here."

"Leonard, I don't mean anything personal about this, but there's only room for one person on my side. Today your side is supposed to be our side. But maybe tomorrow, your boss might send you up here with a suitcase full of dope and money, which you always seem to have an unlimited supply of. Maybe he'd tell you to find some dumb coppers, with five kids and two ex-wives, who never seem to make enough money, and offer them fifty grand to do something stupid and incriminate themselves.

He just stared at me, as if I could believe the 'G' would do something like that. "I've seen enough promotions given out and US Attorneys get elected to public office, over the bodies of dead and convicted policemen." Their methods disgusted me and I made it clear.

"Now, if in the interest of law enforcement agency cooperation, you gentlemen would like to answer the questions that I put to Detective Voltz the other day, I would appreciate that." I looked at Pace, just as disappointed in his technique as he was.

"We will..." Vandeveer started to shuffle papers in front of him, as if he was going to threaten me with them or hopefully take me up on my offer to go out to the sand lot.

"Just a minute." Jurkov said it quietly but with such authority that everyone was willing to give him all the minutes he wanted.

"Hop, we're having trouble figuring out that list of names. What we do know is that you have exposed a North Korean deep cover agent." Vandeveer was obviously afraid to interrupt this guy, so was I.

"About the deaths of the Korean couple in the jewelry store, we still don't know how it all fits together. We were hoping that you could give us a hand." This guy I was willing to help. Or was he just so compelling that no one could refuse him?

"You guys know more about it than I do, Stan, I don't understand anything that's going on, really. I'd appreciate anything you could explain to me." That was the truth.

"That list is what we can't explain. There is no reason for those names to be listed together. Two of the people on the list are big bankers in Zurich. Another is a wealthy naturalized American who is a retired industrialist. Another, we believe was killed in Los Angeles, twenty years ago. And the last is a government official, in our own government, who does not know why he is on the list with the others. Or he does know and will not say. As for the addresses, they are all previous residences, and we can't figure out what the dollar amounts mean at all." He gave me all the information he had. Sorry, I couldn't do the same.

That answered none of my questions. "Stan, all I know for sure is that the leader of the local Asian gang jumped out a window trying to get away with those names. Moon was with him, you can see what he did to me trying to get away." I had two slightly black eyes and the scratches on my forehead looked worst than they were. I almost said, 'then he came back, and tried to kill me again, and again'.

"When was the last time you saw Tae Cho Han?" Agent leaned forward, blocking my view of Jurkov, picked up the picture of Moon and shook it in my face.

I snatched it out of his hand, he wasn't behaving at all. "I had a drink with him last night, rubberneck." He didn't believe me and tried to grab the picture back. I held it away from him just to aggravate him.

"I'll bring charges against you, Cassidy. I'll...I'll" Vandeveer raged, looking over at his partner for support with his charges. Pace didn't say a thing. Jurkov shook his head imperceptibly, there would be no charges.

"Well, you do what you have to do, Junior. The next time we meet, I hope you'll allow me a few civil rights and let me have a lawyer present." I said to his beet red face.

William J. O'Shea

"Now I've got my own job to attend to. Thank you for answering my questions, Mister Jerk-O. If you'll excuse me, Commander." Mulligan nodded and I got up, he tried to act nonchalant but I could tell he'd loved it. Nobody stopped me from leaving, not a word was spoken, but the looks that followed me were varied and not all benign.

I stayed around the desk, filling out my ticket books so all I would have to do was put the numbers in. They walked out of the office, everyone ignored me but Voltz and Jurkov, who both caught my eye and smiled. I went out the revolving door of the station and was stuck for a moment on choice of paths. The last time I'd done this it had been the wrong choice.

Jurkov came up to me as Vandeveer and Pace headed toward their powder blue government Ford. It was parked in front of the station, in the 'NO PARKING ZONE', the bumper on a fire hydrant.

"Hop, are there any more of those names around? Any more pages of lists? We've gone over the jewelry store and their apartment upstairs, both were clean." Jurkov waited until the other two were out of hearing range before asking me the big question.

He didn't really expect me to answer, he just looked at me, measuring every muscle in my face, with his black soul-searching eyes. "Because if there were more names, a lot of people could be hurt by their getting into the wrong hands."

We just stood there trying to read each others minds. Then it seemed that he had made a decision. He reached into his side pocket and produced a business card, handing it to me. It was just a plain card with his name and an '800' number on it.

He patted me on the back, (is) if he was transferring some great responsibility to me and wishing me luck. "This is your beat. Take care of it in your own way. That's a voice mail number, call me if you need any help or have any information you'd like to pass on." He let all the implications of what he said hang in the air before me, dangling like a mobile.

210

Just as he was turning toward the waiting automobile, Vandeveer's patience ran out and he leaned on the horn. He was behind the wheel of the Ford and we could see his angry face clearly, through the glass.

Pace had gotten in the back, leaving the front passenger seat to the larger, in many ways, National Security Agent. I walked him over to the curb and when he was getting in the car I finished the ticket I had been working on, adding the charge numbers for blocking a fire hydrant. Jurkov rolled the window down when he saw what I was doing, trying to stifle a smile.

"Next time you visit, there's a parking lot in the back." I handed Jurkov the ticket which he passed over to Vandeveer, who threw it on the floor of the car, disgustedly.

When Vandeveer pulled quickly away from the curb, I shouted to the retreating car, "and if it isn't paid, Jimmy boy, I'm going to get a warrant for you. We can bring certain leverage to bear here in Chicago..." I think he missed the punch line, but I could hear Jurkov laughing as they drove out of sight.

My smile faded when the weight of the assignment Jurkov had just given me became clear. Suddenly I was very tired again. It was my beat, my job all along, but now the responsibility had been placed squarely on my shoulders. By someone who I didn't think anybody refused.

Chapter 23

Choosing the right path, I headed south on Clark, trying to remember if they had named a new Patron Saint of Cars, so I could say a little prayer that my car could be fixed. I still had a 'glow in the dark' Saint Christopher statue in my glove box, in case he got reinstated. My saint turned out to be a little Cuban with thick salt and pepper hair and a dark complexion.

Balarto's garage is about a block from the station, around the corner on Devon Ave. It was actually an old gas station, with antique pumps still in the driveway. Junk cars, in various stages of disrepair were everywhere. They blocked the sidewalk and the parkway. Balarto gets citations from city inspectors all the time. He pays them and gets more. It was a sort of rent that he paid the city. His neighbors weren't too crazy about it though. When they brought it to my attention, I told them that it wasn't my job. You couldn't be friends with everybody.

Behind the building was a small lot which was piled high with unrecognizable car parts, a rust heap with a sagging fence barely containing it. The ground, where you could see it, and the floor of the station were inches thick with grease and grime that created a slick and lumpy surface.

You had to watch where you walked, if you fell down around here you would have to throw all your clothes away. Balarto came out of the office and greeted me in his heavily accented English. He never offered to shake hands, because they were perpetually black with greasy dirt.

"You'r crazy, 'oppy. You drive in the lake. We have mucho travajo to get it out, but she not so bad. Me, Balarto, I fix. Come back seven-tirty, you pick up." I couldn't believe my ears, if I was hearing him right that is. I'd expected to pay him for the tow and ask him to find me another old plug to drive. Now he was telling me that my car could be fixed, and picked up at 7:30. I had to be getting screwed here somewhere, it sounded too good. I knew that these alley mechanics weren't afraid to rip off a police officer. They hadn't been afraid of Castro, nothing could scare them after that.

"You fixed it, Balarto? My car still runs?" It was like the doctor telling you that a family member was going to pull through.

"Sure, 'oppy,'" he smiled broadly, he was ugly as a goat with a four day beard, but I wanted to kiss him anyway. If I could have found a clean spot on his face I might have.

"We dry the plugs, new filters, change the oil. A lot of tings we must put new." 'Here it comes', I thought. I knew I was going to get raked.

"How much, amigo? You know my rule." I couldn't allow myself to be so happy that I was going to let him go over my fixed ceiling prices on repairs.

"Jes, I remember. 'If it over one hundred dollars, you want another car'. But this is good car. I fix her good." I knitted my eyebrows together.

"Quando est, amigo?"

He cursed in Spanish, then looked up at me sourly. "Ninety-nine dollars. Okay, 'oppy?" I smiled and he grinned back at me. I should have known that I wasn't through when he gave in so easily.

"But you have to pay Papito extra for using his tow truck to pull it out of the water. It was very dangerous. He almost go in the lake." He made a wave motion with his arm, demonstrating Papito going under for the last time. We were past the limit now and climbing steadily.

"Now if you want to put the windows. Then we must ask Ramon, because they are from his car..." My eyes lit up, stopping his sales pitch.

"Windows? You have windows?" For windows I'd be willing to go a little higher. He smiled broadly, he had me by the short hairs now.

He walked me over to the farthest repair bay. My old white stallion was in the stall, with the doors open and fans blowing through the interior. "She almost dry inside." Balarto commented. I tried to hide my delight at the old car being up on dry land.

Ramon, who was a younger copy of his uncle Balarto, was polishing a piece of glass that lay across his knees. It was a side window for my Chevy and he carefully went over it with what must have been the cleanest dirty rag in the place. He turned when we walked in, acting surprised, as if I was supposed to believe that he sat around all day caressing this valuable piece of glass.

The play continued for awhile, Ramon refusing to part with his favorite twenty year old car parts. Finally we agreed on three hundred for everything, including the tow truck driver's brush with death. I could tell them a few stories.

Before he shooed me out of the shop, telling me to come back in a few hours, he remembered something and reached into his desk drawer, pulling out a thin black piece of metal. It was about 8 inches long, pointed, and sharp on the edges above where a handle was shaped into the metal. Balarto said he found it stuck in the back of the driver's seat. I told him to keep it.

At first I looked around myself constantly as I walked my beat. Then after awhile the routine of being back on my street started to relax me. There was spring in the air, my car was going to survive, and I had Jurkov's card in my pocket to give me a kind of support. Maybe I could trust him, maybe he could help me.

Maybe if I got the papers from Georgos and gave them to Jurkov, he would do the right thing with them. Whatever that was. Then maybe they could catch Moon and I might be able to get back to what I considered a normal life. Sure, and maybe the sun was going to come up in the west tomorrow. This was my job, Jurkov had given me the responsibility. Sung and Sui Park, were the job, I couldn't get out from under that.

The papers were Park's. What would he have me do with them? Was giving them to Jurkov going to hurt people who were the opposite of the ones that would be hurt if Moon got his hands on them? Most of the people on the lists were probably dead anyway, I told myself. I didn't know any of them. I tried, but I couldn't talk myself out of it.

When I got to Pratt, the sun had just set, leaving purple traces in the few clouds that I could see between the buildings. I watched for a while to see if it would come back up in the west. It just got darker.

As soon as the sun went down, the breeze from the lake got chilly and when a call of a disturbance came out at the Convenient Store down the block, I told the dispatcher that I'd check it out.

He gave the car he was assigning it to, 2423, a disregard. "Let me know what you've got over there '96." The dispatcher was a vital part of any police force. Most people didn't know just how much they did, how many lives they protected and saved. I knew this dispatcher, not by sight but by voice, just like I knew that the voice on 2423 wasn't Brian White's. As I turned around to head back south, I could see the lighted flags in front of the station. Nobody would be hearing Brian White's voice on the radio again. The drunk driving and moving citation indexes would suffer in this area, among other things.

The convenient store on Clark was owned by an Indian from New Delhi, (I'd never met any Old Delhians), named Nasim Patel. The Indians in my area stayed mostly away from the liquor business. But they had just as many problems as the Arabs or Koreans.

Nasim came running out the front door when he saw me come around the end of the building that was next to his parking lot. "They ran down Albion, Cassidy." He gestured wildly in the direction that the offenders had fled. His colonial accent was very pronounced when he was upset, which was most of the time. "Hurry, go after them. You must arrest them."

I wasn't running down any dark side street after anyone. Not until I found out who I was after. "Nasim, calm down and tell me who they were and what they did."

I saw that he had a small steak knife in his hand. Taking him by the arm, I steered him across the parking lot and into the former Chicken Shack that now housed his grocery store. I took the knife away from him and he looked down sheepishly.

"They steal, they threaten me." He referred to the knife. "I need to have a pistol." He said finally recovering his anger. The last thing this guy needed was a gun.

"I'll take care of it, Nasim. Tell me how many there were and what they looked like." I had my radio in my hand for emphasis, ready to give out a flash message on the criminals.

"Three of them. The same ones all the time. The kids from down on Ashland." I snapped the radio back onto my epaulet. I knew most of the gang bangers that hung around Albion and Ashland. They called themselves 'folks', better known as the Disciples.

Directing him to stay in the store, I went around the edge of his building and took a few wily steps east on Albion, stopping at the alley. Looking in all directions before I stuck me head around the corner, I just caught a glimpse of three little black heads disappearing into a doorway across the street.

I passed the alley and crossed Albion heading for the door of the hallway that they were hiding in. Just as I reached the grass of the parkway on the south side of the street one of the heads popped out to see if the coast was clear. The little eyes and mouth opened wide with shock and the head disappeared to relate his observations to the other two.

They were trapped in the hallway and I could hear them having a fire drill in there when I grabbed the knob on the door. I opened it and the three kids fought to push each other to the forefront. Two little boys and a girl.

She lost and wound up closest to me. When she started to cry, the boys broke down too. I guessed that these were the culprits. They couldn't have been more that six or seven years old, not dressed well enough for the cold night and out later than children their age should be.

"What are your names?" I asked, not too fiercely so as not to increase the crying symphony.

The biggest boy found his courage first and wiped his nose on his sleeve saying, "DeShaun," as he did it.

"And where do you live, DeShaun?" He got a little braver and answered without having to hide under his arm or wipe anything off his face.

"1420 West Albion," he said, reciting it from practiced memory. They were just a block from home.

"Come on, guys, let's take a walk. I won't hurt you." I told the dispatcher what I had and where I was going. There was some chuckling in the background down at the Communications Center. As we walked east toward home, I found out that the other boy was his brother, his name was DeShane, but everybody called him 'Boogie'. The girl was their cousin, Leisa.

"Did you guys take anything from that store?" They all denied taking anything, saying that the man had chased them out before they could show him that they had money.

I asked them about the money and DeShaun produced a wrinkled dollar bill. It was Leisa's and he was apparently guarding it for her, until they decided what they were going to spent it on.

"Okay, you said that you didn't take anything from the store, and I believe you," I'd surreptitiously checked them out already, "but have you ever taken anything from that store before and not paid for it?"

I got a no answer from the boys, but their faces told on them. They were willing, however, to tell on everybody else in the neighborhood who had stolen things from Nasim. Leisa was just along for the ride, she didn't live around here and was new to the shoplifting racket. "You see what happened. You took things before and now the man suspects you every time you go in there, whether you have money or not."

We'd reached their apartment building and they just looked up at me, the wisdom of Solomon wasn't sinking very far into these little heads, it seemed. "You're getting a bad reputation. Listen to what I'm saying. If you take things without paying for them you're going to end up in jail. Do you understand that?"

Either my voice had lost it's 'Officer Friendliness', or they had gotten the point because the tears started flowing again.

"He called us niggers," Boogie said through a torrent of tears and snot. Solomon leaned back on his throne for a moment, trying to figure how to divide this baby up. Divine inspiration was not forthcoming.

Boogie had thrown me a curve and I had trouble handling it. I knelt down so their faces were level with mine. "Name calling is also a bad thing. And I can't say that if you don't call people names, they won't call you names. But nobody has the right to call you niggers or anything else that you don't like. I'm going to talk to the man at the store about it and we're going to have a meeting with your parents. Okay?" I got some uncertain wet smiles from them and we went upstairs. I left them in the custody of an older sister, who I threatened a little about the responsibilities of being a baby sitter, and the consequences of not watching her charges closely. She couldn't have cared less.

I walked back up to Clark Street and went in to see the waiting Nasim Patel. There were a few customers at the counter. I waited as he hurried with their purchases so he could find out what I'd done about his thieves.

"Did you find them? Did you arrest them?" He asked anxiously, while the last customer, a black man, lingered by the door, looking at a magazine. I waited until he left.

"I found them and I know who they are, but they didn't have any stolen merchandise in their possession. Are you sure that you saw them stealing?" His look answered my question.

"I have seen them before, they steal every time they come in here. I don't want them in my store. I call police, but they do nothing." He took a little shot below the belt, I hit back.

"Nasim, did you call them 'niggers'?" He showed resignation, then defiance.

"They call me 'camel'! There is no camel in my country. I am no Camel Jockey!" I had to remind myself that everyone involved considered this a serious thing so that I wouldn't laugh at the scene that presented itself to my mind.

218

"So they called you a Camel Jockey and you found out what the word is that really hurts these children and you call them that?" He looked down again, and didn't answer.

"They're little kids, Nasim. You might not want them in your store, but I'm sure that their parents shop here. You don't call them names. Do you want me to find out what the worst thing that you can be called in your country is, and tell them to call you that?" He looked up at me with a shamed face.

"Just like Gandhi suffered and died so that your people could be free, people here did the same thing so that those children wouldn't have to listen to people call them niggers." He was sufficiently cowed now.

"I have their phone number and later we can call their parents and have a meeting with them. We'll set up some rules, then the kids will only be able to come in here when they have money to spend and you won't need that pistol that you were talking about." He smiled and we talked some more about how he could prevent theft and do business in a community that was not the best in the city, by any measure.

After I gave the dispatcher a code and came up clear, I continued my tour. It was after 7:00, all the street lights were on, illuminating the busy Monday evening street so it's citizens could go about their evening's business.

When I'd gone by Chung's place, the lights were on but I didn't look in, afraid that he would be looking out at the same time and give me a heart attack. I did want to caution him about what Moon had said though, so I stopped at Ah's 'Sun Liquor Store' so he could call the old man and tell him to be careful. I told myself that I wasn't really afraid to go into the martial arts school, it was just the cultural differences that made me nervous.

The liquor sale signs still covered the door and windows and Ah was behind the cash register when I finally managed to grunt the heavy door open. I felt much more at home in a liquor store than a karate school anyway, (I knew that it wasn't called karate, but it all seemed the same to me at the time). He smiled at me just like he had always done in the past.

William J. O'Shea

"Hello, Cassidy." He said in his familiar accent.

I indicated the windows, forgetting why I'd come in here for a moment. "Ah. Please take some of these papers off the windows, will ya?" He bowed just a bit, acknowledging that I had warned him, again.

"You want something?" He gestured toward the soda case behind me.

"No. No thanks. I only came in here to have you pass a message on for me." I leaned over the counter, there was no one else in the store, but his smile vanished when he realized that I was being over cautious in my desire to relate a secret to him.

"Last night I saw Moon. He tried to stick a knife in my neck." I turned my head a bit showing him the bandage at my collar line.

He was startled and looked back at me compassionately, saying nothing. "Moon asked me about the papers. He saw me take them. He asked me what I'd done with them. When I didn't tell him, he asked me if I'd given them to Chung."

"I want you to tell Chung to be careful. If Moon thinks that he has the papers..." I let him furnish his own conclusions.

His conclusions were similar to mine because he picked up the phone and dialed. While he was doing that I looked around and some of his pictures caught my eye. They were mostly snap shots and postcards, clipped and taped to the counter and the side of the cash register.

It reminded me to run over to the drugstore on Lunt, and pick up pictures that I really didn't want to look at. On the side of the register there was a picture of Sung Park. It was a Polaroid of Sung, smiling, standing behind the counter next to his workbench, proudly displaying the tools of his trade.

Behind Park, on the green wall, was the familiar display of photos that he had posted where he could look up at them while he worked at his bench. I tried to look closely at them, to see if they were the same ones that were up there the night of the homicides, but they were too small. I looked at the rest of Ah's

220

photos, several of which were of Sung or Sui Park at different ages, trying to draw inspiration from their smiling faces.

Ah finished his conversation, none of which I had understood, and put the phone back in its cradle. He shook his head wearily.

"It's hard to tell him to something," he said dejectedly.

"You mean it's hard to tell him anything." He nodded.

"Don't worry, Ah, there're people working on catching Moon. Everything will turn out alright." Neither one of us believed what I was saying.

"You give them..." I knew what he was talking about.

"No...not all. But I had to give them some idea of what was going on." He looked at me like I had betrayed him.

"Why would Moon be worried if I gave the names to Chung? What would Chung do if I did gave him the papers?" His expression became a thoughtful one, as if he wanted to give me a truthful answer.

"I do not know," was what he finally said, bursting any bubble of hope that might have been forming in my mind. It was a truthful answer, though. I knew because it was the same answer that I kept coming up with.

Chapter 24

When I went into the drugstore, Candell Drugs, Leo Rosenberg was behind the front counter. The major chain drugstores were putting these independents out of business. Leo could only afford to hire a counter girl part time. So most of the time he spent running from the drug counter in the back to the checkout counter at the front. He fought to survive, but he was losing the battle.

"Did they come up with anything on the murders over at the jewelry store last week, Hop?" He asked, trying to start a conversation. It was obvious that he had looked at the photos. I didn't want to talk about it, and I knew that if I said anything, he'd want to go through the pictures, with me narrating each one. That wasn't going to happen.

Leo was my age, much shorter and thinner. He wore a hairpiece that was darker than the graying fringe of his real hair that stuck out from under the toupe. I could never understand why he wore that ratty looking thing, but I wasn't bald.

"Not that I've heard, Leo." I put $4.50 on the counter and avoided any further conversation. He was disappointed but my mood had turned chill with the wind blowing off the cold lake, and the prospect of revisiting a nightmare.

The packet of pictures created a pressure under my coat, similar to the way the lists had felt the other night. Like some high explosives, barely contained.

I needed a place to look at the pictures unmolested, and went across the street to the Middle Eastern Grocery. Muhammad was behind the counter, stacked with fresh flat breads. Over in the corner was his father, a wrinkled old man, whose name was also Muhammad, as far as I could tell.

Whenever I came into the little grocery, the old man's eyes would twinkle, he'd grin a toothless smile and say something to me in Arabic. He never said anything that I could understand, but we communicated our respect for each other in a universal language of smiles and gestures.

Muhammad was from the land between the Tigris and Euphrates rivers, now called Iraq. The political situation being what it is, Muhammad usually identified himself as an Assyrian whenever he was asked. It was the same with Iranians in this country. Most of them referred to themselves as Persians to deflect some of the built in prejudice.

I didn't care what Muhammad called himself, he was a good man. I accepted a cup of tea from his ever present teapot, chatting with him until he got busy with customers. Taking the picture folder out of my inside pocket, I sat down with my sweet creamy tea and started looking through the photos, hands trembling slightly.

They were in black and white but my memory added in all the colors. There was a picture of the black and blue bandanna on the floor near Sung's body. I could tell it was a gang scarf by the way it was folded, corner to corner, then rolled to an inch wide. Gang bangers usually wore it around the knee, or hanging from a loop of their baggy pants, to signify their affiliation.

It made me think about Gilly Rodriquez, and not too kindly. I thought about what Georgos had told me about Gilly's actions on the day of the murders, right around the time of the murders. I was going to get my hands on him if it was the last thing I did. It almost was.

Jim Geery had provided me with 36 potential clue bearing photos. I tried to look at them professionally. There were feathers on the floor, could have been from the day bed that Mrs. Park died on. I flipped quickly through the ones that showed her twisted body lying there.

There were several close ups of the workbench and now I saw the molds that Dolecki had mentioned. I had never noticed the little electric smelter, that Park had supposedly used to melt down stolen gold. Maybe he had covered it when I came into the shop, or maybe I had just never looked closely at his work bench before.

The pictures of men, women, and children, most of them Korean, were on the wall behind the bench. Some of them had snow covered mountains in the background, they looked like the same snap shots that Ah had tacked up around his store. None of it told me anything.

Finally, giving up, I saw that Muhammad and his father had sat quietly watching me for the last few minutes allowing me to study the photos. When I looked up at them, they had sad serious expressions on their faces. They were only a few feet from me and could probably see some of the pictured carnage that I held in my hand.

"These are from the other night, Muhammad. From the jewelry store on Farwell." I gestured with the stack of photos. The 'question' was on his lips but he was too polite to ask it.

"We haven't found out who killed them, but I wish I...knew..." I couldn't think for a second. The picture that had ended up on top of the stack was one of Sung Park's distorted face. The bullet had struck him in the left temple and taken the right side of his skull off when it exited. His eyes were open and he stared into my heart.

I didn't realize that I had stopped in mid sentence until the old man said something. It was just a whisper in Arabic, I think, but I knew that it was directed toward me. The old man always wore his little cap, covering his bald pate, and flowing Arab clothing. His dark skin looked desert worn. A circle of prayer beads moved constantly between boney fingers.

Muhammad looked at his father with a little surprise, then at me. I just sat there, not knowing what had transpired, but realizing that it had been something serious. Muhammad thought about how to translate his father's comment for a moment.

"My father says that you will find the path, Cassidy. He says it in a strange way though, I don't know how to put it. He said he prayed for you and saw you find your path." I looked over to the well thumbed copy of the Koran that was always at the old man's elbow.

How can you choose your own direction when Oba-women and old prophets kept telling you that your path was chosen for you? I thanked them sincerely and went out in the chilly night air to try and find my path. The one that was obvious to everyone else.

Without realizing that I hadn't eaten all day, my feet led me up to Cyril's and my usual bowl of soup and a half of a turkey breast on whole wheat. After oatmeal, it was my stomach's favorite meal.

"Oh my god! Hoppy you look terrible. What happened to you?" Irene exclaimed, when I walked into the little delicatessen and took off my hat. She waited for an answer, holding her face with a worried look.

"I don't know. I was fine a minute ago." I looked over at Cyril, who's face showed concern but maintained a man to man smile. I had manly bruises.

"Your face, it's cut and...your eyes...And there's something else that's wrong? Yes? What's bothering you so?" You couldn't put anything past a Jewish mother, a grandmother even less. I liked little old Jewish ladies. They could be a pain in the ass, but I liked them anyway.

"Are you going to give me some of that Jewish penicillin you're brewing in the back, or are you going to starve me on top of everything?" I tried my best Yiddish accent. She ran into the kitchen for a bowl of her rich chicken soup.

"So what happened, Hoppy?" Cyril had a real Yiddish accent. Now that his wife was out of the room, he felt sure that I would give him the inside story on everything that was going on. I looked at my face in one of the mirror tiles on the wall, and saw that Irene might have overreacted, but that I did have some angry marks on my puss. The blueness in the corners of my eyes gave me sort of a sinister look.

I wondered what kind of impressions I must have made on the people that I'd come into contact with today? But then, I didn't have to wonder about some of them. "Believe it or not,

Cyril, I ran into a door." He wasn't happy with the truth, and went to make my sandwich.

While I ate, I let them ask me questions about what most of the people on the street had heard. I gave them some answers, changing the subject whenever I could.

"And how is Officer Benjamin Cohen? Doing a good job, Hoppy?" Irene asked. I couldn't tell how many questions were in the statement. And I couldn't think of any answers.

"I'm sure that whatever he does, he'll always be a nice Jewish boy," I said, not being able to think of anything more stupid to say.

"Oh, of course," Irene said, agreeing with my ridiculous comment immediately. "Do you know his mother, Hoppy? I think that she might know my niece, Miriam..." Cyril smiled a knowing smile at me, and we both tuned her out.

After I left the little restaurant, I stuck my thumb out and a CTA bus stopped in the middle of the block for me. The driver's name was Tony Rivera and Clark was his regular run.

"Last run tonight, Tony?" I asked him while he filled out a 'bus check' for me, writing it out on the hub of the big steering wheel as we headed south on Clark.

"Naw, one more after this one, Hoppy." He sighed, not even half way through his shift.

The bus had a few teens sitting in the back, and eight or nine other people spaced around, some of them together. I asked Tony if he had any problems and he said no. I moved toward the rear and took a seat, not wanting to discuss my earlier mass transit experience, which had come to mind, with Tony.

Everybody was nice and quiet, minding their own business. There wasn't usually any problems when I got on the bus in uniform. The blue hat with the checked band, and silver city emblem, added inches to my six foot frame. My bullet proof vest made me look bigger than my 185 pounds. The bruises, and extra gun rounded out the picture tonight, pretty much assuring calm on the bus by appearance alone. Since Irene had pointed out that I looked like the 'cop from hell', I was starting to feel like it as well.

Balarto had my car finished, clear glass gleamed in every window. He didn't want to take a check. I didn't usually carry more than a couple of bucks on me, to buy a paper or some coffee on the way to work, and I never had three hundred dollars in my pocket. Now it was my turn to twist the screws on him. I didn't care what his schemes to defraud the government were, I was leaving with my car. He could take the check or he could wait for the cash, when I decided to bring it around. He took the check. It was hard to do business these days.

By the time I drove the one block to the station, my pants were soaked through to my skin from the wet seat that hadn't dried much at all. I felt less sympathy for Balarto coldly seeping into my posterior. I only had one pair of uniform pants left. They were winter woolys and I usually only wore them in sub-zero weather with long John's under them. At least they were dry and warm when I changed into them, although more than a little itchy.

There was no one in the locker room and I got in and out as fast as I could. I told myself that I was stupid to continue wearing the heavy, nickel plated .44 magnum, but there were too many monsters under my bed these days. I strapped on all the hardware I could carry and ducked back out the rear doors, scratching at the thick wool like I had fleas.

The bus turnaround is across the street from the station. I found a northbound Clark Street bus, parked and running. It was empty and I pulled on the front doors until they opened. I guessed the driver was using the little bathroom that was in the block house at the rear of the big lot. I knew the trick of how to pull the doors open, but couldn't get them to close. I knew it was one of the buttons on the panel, but the words were worn off from repeated use of the switches. Deciding not to cause any more trouble than I already might have, I took a seat.

I avoided the driver's frowning gaze when he hurried across the pavement to his bus to find the door open and all his heat dissipated. He waited longer than he should have, then started driving slowly up Clark without acknowledging my presence. I didn't bother asking him to make out a 'bus check' for me. From his expression I figured, either he didn't like me very much or things hadn't worked out in the bathroom.

Looking at my watch, the one with the Sung Park band on it, I noticed that it was going on ten o'clock. Another hour or so and I'd be off duty. I decided to run up and see Claire, maybe I could catch her before she finished cleaning up and went home. I needed to end my day on a bright note.

Chapter 25

Pulling on the call wire, I exited the rear of the bus when it got to Jarvis. As I started across the street, angling towards Mama Lea's restaurant, I turned and looked over my shoulder at the game room where the Royals hung out sometimes. I never made it across the yellow line. I turned back, it would only take a second to look in and see if any of the bums were in there.

The front of the building, it was two stories, was red brick and iron bars. The place was built like a fortress. When I had first gotten the foot post, and met the owner of this arcade, he had the impression that all policemen took money. There's a difference between a free donut and a fifty dollar bill.

He didn't impress me. I told him that if he wanted to pay someone to protect his business he should hire a security guard. We despised each other instantly and our hatred for each other has grown steadily over the years. He protected the gang members. I also knew that he fenced their stolen property and was possibly one of Gilly's heroin suppliers.

He'd complained about me regularly, to anyone who would listen, and I gave him as many tickets as I could. Twice, I had gone in there on the day that I knew that the new license stickers were supposed to be posted on his machines and closed him down for license violations. For his second violation, the judge fined him five thousand dollars. His name was Victor Turkonias, but he was known to his friends and enemies alike, as 'The Turk'.

He wasn't really from Turkey. Georgos told me that he was an old smuggler from Bulgaria who had smuggled himself out, when it got too hot for him behind the Iron Curtain. There were surveillance cameras inside the arcade and some mounted in armored boxes on the outside, viewing the street. If he was in his office, in back on the first floor, the Turk would see me coming on his monitors. But I didn't care, all of a sudden, I was in the mood for some Turk tonight.

William J. O'Shea

When I opened the metal grated door and looked in, I forgot all about going over to see Claire and brightening up my day. Someone had really put my foot on the path. The joint was full of Royals. They were all there, Pinchy, Dardo, Dukie. There were four or five Royals that I didn't even recognize, they had hundreds of members citywide.

I knew they were Royals because they were all wearing Royal colors. Royal blue and black. Not just casually, what they referred to as 'party colors', they were wearing prominent colors, 'war colors'.

One of the slime balls, that I didn't recognize, had a sweater over his arm. It was a black, high school type, sweater with a big blue 'R' patch on it, like he'd been on the varsity track team. The words 'All Mighty' were embroidered above it with a bunch of pins and other crap that was supposed to have significance.

The others wore nothing but black and blue, accented with scarves and shiny junk, like a bunch of barbarians. A few had shaved wild designs in their hair to make them look even more bizarre. It sounds ridiculous but these boys were serious, they were at war with someone, and I had stumbled into it. The only thing missing was their commander, the Napoleon of this little army, Gilly Rodriquez.

In the seconds that I used to size them up, they did the same. Nobody moved. I reached slowly for my radio, holding the door with my other hand, and asked the squad operator if he could send a Tact team over here. There had to be more guns in this room than I was carrying, and I was blocking the only way out.

The blaring music made it hard for me to hear him call for a team, but I did hear him tell me that everybody was down on other assignments. I snapped the radio back onto my epaulet and turned up the volume. Casually unzipping my coat, I exposed the handles of my guns, their weapons still unseen. The dispatcher asked if there was any unit up, I didn't care if it was the dog catchers, near Jarvis and Clark to give 2496 an assist. He got no response.

230

At least the Royals couldn't hear that there was no help on the way. I just stood there with the door in my hand, playing a foolish game against superior odds. I realized that I had better get my butt out of there. A few of them sensed my hesitation and smirked. The Turk was the one that got me though, he smiled at me like the Cheshire Cat. Who are you? He smiled at me. Nobody.

Sometimes you win and sometimes you lose. There was a time good sense had to take over. When reputation and responsibility, in the face of imminent defeat, took a back seat to self preservation. Not today. Trying not to snap all the way I mimicked the Turk's smile and took two deliberate steps into the game room, so the closing door wouldn't hit me in the ass.

The place was a cacophony of bells, buzzers, and beeps. Each machine trying to be louder than it's neighbor. The booming music fought with the sounds of space wars and dinosaur battles to be the most prominent.

The video games, some with guns, some you sat in and flew, were arranged around the walls with a double row in the center. On my right was the counter where paper money could be exchanged for tokens to play the games.

The Royals were spaced around both sides of the room, where they had been playing this or that game. Now they just stood there watching me, the games playing with themselves. The Turk was behind the counter. There was a lot of sparkling junk for sale, arranged around him. The door in the rear, that led to the Turk's private office, was closed. It was the only place where someone could be hiding.

I never took my eyes off the Turk, he had a face like a cow and he chewed the stub of a fat black cigar to add to the effect. Swarthy didn't begin to describe this guy. I could smell him from ten feet away. He had black curly hair covering all of the exposed parts of his body, growing out of his ears, even his nose. When he shaved, occasionally, he just picked a line on his neck and shaved up from there. I assumed the rest of him was hairy too, but didn't want to find out.

Always dirty and greasy looking, there were the usual brown stains down the front of his shirt, where tobacco juice would drip onto his fat gut when he spit. He chewed tobacco, smoked cigars and cigarettes too. He just stared at me arrogantly. I took a few more cautious steps toward the counter, trying to watch everything at once, without breaking our eye contact.

"Turn the music down!" I shouted over the noise, making a twisting motion with my thumb and index finger to pantomime what I wanted done.

He looked around at the punks that lined the room, then back at me defiantly. Then he smiled, that smile that I despised, and shrugged his shoulders, pantomiming back to me that he couldn't hear me.

I knew how to deal with this slob. His heart was in his pocketbook. The Juke Box was in front of me. It was one of the new ones that played C.D.s and had enough wattage to power big column speakers that were mounted on the ceiling.

I knew that the volume control was next to him, behind the counter, but since he wanted to play games, I thought of another way to lower the volume. I took two steps and kicked the glittering machine where I thought it's heart would be, as hard as I could, bouncing it off the wall. There was an ear piercing screech and a wailing feedback as the music finally died, along with the Juke Box.

"Hey! You can't..." The cigar dropped from his mouth and rolled off his stomach as he protested.

"Can you hear me now, Turk?" I hollered back at him. It wasn't exactly quiet in there, even with the music off. He just glared at me. I tried to watch everybody around me. Some of the Royals smiled openly now, either at my foolish actions or at the Turk's frustration. The only thing keeping the Royals in their places was lack of leadership. I was looking for their leader, too.

"Where's Gilly?" I stared hard at the Turk. He wasn't so sure of himself, now that he had gotten an idea of the mood I was in.

It was just a flick of the eye, he didn't really look at the office door. Maybe one of the kids over that way moved and I'd caught it peripherally, I don't know, but Gilly was hiding in the back office. Everybody knew it now, and Gilly, watching on the monitors in the office, knew that I knew. What he didn't know was that I wasn't leaving without him.

There was no time like the present, nobody expected me to do what I did. They must have thought that their fierce looks and superior numbers would keep me talking while I waited for the backup that wasn't coming.

I ran for the office door, everyone else was frozen for a second, that was long enough. Then it became obvious that I was going to crash into the office door. It was a strong looking wooden door, but if I hit it the right way, maybe. Standing next to one of the machines, that displayed a dinosaur eating a man, was Javier (Pinchy) Sanchez.

Pinchy was about 20 years old, 5 foot 6, 160 pounds. Skinny legs and big 'V' chest with what I called 'prison muscles'. Whenever the weather permitted he wore muscle shirts to show them off. As I stepped past him and he tried to grab me, I caught his arm and whipped him around in a circle like we used to do when we were kids.

When I had 'cracked the whip' just right, and had him between the office door and myself, I added my shoulder to his back with all the force I had. He crashed through the door, part of the frame, locks, chains and all went with him.

A whizzing baseball bat appeared from the right of the doorway and before he could stop his swing, Gilly whacked Pinchy in the back of the head. Pinchy flew into the shelves, lined with electronic equipment, slid to the floor and lay quietly bleeding.

Before Gilly could recover, I had the bat away from him and pushed him up against the wall with a forearm. He kneed me in the groin and squirmed out of my grasp. I stepped back for a moment and gasped for air, stupidly falling for the oldest move in the book.

Gilly was out the door in a flash and I forced my rubbery legs into action, running after him. He called out something to the rest of the gang, as he crossed the room, running for the front door, but it was drowned out by the Turk's screaming something and wildly waving his arms.

I ran after Gilly, heading for the door. Someone tried to step in my way and I shouldered him into one of the machines like a half back breaking through the line. As he tumbled to the floor, the machine lit up and let out a whistle, I think I scored a goal, or whatever. Not waiting to find out if I'd won anything, I was out the door before the rest of them could mobilize.

I don't know why Gilly didn't just gather his boys around him and make a stand in the game room. I would never know if I didn't catch him. I pounded down Clark Street after him, trying not to think of what this reminded me of.

*   *   *

We were running south on Clark. After about half a block, Gilly pulled his, 'cut into traffic' trick, and I followed him recklessly. When we reached the west side of the street, I risked a look over my shoulder and saw a wave of royal blue and black. They poured out of the arcade, flowing like an oil spill down the street after us.

Luckily traffic had gotten heavy in both directions for a moment, and became a temporary barrier to their pursuit. Before I knew it we had reached Touhy, and Gilly cut right around the corner. It was a few steps before I reached the same spot, but I saw him darting across the street and into the alley that ran behind Clark.

I crossed the busy street, not looking for traffic, and ran down the alley after him. My mouth was dry and blood pounded in my ears. Gilly looked over his shoulder at that point and tried to redouble his efforts when he saw that his little diversion hadn't worked. The first block went fast, when we got to the next cross street, he cut over west a half block, to Ravenswood. It paralleled the wall of the Northwestern commuter train tracks.

With each step, the extra weight that I carried made me feel as though I would crash to the ground. The night stick banged against my leg and the straps of my heavy vest grated on my neck. Handcuffs clanked and keys rattled, until I must have sounded like an old wagon rolling down a dry riverbed.

Just as Gilly looked back in fear of his pursuer, I did the same. Five or six figures were keeping pace, only a half block behind me. I searched for reserved strength to redouble my own efforts, but found I was barely able to keep up the distance between us.

I tried to concentrate on strength and stamina. The graffiti painted and repainted along the cement wall on my right jumped out at me, declaring who's neighborhood this was. Who ran this territory? The blue and black paint said 'Royals'. Funny things went through my mind as I tried not to think about the pain in my shins. I thought of the rabbit who was chased by the wily silver fox, only to be saved when a pack of wild black and blue dogs ate the fox.

My lungs couldn't gasp enough air to keep my legs from burning and my side from starting to hurt. Gilly started back toward Clark when he got to Greenleaf, maybe thinking to hide at Marie's house, then cut back into the alley that ran behind Clark Street, still going south.

He was less than a hundred feet away from me now. How many steps would I have to take, for each one of his, to overtake him? How many did I have left? He was half my age. Even though I had been working out and running for years now, I had never run like this. Not since I was a kid at least. I remembered running from the police for breaking street lamps, and how the thought of capture had spurred me on to escape.

I couldn't risk a look over my shoulder now, if they were closing on me I would just have to deal with them when they got here. I wasn't worried about them shooting, besides making too much noise, even gang bangers know that you can't hit anything when you're running.

I thought about the fleeing figure of Gilly Rodriquez and how he was the only person who might have seen what happened to the Parks on the afternoon that they were murdered. He may have even been involved. Although I couldn't see this little Puerto Rican half breed breaking someone's neck, he could pull trigger. I found a few more coals in the bottom of the bucket and added them to the fire.

By the time we got to Morse Avenue both of us were staggering. Gilly crossed the street and continued on down the alley toward Farwell. Neither one of us could really run anymore. I chanced a look over my shoulder and didn't see anyone directly behind me. I didn't have time to focus farther away. At Farwell he turned east and headed for the lights of Clark Street.

I'd have given anything for a squad car to be waiting up at the corner. Anything to stop Gilly from running, because I couldn't run anymore. Not a step. I hadn't called for help, because it might have slowed me down enough for the dogs to catch up and I wouldn't have been able to talk anyway, I was breathing so heavily.

When I rounded the corner of the alley, hoping that someone I knew might be coming out of the Limelight Pub up on Clark, there was no Gilly in sight. I knew he couldn't have made it up to the corner yet, so he must have ducked, either into the doorway of the apartment building here on the alley, or gone behind Georgos' place. Had the rabbit gone to ground, trapping himself in a hallway, or was he trying to double back and call the dogs?

Passing up the building entrance, I ran into the little alleyway that they shared with the Limelight Pub. Gilly must have gone this way last Thursday when Georgos threw him out of the pub. After he had seen or been involved in the murders. This was a short cut that he would know because it was his territory. It was also my beat and I knew that.

I knew that by this time of night Georgos would have locked the back gates, closing off access to the lane that led back out behind the six flat to the alley. If he had come this way, Gilly had found his escape route blocked by a ten foot chain link fence. I hoped that he hadn't been able to climb over the fence, because I couldn't even breathe. I had a side pain that felt like 'The Big One'.

I tried to take stock of the situation. I was in a ten foot wide gangway (poor choice of words), lined with garbage cans and dumpsters. On my left, twenty feet down, I could see light coming from the alley, shining through the links of the closed gates. Listening for footsteps pursuing me, I asked myself if I had heard the clanking noise of someone climbing over the fence. I didn't get an answer, everything was quiet, but I got a break.

A cardboard box between two big blue dumpsters quivered, there was no wind. I still hadn't caught my breath yet but my side pain was starting to feel like it wasn't a heart attack. What could be in the box? A rabbit? A rat? A combination of the two.

After I rested for a moment more to catch my breath, I wound up my black Oxford and kicked the box as hard as I could. I was rewarded by the body of a yelping Gilly Rodriquez squirting out the other end.

He smacked his head into the back wall of the Limelight Pub and fell over, temporarily stunned. I ripped the cardboard box out of my way and knelt, none to gently, on his back.

Chapter 26

"Hello, Gilly." My cuffs hadn't fallen out of my belt during the chase and I snapped them onto Gilly's wrists as quickly as I could wrestle his hands behind his back. I searched him carefully and found no weapons.

We both heard it at the same time. It was just a word in Spanish, but I knew that it wasn't my guys. With my left hand, I pulled Gilly's little pony tail braid until I had his head back. Then I stifled his cry for help with my right hand, covering his mouth.

Frozen in place, I prayed that my radio wouldn't give me away. Shadows crossed the alley light that came into our little hiding place. I hunkered down over the prostrated gang leader, trying to look like just that much more garbage. More voices calling, then figures ran across the only exit from this cubbyhole. I was even afraid to reach for my gun, thinking that I would draw their attention. All I could do was pray. Did I pray? Hell yes, I prayed.

They went up toward Farwell, nobody came into the gangway. Gilly relaxed under me and I realized that with my knee in his back and my hand over his face, he couldn't breathe very well. Letting up on the pressure a bit, I turned his head halfway around, as far as I could turn it without snapping his neck, and saw the white of his right eye bulging out at me wildly.

I made a 'shushing' sound, quietly asking him not to make any noise. He seemed to understand perfectly. I let up on some of the extreme positions that I held him in, but kept my hand over his mouth.

"Home boys!!!" Gilly bit my hand and got the words out before I could stop him. I found a new use for his braid and played paddle ball with his head and the ground until he understood that I was upset with his failure to obey my request. Then a couple extra times to stun him out of attempting it again.

I unsnapped the 44 but didn't draw it, my hands were pretty full already. We waited in silence for an answer to his call. After a few minutes, when they didn't return, I figured that we were in the clear, at least for the moment. Unsnapping my radio, the air had been quiet, thank God, I called for help.

"All units. Stand by!" The squad operator had to ask for quiet, when the urgency of my need became obvious by the tone of my voice and heavy breathing. It seems that whenever someone's in trouble everybody starts talking all at once.

"Clark and Farwell? 2496, I have you down at 7353 on Clark." I had moved a little since my last communication.

"Clark and Farwell. That's a ten-four, Squad. I'm alright, I just need a car to transport a prisoner." And me too. The words stammered out through ragged breaths. I was in no mood to discuss how I had gotten to where I was. My heart was only beating at 200 beats per minute now.

"All units in 24 are down, 2496. 2472? 2423? Any unit in the area of Clark and Farwell to assist the foot man with a prisoner?" There was just static in answer to his inquiries.

"Keep trying, Squad. I'll start walking him down Clark." At this time of night everybody tried to stay down on their last job so they wouldn't chance getting an assignment that would run late. The wagon men and the personnel on 2423 acted like they didn't even hear the request. The dispatcher kept trying though.

Tuning him out for the moment, I used the handy pony tail to get Gilly to his feet. He was a little wobbly. He tried to kick me and I bounced him off the dumpster a few times, stopping myself before I started to enjoy it, like Brian White used to.

"You're dead, Cassidy, you mother..." A good yank on my Gilly handle cut his tirade short.

"Gilly, shut up or I'm going to rip this thing off." I lifted up on the braid, pulling him to his tip toes, for emphasis. He shut up.

Peeking out of the little alleyway before stepping out, I pushed Gilly ahead of me when I saw that the coast seemed clear. I held him by the cuffs now, my left hand between his wrists. Simply lifting up on them would put him off balance, not to mention the pain that he would feel in his shoulders.

When I got to the corner, Georgos was standing on the front stoop of the Limelight Pub, looking around, trying to figure out what had caused him to come outside on such a chilly night. He had his usual white apron around his waist with his shirt sleeves rolled halfway up. When he saw me walking up towards Clark, his extra sensory perception was satisfied, then he pointed at Gilly.

"Basilli! You caught him. That's the one who was in here the other day!" He came towards us as though he would throttle Gilly on the spot. Gilly, seeing the same look as I did in the Greek's eyes, tried to hide behind me. I yanked on his cuffs and got him where I could handle him.

"Georgos, go back inside." I was having enough problems.

"You're dead to, you fat son of a bitch." Gilly got brave when he realized that I wasn't going to let Georgos do anything to him. Georgos came after Gilly, not realizing anything.

"Please, Georgos. Just go back inside and I'll take care of him." I said it in a way that I hoped conveyed several things to my friend. He saw the determined look on my face and the bruises on both Gilly and myself, and backed off a step.

"But you're by yourself. I help you." He insisted.

I thought about taking Gilly into the pub but I didn't want to draw attention to Georgos or the fact that he was hiding the Korean Papers for me. "There's help on the way, Georgos," I said as sincerely as I could.

"They're going to meet me down at the next corner." He looked at me, knowing me better than I wished.

"Go back and watch what you're supposed to be watching." I gave him one of his telepathic looks, and he reluctantly went back into the bar.

I started south on Clark, dragging a protesting Gilly Rodriquez along with me. "What you lockin' me up for, Cassidy? You searched me. I ain't got nuttin on me."

"Maybe I'm not locking you up, Gilly. Maybe I'm taking you into the station because you're a material witness in a homicide. Then again, maybe I'm taking the murderer himself to the station." He didn't say anything, there were a lot of maybes in that nonsense. I looked around, not sure that I had ditched the Royals.

Gilly's 'home boys' never materialized. When we got to Pratt, the end of his territory, Gilly started to fight with me again. The Royals wouldn't cross this street if they were at war with the Disciples. He twisted out of my grasp and ran into the street with his hands cuffed behind him.

I ran after him, thinking of what they would do to me if he got hit by a car with my cuffs on his wrists. Catching him in the middle of the intersection, I took my night stick and poked him in the back with it a few times, to get him moving out of the street.

We ended up on the east side of Clark. I put the night stick between the cuffs and his wrists. Any movement in a direction that I didn't want him to go, brought him course-correcting pain. People passing by on the street turned and stared, cars slowed down to watch the spectacle.

After we'd gone about a block. Gilly started shouting. "Folks! Folks! Come help a brother!"

At first I didn't know what the hell he was shouting about. There was no one around, Royals or Disciples. Then I caught the license plate of a passing car. The Disciples had affected the use of Illinois Conservation plates to identify their gang cars.

The plate had a red Cardinal on it. I don't know if it was the red color, or the bird that signified their gang, and didn't care. Now I had the Disciples to worry about. The car immediately turned west at the next corner, possibly going around the block.

It was only four short blocks to the station now, but they were getting longer all the time. "Why are you calling out to the Disciples for help, Gilly?" I had him in front of me, holding him with my left hand as we walked.

"I thought you guys were at war?" He tried to turn to speak to me and I turned him back, pushing him south.

"We ain't at war with the Folks," he said sarcastically, as though I had said something ridiculous.

"You're at war with somebody. Who?" He told me to go and do something, that is physically impossible, to myself.

The car with the conservation plates didn't return, I guessed that the Disciples had enough brothers in their own gang. That was the second time that the 'Folks' had minded their own business, and done me a favor by it, today. We were in the middle of the next block, when Gilly pulled up short, causing me to walk into the back of him.

"What do we got to walk for? Ain't you pigs got no cars?" I pushed him ahead of me, but couldn't argue with his logic.

He held back again and I saw what was really holding him when I looked over his shoulder. There was a car, double parked, down the street. It was on our side of Clark, facing north, and it was a black Honda. I couldn't see if there were any passengers, but it looked like someone was sitting behind the wheel.

"Friends of yours, Gilly?" I asked the now struggling gang leader. He was wearing the same kind of wild bright blue and black as the rest of the slobs that were in the arcade. If these were my friends the Gray Eagles, they would be sure to recognize Gilly as a New City Royal.

I stopped walking, thinking that he might not have such a bad idea. We were in front of the Nigerian television repair shop and I pulled Gilly into the doorway. Oboda, the Nigerian who owned the shop, had closed much earlier. He never had any business anyway. I think that he must have taken a TV repair course off of a match book cover, then come to America to make his fortune. He'd better find a new business or he'd be going home soon.

"You tricked, man! I know you did! Mother fuckin' tricked me off to the Eagles!!" Gilly found new strength and we had another tussle in the little space between the sidewalk and the door. I had him pushed up against the window now, with the ancient televisions on display beyond it, but he wouldn't stop screaming. If he knew what kind of guns those Eagles carried he would shut up, I was sure.

"You pigs. You're the fuckin' killers. You killed Razor!!!"

"Who the hell is Razor?" I thought that I knew all the dead people around here.

"You killed him, man, you ought to know who he is. You threw him out the window. Now you tricked me off to the Eagles. Don't let them get me man. I didn't know they were in it when I told you they did it." He was whimpering now, practically in tears.

Well, now I knew who Razor was, David Tso. The ex-leader of the Gray Eagles. They all had these tough names, or secret names or other childish nonsense. I didn't have time to find out everybody's gang name, David Tso, or Gilly Rodriquez identified them well enough for me.

Gilly had his head stuffed in the crack between the window and the door, so he didn't see the activity when it began. And it began with a flourish. A body flew from left to right, across my field of vision, about four doors down, on our side of the street. The body went from where it had emerged from the line of store fronts, about five feet off the ground, sailing over the sidewalk to land on the hood of a car parked at the curb. Next to that car, double parked in the street, was the black Honda. That sent a chill up my spine.

The body lay quietly on the hood, (where had I seen this picture before?). Then it dawned on me which storefront doorway this guy had just been launched from. Chung's Tai Kwon Do Academy.

"2496, I need assistance here at 6625 north on Clark. There's a major gang disturbance happening here, Squad." I tried to sound calm and professional, but I was trying to run and drag Gilly along with me, while I was calling for help.

"All units STAND BY!" I heard him say. "All units, we have an officer in need of assistance..." I tuned him out, if help came fine, right now I was nearing the school and another body came flying out. It was Chung. He had managed to hold onto his stick when they tossed him out the door. Actually the door was still closed, the glass was missing, apparently taken out by the first person to be thrown out of the school. Three dark clothed figures came out after the old man. He fought them from where he lay on the ground.

Chung was unbelievable. He kicked and twirled, fighting with his feet and the stick, spinning on his shoulders, almost standing on his head. He obviously couldn't stand up. If he had been able to, he surely would have made short work of these gang bangers. He kept the three off of him, each receiving blow after blow, but I couldn't see how the old man could hold out much longer.

When I finally managed to drag Gilly, fighting and screaming, over to where Chung lay on the sidewalk, I got a better grip on him. There was glass all over the ground and I hoped that I wouldn't fall. Sure. Putting my left arm up under his cuffs, I grabbed his collar and had a useful shield for my left side. The first blow that he received was a karate kick, it rocked us both and I was glad that he had taken the brunt of it.

Taking my stick in my right hand, I struck out over Gilly and effectively used him to push back the three attackers. I now saw them to be all Asian, one of them was Key, the L.S.D. freak. The one that had landed on the car hood, probably launched there by Chung, came back to life and soon they were moving into position to surround us. Chung was on the ground behind me, I kept moving Gilly around to keep them off of us.

Gilly took a few more kicks and punches from the two on my left, and I poked my stick into the face of the third. Gilly started to sag, I think that they enjoyed kicking him as much as trying to get to me. I didn't mind, except that Gilly was getting quite heavy now, he was a junkie and weighed almost nothing, but my arm was tiring.

I had forgotten about a possible driver of the black Honda, but Chung hadn't. He let out a string of what sounded like curses and the direction of his ire caused me to look away from my four immediate attackers, to the street.

Inon Moon, or Tae Cho Han as he was apparently known in North Korea, stood there in the street between the parked cars and the Honda. He still looked like he'd been living in a sewer and he had one of those square looking little machine guns in his hands. He was pointing it right at us.

Moon said something I didn't understand and our four attackers backed away, obviously moving out of the line of fire. I dropped the night stick and tried to pull the .44 mag, but he had me dead. He had us all dead.

Just then Master Chung, and I will call him Master from now on, let loose with one of those scary karate yells. It froze Moon for a split-second, which was long enough for the man who had killed dozens in death matches. Master Chung took his walking stick and broke it in half. Actually it only looked to me as though he had broken it in two, it was designed to come apart. There was now a thin blade protruding from the end of the walking stick.

Master Chung was injured and couldn't get up, but that didn't mean that he wasn't deadly. The sharp point gleamed in the street light. Things happened fast, but the events burned into my memory. The old man said something that sounded like the equivalent of spitting on the ground.

All in the same split second, he threw the spear, that's what it had become, straight at Moon's face. I could almost trace it's path to where it would plunge into Moon's eye. I knew that they could create anything they wanted in Hollywood, make superhuman feats look natural, but there was no film editor on the street that day. I'm still not sure that I believe what I saw.

Inon Moon, the ex-laundry man, moved his head, only a bit, but just enough. His right hand shot up from where it held the back of the 'street sweeper', and he grabbed the spear out of the air. He caught the damn thing as it went past his ear. I didn't even have time to register my shock. At the same time, he let out a triumphant answering scream and jumped over the parked car. He seemed to defy gravity. One second he was in the street, then he just sort of rose up from the ground, sailed over the car and was standing over Chung with the spear in his hand.

Gilly was useless, dragging me down to the pavement with him. Moon had managed to reverse the point of the spear while he was doing all these other magic tricks, and was poised to plunge it into the old man lying helplessly before him.

Moon yelled again, something that sounded like, 'NOW YOU DIE!' in any language, and started to drive the gleaming point down into his prostrated victim. The nickel plated .44 Magnum was in my hand, Gilly was pulling me down with him, I didn't aim, I just fired.

The boom was louder than I ever remembered it being at the shooting range. The hollow pointed slug, as big as the tip of my thumb, thundered out of the short barrel and struck Moon before he could impale the old man on his own weapon.

Moon had sought to kill Master Chung with his own weapon, a traditional weapon. Why didn't he just spray us with the machine gun when he had us cold? What had the old man said that changed Moon's mind? Did the South challenge the North, did Master challenge Master? I didn't think about those things at the time. The gleaming tip of that spear held my attention like a dancing cobra, and that was what I had unconsciously fired at.

Moon's right hand practically disappeared. Pieces of the spear skittered down the sidewalk. Blood leaked from the stump that had only ragged tissue hanging from it. Moon grabbed his bloody right wrist with his left hand and knelt down in front of Chung. He bowed low and whispered something to Chung. Then he looked at me and said a few more words in Korean. Moon lowered his head until it rested on his folded knees and just stayed in that humble position.

The rest of the Eagles had regained their ability to move and were starting to run for the car. I hadn't heard the sirens or noticed the blue lights, but suddenly there were more coppers around than you could shake a spear at.

Alex Garcia tackled one of the fleeing offenders and another one came flying at me backwards. He landed on me, pushing me all the way to the ground, grinding me into the broken glass. I looked at the face, it was Key, and he was out cold. Looking up, I saw the smiling face of Mike Pape standing in the street.

"Got here as soon as we could, Hop!" He laughed as he grabbed another fleeing Eagle by the hair and practically lifted him off the ground. "And where do you think you're going, young man?" He said, laughing gaily. The cavalry had arrived.

Sapper was there, but he was useless in a fight. He came over to me, smiled, and lifted the inert body of Key off of me. I let go of the almost unconscious Gilly Rodriquez. Sapper turned to Master Chung, who ignored Bruce's attempts to assist the injured man.

"You all right, old man?" He grunted when he got no answer from Master Chung. The old man just stared at Moon, kneeling their motionless. Sapper bent over the kneeling, or was he praying, Inon Moon. He touched the laundry man's neck, then turned to me.

"This one's dead, Hop. Had to shoot this one, huh. Couldn't find a window high enough to throw him out of?" He laughed jiggling. I just looked down at the cannon in my hand, not believing what I had done.

Chapter 27

Everybody went to jail. When they dragged a beaten and sorry looking Gilly Rodriquez to the wagon, cuffed to the rest of the wobbly Gray Eagles, he pleaded with me. "Cassidy, don't let me go with them! Please, man, I'll tell you anything you want to know!"

Sapper told him to shut up or he was going to do, something that I couldn't hear, to him. Gilly went into the wagon protesting all the way. I wasn't really listening though. I didn't really care what Sapper did to him, my attention was fixed on something at my feet..

He was just a small heap on the sidewalk. How could he be dead? I fired, sure. But I hit his hand, didn't I? Maybe he was hit by a splinter of bone, or could it have been a ricochet? I couldn't bring myself to examine the body, there was a pool of blood forming around it.

A Fire Department Ambulance was on the scene and they were putting Master Chung on a stretcher, it was obvious that his bad hip was totally useless now. He seemed to be in great pain, but he met my eye with a fierce glare. It seared me to the bone; talk about telepathic looks. I think that even if I'd had a picture of his stare, to study at length, I still would never understand all of what was in that look. The one thing that I did understand, clearly, was that some kind of bond had been forged between us.

The Sergeant had a piece of blue plastic and was unfolding it over Moon's body. For a second I didn't realize that he was waiting for me to catch the other end, so we could cover the body. When we had covered him, Moon looked like a small lump under the square tarp. Like a bag of laundry, only half full.

Sergeant Davis walked away from me, pretending to be interested in the traffic control situation, and talking on the radio. Everybody was distancing themselves from me. Collateral liability was heavy in the air. I could imagine what the comments would be. 'Cassidy shot his gun. Where? Up on

Clark Street.   But that's not all.   He didn't use his service revolver with department issued ammo.   He used a .44 Magnum, and now there's a guy lying on the street dead'.

'This blocking Clark Street with dead bodies, is getting to be a regular thing with Cassidy, isn't it?   Sure is.   He won't be around for very long'.   It seemed as though even the civilians, who managed to get close enough to view the scene, looked at me as though I was guilty of something.

The ambulance, carrying the old man, pulled away.   He couldn't help me, even though he might want to now.   He'd seen the same thing that I saw.   I shot the guy in the hand and he died. The problem was that nobody was going to believe that.

I had the Tact Teams out looking for any gang bangers dressed up like they were extras in a Kung Fu movie, especially anyone dressed in blue and black.   There were a bunch of prisoners already.   I wouldn't be handling any of them once we got into the station however.   Knowing that I was soon to be on the hot seat, I slipped into Master Chung's Tai Kwon Do Academy to make a phone call, brushing shards of glass from my pants as I went.

The Lieutenant was out in front, and was talking to Sergeant Davis now, after only the briefest glance at me and the pile of laundry on the sidewalk.   He was probably trying to decide whether he should disarm me right now, or have me driven into the station and do it there.   While he struggled with the decision making process, I looked around for a phone.   I guessed that I could do anything that I wanted until he finished flipping his coins.   The office was dark but I could see that a battle had taken place here.   The buzzing phone led me to where it lay, upside down on the office floor.

Holding the base in my hand, and the receiver to my ear with my shoulder, I fumbled the business card out of my pocket. Jurkov's number was hard to see and I had to hold it up to the light that came in from the street to read it.

A digital female voice verified the '800' number and told me to speak at the tone.   "This is Basil Cassidy.   I have your boy,

Moon, up here on Clark Street. He's under a tarp. I'll probably be at the station when you get this message, being fitted for my own tarp."

Had this card been just a piece of paper or was it really what I hoped it was, help? Or was it in between? Lieutenant Franklin came into the school and called out to me in the semi-darkness.

"Cassidy? What are you doing in here?" He asked.

"Looking for possible additional victims, or offenders, Sir," I answered. You were always supposed to be on the lookout for victims, but you only got credit for any offenders you found.

"There are people assigned to this scene." I wasn't one of them, apparently. "I want you to go into the station with me." At least he wasn't going to strip me in the street. I hung up the phone and placed it on the desk.

Following him out of the building, I realized that I could hardly walk, every nerve in my body was protesting. Franklin, a big man who had to bend in half to step through the broken door, took long strides. He waited impatiently for me at his car. I walked slowly, resigned to my fate but not rushing toward it.

I don't remember if that was when I decided to retire, but I hope that it wasn't. Though it was definitely sometime that night. The somber atmosphere, caused by White's death, was gone when we reached the station. It didn't take long for something to happen to force everybody back into the old groove. A police shooting was just the thing. People bustled about during the shift change, going around me like a school of fish goes around a rock.

Cohen was in the station and was one of only a few who talked to me. He asked me, lamely, if there was anything he could do to help. Knowing that he couldn't do anything for me, he was alarmed and happy to go to the hospital and look after the old man.

Two television trucks, with the telescopic antennas sticking through the roofs, pulled up just ahead of the Deputy Superintendent's car. They were out of their little vans with cameras rolling and microphones ready. Six people surrounded the unmarked car, jockeying for position while the transmitters on top of their trucks extended and began to scan the heavens.

There were two teams. Each had a camera man, a person who held a bank of lights, and the live reporter. That person, the only one that didn't look like a derelict, was the one who asked the questions. The one that you saw on T.V.

There were both men and women. They were all good at their jobs. They blocked the Deputy's path, bobbing and weaving, keeping him off balance and in the lights. It was a fire drill in the revolving door, but when they had all fallen over each other and gotten into the lobby area, they regrouped and attacked again.

"Deputy Kurwicki, has the police officer been charged with any department violations? Has he ever shot anyone before? How is this incident related to the suicide of Officer Brian White and the increase in fatalities in the Asian Community?" That last stupid question was from the cute little blonde, that I didn't like anymore, on Channel 3.

"I have to repeat that I have no comment...at this time." Kurwicki, smiled into the camera. He was loving it. He'd have a comment later, that was obvious.

"We understand that the latest victim," now Moon was a victim, "was not a gang member but another Korean businessman who was caught in the officer's crossfire," the other newscaster said, reaching over his counterpart's shoulder with his microphone. I was definitely not watching Channel 12 anymore either.

"We're still investigating, Jim. I'm sure I'll know more in a little while." 'Jim'? The Deputy was on a first name basis with the guy from Channel 12. I was sure that he would know more in a little while, too. I was sitting in the Watch Commander's office, able to see the entire scene through the window and hear it through the open door.

The deputy asked the sharks to wait, 'just a few minutes', while he conferred with 'his officers'. Lt. Franklin, who was the Watch Commander tonight, met him outside the office and they talked for about a minute, standing behind the desk. Then Kurwicki stalked into the office, glared at me with handsome blue eyes and went into the Captain's private bathroom. He didn't flush the toilet, but the dent that his hat had made in his movie star hair had been finely combed out when he came back.

Franklin came into the office and closed the door. All of a sudden everybody wanted to talk to me. Kurwicki and Franklin barraged me with questions. The answers to all of them were nails in my coffin. I acted dumbfounded, it was easy. When I found my voice I asked them to allow me to call the Fraternal Order of Police and have them send me some legal advice. I ignored their looks and started to read the little notice on the inside of our Union hand book on what to do when involved in the 'Use of Deadly Force'.

Deputy Kurwicki was very upset when I didn't break down and confess to murder. His threats fell on deaf ears. I knew what was bothering him. The time it would take for the F.O.P. to send me a lawyer would probably cause the news teams to rush off to another part of the city. There was always some juicy mayhem happening somewhere around Chicago.

"Lieutenant Franklin, take Officer Cassidy's star and I.D. Also, I want his weapon inventoried and sent down to the Crime Lab for testing." The news people were filming from the other side of the desk and Kurwicki used hand gestures to accentuate his orders. Relieving me of duty in pantomime.

If the Deputy hadn't made it clear that he was currying the attention of the media, the Desk Sergeant would already have put them out in the cold. There are mini-blinds on the floor to ceiling windows in the watch commander's office, I wondered if the Deputy would mind if I closed them?

"Aren't you supposed to give me some kind of written notice, or advise me of my rights?" I said after reading it in my little book. Kurwicki looked at me with revulsion in his eyes.

"You'll have your 'lawyer', Officer, and all of your contracted rights." He spit the words out at me, as if all the lawyers and Union contracts in the world weren't going to save me.

I had just made up with George Stokes and of course he was gone when all this happened. Now this guy wanted to use me to get his puss on television. I could tell that Lt. Franklin was afraid of this 'heavy' from downtown and was going to let the Deputy do anything he wanted to me.

"Have you actually done any of the investigating that you told Jim you were going to do?...Sir." I amended, when he looked at me wildly. Who was I to question him?

"What? What investigation? Jim who?" Then he looked out the window at the now milling throng of news goons.

I smiled at him. "You're not the only one who's on a first name basis with the media. Sir." He went wild, screaming at the top of his lungs. The cameras came up and the lights went on. He rushed over to the window and practically ripped the blinds down trying to close them.

"You're a real wise guy, aren't you, Cassidy?" He said, after he had composed himself a little. Kurwicki was one of the guys who had been promoted, 'within the building', as it was called. He'd spent most of his career working downtown, at Police Headquarters. They considered the men in the Patrol Division the lowest form of humanity and a constant embarrassment to the 'Department', which they ruled from their tower on State Street.

"Would you listen to me if I told you that you're doing the wrong thing. Not establishing the facts before you promise a 'big story' to the press?" He was a little taller than I and stood over me with his fists clenched while I sat comfortably in the visitor's chair.

I smiled up at him. "Or should I just tell you to 'kiss my ass' right now, and get to the end of our conversation right away?"

I thought I had him with that one, but he didn't flip. He agreed that he should get more facts before 'we go any further', and asked me to wait outside. My false confidence must have given him food for thought. It wasn't doing me any good, however. Lt. Franklin was sure going to have a hell of a story to tell when this was over, if he wasn't afraid to tell it.

The voices in the office rose as soon as the door pulled itself closed. The cameras panned me as I left the office, heading for the locker room. I still had my service revolver and apparently no permission to carry it. I was half way down the hallway when I heard Donny Cramer's voice over the PA system.

"Officer...Hopper...you've got a call on line one, Hop." Good old Donny was trying to give me a message without letting the media know that it was for me. At least I thought he was, I knew that there was no Hopper in our district.

There are no phones in the locker room, for obvious reasons. Coppers had the most creative minds. So I had to go elsewhere. Cutting through the roll call room into the sergeant's office I sat at one of the battered desks and saw that there was no light on line one. I picked it up just in case the phone lights were broken and got a dial tone.

Shrugging it off, I went back to the locker room, to put my gun away. I wondered if I could change out of uniform. The wool pants still had me scratching like a dog with fleas and now they were ripped and dirty. So what else was new? Standing by my locker, I started to reflect on my killing a man and how I felt about it. I thought about telling Claire what I had done, expecting her to look at me either sadly, or with revulsion. Maybe she had been the one who had just called me and hung up. What happened to my plan to brighten up my day. It was dark outside now, and inside too.

The door opened, I could see who it was if I leaned over a bit. Mike Pape came around the jamb and walked over to me. "We're down on the paper, I'm not going back out there and get that body now. I don't care what they say." I didn't know if he was talking to me, or just talking.

"What are you talking about, Mike?" I said, smiling at one of the guys who had just saved my bacon.

"Damn detectives think that they can order us back on the street. Something about the body. Let somebody else do it, we get stuck all the time. I'm gonna put our names on a couple of those arrests, okay, Hop?" He wanted to stay down on the arrests and not be available for assignment to transport the body. As far as I was concerned he could have all the arrests. I told him as much.

He had a big sloppy grin on his huge, Saint Bernard, dog face. "Thanks, Hoppy. I can use the overtime when it goes to court.

Pape just stood there, across from my locker, looking at me. I was undressed and had other things to worry about. "Well, if you're going to get some court time in you better go put your name on some of that paperwork." I said.

He didn't get the hint, big as it was. "I've got to get dressed and do some report writing myself. They just took my star and ID." That got a reaction out of him. I decided to change the pants at least.

"They had no right to do that! Did you call the Union?" I nodded.

"Are you suspended, or what?" He asked. Mike was a nice guy, but I was tired.

"I guess. I'm still waiting for the F.O.P. lawyer, or whatever they're supposed to send me." I felt like I was standing in a hole, (that I'd dug for myself), waiting for them to start throwing the dirt on my head.

"But I thought it was all over now?" He said to me, I just looked at him wearily. "I mean that the whole thing is solved now. That guy out there killed the people in the jewelry store, and you killed him. That's the end of it now, right?" It sounded so simple. He was rambling, trying to console me in some convoluted manner, I just couldn't answer him was all.

"I'd better go give Bruce a hand," Mike said uneasily, after he watched me stare into space for a minute, suddenly more tired than I'd ever been before. I must have looked it too.

"Officer Cassidy. Please come to the desk." It was Donny again, but this time it meant something else. Some one had given him an order, and me too.

The lobby was still packed, although the cameras weren't rolling and the lights were off. Jim and 'what's her name', the blond from Channel 3, were having a private conversation with Kurwicki, who was probably begging them to wait around until he could get my head in a noose.

There was a nerdy looking man in the Watch Commander's office. He had a baby face, was about 5 foot 7, thin as a picture in a missionary magazine, with wispy brown hair. He wore a thread bare overcoat and brown shoes that were worn out on the top. He turned out to be my lawyer.

Burnbach, that was his name, was in a 'wait and see' mode. He listened to my story attentively, making notes on a long yellow pad. His wire rimmed glasses had fingerprints all over the lenses, but that apparently didn't obscure his vision. What vision there is when your prescription is 20/400. When I told him that Kurwicki had taken my star and ID, he said that they weren't supposed to do that. The stupid Union handbook had already told me that.

My lawyer was sort of new at this game. He told me that he had recently left his first job at the Public Defender's Office to begin working as a junior attorney for the Union, and might not be defending me in any upcoming hearings. That was a relief. What hearings? Apparently I had already been convicted, and this guy was planning the appeal. Every time Burnbach lost a case as a Public Defender his last words to his client, as they led him off to jail, were probably 'don't worry, we'll appeal'. I'd heard mostly good things about the F.O.P. lawyers, but that must have been the ones that worked during the day. The night shift was woefully lacking.

Lt. Franklin had given us the office for our 'conference'. He must have been laughing his ass off. I knew now what Kurwicki was telling the media people. 'I'll have him served up on a silver platter for you, as soon as he's finished conferring with his attorney, ha ha'.

I noticed some movement through the now open blinds covering the big windows. It got my attention easily, as Mr.

Burnbach, with his fatalistic counsel and gravy stained brown suit, weren't making it.

Kurwicki was standing just outside the door, with Franklin flanking him, talking to a civilian who had his back to me. Kurwicki became animated and I could see why the cameras liked him so much. He was the picture of authority, giving orders, not taking them.

I was just about to step over to the door to get a closer look, when Kurwicki opened the door, stepping in front of the man he had been having the animated conversation with. The man stepped aside, giving way for Kurwicki, but the Deputy stopped when he had come face to face with the civilian. Kurwicki towered over the man, obviously feeling superior. His only problem was that the man was Stanley Jurkov.

"I am the ranking authority in the City of Chicago! Mr..." His voice reeked authority.

"Jerk-O." Stanley helped him out, prodding him at the same time. I could tell from Stan's voice that the Deputy had the 'bear' by the tail. It didn't look like the Deputy was going to have a very good night, if Jurkov had anything to say about it. Mine, however, was looking up.

"Yes, uh. Now see here, you have no jurisdiction here. I don't care what agency you're with. The victim is a local businessman who owns a cleaners just down the street from where he was shot. There is no Federal crime here." Kurwicki was building confidence. Jurkov was just calmly listening to the Deputy.

"And who do you think you are to give my people orders at the scene of a homicide? You can't interfere in a police investigation. I'll have you locked up." Kurwicki's voice was commanding now. He had his downtown 'we run this city' attitude, turned up all the way.

Kurwicki looked down at his pure white shirt and perfectly pressed uniform pants, gold badge, patent leather shoes. It was obvious who commanded here, especially when you compared him to the haphazard appearance of the National Security man.

William J. O'Shea

"Where's your authority to do anything in this city? I doubt that you can produce it at this time of night. Now, I strongly suggest that you leave, and take it up with Headquarters, in the morning." It was a threat.

The grin faded from Jurkov's face and Kurwicki took a step back when he saw what was under it. Burnbach and I took steps back also, away from the man with the strange look on his dark semi-bearded face and the Deputy who looked like he might bolt and run.. I could see Cohen now, smiling like an idiot, standing behind Jurkov.

"Is there a private line in this office, Lieutenant?" Franklin nodded. "What's the number?" The lieutenant gave it to him without comment, or without asking Kurwicki's permission.

The lieutenant told my attorney and me to wait outside. We almost ran out of the office. Kurwicki went over to the phone, his superior attitude shaken slightly. He picked it up and started to dial for more confidence. Probably waking his mother up.

"I heard that you had a bunch of arrests, Hop. Done with all the paperwork already?" Stanley said to me smiling, as he gestured toward my semi-civilian clothing.

"I've been relieved of duty. No star, no gun, no paperwork." I shrugged. My lawyer just stood there like a coat rack.

"Oh, yes." That reminded him of what he was going to do when I'd walked out of the office and he had joked with me. "Excuse me a minute, will you?" He took a small portable phone out of his coat pocket.

Stanley Jurkov was wearing a crew neck sweater and slacks, that didn't go together, under his topcoat. Obviously living out of a suitcase, I remembered that his driver's license was issued in Virginia. Turning his back, he walked over to the side door that was just a few feet from us and stepped outside. Better reception and less chance of being overheard, I guessed.

Cohen was buzzing with the desire to say something, but was wisely keeping his mouth shut in the presence of a stranger. When I noticed that the 'coat rack' was keeping Cohen from speaking, I introduced my attorney to the rookie.

"Steve Burnbach, Benjamin Cohen. Landsmen." I just pointed at each of them.

"You can say anything you want in front of him, Ben. This is my attorney." Burnbach came to life, nodding to Cohen and trying to look competent.

"Nice to meet you, Sir." Cohen was a rookie. They thought that everybody was their superior.

"Besides, I don't think he understands anything that's going on anyway." When I finished my statement, Burnbach looked at me as if he didn't understand what I had said.

"So?" I had to coax the information out of Cohen. "Were you trying to tell me something, or do you want to go to the bathroom?" I joked with him a little, to get him going.

"Yes...No. Do you know that guy?" Cohen asked me referring to Jurkov.

"Just tell me." I gave him my best fatherly look.

"Oh. Well, he came to the hospital and talked with Master Chung." Cohen paused, amazed.

"Okay. Did you hear what they said?" I wanted to shake him a little.

"Yes, I did." He was watching Jurkov through the plate glass, as the man talked on his little phone.

"Well what did they say?" I wanted to throttle him.

"I don't know. Did you know that he speaks fluent Korean? I couldn't understand a word of what they said. But they got along just like old friends." Cohen had a new person to admire. Good, I didn't feel very admirable at the moment.

"I'm not surprised." I touched his arm to get his attention, I wanted to sock him one. Talking to this kid was like pulling teeth. "What else happened, Ben?"

"Well, he made me go with him in his government car. I had to leave my car at the hospital...I tried to call you...but, he said..." Cohen was worried about his car.

"I'll take you back to the hospital myself, to get your car. Now will you get to the point?" I was reaching for him.

"Well, you know that phone he has? Somehow they cut him in on our zone and he spoke to the Sergeant. Told him not to do another thing until we got there. He drives like a maniac. When we got there, Sergeant Davis was ordered to turn over the scene to Mr. Jerko. That's not his real name is it?" Cohen hadn't told me anything yet and if he was going to, he didn't get the chance. Jurkov came back into the building.

He shook himself like a huge black wolf. "Not used to this cold weather, been spending too much time in the desert." He smiled knowingly at me. I didn't know what the hell he was talking about and didn't want to speculate on it. At the moment I couldn't care less what happened in the deserts of the world, I had the whole world on my shoulders, right here on Clark Street.

"We should have some movement soon." He said confidently. I was doing my own version of a coat rack. Cohen was beaming at Jurkov, reeking adoration.

The phone rang in the Watch Commander's office. It was loud, so that it could be heard when they weren't in there. We all jumped. Not Jurkov.

Lt. Franklin answered it, like a secretary, while Kurwicki composed himself. When he took the mouse eared receiver in his hand, he had his television look on his face. He listened for a moment, then tried to say something but was cut off by the person on the other end of the line. Kurwicki's confident look faded and he nodded his head repeatedly, then answered 'yes' a few times and hung up. He didn't look up at us, but Jurkov took the end of the phone call as a signal. He motioned for his ragtag bunch to follow him and walked into the watch commander's office, without knocking.

Kurwicki just stood there looking down at the old time telephone, as though it was a lifeline that had just been cut and was out of reach. "Do we have an understanding of the chain of command, Sir?" Jurkov said, 'sir', like you would say it to someone who was not your superior.

"What? Oh yes. You seem to be in charge, Mister..." Kurwicki still couldn't remember Jurkov's name. It didn't matter.

"Fine. I'm in charge, and you, sir?" Jurkov said the same way.

"Me. Uh..." He couldn't believe it, whatever it was. "I'm relieved of duty. He relieved me and I'm to be reassigned to the Patrol Division." I felt sorry for his new men at the district where he would be assigned. Kurwicki kept looking down at the black plastic phone, thinking maybe it might ring again and the caller would say it had all been a mistake.

"No. You're not relieved, yet." Jurkov had that mischievous look on his face. Kurwicki looked up at him.

"First, you will return whatever you took from this officer, then apologize to him." Jurkov was enjoying putting Kurwicki in his place. I was starting to feel sorry for the guy, even though he had tried to throw me to the sharks. Burnbach didn't know what the hell was going on. I wondered if Kurwicki needed a lawyer.

"What? Oh, of course. Lieutenant, return the items to Officer..ah..Cassidy. I'm sorry, Cassidy, a misunderstanding, I'm sure..." I said, it was 'Okay' quickly to stop his embarrassment and mine.

"But the weapon has been fired, sir. Any time an officer on duty..." Franklin started to quote regulations. He hadn't been ordered by any telephone caller to break department regs. Jurkov held up his hand and turned to me. Kurwicki didn't say anything, he was relieved.

"You want the gun, Hop?" Jurkov asked me casually, as if it was a cup of coffee. He cared nothing for Chicago Police rules and regulations. I had them ingrained in me, I was a cop.

"No. You better let them take it and check it out. I did shoot the man." I thought back to the shooting grimly.

Franklin handed over my star and ID and Kurwicki picked up his gold checked hat with the scrambled eggs on the bill. Running his fingers through his luxurious hair with a sigh, messing it up, he prepared to leave. He moved toward the door, but Jurkov wasn't through with him yet.

"And before you leave, clean up that mess you made with those media people. Tell them it was all a mistake, and you made it. Tell them that Officer Cassidy is a fine policeman and a credit to the department. Tell them that," he ordered. Kurwicki stepped out the door to the waiting lights and cameras, a little out of character.

"Thanks, Stan." I said smiling, and as sincerely as I could, he smiled back warmly. Jurkov asked Franklin to do a few things for him and requested the use of the office for a little while. Franklin got the message, he changed gears smoothly, and took the befuddled Burnbach and Cohen with him when he left.

"It's a good thing that I stayed in town. I had a feeling that you were going to get some movement on the situation soon." Jurkov grinned broadly at his intuition.

"Good thing. The movement was almost in my pants." We laughed together and then he gave me one of those pats on the back again. The one with all the responsibility attached to it.

"Phew. That stuff really stinks." Jurkov was holding a handkerchief at arms length, talking to himself more than me.

"What?" I said, but could now recognize an odor that had been faintly in the air ever since...?

"Almonds, can you smell the bitter almonds?" Now that he put a description to the smell it was clearly there. He tossed the handkerchief on the desk in front of me. Then he started looking through the Captain's desk, as though it was his own.

"What's it for?" I said stupidly.

"It's for killing yourself. I wiped this over your boy Moon's lips." He smiled and continued rummaging through the drawers.

"They watch too many old spy movies in North Korea, I guess. Ahh..." He found a pair of dress uniform white gloves in the bottom drawer and took the plastic bag that they were in, putting the almond stinking cloth in the baggy.

"You mean...?" The light was flickering in my numb brain.

"That Moon committed suicide? Yes. Prussic Acid. Very deadly stuff. Even if nobody uses it anymore." He looked up at my stupefied expression.

"You mean that I didn't...?" I tried to ask again.

"No, you're still a virgin. Still shooting the guns out of the 'bad guy's' hands, Hop-Along." I sat down in the chair unable to stand the relief that went through me.

Chapter 28

"We caught Moon's wife in Seattle, trying to board a plane for Japan. I don't know where she thought she was escaping to. Pyongyang has already abandoned them. North Korea claims, through unofficial channels, that the whole thing is a South Korean/American plot. She's better off, we'll take better care of her than they would have anyway," he said, trying to bring me back to reality.

"She's already been...disarmed, I guess you could call it that. We relieved her of a ceramic tooth, a rear molar, that had the same stuff in it." He picked up the deadly plastic bag and put it in his pocket.

"She was glad to get rid of it, I'm sure. She had every opportunity to use it, and didn't. I know I would be chewing lightly myself, if I had one of those things in my bridgework." He laughed, and I tried to laugh with him.

"All this spy stuff is too much for me." I turned and saw Cohen's baby face, grinning widely and practically pressed up against the glass.

"I see that you've appropriated my side kick. Where's Agent Trigger and Nellie Bell?" I said, referring to Vandeveer and Leonard Pace.

"They went to Seattle to capture Mrs. Moon." He smiled, I thought about the pinched faced old witch.

"I know the woman. They should all get along well together," I said, laughing for real.

"She's small potatoes. I think he was too. Sometimes these deep cover agents get smuggled in here, and then just sort of forget that they're supposed to be spies. They start to like the life here in America, and sort of forget to check in from then on. Sometimes they 'come in' and start working for us, we also pay better than anyone else." He was thoughtful.

"Moon and she have been here since 1975. She's told us everything she knows, and it seems that she doesn't know very much. The husband was the real spy, she was just added for color. She wasn't even sure of what their assignment was. They may have been here just to keep an eye on the Colonel. I don't know..." I squinted at him for a second, part of what he'd said just registering.

"Colonel? Sung Park was a Colonel?" I said, when I finally got it. I acted as though I hadn't just remembered what Ah had told me of Park's background. I didn't have to change the stupid expression on my face at all.

"Yea, he used to be a big shot in the South Korean Army. Back in the fifties." He looked away again, then back again with a question in his expression.

"Hop, I can't see why Moon would watch Park for over twenty years and then kill him. What can you tell me about the murders of Sung and his wife?" I tried not to look like I had a lot to tell.

I reached in my pocket, took out the picture folder, and tossed it on the desk. "I don't know what I can tell you. Here's the whole thing, in black and white. Take a look at them and tell me if you can see anything there that I can't." I didn't want to look at them any more. They only told me things that made my eyes water.

"One of these gang bangers in the back, Gilly Rodriquez, promised me that he would 'tell me anything that I wanted to know', which is quite a lot. I'm not sure what he has to tell, but he was around at the time of the murders. I think I'll go have a little chat with him." I got up to leave.

He was still looking carefully at the first picture, one of the little back room, with a rickety metal legged table, worn vinyl covered chairs, and a hot plate with a cold tea pot resting on it. "It doesn't look like they were exactly living in the lap of luxury, does it? You want me to go with you, Hop?" Jurkov looked up at me from under shaggy eyebrows.

"If you want. But I'd rather not scare him too much to start." I smiled, and by his look, he conceded that he could scare the wax off the floor.

I left the office and started down the hallway after winking at a concerned Donny Cramer, who smiled relief in return. Cohen was standing there buzzing in place and I told him to 'stay'.

I went down the side hall to the lockup, passing up the little rooms where prisoners were processed, among other things. Mounted in the wall next to the big steel door of the detention area is a door bell and a grill with a speaker behind it. This enabled the lockup keeper to speak with anyone wishing to gain access.

I pressed the button and heard a loud buzz on the other side of the heavy door. After a second, without anyone checking who was ringing, the lock in the door clicked. It opened when I pulled on the thick metal handle.

Inside was an anteroom where you were still surrounded by bars. On my left, in the wall, was a number of lock boxes for visitor's weapons. They were mostly unused, some had keys missing. Over the years many officers had been shot with their own guns, by prisoners, even though there was a rule against guns in the lockup.

It still happened. The barred door, that was supposed to be locked until I put my gun in a locker, was open as usual. I had no gun, so I just walked into the lockup. These were not serious violations of actual penal security, nobody was escaping from this lockup. Rules and regulations were always designed for overkill.

Across from me were the banks of cell blocks, on the left was a little kitchen. On the right was the counter with several desks behind it, and beyond that was a big barred room, sometimes referred to as the drunk tank. There were a few customers in there. The lockup keeper, Alvin Lee was sitting at one of the desks behind the counter, tying a trout fly with a piece of thin plastic line.

"Hi, Hop. What's up?" He said, trying not to show annoyance at having to look up from the feathers and hook that he was working on. The fly was clipped to a bracket that attached to the edge of the desktop.

The top of the counter, it was about chest high, had a number of prisoner's property envelopes on it. The packages were clear plastic, that had been heat sealed by Alvin, after he'd filled them with all the possessions of each prisoner.

Through the plastic, I could see all of the keys, belts, wallets, and junk that had been taken from the arrestees. I saw the package that had 'Guillermo Rodriquez' written on it along with his case booking number. I copied the number in my little police handbook.

"Alvin, I want to talk to one of these assholes."

"I don't care what you do with them, Hop." He was a 'good old boy', from back in the 'holler' in West Virginia. He knew that my mother had also come from somewhere back there. Although she'd left the hills thirty years before Alvin, he still considered me some kind of relation.

He had his tongue hanging out, and was screwing it around as he used the needle nosed pliers to wrap the fishing fly. I hoped that we weren't 'that' closely related.

Also written on Gilly's property envelope, was the block number and cell that he was in. When I started toward the door with a big 3 painted over it, I noticed all the shoes lined up along the wall. They were an odd collection of gym shoes. Manufacturer's had so many gadgets on shoes these days, and the laces were considered a suicide threat, that it was easier to just take their shoes away than searching every smelly pair.

I could tell which shoes were Gilly's, they were black and blue. Shoes were made in every color of the rainbow so they could fit the Gang's decor. The big door to block 3 was open. Inside, there were six cells, three to a side, all bars, so the ceiling cameras could view all activity in each block. The cameras watched everything, nobody watched the monitors much.

Gilly was lying on the stainless steel bench, that was attached to the back wall, in the first cell on my left. The rest of the cells in block 3 were empty. I had asked Alex Garcia to make sure Gilly was kept separate from other prisoners.

"I ain't sayin nuttin widout my attorney's presence." Gilly spoke from a prone position, without looking up at me. He must have heard me out by the desk talking with Alvin. He tried to play it cool, but it was difficult when you were behind bars, in your dirty stocking feet.

"You should be asking for your school teacher instead of your lawyer, Gilly. The Disciples are continuing their education, something you should consider," I said, shaking my head at one of societies failures.

"Dem 'Folks' ain't shit, man." I vowed to watch my pronunciation more closely when I listened to him speak. He was apparently willing to say a few things, 'widout his attorney's presence'.

"You promised to tell me 'anything that I wanted to know' up on Clark Street. I only have a couple of questions to ask, and then you can go back to sleep." He was going to answer my questions, right now, without anyone else being present.

"Tell me what happened at the jewelry store last Thursday?" I really only had one question. I was holding onto the bars anxiously, looking between them, so I could watch his reaction.

He sat up quickly. "You had a lot of fun lettin dem Eagles beat the shit out of me while you hid behind me, like a pussy. Now you can kiss my ass, Cassidy." I could see some scrapes and bruising on his face now, but he obviously wasn't hurt badly at all. I knew that he wasn't hurting as much as I was. I thought about what I said to Kurwicki. How did it feel to have someone tell 'you' to kiss 'their' ass? It had only taken me an hour to find out. When was I going to learn?

"I'm going to put you in the cell with the Eagles, and let them soften you up some more, if you don't start talking." I tried not to let it show that I was bluffing.

"Fuck you, Cassidy. You ain't the boss in here, this ain't Clark Street. That red-neck out there runs this jail, and he ain't gonna let you do nuttin to me. And I ain't answerin' no fuckin questions widout I talk to my lawyer first."

"You know me Gilly." I gave him my fiercest glare. "If you don't tell me and I find out later that you were involved..." I let his imagination take over. He looked at me. I thought he was going to flip.

"Go ahead and try somethin', Cassidy, I know my rights." That was about the only thing he knew. The jails were full of innocent people who were all legal experts. Gilly had no rights unless somebody wanted to give them to him. I could strangle the information out of him, and hang him from the bars with his shirt if I wanted to. It would probably upset Alvin, because he would have to stop tying trout flies to clean up the mess. Other than that, it was just a suicide report.

Gilly was right, though not for the reasons that he thought. I was not going to, or have someone else, beat information out of him. That was just not my style, but I wasn't giving up. "No, I have a better idea. I'm going to turn you over to the Federal boys, who are waiting outside. They'll take you down to the federal detention center and in a little while you'll be begging them to let you talk." I wished.

Gilly, I hoped, was not so sure of himself any longer. He shouted after me as I left. Whether to impress himself or other gang bangers within hearing, I wasn't sure. "Boracion!!! Ha, ha, ha."

"You'ns want the key, Hop?" Alvin looked up at me, his half glasses down at the tip of his nose, when I came out of the cellblock. He motioned toward the ring of giant keys that was on the desk next to him. If I wanted them I'd have to get them myself, he was winding line around a new hook and a little piece of brown fur.

"No. I'm too exhausted. I'm going to see if I can get someone else to question him, though." Alvin smiled, misunderstanding my meaning.

"Somebody needs to teach that boy a lesson. Thinks he's a big shot or something. Nothing but a smart mouth dope addict is all. Gold chains don't mean nothing to me." I was thinking about going home to a cool pillow.

"Gold chains? What gold chains?" The light went on again. I had a little surge of energy.

"Look for yerself." He motioned toward the row of personal property envelopes. "He had five or six gold chains. Acted like they was worth a million bucks. Looked like cheap shit to me."

"At first he refused to give them up. Then I told him how I enforce the rules around here." He gave me a crooked grin. Alvin was a skinny guy. He carried a lead slap jack in his back pocket to add a little weight. He wasn't a sadist, but you couldn't work the lockup without having to fight with an occasional prisoner. And you couldn't lose any of those fights.

I found Gilly's plastic envelope and held it up so I could see what was in it. After I pushed the contents around a bit, I saw a smaller plastic bag emerge from under his wallet. It contained a small gold ring, that I had seen him wear before, and a bunch of little yellow squiggles that glinted brightly at me. I had him.

Gilly was lying calmly on the bench when I marched confidently back into the cell block. "Where'd you get all these gold chains, Gilly?" I could hardly contain my elation at finding a real clue to the Park murders. Every word I said, hit a nerve.

"I want my lawyer," he said, like a baby asks for a bottle.

"I'm as anxious as you are for him to get on the case, Gilly. Then, when he's standing there next to you in court, I'm going to have the judge ask you where you got these gold chains. And by that time, I'm going to be able to prove that they are from the scene of a homicide. Ha, ha, ha." I accentuated each phoney laugh, spitting the words at him.

He jumped up from the bench like an electric charge had just gone through it, and ran at the bars, the toes of his socks flapping. He grabbed the bars as if he would tear them open.

"Them chains ain't from no murder. I got them from Marie. Ask her. Them chains ain't stolen...I mean they ain't from that jewelry store." I laughed some more to let him know what I thought of that theory.

"Murder, Gilly. Double murder. And I'm going to put you at the scene of the crime." I smiled as broadly as I could. "You have anything to volunteer now, Gilly?" He slumped against the bars.

"You pigs are shit. You're gonna frame me with dem murders. I want my lawyer!" He cried for his lawyer, who I was sure wouldn't answer the phone if he knew that it was Gilly Rodriquez calling at 2 in the morning. From the lockup.

As I was leaving, I had another thought. "You won't be getting out, Gilly. Not tonight, not tomorrow. When was the last time you got high?" I laughed, and left the sad looking junkie scratching his elbow 'pit' unconsciously, and probably thinking that it had been too long already.

*   *   *

I told Jurkov about the interview, but he didn't seem very impressed with my evidence of gold chains and Greek bartenders seeing Gilly around the time of the murders. I thought that I had something at least. He just shrugged off my theories.

He handed the packet of photos back to me. "I don't know what you're going to get out of these gang members, but at least one of those pictures looks suspicious to me."

"Which one? What did you see?" I took the stack out, the one he was referring to was on top. It was the photo of the bandanna, folded in the gang style, lying next to Sung's body. I remembered that the colors were black and blue, royal blue.

"You see that spot next to that handkerchief. It looks like a stain on the carpet." He pointed with a pencil that had been on the captain's desk and was now Jurkov's.

The bandanna was folded to about an inch wide, pressed flat and tied in a loop. I could see what he referred to as a 'spot' next to the gang scarf. It was about the size of a dime, cut in half. Sung's old brown loafer was in the corner of the picture, lying just over the top edge of the scarf. I said I saw the half moon shaped spot, but didn't understand what he was trying to tell me.

"If that's a drop of blood, and I think it is, then half of it is under the handkerchief.   But his foot is on top of the handkerchief at the opposite end. That says to me that the body fell and the blood splattered there first. Then someone lifted his foot and put the gang scarf under it to make it look like the gang was involved." My hopes were fading into a familiar fog of confusion.

"A little too convenient, that gang members would leave such a strong piece of evidence against themselves, in any case." I'd asked him to look for something that I couldn't see in the photos, but I didn't ask him to shoot my only lead to pieces at the same time.

"Maybe it's one gang trying to frame the other." I threw that out, hoping it might float, doubting it would fly.

"Maybe, Hop. But I think that they're all too smart for that. You know there may be more than one false clue...you have to be ready for anything." He looked at me seriously, trying to fortify his comment.

"What do 'I' have to be ready for?" That look made me nervous.

"Now that we have Moon and his lovely wife, we've already gone over his house and business with fine tooth combs, I've got to go back to Washington." He looked at me, knowing that he was giving me what I considered bad news.

"The murders of the Park's, the gangs, or whatever else is happening regarding all of that is your job. I have to agree with your Deputy Superintendent on that." I could feel that symbolic pat on the back that he liked to give me.

I tried to get him to take Gilly and the Eagles down to the Federal building for interrogation or possibly lie detector examinations, but he said that he didn't think it was worth the effort. The Eagles were just hired mercenaries and he didn't think Gilly was worth the powder to blow him away. Neither did I, but I didn't know what else to do.

"There'll be someone keeping an eye on these gang members. I'll be kept informed. You know how to get a hold of me if you need anything," he said, trying not to make me feel totally deserted.

He made sure that he said goodbye to his newest fan, Ben Cohen. The kid looked like he was losing his best friend. I sort of felt the same way.

"Be careful, Hop," Jurkov said to me, when I walked him to the revolving door. It wasn't the kind of 'be careful' that you say casually to someone, not really meaning anything. He gave me a look that was half Georgos' telepathy and half Master Chung's eerie mysticism.

"Careful of what?" I was shaken into another stupid comment by his two word warning.

"I'm not sure...but it's not over, is it?" He hesitated, standing there with his hand on the edge of the door panel.

It wasn't a question. "No," I said resignedly, "I guess it's not." He shook my hand and told me that he was sure that everything would work out for me. Another prophet.

Chapter 29

As I watched him walk to his car, which was parked in the same place as the last time he'd been here, I thought about what my next move should be. I decided that I had to get those papers from Georgos. Even though Moon was dead, I still didn't want to take any chances with the Greek's safety. I decided to take them, and...what?...I was back to square one.

What would Park want me to do? If I gave Jurkov the papers, someone would get hurt. Sure, it might be someone who deserved it, but it would be because of me. Because I had given the lists to the wrong person maybe. If Sung Park had wanted anyone on those lists hurt, he could have done it himself.

Knowing that I had court in the morning, I went into the tactical office, where Cohen had found someone that was willing to take advantage of his enthusiasm. Doug James had him stapling copies of Case Reports together and filling out log books. Cohen was playing 'Tactical Officer'.

I looked over his shoulder to see what court the arrestees were going to, and what the charges were on each. "Simple Battery? Is that the best you could do on Rodriquez?" I asked James. I felt that Gilly should have at least been charged with 'Aggravated Battery on a Police Officer', a felony. I thought they all should have been charged with battery on me. Someone had battered the hell out of me, that's for sure.

"Sorry, Hop. We had so many other pinches...and he had your cuffs on him...so we didn't know..." They didn't know if I was going to be around after the Deputy got through with me. He handed me back my cuffs. More collateral liability concerns. I couldn't blame them. Nobody wanted to have anything to do with somebody that I'd arrested. Especially after I'd supposedly shot a passer-by, trying to arrest Guillermo Rodriquez.

"Okay, Doug," I said. He looked relieved. "I was going to ask the State's Attorney to upgrade the charges in court tomorrow anyway."

"You better add your name to the arrest report if you're going to go to court on Rodriquez. Sapper and Pape took that arrest. You know that they don't like two guys going on the same case unless they have different testimony." There was a lot of abuse of overtime, and court was a good place to cheat. It didn't matter, because I no longer cared about overtime. Sapper and Pape could have it all.

"What else did you get out there?" I said, changing the subject slightly when I saw Cohen playing with a little machine gun like the one that Moon had pointed at me.

"Three of those nine millimeter 'street sweepers', a couple of hand guns from the Royals that we found wandering around. Between us and the other teams, we got nine heads and six guns." He was thanking me in a way, smiling at their success. This was a major arrest, there would be citations given out. I was thinking about being pursued by gang bangers, who I now knew for sure had been carrying guns. I'd come close to being awarded posthumous citations, again.

Garcia came over to put another completed report on the desk in front of Cohen. "We couldn't find the Turk, Hop. He was closed up tight when we got there. Do you think that we have enough to get a search warrant?" These young coppers didn't know when to quit, thank God. I, however, had had enough.

"No, I don't think so. And I'm not going to be waking Judge Presser up in the middle of the night. Us 'old guys' need sleep, and that's just what I'm going to do. We'll get the Turk tomorrow, or the next day." Judge Eric Presser was an old friend and the 'go to' guy when there was a quick warrant needed in the district. He'd signed more than one, while in his pajamas, in the wee hours of the morning. He never acted as though he minded being woken up by these 'gung ho' young men at all hours.

I couldn't see how he could not mind, but I also knew that he was a good man and public servant. Sometimes you did things that were not included in the usual days work, for the good of the community. Or just because there was something in you that made you do it.

"Don't forget, you said that you would drop me off at the hospital, to get my car," Cohen reminded me. I sunk down another rung, barely able to keep my eyes open now.

"Yea. Okay, rookie, let's go." When I called him a rookie, Garcia and one of the other tact team guys snickered. It was unkind of me to embarrass the kid like that, but I was in an unkind mood.

I forgot to get some plastic bags and lay them on the seats so we were both soaked by the time we got to the parking lot behind St. Francis' Hospital, in Evanston. Cohen said he wanted to look in on Master Chung, and I declined the invitation to wake another old man up in the middle of the night.

It was 2:30 a.m., and I was totally exhausted. Feeling badly for doing so, I called Claire and asked her if I could come over to her house instead of driving all the way home. In a sleepy voice, she asked me where I was calling from, and when I told her I was just a couple of blocks away, she said she'd leave the door open. But I had better not have any ideas of tapping her on the shoulder, once I came to bed. I assured her of my trustworthiness, and my exhaustion.

When I got there, and tiptoed into her house, she was sitting on the sofa, wearing a silk bathrobe. "Well, now that you've awakened me, you may as well tell me what happened tonight."

I was startled, shoes in hand. "What?" I said stupidly.

"I was having a dream about running, a bad dream. You were in it. Then you called and wanted to come over, to sleep. Since you're here I'm not worried any longer, but I still want to know what I was worrying about. So before you go 'to sleep' I want to hear the story." These Oba-people were getting the best of me. She looked beautiful sitting there. I laughed when she tried to make a stern face, but she wouldn't give in until I told her something.

"Well, your dream was partly right, but I'm just going to give you an outline. I really am tired, okay?" She agreed, I must have looked pitiful enough. I filled her in, and when I told her that I was thinking about retiring, she was delighted. Not as though she was happy with my decision, or maybe decision, it was as though one of these nuts in her family had another dream and everybody knew about it before I did, again.

At that moment, all the prophets and soothsayers in the world, would only have been able to predict one thing about me, and that would have been that I was going to sleep. Claire even had to wrestle my clothes off when I crashed on the bed fully dressed.

Eight o'clock came soon enough, and I woke to the smell of bacon and coffee cooking. I don't care how bad it is for you, that's one of the best smells in the world. The next thing I thought about was, did I have any of my stomach pills so I could counteract Claire's cooking. Then I thought about going to court. My body wasn't answering the signals that my brain was sending, and when it did start to move, every nerve ending screamed in protest.

Claire's shower was a rubber hose, hanging over a pole, surrounded by plastic curtains. It was crude, but it brought me back to reality somewhat, as I scrubbed my skin with a loofa sponge and shampooed the white mop with some smelly female stuff.

"Well, you look better," she said smiling, when I had dressed, in my still damp clothes, and walked into the kitchen searching for smells.

"I had only one direction to go." Smiling, I fingered my too long hair back on top of my head when a damp lock fell down. She handed me a cup of coffee, island style. It was so thick that even after I had filled the cup to the brim with milk, it was still a dark brown color. Well, at least I'd be wide awake at court.

The little television, that she had on the counter, was on and tuned to one of the local morning news programs. Claire put a plate of sunny side up eggs, bacon, and slices of fresh papaya in front of me. My mouth started watering. I told myself that I'd

William J. O'Shea

run enough last night to deserve this hearty breakfast, my stomach agreed with me.

While I was sending a stomach pill down with a mouthful of breakfast, something familiar on the TV caught my eye. "This is the scene of an explosion and fire that occurred early this morning."

It was my buddy 'Jim' from Channel 12. He was standing in front of a burned out building, out of focus in the background, while the camera zoomed in on the newscaster. The scene behind him was dark, indicating that this was a tape and not live.

"Just before 4 a.m. this morning, the residents of this quiet community were awaken by a blast. The huge explosion was followed by a fire that engulfed an entire building. The family on the first floor, of what used to be this two story building behind me, all escaped without injury. The Fire Marshall stated that they will have to wait until the ruins cool before searching for possible victims." Jim was wearing the same cheap suit that I'd seen him in at the station, so I figured that he had gotten stuck all night on this fire.

"It is suspected that there is at least one death involved in this incident. We have a citizen here with us, who was next door when the blast occurred. He states that he saw another resident, who has not been accounted for, enter the building shortly before the explosion and fire." I wondered why he was telling us what the guy had to say if he had the person standing there with him.

The camera angle changed, to pick up the person who Jim was talking about. It was another person I knew. It was Jack Bailey, and he was stinking drunk. Jack was a roofer, who I used to 'tip a few' with, in my drinking days. Being a roofer was a job that was also conducive to drinking. When it rained you spent the day in the tavern.

Jack looked like he had been drinking all day and night. He tried to compose himself when the camera panned over to him, as most people do, which only made him look more intoxicated. Jim was really scrapping the bottom of the barrel if he could only get Jack Bailey to interview. I sort of felt sorry for the tired

278

looking newsman. "Mr. Bailey. What can you tell me about the explosion and fire that occurred here early this morning?" Jim stuck the microphone in Jack's face, a move that I'd seen before.

Jack was small and muscular, like most aerial workers, and stammered when he answered. I was paying close attention now. "I don't know how it happened", he said slurring. "We was just closin' up the tavern when we heard it. BOOM. It shook the whole building. Then we ran outside and it was already all flames. We got the people out of the first floor, but we couldn't get upstairs to the attic apartment. We called out, hoping that we could wake him up. I tried to go in there myself, but it was just too hot." He was really upset, I was getting upset myself.

"And who lived on the second floor of this building? Who was it, that you tried to rescue, but couldn't?" Jim was setting the viewers up for the dramatic conclusion. Jack was weaving. It looked like he'd had a few shots since the fire to bolster his courage.

The camera panned from Jack to the smoldering ruins behind him. I couldn't recognize what it used to be, but I had a hunch. "The guy who lived there, was Hop...I mean Basil Cassidy, he was a Chicago cop." The look on Jack's anguished face matched my own. The smoldering ruins of my house. The only thing good about it, besides my landlord and his family being unharmed, was that they weren't going to find my body when it cooled. And that wasn't very good.

*   *   *

Strange place, the mind. The first thing that I thought of was the huge pile of dirty clothes that had been building up on the chair next to my bed. There was no need to find a new cleaners now, I didn't have any dirty clothes, or clean ones either.

Claire was looking over my shoulder and figured out everything that had happened. She squeezed my shoulder, I saw her biting her knuckle when she turned away, heading for the bedroom. I started switching channels on the television frantically, trying to find one that would tell me the story again, or better yet, one that would tell me that it hadn't happened.

Claire came back into the kitchen. She had been crying, but there was pure happiness in her eyes now. She stopped smiling long enough to kiss me, wetly, and hug me like a child. I didn't feel very happy, but the look on her face was so comical, I had to laugh.

I figured it was more Oba-stuff, and was beginning to appreciate it if it kept me from going home last night. Then she gave me a key and told me that it was because she didn't want to be awakened in the middle of the night. When I came home.

What did I do to deserve people this wonderful in my life? Just as I had started to realize the panic of 'homelessness' she throws me a life preserver, happy as a lark. For a moment we just held each other, for slightly different reasons, as tightly as we could. I thanked her and asked her if this was what it was like to have her grandmother have dreams about you. She acted like I was joking and started the dishes.

At this point I was willing to believe that I was in the twilight zone. If her grandmother, up on the side of a mountain in a mahogany forest had done something to help me survive last night, God bless her. While I was asking for a blessing for Grandma, I quietly gave thanks for the lives of my downstairs neighbors and tried to count my blessings. Hell, I'd been in worse shape before and made it. I was beating alcoholism, I could handle anything.

Making some phone calls, I found out that I was able to brighten several peoples days, just like the commercials said you could. Georgos thanked every god that he had ever heard of, when I called him. He started singing, but he sounded like he had been crying too. He immediately offered me a place to stay and when I told him about Claire's offer he was even happier.

When I called the station, Jerry Manning, the desk sergeant, went crazy. He started hollering, "Cassidy ain't dead! Cassidy ain't dead!", at the top of his lungs. I could picture his smiling freckled face, and pencil thin mustache, when I thought of the feisty little Southerner. It brought a smile to my own face.

Many people had once had a superior, or in my profession a sergeant, who had made such a great impression on their lives that you would risk anything if that person told you 'it would be okay'. Jerry Manning and I went back to my rookie days, when we were both possessed of all the things that went with youth. He had been 'my sergeant' and I would always be one of 'his men'. I could understand his joy at my being alive, I wouldn't want to lose him either. The loss of my meager possessions had brought about quite a bit of happiness. I still wasn't too thrilled about it, though.

When he calmed down, he'd started choking, maybe on some of that foul tobacco that he chewed, he told me to call Bomb and Arson right away. "The detective that's been assigned is Timothy Dolan. Call him so he can stop looking for your body." Manning laughed at his joke, I didn't, and he gave me the number.

"Hello. My name is Basil Cassidy...I" That was as far as I got.

"Just what the fuck are you, Cassidy?" Dolan asked me without any cordialities. It had taken a dozen rings and he sounded like he was on a mobile phone.

"What?" I said, a little startled by the unique way that he answered the phone.

"First you're dead. Not just regular dead, blown up and cremated. I'm covered with soot, looking for your damn teeth in a hot bed of ashes. Then I find out that you're shooting people last night and had a Deputy fired. This god damn portable phone, that they make me carry now, hasn't stopped ringing for five minutes. Some fucking guy called me from an airplane, for Christ's sake. I asked him where he's calling from, and he tells me he's 30,000 feet over the Virginia. At the time, you were only dead about an hour. How the hell did he know? Now you're alive! Bullshit! I want to see the body alive or dead,

281

before I do another fucking thing!" He sounded like he'd been under a bit of stress.

I didn't give a damn. "I've got to go to court, at Belmont and Western, in a few minutes." I looked at my watch and saw that I had twenty minutes before the first call. I'd be late for court. "I'll meet you up stairs at the Area headquarters after court."

"Hell, no!" He shouted. "I'm not waiting until after you go to court. I'll be waiting for you in the lobby of Branch 29. Is that the branch you're going to?" It was. That was because they had only charged Gilly with a misdemeanor, if I had my way, he'd soon be across the hall in Branch 42. Felony court.

"Yes," I said. Dolan tried to sound as mad as hell, but I could tell that he was glad that he didn't have to keep sifting through the ashes for my bridgework.

"Okay, I'll look for you," he said, then added, "do you really look like Hop-Along Cassidy?"

"That's what I've heard."

"That's what they tell me, too. All right, I'll see ya in a little while. Hoppy," he added.

"What do you look like?" I asked.

"Me? I look like John Wayne, of course. I'll find you, Cassidy," he said, then added an afterthought. "Cassidy?"

"Yeah?" I was already getting up from the table.

"I really have only one question. Why would someone put a bomb under your bed? Like I said when you called. 'Who the fuck are you, Cassidy?'" That was two questions, but he hung up before I could answer. It would have taken me a long time to answer anyway.

Claire was getting dressed, after her shower. She was in the bedroom, humming softly. I thought that maybe I should start counting the people who wouldn't want to put a bomb under my bed instead. One.

When I got to court, after driving madly, there were no parking places in any of the lots where police officers were allowed to park. The parking lot for the judges and court personnel had some serious threatening signs guarding the entrance. It also had an open spot in it, next to a brand new Cadillac. My old white stallion fit nicely next to the big green beauty.

A big blue city tow truck was pulling into the back of the Area Headquarters/Court building, I waved at the driver, as if that might keep him from hooking my car. Really, I knew better. Tow truck drivers in Chicago would tow their mothers away. If the owner of the Cadillac complained, my beater would be unceremoniously dragged to the pound.

The first floor of the building was divided into the 19th Police District and two Court Branches, 42 & 29. The second floor was all detective divisions. Standing inside the lobby of the court room, I craned my neck a little, acting like a person who stands at an airline gate looking for someone they've never met. There were a lot of unusual characters around, but no John Waynes.

Well, Timothy Dolan would have to find me. I was already late for court, so I went into the packed Branch 29. Two bailiffs, a stout little Latin woman and a scrawny Italian looking guy, were going up and down the side aisles, packing people into the pew like benches. I nodded to the woman, who wore the blue Sheriff's uniform, and walked over to the right side of the judges bench. The court sergeant stood there, behind the counter, shuffling a huge stack of arrest reports. He handed me a clipboard and I signed in.

There were a number of police officers, sitting in the first row, and standing around the sign-in area. I nodded to a couple of guys that recognized me. Most were in uniform, some in civilian courtroom attire; sport coat, blue jeans, a collared shirt, with a clashing tie. I was in damp casual clothing.

"Where's your uniform, Cassidy?" Sergeant Borge knew me, and knew that I wore a uniform now. Whatever you were wearing when making an arrest dictated what you were supposed to wear for the court appearance.

"My house blew up last night," I whispered to him. The judge was issuing orders to his clerk, who stood opposite the sergeant, on the other side of the bench. He paused and looked over at me, hearing everything that went on around him. It was never fun to have the judge stop court and holler at you for disrupting his courtroom. I'd seen people, even attorneys and police officers, held in contempt, although briefly, when a judge was having a bad day. They sometimes needed to let everyone know who was boss in their court.

The sergeant and I stepped over to the wall. Borge looked down at my clothes. "So your house blew up, that's a new one. At least zip up your jacket," he said. He thought that I was pulling his leg, but was willing to give me a pass regardless of the lameness of my excuse. I didn't feel like going into it any more, so I zipped my jacket and changed the subject.

"I made a pinch last yesterday, Guillermo Rodriquez. Did they call the case yet? He was a hold over from last night." The prisoners who didn't make bond were first on the call in the morning.

He handed me the stack of buff colored court copies, of the arrest reports for the day. "We're only up to the 'D's," he said to me tiredly.

I took the stack and started to page through them. I looked at a few, there was always some interesting and sad cases in a stack this thick. When I got to the 'R's, there were several Rodriquez's, but no Gilly.

I looked again, finding reports that were on some of the others who were arrested with Gilly last night. I was on my fifth search of the stack when the sergeant grabbed it away from me. Apparently everyone, including the judge again, had noticed me frantically ripping through the onion skin copies. "What's that name again, Cassidy?" Borge asked, humoring me.

I told him, again, and he quickly looked through the stack and then shook his head at me. A second thought crossed his face and he picked up a vinyl zippered envelope, from his desk.

Borge opened it and fingered through the papers inside. He pulled out an arrest report, which had some papers stapled to it.

"He made bond." Was all he said to me. I couldn't believe it.

"How could he make bond?" I said, a little too loudly.

"You give the desk sergeant a hundred bucks, and he lets you go home," he said, becoming frustrated with me. "His new court date is May 19th. See ya then, Cassidy."

Everybody ignored me after that. The stupefied expression on my face made it clear to everyone, including the judge, that I was just a harmless, confused, white headed old man. And they were right.

How could Gilly have made bond? I had examined all of his personal property, closely, and I knew that he didn't have any money. Especially not a hundred dollars. For a second, I thought maybe his girlfriend, Marie, had brought him some money early this morning. I doubted it though. She had never been able to raise bond money whenever I had arrested Gilly, for various misdemeanors, in the past.

What about the gold chains? I'd added that information to the report and made a separate inventory, indicating that Robbery and Homicide might be involved in this case. If I went up to the counter and insisted that there was no way that Guillermo Rodriquez should have made bond, I was going out of here with a boot mark on the seat of my pants. Or, even worse, I'd be cooling my heels in a holding cell for 'contempt of court'. What was I supposed to do now? Start looking for Gilly all over again. I just walked out of the crowded room, trying to hold my weary head up.

"Cassidy?" Someone half shouted to me when I stepped into the noisier lobby. I turned and looked down at the perfectly round, cue ball head of a rotund little man. He ran his finger under a dark walrus mustache, trying in vain to keep the huge thing out of his mouth.

"Dolan?" He nodded. "You don't look much like John Wayne."

"I do on the inside," I couldn't see his lips move under the profusion of bristles hiding his mouth.

"Let's go next door, where we can talk," he said, showing disdain for the mass of criminal humanity that milled around us.

We walked past the metal detectors, and out the front doors of the court, then went back into the building through the district entrance. The station lobby was bustling, as usual, and we found a corner out of the traffic lanes where we wouldn't be saying 'hello' to someone we knew every other minute.

"Did you think about my question?" He asked. It took me a second to stop thinking about where Gilly could be, and remember his question.

"The only person I can think of, is the guy that died last night up on Clark. Inon Moon." I said truthfully.

"Yea, my best lead and you killed him," he responded. I didn't feel like explaining it to him. I knew that he probably wouldn't believe me if I bothered to try. The scuttlebutt would develop on its own. The facts would be disregarded for rumor and grow from there.

"So you have other leads?" I asked him.

"Not really. And I'm not trying to develop any. As far as I'm concerned, this guy Moon put a bomb under your bed, for 'unknown' reasons, and you blew him away because...let's say he put too much starch in your shirts." I wondered if his head would have a hollow ring if I hit it with something.

"That's it?" I said, disappointed in his desire to find out exactly how it happened. "Was there any evidence to prove that Moon was around my house? Did they find any bomb making equipment in his car or on the Eagles? What kind of bomb was it?"

"The kind that blows up. Your fucking bed was across the street. If you were dead, they might have sent out some A.T.F. bomb technicians, but you're not dead, are you? So now I have to collect and send them samples myself. Then they send me a report in six months." He ran his finger under his mustache again, probably trying to dislodge a half of a hamburger or something that was caught in there.

"So that's it, case closed?" I asked, frustrated with the whole system.

"What the fuck do you want? Whatever they put under your bed was big enough to take the whole top of the building off. If there's any evidence, it's microscopic. It was a miracle that your landlord and his family escaped with their lives."

I guessed that one miracle was all I could expect. "Look, Cassidy," his voice took on a placating tone, "I've got thirty cases open now, with no suspects. Shit, anytime these jaggoffs want to blow someone up all they have to do is sit down at a computer and type, 'How do I make a bomb?'. So much information comes off that damned Internet that the computer practically blows up. Everybody's a fucking bomber these days, it's the latest fashion. I even thought about leaving the bomb squad and trying to get a nice foot post somewhere, until I heard about you, that is. This job sucks."

I had to agree with him there. I zipped my jacket up a little more and put my hands in my pockets. A move designed to precipitate my getting away from this maniac, but he wasn't through bitching about the world yet. "And when you talk to your fucking buddy, Mister Jerk-O, tell him to stop calling me. He called me again, when I was on the way over here. Sounded relieved that you weren't dead, but that prick scares the shit out of me anyway. I don't like mother fuckers who can see things from 30,000 feet up. Who are these guys you're fucking with, Cassidy? I know one thing they're not, amateurs. That cracker they put under your bed was some professional shit, military."

I tried to walk away, but he held my arm. "Where were you anyway? You couldn't have been on the second floor when it blew."

I pulled my arm away and started for the doors. "I didn't go home last night." I thought about how close I had come to being asleep in that bed when it got launched across the street.

"I knew that fucking drunk was yanking my joint." That stopped me.

"What drunk?"

"That's what started all the shit about you being killed in the fire," he said. "One of them drunks from the bar next door swore up and down that he saw you go into the house about an hour before the blast. If he'd have said he saw pink elephants, I would have believed it more." he said laughing, and walked away. Leaving me standing there in the doorway with my now familiar awestruck expression on my face.

The questions got harder and harder to even contemplate. I knew that they would let me have the day off if I wanted it, I had a damn good excuse, but I didn't have anywhere to go. To clear my mind, I decided to take care of essentials. There were still several hours before I had to be at work. I went to a couple of stores and picked up some necessities. Suddenly, I decided that I would take some serious strides in one direction at least, and went down to the Annuity and Retirement Board to find out what I needed to do to get the ball rolling on retiring. It was strange, one minute I didn't know what size underwear to buy, and the next I was making the biggest move of my life.

All the things that need to be done when your home burns filled my mind on the way back up north. The Post Office, insurance companies that you no longer had the phone numbers of, pictures of my kids, there was a lot of stuff. It was about 2:15 when I got to the station and parked in back.

I needed to talk to the commander's secretary, and have him figure out how much time-due I had on the books, vacation days, and whatever else I might have forgotten. Total it all up and subtract it from my appointment date, 32 years ago next June 23rd, and then I'd know when my last day of work would be.

It would be soon, but I knew it wasn't today. There were a few things that I needed to find out before I was leaving Clark Street. Before I could get to the front office, George Stokes came out of his office and called me over.

"Come in here, I want to talk to you for a second, Cassidy," he said in his official voice. Once we were in his office, his tone changed.

"Now that all this crap is over, maybe we can get back to normal around here." He sounded relieved. I just smiled at him, not knowing where all this was going.

"I heard about that scene with Kurwicki," he chuckled, "I'm glad that I'd left by that time."

"Kurwicki didn't get fired, did he?" I asked him, remembering something that Dolan had said between curse words.

Stokes looked at me puzzled. "No. What did you hear?"

"Just scuttlebutt, I hope. He really didn't deserve to be disciplined or anything." I said, remembering how it felt to have Gilly tell me to 'kiss his ass'.

"That's not what I heard. I heard that he was a real beaut. He should get dumped back into Patrol. Here." He thrust an envelope at me, apparently the purpose for his calling me into his office in the first place.

"What's this?" I said, opening the envelope and finding it full of money, mostly wrinkled up ones, fives and tens.

"Well, it started out as a flower fund," he said smiling now. "But now I guess that it could be called a 'fire fund'. We took up a collection around the station."

"Looks like you took it at the point of a gun." I said, trying to be comical, when I was actually swelling with pride at the generosity of the people who, besides their own problems, could also dig down and help a fellow officer.

Staring down at the stack of bills, misty eyed again, I almost missed it when he told me that I was on the wagon tonight. "The wagon!" I was clear headed instantly. "I'm dead for five minutes and you give my post away?"

"Sorry, Hop. Nobody's on foot tonight. Pape took time-due, something with the kids again, and I thought that I had enough personnel, until they called Cohen down to the Chief of Detectives office. I'm really in a jamb, Hop, I can't put the wagon down." He looked at me pleadingly, how could I refuse him when he could order me to do it.

"Sure, George." I said quickly, more concerned with the other thing that he had mentioned. I tried not to sound too interested. "Why did they call Cohen downtown?"

"I don't know." he said, lying badly.

"What do you 'think' it is, George." I stuck him with my best hypnotic look.

He looked down at the desk, purposely breaking eye contact. "I...don't know...but I think it has to do with Brian White." Then he added quickly, "but don't repeat that."

Cohen was a Probationary Police Officer, he had no rights. The Union couldn't represent him until he had nine months on the job. I hoped he was alright. I had Jurkov's card in my pocket, but didn't think it would do us any good until I found out what they were doing to Cohen downtown.

"Sure, Captain. Thanks for the envelope, I really appreciate it. Tell everybody for me, will ya?" Putting the money in my pocket, I left the office thinking about how to kill some time. Not only was I now on the wagon, I was on the late wagon. I'd be even later coming 'home' to Claire's. But the worst thing was that I was working with Bruce Sapper.

When I went to my locker, I had trouble with the lock. It was just a cheap combination lock, but it had always worked smoothly before. Then I noticed a small dent in the top of the casing, between where the hasp snapped in.

Doing the combination carefully, when I got to the last number, I yanked on the lock as hard as I could, and it popped open. When I opened the door, everything inside looked like it had been through a food processor. All the ticket books in the bottom had been tossed every which way, and what was left of my uniform was mixed in with them. Everything was still in there, my service revolver was on the bottom, the locker had just been torn apart. Searched to the most minute degree, even the pockets of my uniform pants had been ripped out.

There were a couple of guys in the locker room and I managed to borrow a shirt here, and a pair of pants there. Everyone assumed my uniforms were destroyed in the fire, they were mostly right, so I didn't explain. I couldn't explain it anyway.

Chapter 30

The cigarette smoke was stifling, here in the back of the roll call room. I had gotten steered here after inspection by all the comments, questions, and pats on the back from the other coppers. "Sorry about your house, Hop." "You don't look dead to me, ha, ha". Sapper, thankfully, was willing to tell the story of the 'gang war' on Clark Street, to anybody who would listen. I let him draw much of the attention.

I was some kind of weird celebrity, and being my partner tonight made Sapper my unofficial spokesman. Everybody crowded around to see his vicarious demonstration of all the action, most of which he hadn't seen. His finger gun looked deadly when he pointed it at the imaginary gang members. The story now was that Moon had been the secret leader of the Gray Eagles street gang. Again, just a sprinkle of truth over a pile of horse apples.

When he got to the good part, where 'Cassidy killed the bad guy', I walked away, pretending to check my mailbox. Let them think that I didn't want to relive the experience, I didn't. Now I'd been in a running gun fight with machine guns blazing at me, and at Sapper. Somehow he had gotten into the thick of the battle, which seemed to last for hours.

Even if the truth of Moon's suicide by cyanide poisoning came out, the story would still be told Sapper's way. Had Jurkov decided that the suicide would remain a secret? He didn't tell me that it was a secret. The eternal 'they' downtown would have to know what happened. They should be arranging all the real facts and evidence to put the incident in perspective.

They would have to come out with some kind of determination. 'Inon Moon was some sort of super bad guy, who killed the Parks, blew up my house, among other things, and now it's all over'. That would be perfect. And Cohen was downtown having a friendly chat with the Chief of Detectives. And pigs can fly. And Oba-women really do exist.

Was I so confused that I didn't know what was going on, if anything? Absolutely. There was stuff in my mailbox from three years ago. Which was the last time I'd looked in here. I started to clean it out, taking all the rolled up papers over to the circular file.

Instead of dumping the whole wad, I started to peel through the stack, needing some more time until Sapper finished his act. General Orders, Department Notices, Training Bulletins, these were all the things that you needed to take home and study if you ever wanted to be promoted. I glanced at them as I slid them into the can, one at a time.

There was a bunch of advertisements and some unsigned hate mail. Some officers had resorted to printing up their own rumor, scandal, and downright lying, hate mail. This stuff ran the gamut, from supposedly exposing a certain person's homosexuality, to advocating insurrection or racial genocide. Desktop publishing had given method to more than a few individuals' madness.

I tried not to look at the victim's names, as I slid them through my fingers to float down into the garbage where they belonged. They had about the same interest for me as studying for the Sergeant's exam.

When you make an arrest, they were supposed to put copies of the paperwork in your mailbox so you could keep personal records. In three years I had probably made over a couple of hundred arrests, for just about everything in the book, and no one had ever put any copies of anything in my mailbox.

The last paper that was in my box, or actually the first one, had I started from the inside of the roll, was a copy of an arrest report. The only arrest report in the whole pile. Guillermo Rodriquez. I was seized with new direction.

Crushing the page in my hand I turned and grabbed Sapper by the arm, stopping him from finishing his discourse on bomb theory and his opinion of the type that they'd put under my bed. "Come on, 'hero', we've got work to do if we're going to have a good story for you to tell tomorrow."

The look on Sapper's face clearly stated that he didn't want to be the hero in any 'real' stories, but he had to act like he was ready for action so he followed me reluctantly out of the room, urged on by a few jeers and 'hero' comments from his tired audience.

Pulling a Cohen, I grabbed the keys to the wagon and handed Sapper the radio. I knew that he usually drove the truck, all his uniform shirts were worn out in the front, where the steering wheel rubbed against his gigantic stomach. He liked to cruise up and down the alleys, looking for 'good stuff' that people had discarded in the trash. This was the basis for his supposed 'antique' business. He wasn't driving tonight.

Heading out the door to the parking lot, I didn't look twice at his frown or stay around to hear any complaints from him. If he came, fine. Otherwise I was going looking for Gilly by myself.

The big blue and white truck was parked in the gas line, and I filled the tank while Sapper checked the equipment. The new, modern prisoner vans have special locks and restraining bars, and a whole collection of equipment which is locked in metal compartments. Everything is supposed to be inspected on each shift. To me it was still a top heavy pick-up truck with a big metal box on the back. When I was a rookie I'd even tipped one of them over, driving like a fool.

Stretchers, body bags, sledge hammers, dog nooses, fire hydrant keys, the list was two pages long. Sapper checked 'yes' on everything without moving from the passenger seat, and signed the inventory sheet, which he would turn into the sergeant when we ran into him sometime during the night.

"What's the big hurry, Hop. I had a few things that I wanted to pick up..." Sapper said sheepishly, as if he was worried that I wasn't going to let him do his junk hauling with the wagon tonight. He was right.

I handed him the crinkled arrest report that had his name, along with Pape's and mine, on the bottom of it. "Did you know that he made bond last night?" I looked at him closely.

Glancing at the photo copy he said "no, so what?" Then he added, "Pape takes all the court. If you want some overtime, we'll lock up some other jaggoff tonight and you can go on that."

A simple solution from a simple mind. "Well, we're going to find this particular 'jaggoff' and lock him up again. And then maybe I'm going to have you sit on him while I ask him a few questions." Sapper liked the sound of that, but he didn't want to do much more work than sitting down.

As I drove ponderously up and down Clark Street, with my new underwear pinching my butt, I couldn't help thinking that it had changed for me. It wasn't my street anymore. The things that had happened on the street couldn't be dismissed in my mind. I wasn't too old for the foot post, I had just gotten too involved with the people. I'd gotten soft. Maybe younger men were tougher. Things had happened that would make me steer my path away from the Street.

The lights were off at Master Chung's school. A sheet of plywood had been used to replace the glass that was broken out of the door last night. Sun Liquor Mart was open for business, the jewelry store was dark.

The winding stream, that was Clark Street, meandered at it's own whim etching away at the people as it flowed. Wearing them down. It moved slowly, the changes were subtle, like the movement of the glacier that had created this ridge that was a street now, paralleling Lake Michigan.

Up near the corner, there were some Latin children riding a tricycle down the sidewalk. Well, one riding and the others trying to get their turn. An East Indian man, wearing his flowing native clothing, almost got run over by the children while trying to get into Muhammad's Assyrian grocery store. Jose, in the window of the Mexican restaurant on the next block, was sweating over his flaming gob of pigskin and fat, slicing it with his sword. Everything seemed normal.

They didn't realize it but Clark Street was changing them all. They had become part of the street and therefore subject to it's evolution. I had never noticed the movement before, not until it had gone into high gear for me.

With all the time I had to kill today I hadn't eaten since breakfast. My stomach growled loudly, making me suggest we get a quick sandwich somewhere. Sapper said he wasn't really hungry, but he would go with me if I was.

I couldn't get Gilly out of my mind though, and I continued to ride around and around looking for him. The Turk still had the bars locked across his darkened arcade doors. Too bad, because I was driving the perfect vehicle for visiting.

After awhile, I realized that Sapper was now pestering me to go and eat. The mention of food must have started a chain reaction in his huge body. My regular body was pestering me also, now that I thought about it again.

I parked right in front of the Bagel Nook, in the bus stop. Driving this big truck gave me sort of an attitude. As though there was us 'truck people' and you 'car' people. I think my hillbilly heritage was showing a little. I guess I secretly liked driving the wagon, people got out of your way, and you parked where ever you liked. Two of my favorite things.

"Hello, Hoppy!" Cyril called out happily from behind the register, when we walked in. "Hello...Officer..." Cyril stammered when he saw Sapper fill the doorway behind me, probably wondering how hungry the giant was.

I always sat at the counter, on the red vinyl stools, but Cyril steered us to a table. Picking what he thought to be his strongest chair, he held it out for Bruce, silencing Irene with a sharp glance knowing that she was about to make an awkward comment. They read each others thoughts pretty easily, they'd been together a long time.

"I have some nice soup today, Hoppy. You know how Mama puts it in the refrigerator so the fat gets hard, then she just scrapes it off..." He went on, making his own awkward comments, while I watched Sapper study the menu. I didn't usually bring guys with me when I came in here, especially ones that easily topped three hundred pounds. People took notice when you went somewhere with Sapper.

Irene came out from behind the counter carrying two cups and a pot of coffee. There were a few customers. The two Russian guys, that she frowned at when I'd brought Cohen in here, were sitting at the same table, looking out the window, drinking coffee. One had dusty red hair, the other was a black bear like Jurkov.

Smiling, she put the cups down in front of us, not asking if we wanted any coffee, and filled them with her thin brew. "There's cream," she said pointing at a little metal pitcher that had 'fake cream' in it.

"Let me have a bowl of soup and half a turkey on whole wheat. Okay beautiful?" I said, flattering her in my usual manner.

"I know what your having by heart, Hoppy...you liar." She smiled coyly and slapped at me with her receipt pad.

"I'll have the boiled chicken." Sapper said, finally coming to a decision.

The boiled chicken is the speciality of the house at the Bagel Nook. It can also feed four people. The thing comes in a big ceramic pot, with noodles, matzo balls, potatoes, carrots, and of course, a whole chicken. The pot is served filled to the brim with boiling Jewish Penicillin, that's had the fat scraped off. I was about to point out how much food he was ordering, when Irene noticed Sapper's ring.

"What a beautiful ring." She took Sapper's huge hand and lifted it up, so she could look at the ring closely, then twisted his hand so Cyril could see it. "Cyril, look," she called out to him.

"It's a lion." Sapper said, a bit embarrassed by Irene's 'hands on' familiarity. "I'm a Leo."

"Yes, I can see that it's a lion. It's beautiful. Cyril was born under Leo also, that's why I noticed it. See, Cyril." She wrung Sapper's flipper some more and Cyril commented on how nice the ring was to keep her from continuing to torture the blushing giant.

Sapper recovered his hand, twisted the ring off his finger and handed it to her. Irene weighed it in her hand for a second, marveling at how heavy it was. Then she went over to the counter to show it to Cyril. When she brought it back, I put my hand over Sapper's and grabbed it when she tried to give it back to him.

It was heavy, and large. I put it over my thumb and it was still loose. Beautifully formed, the lion had two sparkling diamonds for eyes, they must have been a half carat each. The face of the animal seemed alive, the glaring eyes frozen in gold. I wondered how I had never noticed such a large and beautiful piece of jewelry on Sapper's hand before. Then, I had never tried to get to close to the guy either.

"Where did you get it?" She asked him as I dropped it into his hand and he screwed it back onto his finger. "I'd love to have something like that made for Cyril."

"I picked it up at an antique show," he said. I thought about Irene's comment, about having a ring like that 'made'. I saw that it must have been a one-of-a-kind piece, now that she had pointed it out. It made me think about how jewelry was made. You got some gold, melted it down in a smelter and then you poured in into a mold...what was I going to do with those papers? I had to get rid of them. Everything made me think about the Park's, it was driving me nuts. I wondered what was going on with Cohen and I was glad that Irene neglected to ask about him. Should I call Jurkov and...?

The next thing I knew Irene was putting 'the pot' in front of a smiling Bruce Sapper, along with a second basket of onion rolls. I'd always heard that heavy people really didn't eat a lot, but I was apparently wrong. Sapper started into the pot like a propeller on a motor boat. Spoon in one hand and roll in the other.

"These Russians, all they do is sit around and drink coffee. They want to get paid for breathing. Free, free, free. They think that because America is 'free country', everything is free here." Irene fumed and bitched when one of the men at the table lifted his cup, signaling for more coffee. When she poured it, they ignored her obvious dislike of them, and thanked her for the coffee, enjoying their freedom.

She made a point of telling Cyril to be sure that he charged them for the coffee, then went into the back room to fume some more. Cyril waved away her dramatics and winked at me.

"What's she got against Russians? You'd think she would hate Germans. Did you see the number on her forearm?" Sapper whispered to me conspiratorially.

"535779?" When I repeated the number, he stopped eating and looked at me. I knew the number well, Irene wore it like a badge of honor. Sloppily done in Indian ink, the sevens had little lines through the middle of them, in the European style.

"You know the number?" He asked incredulous.

"Sure, I've seen it a thousand times. She always wears short sleeves so it can be seen. Cyril has one too, but he chooses not to show it." I said quietly.

"You mean, they were both...?" His mouth was half full, and he was spraying food around when he talked. This guy was not a very appetizing dinner companion.

"Yes. They were both in Nazi concentration camps when they were children. That's where they met, they've been together ever since. They had no other family left after the war."

"And she hates Russians?"

"Irene is a German, regardless of what some Germans did to her people years ago, she's always been proud to be a German. The Germans have been feuding with the Russians for a thousand years. What happened between 1939 and 1944 in her own country doesn't wipe away a thousand years of hatred. The world is a funny place, everybody loves to hate the neighbors."

I finished my sandwich, trying not to watch Sapper eat. My little history lesson had dampened his appetite but he had still managed to finish almost half of the pot. The second basket of rolls was history too. When he asked Irene to give him a doggy bag for the what was left, I wanted to put the pot over his head. He even asked her to put some more onion rolls in with it.

He was with me, so Irene didn't say anything, but I could tell that Sapper had just been categorized with the Russians. Irene put the chicken, the noodles, potatoes, and all the other smutz, including the broth, in foil containers. She crimped the edges down loosely around the paper lids and put the two boxes in a paper bag.

When we got into the wagon, he put the bag on the floor between his feet. The whole thing looked extremely precarious to me, but Sapper waved off my protestations stating that he could never let such good food go to waste.

After a short while on patrol, Sapper's conversation was getting on my nerves, we didn't have much in common. On top of that, every time we started or stopped, the bag, which was soaked with chicken juice now, slid around the floor of the wagon. I tried to concentrate on finding Gilly.

I couldn't even find one Royal. All their hangouts were empty. Everybody's girlfriend Angie wasn't on the front stoop from which she usually made herself available. I drove up and down every street in their territory looking hard at regular citizens just because they were wearing blue or black.

"There, in the alley!" Sapper exclaimed, pointing to my right. I practically hit a parked car trying to turn the cumbersome vehicle on a dime.

"Where?" I asked, anxiously looking for any movement in the alley.

"There, that dresser. See it? That's Early American!" He was pointing excitedly to a broken down wooden box with three drawers and wooden uprights that might have once held a mirror between them. I was immediately sorry that I'd stopped Donny Cramer from breaking Sapper's jaw.

"So?" I said, instead of what I wanted to say.

"So! Do you know what that's worth?" He was astonished by my ignorance.

"No, but I know that kindling is cheap." We still had more than half the night to go, I was starting to groan inside.

"You have to help me put it in the back of the wagon." He said it like there was no other choice.

"Forget it, Bruce. I'm not hauling any junk around for you. Come back after work and get it." He drove an old Ford pickup, apparently for just such an occasion.

"No, Hop, we can't let it sit out here until then. Somebody else will grab it." He said it as though people were lining up to pick this trash out of the alley.

"Forget it." I said with finality, and drove past the valuable item, exiting the alley on the other side and resuming my search for Gilly.

"Then I'm not looking for your guy anymore." He said it like a child, trying to punish me for not letting him have his way. He probably didn't even know what Gilly looked like.

I continued my patrol up and down Clark Street. Sapper kept commenting that it looked like rain, and it might even snow, which would ruin that valuable piece of furniture. The floor, on his side of the truck was awash with chicken soup that sloshed around with the movement of the wagon. I couldn't figure out which aggravated me more, the greasy bag sliding around or the whining mountain of humanity that sat next to me.

When I turned the corner at Ashland and Pratt, heading back up towards Clark, there was an old man picking through a garbage can that was next to the traffic signal. He wasn't the kind of bum that stands around in the subway and begs for food money, then goes and buys wine with it. This man was hungry, he had a discarded hamburger bag and was about to feast on a few cold fries, and the crust of a bun.

When I stopped the truck, Sapper said, "good, we'll lock this asshole up and stay off the air for awhile. We're overdue for a job." When there were only two wagons, it became a contest to see who worked the most on any given night.

Getting out of the wagon, I went around the front and when the old man saw me he held up his hands in a frightened manner, as though I was going to strike him. That only made me feel even more sorry for the old fellow. He dropped the bag back into the can, maybe thinking that I would accuse him of stealing garbage.

He was really a sorry sight. It was terrible to find relief in his plight, but this man made me put my own problems into perspective. Sapper had his door open when I came around to his side and I told him to stay in the truck. Then I reached under his legs and took the soaking bag from the floor.

The old man hadn't moved, he just stood frozen next to the can, watching me, fear in his eyes. "Here, Pops. Here's a nice chicken dinner for you. I hear that it's pretty good. Sorry it's so wet."

I started to turn away from the startled man, when I had another thought. I never carried much money, which reminded me to go to the cash station, but I had a couple of bucks and I took it out of my pocket.

I turned back to the grubby little wino, and stuffed the few singles into the pocket of the worn overcoat he was wearing. He just stood there, holding the greasy bag. "And get yourself some dessert." I smiled at him and saw a twinkle in his eyes flicker to life. If he needed a drink as much as a meal, I could understand that too. He never said a word, but a smile started to cautiously form on his lips when I got into the truck and started to pull away, indicating to him that I was not pulling some kind of cruel hoax.

"You know something, Cassidy, you're crazy," Sapper kidded me smiling.

"You're absolutely right, Bruce," I said, and pulled into an alley, the other end of which contained his 'Chippendale' dresser. As I passed the questionable antique I stopped so that the back of the wagon was even with it.

"Come on, asshole," I said, getting out of the truck. Sapper was so happy he was giggling. We opened the back of the prisoner van and hefted the rickety piece of junk into the dark space. There was no one around to see us alley-picking this junk, but I was more worried about someone seeing us unloading it when we took it to the station, just a few block from here.

302

"2472." We got a call the minute we got back into the cab. I immediately started thinking of something to say to put the job off long enough for us to dump this junk out of the back. 'I have to go to the bathroom', was the only thing that I could think of. There was an inspection tag crawling around in my underwear that had focused my thoughts on that area.

Before I could tell Sapper my plan, such as it was, he answered the call. "2472," he said, probably thinking we would accept the assignment and then dispose of the trash, before going to the call.

The dispatcher wasn't giving us much room to maneuver. "The Fire Department operator is asking if we can back them up on a 'sick person' at 1712 West Greenleaf, apartment 3b. Both of their ambulances are tied up on other jobs. Check it out, will you?" It wasn't a question. "The name on the bell should be Barksdale."

"Third floor. Bullshit! I ain't walking up no three flights of stairs for no Smoke Eaters." Sapper started complaining, refusing to acknowledge the call while he bitched at me. I reached over and squeezed the mike where it was attached to his epaulet.

"Ten-four, Squad. 2472, we'll check it out." I acknowledged the call.

"We ain't gonna check nothin out, Cassidy. If you're so anxious to get some exercise, you can go up there by yourself."

"I will. The girlfriend of the guy that you refused to look for lives in that building, and her last name is Barksdale." I spun out of the alley, the Chippendale all but forgotten. When I hit the street with my foot to the floor, the banging in the back made Sapper cringe. But he knew better than to say anything to me.

When I pulled up in front of the address, lights and siren going, I double-parked the wagon facing the wrong way. The sidewalk was on my side and I jumped out of the truck, heading for the entrance, not caring what Sapper was going to do. The downstairs door buzzed before I could look for a bell. I pulled the heavy door open and ran up the stairs, the lock continued to buzz loudly behind me.

Taking the first flight two steps at a time; by the second landing I had slowed down to one stair at a time, clutching the rail. When I got to the third landing, Marie was standing there, jumping up and down, crying hysterically. Her pretty face was flushed with color, tears streamed down her checks.

She was wearing a 'T' shirt and sweat pants, pulled up over her basketball stomach. Marie was a tall girl, so slender that from the front or side, her pregnancy was all the more obvious. She was trying to talk and scream and sob all at once. I couldn't understand a word.

"Marie!" I held her arms to stop her from jumping up and down. If she was having labor pains, the jumping wouldn't help. "What happened!" I shouted into her face, trying to shock her into talking intelligibly.

"Gilly! Gilly...He..." Her nose was running and she was gasping for air, hyperventilating. If Gilly had hurt this girl...or the baby...I was going to...Rage started to surge in me, it hadn't been too far beneath the surface.

Reaching for my radio, that wasn't there, only made it worse. I turned and looked down the stairway for Sapper, who was carrying the radio. He was nowhere in sight and I called down, my voice becoming infected with Marie's panic. "Sapper! Sapper!"

"I'm commin." I heard him answer sarcastically, just before I saw the top of his head come around the corner of the lower landing. He lumbered to the top of the stairs, breathing heavily.

Marie was still screaming and pointing down the hallway now. I wanted Sapper to put out a 'flash message' on Gilly, but he walked right past me, down the hall, and into the open doorway of apartment 3b.

Marie was sobbing and crying out Gilly's name when I gave up on her and took her by the arm, following Sapper into the apartment. The door of 3b opened into the kitchen, probably being half of what was a larger apartment at one time.

Marie's mother was standing by the stove, with a dish towel twisted up around her fingers, held to her mouth. She was tall and thin like Marie, but worn with the hard work that she'd been forced to do all her life. Her wrinkled hands were strong, and no nonsense looking. Her long hair, piled on top of her head, was a dingy yellow gray, only hinting at the former golden color of her daughter's beautiful hair.

She looked at me, she wasn't crying or upset, she was afraid. "I didn't know what he was doing, Officer." She said to me and then pointed towards a doorway on her right. Just then Sapper's voice came from the room she was indicating.

"Hey, Cassidy!" He said loudly, I was already running towards the door. "Is this your boy? Looks like an overdose. Fired a 'hot shot'. He's a DOA."

That froze me in the doorway. Sapper's unique way of breaking bad news elicited screams from behind me. Gilly was on the bed, staring up at the ceiling, a rubber cord in one hand, blood in the crook of his other arm. On the floor was a syringe with a brownish liquid in it. It was snapping time in the city. My only lead was dead, again.

I ran across the room and grabbed Gilly by the arm, yanking his lifeless body from the bed. When he hit the floor, I jumped on him, pounding on his chest and screaming. "Don't you die on me now, you son-of-a-bitch!"

Then I stopped myself. Think! Remember the in-service class on CPR. I got off him and put my hand under his neck, straightening his airway. I checked to see if he was breathing or had a pulse in his neck. Negative. Then I held his forehead with one hand and his jaw with the other. Taking a deep breath, I put my lips over his and blew a lung full of air into his mouth.

When I felt air come out of his nose, I pinched his nostrils closed and continued blowing. Out of the corner of my eye, I watched his chest rise. Good, the air was going in his lungs and not his stomach. For the first time I realized that he felt cold.

I tried to concentrate on what I was doing. Trying to think of Gilly as the rubber doll, 'Resuscitating Suzy', I straightened my elbows, laced my fingers together and put the heel of my bottom hand on his sternum. At any other time I couldn't have cared less if this man lived or died. In fact I only needed him alive long enough to answer a few questions. I said a silent prayer for this piece of trash and for myself too.

Counting to myself, 'and one, and two, and three, and four," I pumped down on his chest, hoping I was doing it right. 'And five. And one, and two, and three, and four, and ten. And one, and two, and three, and four, and fifteen'. Blowing two more breathes into his lungs, I proceeded to pump his chest fifteen more times.

Counting and blowing and pumping. This was my only job now, until I got relieved. It was better with two people, but Sapper wasn't even considering kneeling down. I didn't have time to argue with him.

"Are you nuts, Hop?" He said disgustedly. "Here, at least use this." I glanced up at him and saw that he was holding a little plastic bag out to me. I figured it was one of those mouth protectors, that were for use in a situation such as this. People who used needles, like Gilly, had a high incidence of infectious diseases, including HIV.

It was a little late, I thought, as I put my mouth back over Gilly's cold lips, blowing two more breaths into him, watching his chest rise. Then back to locking my hands together over his sternum and one, and two, and three, and four, and five, and one...

Chapter 31

Some time later, I wasn't counting time, someone tapped me on the shoulder. "Ready to take over on your next breath, Officer. I looked up and saw a paramedic kneeling across from me, he was one of the crew that I thought of only as '41'. "Okay, ready." I broke a rhythm, that I now realized had exhausted me, and tied my shoulders in knots.

The other EMT, the large woman, pushed me out of the way and started the chest pressure, when the rhythm came around to 'cardiac stim'. I got up and stretched my sore back. These people were using a proper respirator, and doing several other things at the same time, it seemed. This was their job now, and I was sure that they could do it better than I. When I looked around, I saw that cases of medical equipment had materialized, along with the 41 crew.

Stepping around the three busy people, two giving, one receiving, I looked around the area of the bed. There was a small night stand under the window, next to the bed. It was cigarette burned and glass ring stained. The single drawer was partially open. I snatched a pair of exam gloves from the EMT's medical case, they didn't look up from their job.

Inside the drawer, was Gilly's medical equipment. Several individually wrapped insulin syringes, lengths of rubber tubing, alcohol, cotton balls, and a metal bottle cap burned black on the outside, with a tiny cotton ball inside. The cap had a piece of wire wrapped around it so Gilly could hold it in the flame of the vigil candle, that still burned on the night stand, without burning his fingers.

Fishing carefully in the drawer, (saliva was one thing, getting stuck with a junkie's hypodermic was an entirely different story), I hit the jackpot. Or more precisely, I found Gilly's stash. He had a big bag of dope. It filled half of a clear zippered sandwich bag. A couple of ounces, at least. The brownish color told me that it was probably Gilly's favorite drug, 'Mexican Mud'. I'd arrested him with heroin before, but the most he'd ever had on him was a few 'dime' bags. A few hundred dollars worth. There was thousands of dollars worth of the drug in this bag.

Reaching down, I carefully picked up the syringe that lay on the floor next to the bed. Holding it by the benign end, I looked at it closely. It was about 1/4 full of a cloudy brown liquid. I placed it length wise on the bag of dope and rolled it all up together. Holding it in my hand, afraid to put it in my pocket, I looked back to check the progress of the paramedics.

They were through, wrapping up their equipment. Gilly's little pony tail braid stuck out at a right angle to his head. His eyes stared vacantly, his face was gray, mouth still open, waiting for the next breath. I had pumped and blown air into this guy for about two days, and they were done in two minutes? Oh, no.

"What are you doing? You can't stop!" I said, prepared to continue CPR on the kid myself.

"Look, Officer, it was a good try. But he's been dead for too long. We tried everything." I was furious. He can't be dead.

"Everything? You only worked on him for two minutes. You're not doctors. You can't stop CPR once it's been started. Only a doctor can declare him dead. Only a doctor can stop CPR." I said it as if I was quoting regulations.

"This is the 'street', Officer, we stop CPR when we determine that the subject cannot be resuscitated. This guy's dead. That's it. You can blow air into him all day if you like. He is not coming back to life." I hated firemen. I hated life.

They packed up and left Sapper and me with the two women, one still hysterical, the other happy, I think. Marie wailed and her mother just smirked, seeing all of a mother's warnings to her children come true. 'If you do this or that...something bad will happen to you.' I could still hear my mother saying it, and I still believed her.

Sergeant Davis arrived on the scene, Sapper must have told the dispatcher what was going on over here. I showed him the dope and he told me that we'd have to handle the body, the

Hospitalization Case Report, and the inventory ourselves. He told us to make it 'death by suspected overdose' and to keep the narrative brief. The last was said to me, meaning that the case was closed.

I argued with Davis. There might be fingerprints on the bag, other than Gilly's. I'd wanted all the Tactical teams to start working on this. When I told him that this much dope, in Gilly Rodriquez' possession, had to be just the tip of an iceberg, he told me that there weren't any cars available. He told me I should let the 'dicks' decide what to do as follow-up, and basically to get back to work. They only thing he didn't say, which the captain had, was that I wasn't a detective any longer and should stop investigating, but it hung in the air.

This junkie makes bond, when he had no money, then is found dead with enough dope to choke a horse, and nobody cared. There wasn't enough manpower to assign someone to it. Let some detective that knows nothing about the case get assigned to it tomorrow, and file it in his 'suspense file' the next day. Gilly was gone and so were my hopes of finding out the truth.

I had to face reality. I had to give up now. There was nowhere else to go. Everybody was dead, and I would retire soon, so there would be nobody left to care. Then again the young mother-to-be, that sat crying at the kitchen table, would care. I tried to quietly console her and ask her a few questions at the same time. I couldn't help it. The Park's wouldn't let me rest.

"Marie. Where did Gilly get all this dope?" I asked, sitting next to her and patting her knee awkwardly. The rolled up plastic bag sat in the middle of the wooden kitchen table.

"I don't know," she said between sobs. "He came home early this morning with it. He said that you had let the Eagles beat him up." She looked up at me accusingly.

I didn't have time to explain what had happened between Gilly and me last night, and didn't. "But this much dope is a lot for him to have. Where did he get the money to buy it? Where did he get the money for bond." If Gilly had stayed in jail like he was supposed to, he would be alive now.

"Oh...I don't know." She broke down again, mumbling her words into a wad of tissues. "He said that everything was going to be alright now."

I could tell that she was referring to the baby and her future with Gilly. It wasn't going to be alright. "What was going to happen, Marie? What was going to make everything 'alright'?" I prompted.

"I don't know. He just said that we were going to be really big, and the baby..." She started crying again. Then she stopped and looked up at me. "He said he was tired. He showed me the bag but he wouldn't give me any because of the baby...we argued and then he said that he wasn't going to 'shoot up', just go to sleep...Then, after a little while, I went into the bedroom, and..."

I waited for her to calm down, before I asked the other question that was burning in my mind. "Marie, Gilly had some gold chains on him when he was arrested last night. Where'd he get them?"

"I don't know." She said, lying badly.

"Marie, come on. Don't lie, not now." I pleaded and tried to reason with her. I could have threatened her, and her mother, with arrest for the narcotics, but that wasn't my style. "He said that he got the chains from your mother. Where did he really get them?" I watched her reaction closely.

She sniffled a bit more, and blew her nose, I could tell she'd resigned herself to tell the truth about the gold chains. I clenched my fists and held my breath, in anticipation of finally finding something out.

"He told you the truth. He did take them from my mother. I'm sorry, Ma." She looked over to her mother, who nodded, as though she'd known what had happened to her jewelry all the time.

But that couldn't be right. The gold chains had to come from the murder scene, that was my theory, Gilly knew something, he was involved in the killings. Then I thought, maybe he had been taking the gold over to the Park's to sell it. Maybe he only saw what had happened in the shop last Thursday. Maybe, maybe, maybe. I quit badgering her, Marie wasn't going to be any help.

Sapper was in a hurry, so much so that he walked down to the wagon and back up carrying the stretcher and a body bag while I was talking to Marie. Marie's mother, I now knew her as Kate Barksdale, took Marie into the living room while we did our job in the bedroom.

When I went back into the bedroom, Sapper already had Gilly stretched out next to the open, black plastic bag. He grabbed Gilly by one of his belt loops and rolled him deftly into the bag with one hand. Leaning over, he zipped up the long zipper, straightening and feeding the ends together as he went. Sapper was an obnoxious slob, but he knew how to do his job.

"Come on, Hop." He said gesturing to the stretcher. "This guy don't weigh nothing. We'll have him down in a snap."

Picking up my end of the bag, that was now the earthly remains of Guillermo Rodriquez, I helped put him on the stretcher. Then I pulled the straps up around the bag and strapped Gilly's feet down.

Marie got hysterical when we started to carry him out, running from the living room. She tried to throw herself onto the stretcher, but Sapper elbowed her out of the way roughly.

"Hey! Take it easy, man," I said to him seriously. She didn't deserve that kind of treatment. Guillermo Rodriquez had left something of himself in this world. I told Marie and her mother that I was sorry for their loss and wished her well with the baby. Then I followed Sapper and Gilly out the door, holding my end up.

Sapper was a lot stronger than I'd thought. He practically carried the stretcher by himself, taking the bottom and pulling me with him as he slid the cumbersome shape down the stairs. When we got to the bottom of the roller coaster, Sapper halted abruptly, almost causing me to join Gilly on the stretcher.

311

The sergeant must have sat in his car filling out his log for a few minutes, and was just pulling away from where he had been parked behind the wagon. I didn't understand what was with Sapper, first he's running down the stairs, then he stops at the bottom. When the sergeant's car was out of sight, he looked at me as if the coast was clear, and said, 'let's go'.

When we got to the back of the wagon, and put Gilly down on the pavement, it dawned on me. Sapper opened the back of the van like it was an armored car stuffed with money. He'd even put the padlock on the door. Sitting there in the dark interior, was the Chippendale, which took up all of the space in the back of the wagon.

Throughout this entire event, the thing that had been foremost on his mind was this piece of alley trash. Unfortunately it was now the only thing on my mind also. I was glad that I hadn't opened the back of the truck while the sergeant's headlights were shining on it.

"Just put it here by the curb. Nobody will bother it. I'll come back with you, after we dump the body off, and help you bring it to the station." I could tell that no amount of coercion was going to make Sapper leave this masterpiece lying in the street.

"No, we can make it, Hop. I'll show you." He was going to do it by himself, if he had to. I just shook my head in resignation and let him proceed with his plan.

First he got a blanket out of one of the storage lockers, then carefully covered the dresser, protecting its warped, scratched, and broken frame from further damage. Because he was so fat, I had to lift the stretcher into the back, while crawling over the side bench. Then I couldn't figure out how to get out. After a struggle with the dead man, I squeezed past the body and out of the wagon. Sapper snapped the pad lock on the door, pulling on it to make sure it was secure. He was certainly not worried about somebody stealing the dead junkie, but I didn't want anyone looking in there so I kept my mouth shut.

He wanted to stop at his house first, with Gilly, and drop off the dresser. I vetoed that idea because Sapper lived way out west and I wasn't carting a dead body all over the city. So we headed down Clark Street, going to the morgue, with Gilly Rodriquez riding on top of the dresser. I talked about retiring all the way. I was ready to go right now.

They don't call the place that collects the dead the 'morgue' anymore. The old Dracula's Castle, behind the Cook County Hospital, has been demolished for years now. Now it's called the Medical Examiner's Office, or the Forensic Institute, and they have a shiny new building over on Harrison Street.

Pulling into the parking lot, in back of the new building, I swung the wagon around and backed it up to the dock. There were no other wagons dropping off bodies, so we were able to take our time getting Gilly off the dresser and into the rear entrance. The doors opened automatically, and we wheeled Gilly up to the receiving window. Sapper knew the ropes around here, he'd gone right in and came out with the cart to put the body on, and seemed to know the dark man with the hospital scrubs who sat on the other side of the window, so I let him do the talking.

We signed Gilly in, and then were allowed to take him into the big room with the walk-in refrigerators. Nice clean floors, new paint and a lot of flourescent lighting kept the room looking like a hospital, or a meat locker. I could still smell death in the air. It wasn't as bad as the old morgue where the smell of human beings, killed in a million different ways, had long saturated the very walls and floors, but I could still smell it.

Under the chemical and cleaning fluid odors was the last scent of humanity. There was no such thing as ashes to ashes, dust to dust. When a person died they went back to the earth, stinking rotting goo. We had to undress the body ourselves, Gilly was only wearing jeans and his floppy toed socks, so it was no big deal. He had ropey muscles, no fat on the lean frame, blood still on his arm where he had fired his last shot.

313

There was some bruising on his forehead, and I felt bad about that. Then I noticed something. There was a mark on his right pinky finger. I remembered the little gold ring that had been separate from the gold chains, when I'd looked through his prisoner property envelope. I hadn't been interested in it at the time because I remembered that he always wore it, even before the jewelry store murders. Now there was an indentation that ran around his finger where the ring had been.

When a person dies with a ring on, and someone takes it off after they're dead, the dent the ring made on the finger stays there. There's no blood pressure to make the mark go away, to smooth out the skin. I picked up his now blue hand and showed it to Sapper.

"What happened to his ring?" I asked him accusingly.

"What?" He acted as though he didn't see the indentation around the kids finger. He couldn't miss it. He worked with bodies all the time. I didn't, but I still knew that someone had removed the ring after Gilly had died. "I didn't see no ring." Sapper finished lamely.

I let it go. What was I going to do, accuse him of stealing a two dollar ring, that I couldn't say for sure I'd seen on Gilly's hand at all. There's an old saying, 'the grave digger gets the last search'. In Chicago it's the wagon crew. I wondered how many little gold rings it would take to make a Lion's Head ring, with two diamond eyes, that would fit Sapper's sausage finger.

"Can we go drop off the dresser now?" Sapper asked when we'd gotten back into the wagon. I'd almost left him in the meat locker with Gilly. We were even farther away from his house now and I told him that he would have to wait and take the junk home in his truck. He didn't complain, probably knowing that I was about an inch from strangling him.

"As long as we're downtown, I want to drop this dope off at the Crime Lab." It was just a few blocks away. The brown powder and the syringe were wrapped in paper towels now, and I wanted to get rid of it as fast as possible. I also hoped my friend Phil Roman was around the lab. Phil was the guy that had helped me find out what one of my sons had been fooling around with years ago. He'd done me a favor and kept it between us. Now I needed another favor.

Sapper started moaning and I silenced him with a look. When we got to the lab I parked in front. The inside of the cab was typical of a police prisoner van. Between us was a cardboard box that was filled with blank reports and complaints, extra handcuffs were snapped around the steering column. The fire extinguisher that was supposed to be bolted to the floor, was only half secured and rattled with every bump. That was why the dope was on the dashboard. It was the only place that wasn't filled with junk, and where I could keep an eye on it.

I grabbed the bag carefully and went into the building, leaving Sapper sitting in the truck to finish the case report. Once inside I was in luck, Phil Roman was working the desk. "Don't you have enough seniority to be on the day shift Phil?" I asked him after we shook hands, I was really glad that he wasn't on days though.

"Don't you?" he countered. I had always been an afternoon shift man myself. Which I'm sure was part of the reason that my marriage had failed. I shrugged an answer at him. We were old friends and understood each other.

"I hate working the day shift," he said, "too many bosses around here during the day." Phil Roman, his name had been shortened from Romanowski, and I went back to rookie school, where we'd first met. We were the same age, but Phil had a big belly now, and gray hair, only on the sides. He'd grown a mustache along the way, to distract observers from the balding pate. It was gray too.

"I'm thinking about pulling the plug." I said, referring to my retiring.

"Good for you, Hop. Me, I've always had it too good, working here in the lab." He didn't look too good to me. "I'll probably be here until they kick me out the door. My daughter moved back home, with her three kids, last month. She's getting divorced. What do I get? Monsters running around at 5 am.

screaming, grandpa! grandpa!" He looked to the heavens for guidance. I didn't tell him that I'd been looking too, and none was forthcoming.

Our future roads looking short and bumpy, we stood there for an awkward moment, lost in our own thoughts. "Well, what brings you all the way down from the rich suburbs, Cassidy?" he finally said, breaking the reverie.

"I see that it's been awhile since you've been up north," I answered, smiling at the south-sider, then I got to the point. "Some people on my beat were murdered last week, you may have heard about it, and it's been a can of worms trying to come up with something on the case. I had one lead left and he OD's on me tonight. I found this bag of dope and syringe by his bed. I thought that we might find some fingerprints, or something, on the bag." I opened the paper towels, revealing the plastic bag, rolled up around the syringe.

"This has to be inventoried properly before anything can be done with it." Tossing me a blank evidence envelope, he put on a pair of exam gloves and unrolled the bag, as I reached for my pen.

Holding the syringe up to the light, he said, "See this? This wasn't the first time your OD has injected narcotics. There's a little blood in here, meaning that he hit a vein alright, then drew back on the plunger to make sure. Then he pulled off whatever he was using as a tourniquet, and fired half the load. That's the way a smart junkie does it, incase the heroin is cut less than he's used to. Your junkie shot up half of what he usually takes and it killed him. Too bad. There's been some pure junk going around, he must have copped from a new source."

Roman didn't even know Gilly and he felt sorry for him, there were all kinds of people on this job, Phil was a real humanitarian. "That's why there's still some left in the syringe?" I said, understanding what he was telling me. "He was trying to see how strong the stuff was, when he realized that it was pure, it was too late. Do you think he could have made a mistake, done it wrong or something?"

316

"No. Being a junkie is dangerous," he answered. "These guys know what they're doing, believe me. Sometimes, when they're hospitalized for one thing or another, they won't even let the nurses find veins for intravenous medications. The junkies find the veins themselves, considering doctors and nurses incompetent when it comes to finding their veins. No, Hop, this guy did everything right, as far as I can tell, standing here conjecturing. When the chemist takes a look tomorrow..."

"Phil, this is driving me. I told you my house got blown up last night. I think that it's all involved in some way. Can't you check it out for me? I need to know tomorrow, or sooner, if there's any more that we can find out from this. It's the only thing that I've got to work with. Please." I was willing to play on his sympathies, beg, anything to get to the truth. I was really desperate.

"I can't do it, Hop, I'm just the desk man now. They have real chemical engineer's working up here these days," he said shaking his head.

"Bullshit. You were analyzing this stuff before they had chemical engineers," I tried to stimulate his pride.

He laughed and picked up the bag holding it to the light. "Hop, after thirty years, you're still a pain in the ass." Then I saw his mind click onto something. "Still, this 'mud' doesn't look very pure to me." He opened the bag, holding it away from his face. Anyone who touched his finger into an unknown substance and tasted it or even smelled it, acting like some kind of television 'narc', was crazy.

He took a package out of a drawer and took a slip of paper out of it. There were a number of the multicolored slips in the packet. "It's a lot easier than it was twenty years ago, too," he said smiling.

He broke a tongue depressor in half, opened the bag, and touched the stick to the powder. He shook the stick so just a dusting of the brown dope stayed on the stick. Then he carefully closed the bag and put it aside.

"Don't want to change the weight," he said, I couldn't care less. He scraped the stick along the slip of colored paper. Then he took the filled out evidence envelope from me and put the bag into it. After waiting a second longer, he picked up the multi-colored slip, which hadn't changed to my perception, and examined it. Sliding his glasses down his nose for magnification, he seemed to notice something. "Hummmmm," was his only comment.

"Humm. Humm what?" I asked to be let in on the test results.

"Hum, you can call me tomorrow. That's what hum. Go on, get out of here and leave me alone will you, Cassidy?" he said, still looking at the slip of litmus paper, or whatever it was.

"The prints on the bag. Don't forget to look for prints." I said, trying to get his attention again.

"Yeah, yeah. I'll take a look. Go on, beat it Hop." He shooed me with his gloved hand, without looking up, his mind already traveling away from me at the speed of thought.

Chapter 32

When I got back to the wagon, Sapper was asleep. Being overly paranoid, for a second I thought he was dead, the way his head was back with his mouth gaping slackly. I tapped loudly on his window. He slammed his mouth shut so fast that he started choking. I got a good laugh out of that sick prank and felt much better as we cruised back up north to Rogers Park.

"You gonna help me with the dresser?" he said sheepishly when we got back into our own district. We had killed the whole night fooling around with Gilly, and I still felt bad about scaring him half to death when he was asleep, so I reluctantly agreed to help him. Sergeant Davis caught us trying to get the thing out of the wagon.

"Cassidy, if you weren't retiring, I'd write you up for being so dumb. Or if I could find a way to get a number on Sapper and not involve you, I'd happily do that." Davis was fuming, but I could see that it would be hard to only punish one of us for unauthorized use of a Department vehicle. I could see it because I'd been trying to push the dresser out of the back when he walked up.

"I've told you for the last time, Sapper. I'm going to fix you good if I ever see you transporting anything but prisoners in this wagon again!" I wanted to say 'how about dead bodies', but he was already getting worked up. He wasn't finished with Sapper by a long shot, and kept sticking his finger in Bruce's face for emphasis.

I didn't know if I was more mad at Sapper than embarrassed, both emotions were going strong. I just left them standing in the lot, next to the rickety wooden box, and went into the station. I could still hear the sergeant chewing Sapper out when the door closed behind me. I didn't want to be there when Sapper asked the sergeant to help him put the thing in his pick-up. Which is what, I was certain, that thick headed ignorant bastard was going to do.

William J. O'Shea

Cohen was waiting by my locker when I went to put my stuff away. He had civilian clothing on, blue jeans, a light jacket with a sweatshirt under it. I could see the first numeral of his star number under the edge of the jacket, where they had crudely written it with a black marker on his first day at the academy. "I've been waiting for you," he stated the obvious.

"Don't ask what I've been doing." I said without thinking. He didn't ask. My mind was still someplace else, but I remembered to check the little traps I'd left in my locker after I yanked the lock open. Unless they were very careful, nobody had been in there.

After I got my gun belt and vest off, I felt ten pounds lighter, because I was ten pounds lighter. Cohen maintained a doubtful expression, maybe trying to decide if he should tell me what I was going to make him tell me anyway.

"So what happened downtown?" As usual, I couldn't wait for him to figure out where to start the conversation. He looked relieved at being prompted.

"I didn't know who to talk to," he said haltingly, apologizing for what he hadn't said yet. "My wife...she's sort of nervous...and that lawyer from the Union..."

"Yeah, you wouldn't want him defending you in a murder case, you'd fry for sure." The look on his face told me that I'd chosen a poor example. "What did they ask you about, Ben? Tell me?"

I tried to give him a Georgos' look, but he wouldn't meet my eye. Instead he just stared at the locker in front of him as he sat on the bench. If the lockers hadn't been there, lined up row after row, he'd be looking directly at the spot where Brian White died. I just waited.

"They asked me about Brian. They asked me a lot of questions." He looked up at me, a little of the terror that they must have put him through still in his eyes.

"Did they read you your rights? Allow you to have a lawyer present during the questioning?" I asked the questions that I wanted to know if it came to my turn. If?

320

"They almost insisted on it. But I refused. They made me sign a waiver then."

"Never give up a right kid." I said and sat down next to him.

He looked at me and said forcefully, "but I didn't kill him." He backed off a bit when my eyes must have bugged out of my head.

"Kill him? Kill who? They think you killed Brian White?" I was fumbling over the concept.

"I think so. Well, they think somebody killed him, at least. I took a lie detector test and..." This was knocking me for a loop.

"They put you on the box?" This kid had been stripped of all his rights. Didn't he realize that people who protested their innocence, and were willing to speak freely to defend themselves, often spent the rest of their innocent lives in jail? The best advise, that a lawyer usually never gets to give his client, is 'when they tell you that you have the right to remain silent, do it'.

It was time to call upon professional reserve and ask some intelligent questions. "Why did they think that Brian White had been killed?"

"His trachea had been damaged, crushed they said. And somehow they knew that I knew martial arts and..." 'They' were never to be underestimated.

"Could you crush someone's..trachea? That's the windpipe, right?" He put his finger out and quickly touched it to my Adam's apple. I tried not to flinch even though I trusted him, I think.

"I told them that I have the knowledge and ability to do something like that, but I didn't. I could have done it in the jewelry store that night if I'd wanted to. I didn't like Brian, but I wouldn't kill him. Besides, if I'd crushed Brian's trachea, there wouldn't be any need to shoot him too. Would there?" Here was a deadly weapon that was naive as a person could be and still stumble through life. What was the saying, 'God protects fools and...?'

"Sure, kid." Then, thinking about what he had said, I added, "I almost wish you had done it the other night." It would have saved me a hell of a time fooling around with Moon and I might have a house to go home to tonight.

He looked at me as though I had suggested putting the cat in the microwave. "No. I couldn't have done it. They didn't really know how to fight. I was in no danger, and that would have been the only way I could have delivered killing blows." That was a lot of ethics to be thinking about when two guys were trying to beat your head off. "Master Chung taught me that the more power you accumulate, the more responsibility comes with it." Just what I needed, another lesson in responsibility.

"Speaking of Chung, how is he doing?" I said, taking a different track for a moment, giving myself some time to digest what I'd just heard.

"He's okay," Cohen said brightening. "He'll be going home tomorrow. He won't let them do much for him in the hospital. I'm afraid that he's not a very good patient."

While I tried to fathom the reason for the murder, and feigned suicide, of Brian White, Cohen remembered something else that he wanted to tell me. "Oh, Master Chung gave me a message for you." He waited until I realized the significance of Chung bothering to send messages to anyone.

"A message? What kind of message?" You had to be wary of anything Chung did, even at great distances.

"Well, not a message, exactly. More of a translation. Something that the guy from the cleaners, Moon, said to you just before he..." Cohen wasn't eager to tell me and I didn't think that I wanted to hear it anyway. Just the mention of the incident brought back the images of Inon Moon kneeling on the sidewalk, speaking his last words in life to me.

Tired of prompting information out of him, I just looked at him, conveying my desire for him to get to the point with a frown. "Well, I don't understand it, but Chung said to tell you that Moon said..." He thought about it for a moment longer, his face becoming more puzzled looking. If I wasn't afraid of getting hit back, I would have socked him.

"What the fuck did he say!" I was losing it quickly. He was startled into speech.

"He said that he was sorry, but he would have killed you if he could have, but that he didn't kill them." I could see why he didn't understand the message, I didn't either.

I guessed that Moon considered me a soldier in his little war against the free world, and therefore fair game. So he would have killed me, he'd tried hard enough, but he didn't kill 'them'. Was I supposed to believe that he was a spy and a professional killer but he didn't kill the Park's? And who else could he have been referring to? There was only one 'them' for me.

So, I get sprayed with bullets, stabbed in the neck, he blows up my house, but I should keep looking for the killer who murdered the couple in the jewelry store. I was tired of looking. I couldn't even find a place to look any longer.

Taking the photos from the crime scene out of my leather police jacket, I transferred them to my civilian jacket pocket. I told myself that I was just keeping them with me because of the locker break-in, but I feared that I'd be up late tonight looking at these pictures. They called to me.

Cohen told me he was going back to the academy for his next faze of training, so I gave him Claire's phone number if he wanted to talk or had more problems. I told him not to worry about the assholes downtown, if they were going to charge him with anything they would never have allowed him to leave the building.

I didn't believe it, but he apparently did, which was the point. Cohen left, hopefully feeling a little more secure. I thought of leaving another message for Jurkov, but I figured that he knew more about what was going on from 30,000 feet than I did standing here on the ground. I went to check-off, feeling less sure of anything.

I met Tom Davis in the hallway. His face was beet red. "Do you know what he asked me to do? After everything that I said to him?" His blood pressure must have been soaring.

"He wanted you to help him carry that piece of junk and put it in his truck?" My smile became infectious and Davis started laughing with me. "What do you think I had to put up with all night?" Then I told him about how I'd caught Sapper sleeping, a sergeant's favorite thing to do, and scared him half to death, graphically demonstrating the choking and telling Davis that I was afraid Sapper had swallowed his tongue and almost had to start CPR on him. I practically had him rolling on the floor.

"Thank God I'm off the next two days," he said, feeling much relieved. Then he added, frowning, "The only problem is that Sapper is in the same day off group as I am. When I come back to work on Friday, he'll be back to." He sighed.

Then he took another track. "Hop, are you pulling the plug because they keep taking you off foot patrol and putting you on a car or the wagon?" he said it conversationally, as we walked down the hall.

"No, I don't mind it so much." I half lied. "I don't really know why I decided to look into retirement. 'Mental-pause', maybe." I pointed to my head and we laughed together. I had not come up with a specific reason. I just knew that I wanted/needed something different. I tried to think of it as a kind of change. A big change. A new life? An escape? I hoped that I wasn't running away from...what?

"Good, you're on the wagon again tomorrow." I groaned inwardly, trying not to go back on saying that I didn't mind working on a mobile unit. Though I had to admit it was at least part of the reason for retirement. When I remembered that Sapper was off tomorrow, I brightened a bit. "Who am I working with?"

"You're with Mike Pape. He's in the same day off group as Sapper and I, but the Captain lets him change his days off so he can go to those things with his kids." Well, at least the only thing I would have to endure tomorrow was listening to Pape brag about his kids. Mike wouldn't have me moving furniture all night.

Claire was still up when I quietly walked through her house and stopped to get a drink of water at the kitchen sink. She came up behind me and gave me a hug, startling me so I almost dropped the glass.

Reading me like an open book she said, "Still a little wound up from work, Basil?" She shared my glass, more to steady me and it.

I sat down at the table and gave her an outline of how my night had gone. I made her laugh, against her nature, when I told her about making Sapper almost swallow his tongue, because he had been such a pain in the ass all night. Then she gave me a foot rub which hurt more than I thought would be possible. She said that the more she did it the less it would hurt. I wasn't convinced.

After the foot rub, Claire and I went to bed and she shared her love with me. The words 'thanks, I needed that', didn't begin to describe my feelings and surprise at how much love really does do for you. Before I fell happily to sleep, I knew that I was doing the right thing.

My responsibility to the Parks had become a fleeting thing, far away from where I was. I decided, firmly, to take the Korean papers, as I had begun to think of them, and give them to Chung. That would be the end of it.

Well, not the very end. There was still Brian White. Who killed him? The only person who I could be sure of was myself. There were dozens of people who could have killed him, and might have wanted to. The only problem was that those dozens of people were all policemen.

Not all police officers, not female officers. Police 'men'. Only a man could have walked into that locker room and expect to be unnoticed. I thought of the maintenance man, Jose`, he was a burly little guy, could he crush a bigger man's windpipe? I didn't think that Brian White would just sit calmly and let the little Mexican strangle him. There had been no signs of a struggle.   But I remembered that he had been holding a mop, with a long thick handle, maybe...   Realizing that this would make me more crazy if I kept trashing through it, I thought about the person next to me and escaped into a confused dreamland.

Chapter 33

Wednesday was a day of confusion. I started out trying to find my landlord, Danny Costa. He was camped out at his mother's house with his four children and smiling chubby wife. She and I only spoke in pidgin English/Spanish. Estelle seemed to be handling the tragedy much better than her husband, however. Estelle had lived with her mother-in-law before, I'd met the old battle axe a few times. Having your house blow up was nothing compared to that. Danny wrung his hands and kept apologizing for the explosion and fire, which only made me feel worse.

I did my best to make him understand that it had been because of me that his house was gone and his family had been put in danger. Now I was the one who was apologizing, and justly so. He still couldn't blame me, no matter how hard I tried to take responsibility. I couldn't count the times that they had taken me upstairs and put me to bed when I had only been able to make it to the front porch. They were like family to me and I was happy that they were unharmed, at least.

It welled up in me and I tried to keep from getting emotional, playing with the kids to distract myself from thinking how I had almost been responsible for all their deaths. I talked to Danny's insurance agent, who I found out after a little conversation was a friend of a friend. I told him that I was taking a personal interest in making sure that everything went smoothly with the Costa's claim. He got the message, telling me not to worry. I gave him the 'Bomb and Arson' guy's name and phone number and told him to call Dolan until he drove the detective crazy. The wheel that squeaks the most...

Then I called an attorney friend and told him to get on the insurance agent's back, and told him how to handle Tim Dolan. I gave the lawyer his number and told him to mention Jurkov's name whenever he needed to threaten Dolan into compliance. Once I figured that I had enough checks and balances in place, I explained it all to Danny, who just nodded, but looked much relieved.

More calls, I called my own insurance agent, my ex-brother-in-law. Tom is a great guy and had heard all about it on the news. He was ready to write a check whenever I got around to telling him what the losses were. More work for me to do. It all took most of the day. Danny's mother wasn't smiling when I left, having invaded her home and overused her telephone. By that time I was glad that I was on a late car. I was bone tired. I decided to grab the keys to the wagon again tonight, drive down to the lakefront, park and take a nap. I'd worked with Mike before, I knew he wouldn't mind.

The station, when I got to work, was running normally, chaotic. I didn't see any 'suits' around, there was no word of anyone getting called downtown. Nobody talked about Brian White and it wasn't because they were trying to avoid talking about it. They didn't seem to have heard that there was a suspicion of Brian's being murdered. I wondered if the department grapevine was breaking down.

While I was standing by the desk, people watching, Ernie Perez answered the phone and handed it to me. It was Phil Roman calling me, instead of me calling him later, like he'd told me to.

"Hop. Where did you say you got this stuff from?" he said abruptly, when I said my name into the phone, not bothering to say hello or identify himself.

"I got it from the night stand next to the bed, where we found the body," I said, not knowing where he was going with his directness.

"And he's supposed to have copped this stuff on the street?" Roman asked another strange question.

"Phil. I don't know where he bought the shit." Why was I always dragging information out of people? "What's the story, Roman? Get to the point, will ya?"

"The story is that your boy was poisoned." he said, dropping the bomb directly on me just as I'd asked.

"What!" I said it so loudly that all the activity at the desk stopped, and everybody looked at me. I gave everyone an 'excuse me look' and turned my back to the counter.

"That bag had more than six different drugs in it. Chemicals that are never mixed." I could tell that he was reading from a list.

"Heroin. It was mostly heroin. Methamphetamine Sulfate, that's speed. Phencyclodine, it's called PCP on the street, that stuff was originally used as elephant tranquilizer. They're still analyzing the other chemicals to try and identify them. One of the chemists thinks that there's kitchen cleanser in it too." I just stood there, staring at nothing, saying nothing.

"Whoever Rodriquez got this stuff from didn't want him to get high. He wanted him to die. When he shot up that little amount to test it, his heart and body went six ways at once. Hop, are you still there?" he asked.

I tried to think. "Yes, Phil. Is that all?"

"Isn't that enough?" he kidded. "You should be pretty proud of yourself, you uncovered a murder."

"Lately, that's not very hard to do." I didn't feel very proud. I didn't want to think about it, but I had to ask another question. "How about prints? Did you find any?"

"Oh, yea," he said as if he'd almost forgotten. "I had a copy of the dead guy's prints faxed over, they matched some that were on the bag. We also picked up a few partials that didn't match his." He waited a calculated moment. "Now if you had any suspicions as to who we could match these fragments to..."

Fingerprints can only be useful if you first collect and preserve them; then, and this is what most people don't understand, you need to have a suspect to match the prints with. Even with computer matching, the computer has to have the suspects prints on file to match them. I told Roman that I didn't know who we could match the prints against, thanked him sincerely and hung up. As I walked down the hall to roll call I looked at my fingertips, wondering where I could find the ones that matched the prints on the bag of poisoned dope. Gilly

Rodriquez was murdered. Just thinking about it made me sick to my stomach. Thinking about the last seven days, made me sick, period.

Roll call was conducted by Sergeant Andrews. He walked in with the CO book and a bunch of hand-outs, waving us off when we started to line up for inspection. Andrews didn't usually work the street, being the regular desk sergeant. Man power shortage, days off, whatever. I was on the wagon so I wasn't very sympathetic. He squinted as he read off the names and assignments, a long cigarette hanging from his lips, the smoke that drifted up from the lit end, puffed out when he spoke.

There were no rookies at roll call. Like Cohen, they had all gone back to the academy for their final phase of training. Alex Garcia grumbled when Andrews called on him to pass out the bulletins and other notices.

I sat next to Pape. Two grizzled, white haired veterans, even more veteran than the rest of the fairly regular crew. Garcia and James had been pulled off Tactical and were in uniform tonight, filling vacancies that the rookies had left. I knew they hated it. Tact guys felt that answering domestic calls and doing things like making out 'dog bite' reports, was demeaning. They were the hotshots.

Pape took the radio and gave me the keys, telling me that he was tired. That was fine with me, I was thinking about a nap. There was gas in the truck so we could have gotten onto the street right away, but Pape had to check the equipment properly before he signed the inventory log and gave it to the sergeant. I had no complaints about not doing things Sapper's way. Hopefully, I was just a guest on this wagon for a limited time anyway.

While he did that, I went into the secretary's office and checked on my vacation and accumulated overtime. I could leave anytime after May 31st and receive 75% of my salary in pension. I was living on less than that already, so what was I doing here? I was beginning to look forward to June.

Mike Pape was a little over a year younger than me and we talked about retiring. I tried to steer the conversation away from talk about children.

"I've got the age, but I still have to work another year before I'll be eligible for the full 75 percent." Pape said. He looked good for his age. His light gray hair covered most of his head and he kept it cut short, in a military style. "Even then I won't be able to retire until 63, probably. I've got three little kids, remember. Yours are grown, aren't they, Hop?"

I did remember, and I wanted to tell him about my son graduating from college, but I didn't want to open the door to taking turns bragging about our children. I knew that he would win that debate.

Luckily, we got a call before we could get into any real tedious conversation. "2472, check out a 'man down' at the 'L' station on Granville." The elevated train ran the length of the district, ending in Evanston. Granville was on the south end of 24.

I cruised over there slowly, rush hour traffic was thick in all directions, hoping that the guy would wake up and be gone by the time we arrived. No chance. When we pulled up, we could see our 'call' lying just inside the glass doorway of the CTA station lobby. There was no place to park the wagon so I blocked the south side of the viaduct. Police business.

Pape handed me a pair of latex gloves, which I accepted gratefully, and hastily pulled on, once I got close enough to smell the man. "Come on, old timer," Pape said. Apparently impervious to the repulsiveness of the situation, Pape slid his arms under the semi-conscious man and lifted him effortlessly to his feet. I held the 'citizen' steady while Mike checked his pockets for identification.

The man was in his seventies, he was drunk and his bowels and bladder had let go. His hair was white, and as full as mine, with faint reminisces of red in it. The sky blue eyes and fair complexion told me that he was probably Irish, or a Scotsman.

331

When he spoke, I knew he was an Irishman. He had a brogue so thick that it was hard to tell if he was speaking English. "Get your goddamn hands off me!!" he thundered, trying to focus on us.

Sometimes I think the Irish invented swearing. Cursing with a Irish brogue, made it sound like poetry. The old man was fluent and fluid. He struggled drunkenly, while he cursed us eloquently. I held him firmly, to keep him from falling down again more than anything else.

"All right! Take me in. Ya thieving scoundrels. Ya bloody sons o' bitch mongrels!" Pape laughed, it was sort of funny.

"Take me in. I'll admit it. I killed them both." For a second, I just stared at him, my mouth hanging open.

"Who'd ya kill, old timer?" Pape asked conversationally, not really paying attention. "Where do you live? What's your address?"

"I killed them both." He said again. "Blasted the bastard's head off. Sent 'em straight to 'ell, where they rightly belonged."

Finding no identification, Pape was looking him over, checking to see if he had any name tags on him, or injuries from falling. "Who'd you blow away, old timer?" I said, shaking his arm and forcing him to look at me, hoping that he could understand what I was asking.

"The 'Black and Tan's'," he answered finally. "They killed my uncle, back in '26, and I got my father's shotgun and went and found two o' them. Killed 'em both. Dirty murdering scum." He was confessing to a murder that happened in another country, over sixty years ago. Probably during the 'troubles' that were at their worst around then. My heart was racing, I was finding killers everywhere. I chided myself for being a fool.

"Lock me up, if you must, constable." He put his wrists out in surrender. "I'll not deny it any longer! They needed kill'n, they did." I looked differently now at the frail old man, who'd lived all these years with the blood of two British soldiers on his conscience. I had trouble picturing the angry young man he must have been.

"Come on, Paddy. We'll get you home." Mike took the other arm and we half carried the babbling man out to the wagon. Mike opened the door and we gingerly placed the old 'freedom fighter' in the back.

Mike treated the man like the guy was his father, placing the restraining bar across the old man's chest to keep him from falling off the bench, and telling him to hold on tightly when the truck moved. When we stepped down into the street, Pape looked back to make sure the man was secure, before he closed the door.

"We going to take him over to the 'detox center'?" The hospitals wouldn't take these 'downers' any longer. Usually drunks were taken to the reconverted community center, given something to reverse the effects of the alcohol, some food, and maybe a bath. Our passenger sure needed the latter. I hadn't ever ended up in the 'Detox' center myself, but I knew many other alcoholics who had, it wasn't a very nice place. Most of the temporary inhabitants simply came off the street for a night and then went back to the same alley the next day. I had met some of them in the hospital, when I was recovering.

"No, Hop. These guys are sometimes 'walk aways' from one of the nursing homes down along the lakefront. You can tell from his clothes that he hasn't been on the street for very long." He might be able to tell, I hadn't noticed any of these signs that were obvious to a regular wagon man.

"They won't give him the care that he needs if we take him to 'Detox'. He's drunk, but he's not a street person. He's probably also on medication that he needs to take regularly too. We've got nothing else to do, let's try a few nursing homes down along the lakefront and see if anyone recognizes him. Sometimes these 'unruly' patients, get shipped from one home to another when they cause trouble. And I'll bet that 'old Paddy' causes as much trouble as he can." We laughed. I was all for getting this man the best care we could. As a recovering alcoholic I had empathy for anyone who couldn't control it.

Besides, if he was from one of the local nursing homes, they were getting paid to care for him.

On the third try we found the nursing home that he was living in. Pape was not very nice to the administration people there. He told them that he was going to report the 'walk away' incident to the proper city and state regulators, which got them all moving quickly.

They soon had the old Irishman, Liam Griffin, out of the wagon and were rolling him into the lobby of the two story building. Pape made them call a doctor, to double check Liam's physical condition, which would be an additional cost for their letting him get out in the first place, and not reporting it. I could see from the condition of the place that it was one of the cheapest, and therefore one of the worst. The lobby smelled like Mr. Griffin, even before they brought him in, but the orderlies handled him with care, at least in front of us.

Pape gave the orderlies some threatening advice about how he expected Mr. Griffin to be cared for, and told them to get moving and give the old man a warm bath and some clean clothes. There were a lot of dirty jobs, and someone had to do each one of them. If I had known what our next job would be, I'd have rather stayed right in that smelly old building, given old Liam a sponge bath myself, and let him curse me a blue streak the whole time.

Chapter 34

"2472." Pape asked the operator to acknowledge us.

"Go ahead, '72." The husky female voice, which I didn't recognize, told me that the shift had changed down at the Communications Center. It was becoming more routine to have a female 'in the middle'. It took three people to work a radio zone. They sat in front of a huge lighted map of their section of the city. The person on the left ran the computer, that was the rookie position. The person on the right answered the '911' calls, but the middle chair was the one with the most responsibility. This woman had the lives of every officer on her zone in her hands. She sounded cool as a cucumber, there were veterans in all facets of this job.

"We're clear from the 'man down', took him home. Code that for me, will ya?" He was telling her that there would be no paperwork on this job. "You got any cards, with our number on them, lying there in front of you, Squad?"

"Why, '72, are you looking for work?" she asked jokingly.

"No, squad, I'm looking to wash up after that last job. How about holding us on a personal, up at Clark and Greenleaf?" I realized that I had been unconsciously cruising north on Clark.

"Ten-four, '72." She granted our request and called a car in the neighboring district for an assignment.

"I've got a taste for a bowl of soup and a corned beef on rye. How about we stop up here at the Bagel Nook, Hop?" Pape looked at me questioningly, knowing that the restaurants on my beat were places that I was in every day, and now that I was mobile I might want to eat somewhere else in the district. I really didn't care.

"As long as you don't order the boiled chicken." I said, cringing over the experience with Sapper. Now that I thought of it, the inside of the cab still smelled like chicken soup. I figured that Pape was having a subliminal craving for Jewish food.

"You worked with Bruce last night?" I looked back at him, a little surprise showing on my face.

"Anytime someone has a bad experience while eating, I have to figure that they were with Sapper. And that boiled chicken sounds like something he'd order." He smiled at me knowingly.

"Ordered it, sopped up half of it with a couple dozen onion rolls, and took the rest to go." I said verifying his suspicion. I gave Pape a brief rundown of the 'boiled chicken caper', and how I had given Sapper's dinner to a homeless person.

"Un-fucking-believable." He laughed. "You know, I try to work my days off so that I can get at least one day a week away from Bruce. He's not too bad, but he's not as good a partner as Tim O'Leary was. If you want to eat somewhere else, it's okay with me."

Pape's last partner had died a few years ago, leaving Mike to break in a new wagonman. Not easy, after spending eight hours a day, six days a week with a guy for twenty years, like Pape and O'Leary had done.

"No, it's all right. I have something else to do as long as we're up this way, anyway." I said, thinking of the Korean papers. When we'd cruised past the karate school, there was a light on inside, with a note attached to the board in the door. There would probably be no school for awhile.

"Eating with Bruce isn't exactly a pleasant experience." He said conversationally. " I've been too embarrassed to go back to some of the places that he's eaten out of house and home." He laughed. I had to laugh too, now that I was with someone who really knew what I'd gone through last night.

The street lights were on already, even though it wasn't very dark yet. Clark Street throbbed with the evening traffic. I parked in my favorite spot, in the bus stop in front of the restaurant, and we went into the Bagel Nook.

After we scrubbed our hands in the back, there were a lot of customers and Cyril and Irene were busy, we sat at the counter. Pape was nowhere as big as Sapper, but I figured he still topped 230 pounds. I hoped that Cyril wouldn't mind, and that the stool wouldn't break. Sitting on my usual corner stool, I leaned into the wall a little more to give him elbow room.

Irene greeted us with coffee, and took our orders. I could tell that Pape's sensible request for soup and sandwich passed him. He wouldn't be categorized as 'a pain in the ass' with Sapper and the Russians. The red haired one and the black one, that looked like a bear, where at their regular table by the window, where she had just come from refilling their cups, her frown prominent.

"Hoppy, you have a new partner every night? No more 'foots patrol'?" I couldn't tell if Irene was stating a fact or asking me a question.

"This is Mike Pape, Irene." I pointed over my shoulder, "and that's Cyril over behind the cash register, Mike. He takes the money, counts it, then gives it to Irene." Pape smiled and acknowledged the introductions politely.

"Oh, I know him. He used to come all the time with the old Irishman." Cyril said, seeming to remember Mike and O'Leary coming in, but not remembering Pape's name. Then to me, he said, "She's just the cook, I take charge over here." He pointed down at the register.

"He better give me the money," she said shaking her fist at him. Then to Pape she said, "you're not Jewish?" He obviously wasn't, and didn't know what to say. Irene was just pointing out that there wasn't enough Jewish policemen on the job. One hundred percent 'might' get her approval. She asked me about the nice Jewish boy, Benjamin Cohen, and how his mother was. I lied politely.

"Hoppy, do you think that nice boy, that you brought with you last night, would consider selling his ring?" She called Sapper a 'nice boy', but she really didn't mean it, nobody could.

"I don't know, honey. I'll ask him. It was a little to big for Cyril though, wasn't it?"

"Well, I would have to get it sized for him. My nephew works down on Adams Street. You know where the Jeweler's Building is?" I nodded. "Jacob will know someone who can make it fit Cyril." Every floor of that forty-some story building was occupied by jewelry dealers. There had to be a hundred people in that building who could make her a lion head ring, but I had to admit, the ring that Sapper had was so finely crafted that it looked more like a piece of art than jewelry.

"Hoppy, maybe you could find out who made it for him and I could get one made for Cyril. It was the most beautiful ring I've ever seen." She said the latter to Pape, who was putting some mustard on the sandwich Cyril had delivered. I was sure that she had already been told that the ring had been purchased at an antique show. Was she just wrong, or did she doubt Sapper's statement on some subconscious level. She sighed, and went to check on her customers.

I don't know why I said what I did to Pape. The words just came out without my thinking about what I was saying, or implying. "You know which ring she's talking about, Mike, the Lion's Head with the diamonds for eyes."

He just looked at me, chewing a huge bite of his sandwich, and nodded. "Bruce mentioned that the Korean jeweler, who was killed, made the ring for him out of scrap gold and gems that he'd picked up here and there." What was I saying?

"Yeah. I think that he did get it made there," he said, while stuffing a quartered dill pickle into his already full mouth. Working with Sapper hadn't done anything for Pape's table manners either.

"She won't be able to get one like that made again," he shook his head sadly, looking over his shoulder to where Irene was cleaning tables.

I finished eating in silence, trying to think. We paid our half-priced checks and drove around for awhile, until Pape saw someone go through the light on Sheridan and Pratt. We pulled the woman over with the spot light and Pape gave her a ticket.

The front office didn't have quotas for writing tickets, movers or parkers, but there was a favorite question that the check-off sergeant asked at the end of every shift. 'You mean that you rode around for eight hours and didn't see one traffic violation?'

You couldn't say 'yes' to that question too often and get away with it. Even the wagon was expected to bring in some traffic activity. We had ours for tonight. I sure wasn't writing any tickets, I didn't even have a ticket book with me. My ticket writing days were coming to a close.

I had been trying to rationalize the reason for Sapper not saying where he had gotten the ring. I came to the conclusion that even though he brought gold to Sung Park and had the ring made, it was still a far cry from accusing him of murder.

I looked at my watch band; black alligator skin, twenty bucks easily. Park had given me this band. I hadn't told anyone about it, and didn't know if I would admit to it, should I be asked. It still looked brand new. I could easily be accused of pocketing it at the scene of the homicides.

After Mike gave her the yellow copy of the ticket, the woman drove off in a huff. Traffic violators are all innocent. Pape used a little stapler to poke holes in the woman's driver's license, fixing it to the copies that would go to court. When he got all his rubber bands and junk settled around him, we started rolling again. I headed for the Limelight Pub. I'd made up my mind to do something, finally.

Making a U-turn, I parked on the corner in front of the bar. I jumped out of the cab, telling Pape I'd be right back and to beep the horn if we got a job. I tried not to look at the jewelry store across the street, but of course I did. Just a dark store front.

"Basilli!" Georgos greeted me from behind the bar with a big smile, when I walked into the green room. "How are you doing, my friend? You still have a place to sleep?" He smiled coyly.

"Yes, you sly old Greek, I still have a place to stay, but thank you for asking." I loved this man, he was a real friend.

"Georgos," I whispered to him, drawing him over the bar to hear better, "give me the papers, the ones I gave you last week, will you?"

Winking at me, he went into the back where he kept a little safe in his office. When I heard some furniture move, I knew that he had hidden the papers in his most secure place, a hole in the wall behind the file cabinet. The safe was just for burglars to fool with.

When the Greek came out of the back he was carrying a plain manila envelope. He tossed it on the bar. We were alone, except for Nicko who was cleaning up around the bandstand. I opened it and saw the bloody papers inside, a stack of forty or so, folded lengthwise. I knew that they were all there.

I was glad that he'd put them in an envelope, realizing how it might look to have them out in the open and not relishing hiding them in my jacket again. I closed the flap, securing it with the little metal clips, and thanked Georgos as sincerely as I could, though I knew that friends did things for each other that thanks couldn't cover.

"Basilli, you found them?" He said more, with his eyes. I knew what he meant. He knew that the papers had something to do with the Park murders and wanted to know if I had done my job.

"No, Georgos...I don't know. But I want to get rid of these." I didn't tell him how much blood was on them, besides the obvious red stains. I left before I confessed that I'd almost given up on finding out the answer. Almost.

*   *   *

Tossing the envelope onto the dash board, I pulled the big van into traffic and headed down Clark, toward Chung's school.

"What's that, Hop?" Pape asked, when we stopped at the light at Pratt, referring to the envelope.

"What?...Oh,...it's tax returns. The Greek does them for some of the businessmen on Clark. He asked me to deliver these for him because it's getting late for filing," I said, not being able to come up with a less stupid sounding reason.

"Late is late, Hop. I hope that they filed for an extension. You know how the IRS is." We chatted about government bureaucracy. Pape did most of the talking, my mind on something else.

I only intended to be a minute, to run in and out, I told Pape. I left the wagon running, double-parked in the street, blocking the south bound lane. After running across the north-bound lane and up to the school, I knocked hard on the wooden panel, finding the door locked. I cupped my hand to see in the window, there was no movement inside. The sign on the board, that had replaced the door glass, said 'School Tomorrow'. It was written in English, but still looked like oriental calligraphy. One day out of the hospital and he was back to work.

I held the Korean papers in my hand, as though a normal manila envelope could hide their deadly potential. I'd thought about putting them in my jacket again, to hide their explosive nature, but I didn't want to act too strangely around Pape. It had nothing to do with how much it had scared me to have them concealed there, over my heart.

If someone had sneaked up on me and shouted, 'What are you doing there!', I probably would have dropped the package and ran.

After feeling totally exposed for what seemed like five minutes, I heard a thumping inside the Tae Kwon Do Academy. Looking back through the window, I could see a dark figure shuffling towards the front. The light behind him made the old man just a silhouette, but it was Chung.

He peeked around the edge of the glass before he opened the door a few inches. He didn't invite me in, he just stood there, leaning on his stick. It wasn't the same stick that had gotten inventoried the other night after Moon had almost stabbed him with it, but that didn't mean that this one wasn't more than just a length of wood.

He had a plain, dark maroon Kimono on, his bald head was bare, large ears lying flat. I couldn't believe that he had recovered so rapidly from the fight the other night. He seemed to be standing even straighter than I'd remembered from before.

The look on his face was a questioning one; maybe I was here to have him explain the message from Moon? I could tell that he didn't intend to elaborate on it. He still looked sinister, but I didn't feel threatened by him any longer. Well, not as much at any rate.

"I have something for you." I gestured with the envelope, and put my hand on the door, indicating that what I had wasn't to be discussed here on the street.

He grunted at me and stepped back, allowing me to push the door open enough to enter. Somehow he conveyed his desire for me to precede him to the back of the building. I headed that way, not looking back. I could hear him thumping after me, his gait sounded faster and lighter than it had when I was waiting outside. Someone had cleaned the place. Except for the missing door glass, you couldn't tell there had been a war in here three days ago.

As I approached the office, I could smell the smoke of burning incense. I stopped at the doorway, waiting for Chung to catch up. He was right behind me and pointed into the office, indicating that I was to precede him again.

Once I stepped into the poorly lighted room, I noticed where the smoke was coming from. He had created a small shrine on one of the shelves that had once held some of his many trophies. On the shelf now were two bowls of rice, two pair of chopsticks, and a little metal cup with smoke rising out of it.

Behind the smoldering cup, and to either side of it, were two little vases. When I looked closely at them I realized that they weren't vases, they were urns.

The pictures that were leaning against the wall on the back of the shelf told me what they were. On this shelf, one in a white looking soapstone urn, the other a jade green, were Sui and Sung Park.

Here were the cremated remains of my friends. The people who were my responsibility, my people. Citizens who lived and worked on my beat. People who I had sworn to serve and protect, were just ashes now. I tried to focus on the pictures that were lined up behind the urns because my vision problem was returning.

The photos were the same type of snap shots that Ah had in his store and that Sung had behind his work bench. None of them really matched, being taken on different kinds of film. Some pictures of old people, some with snow covered mountains in for background, some of children at a beach. The only thing that they had in common was that each had a smiling happy face of either Sui or Sung Park in them.

Chung gave me a grunt to get me off the dime, and I cleared my throat a few times to get my voice working. Hoping it wouldn't crack when I spoke, I handed him the envelope and said, "here, these are for you. I don't know what more I can do for them."

He looked up at me, but I felt that he was taller than me. Taking the envelope, he carefully bent the tabs up. Lifting the flap, he looked inside, then he looked at me again, only this time there was more to it, reminding me of the look he had given me the other night just before they had taken him away in the ambulance. The look that had made him my friend.

Taking out just one of the pages, it was the outside one, the one that had most of the blood stains on it, he bowed slightly, then held it up toward the little shrine, as if in salutation. Then he touched the corner of the page to the inside of the incense cup, and it immediately caught fire.

There was a trash can on the floor under the shelf and he held the burning paper over it, until it was well lighted. I watched the cleansing flame grow. When the fire consumed the spots of blood on the page, it seemed to flare up, or maybe it was just my imagination.

Dropping the flaming page into the metal basket, Chung took another page from the envelope. He bowed his head a little more this time, he seemed to be addressing the green urn, the one with a picture of a young Colonel Sung Park in his uniform

343

behind it. When he touched it to the burning coals this time, I thought I heard a whispered sound, or a brief, almost silent cry escape the old man's lips.

After he dropped the second flaming page into the can, he followed it with the rest of the papers, one at a time, making sure that they burned completely. They burned quickly, seeming to flare occasionally until they were all consumed. Then Chung handed me back the empty envelope, and did a very strange thing. He bowed slightly to the urns again, then turned to me and bowed. It wasn't just an exaggerated nod, the old man bent halfway down to the floor and stayed in that position. After a few moments of standing there, feeling like a fool, I realized that he was paying me some kind of homage and I had to bow back before he could release it.

I bowed in return, awkwardly, as low as my gun belt and Kevlar vest would allow, and we just stayed in that position for a while longer. When he thought the time was right, Master Chung straightened up, thankfully giving my back a break when I un-cricked it.

"Hey, Hop?" I heard Mike's voice coming from the other room. "We've got a job."

Chung turned like a cat, his back had been to the door and he now faced it in a fighting stance, the stick held out in front of him offensively. He immediately realized that it wasn't a threat and put the stick back on the floor for feigned support. But even though he relaxed just as quickly as he came 'on guard', for a second I saw the demon that had reeked havoc on his attackers the other night. A shiver ran up the back of my neck.

"Phew! Boy, what you been smokin' in here?" Pape said jokingly, with a little southern twang.

Chung didn't speak, he just stood there looking at Pape when he appeared in the doorway. I could see a little look of fright in Mike's eyes when he saw the expression on Chung's face. The old man had his back to me now, but I didn't have to see 'the Master's' face to sympathize with Pape's fearful look. At least I wasn't the only person who Chung scared the shit out of.

Chapter 35

I followed Pape out of the school, without another word
being said by anyone. He handed me the keys to the wagon.
The street was blocked with traffic, caused by the double parked
truck. We pretended to hurry and got rolling again before Pape
finally broke the silence.

"Scary old bastard," he commented. At first anger started to
well up in me as though I needed to defend Chung or myself.
Then I realized that I agreed with Pape completely and said so.

"...From the beating he took the other night I didn't think
that he'd even be walking this soon," Mike continued
conversationally. I didn't know how badly the old man had been
hurt, but I was sure the Eagles had been hurt worse. Two of
them were still being guarded at Cook County Hospital while
their bones and other broken body parts mended.

"He's apparently a tough old bastard too." I agreed again.

"Hop, pull in at the convenient store for a second, will you?"
He pointed to my left, and I turned into Nasin's parking lot. "I'll
be just a second." He jumped out and went into the store. I
wanted to ask what he was up to, but he hadn't asked me
questions when I'd done the same to him.

When he came out, he was carrying a small bottle of bleach
and two cigars. Twenty-five centers. It wasn't going to be a
very big celebration, I guessed.

"Where are we heading anyway?" I asked him suspiciously
when he got back in the truck, afraid to ask about his purchases.

"1640 Pratt. Apartment 1208. The complainant is Mr.
Harvey Singleton." Pape said in a husky voice, mimicking the
squad operator. There was more to it, he waited for me to ask.

I didn't want to say it, but there was no avoiding it, "And?"

"It seems that there's a 'suspicious odor' coming from Mr.
Singleton's apartment." I groaned inwardly, outwardly, and as
loudly as I could. I knew that the job was probably what we

referred to as 'a stinker'. I hoped that it wouldn't be too bad. Sure.

I double-parked the prisoner van in front of the Pratt Arms, it used to be a hotel and now was the biggest apartment building for several blocks around. I blocked the westbound lanes, even though there was space enough to fit the wagon next to the curb. If we had to put anything, or anyone, in the back, I wanted lots of room to maneuver.

We went into the vestibule and Pape rang the manager's bell instead of 1208. The door buzzed immediately and he pulled the door open, then he turned to me. "Smell it?" He said.

Now that he mentioned it, I did. We were on the first floor, in the building lobby. What we were smelling was on the top floor, in apartment 1208. The manager was a frail little man who was afraid to go up with us but steeled himself and led us to the elevator, master keys in hand, prepared to do his job. I wished I was as prepared to do mine.

The rickety elevator had a scissors gate that was supposed to protect the passengers from the inside of the brick shaft that glided by as we went up. Each floor was announced by a hand painted number on the flowing wall. When we stopped at twelve, the manager opened the gate and pulled on the handle that opened the outside door. The smell was much stronger now. Pape handed me a cigar, tearing the cellophane from the other.

As we walked down to the far end of the long hallway Mike lit his cigar, puffing it up to get it smoking well. Then he handed me a book of matches and I reluctantly did the same. I'd quit smoking years ago and wasn't looking forward to starting again, but this wasn't for smoking enjoyment.

Heads popped out of a few doorways as we walked. Everybody was glad to see the police tonight. When we got to the door marked 1208, the manager's courage failed. He had a handkerchief over his face now, whether from the smell or the cigar smoke, I couldn't tell. He handed me the key, it had a metal tag on it that matched the doorplate.

What the hell, I thought, this is what I get paid for. I wondered if I could retire right now. I probably could get out of this job but I would be letting Pape down, he certainly wasn't intending to try to get out of this nasty situation. I accepted the key from the little green man and turned it in the shaky lock, or maybe I was using a shaky hand.

Pape pushed the door open and a wave of the foulest smell on earth washed over us. The manager fled down the hall, retching into his handkerchief. Mike puffed on his cigar, blowing a cloud of blue smoke into the room ahead of him, then walked into the darkness. I felt around the side of the wall for the light switch.

"Don't turn on the light!" Pape called back to me, apparently having eyes in the back of his head.

"There's methane from the body in here for sure," he said, walking across the room to the window in the opposite wall.

"And there might be cooking gas in here too. Mr. Singleton may by lying in the kitchen with his head in the oven. With all this stink we might not be able to smell the gas. I don't think so, but it's better to be safe than sorry." I knew that the little spark that occurred when a light was switched on could ignite gas fumes, but I'd never heard of a dead body blowing up.

As I stood there, waiting for him to tell me what we had to do next, I puffed on my cigar until I couldn't tell which was making me sicker, Harvey Singleton or Havana Panatella. Apparently the light on the cigar wasn't hot enough to cause an explosion, but at this point I really didn't care.

Pape was struggling with one of the windows, while he told me a story about two old wagon men who had flipped on the lights at a 'natural gas suicide'. "...blew up the building and themselves. Now the methane from a decaying body can ignite, but only with an open flame, so don't worry about the cigars. I've done this plenty of times before." I wondered if he could do it by himself.

When the windows were open, Pape looked into the kitchen, which was on the left of the living room, then walked back across to the opposite doorway, which I figured was a bedroom. "Shew! You in there, Harvey? If you are, you don't smell too good, old buddy." Pape called into the dark room, laughing at his own joke.

"I guess you can turn on the lights now, Hop," he said over his shoulder, trying to see into the bedroom with the dim light that came in from the hall. I pushed the much painted lever into the up position, and one of three dusty bulbs in a ceiling fixture came on dimly.

"When you see this guy, you may wish the joint did blow up." When Pape turned to me smiling, he realized by my expression that he had picked a touchy subject. I didn't like this talk of blowing up places.

"Sorry, Hop. I wasn't thinking," he said more sincerely than was necessary.

"It's okay, Mike. Let's just get this over with." I entered the apartment, until now I had stood in the hall doorway. Pape walked into the bedroom and switched on the night stand light, just as I walked in to the bedroom behind him. Harvey Singleton was in bad shape. He was still in bed, where he had died several weeks ago. I couldn't believe that he had been dead for that long and none of the neighbors had noticed before. Harvey had been about six feet tall in life, and maybe 240 pounds. Now, he was so bloated, he looked like he was five hundred pounds.

It was a single bed, though it looked like a cot with the huge body on it. Laying on it's back, the side of the body that I could see, Pape was on the other side, was hanging off the bed. Well, the body wasn't hanging off the bed, just the skin was. The skin on the left side, had separated from the body and stretched like a balloon. I could see through the skin, it was half filled with a dark fluid. The 'half-filled balloon' effect ran from his ankle to his shoulder. The skin on the left arm, which was hanging of the bed, had already ruptured and a pool of thick goo had formed under the blackened fingertips.

"Hey, this guy was in my old unit, in Nam!" Pape exclaimed, as though he had found an old friend. He was looking at pictures that were framed and standing on the dresser next to the bed.

"I don't ever remember meeting him though, must have been sent in after I was out of country." Pape was reminiscing while I waited for his old buddy to burst and sent a tidal wave of 'yuck' my way.

"And he was in the Reserves for awhile too." Pape acted like this was great. "Too bad he didn't stay in until he got a pension, he might not have ended up in this flea bag building. I've got my twenty years in, I can retire on a Major's pension any time I want." I remembered now that Mike was in the National Guard or Reserves or something, but I just wasn't in the mood to chat over the grotesque figure that lay between us.

"You did a tour in Nam, didn't you, Hop?" He still wanted to talk about the old days. I needed to either get going with this job or get the hell out of there.

"Yeah, and I never shot a gun or even saw a dead body. Especially not one like this." I was trying not to retch, but it was 'erping' up in me.

"Rifle, Hop. In the Army, your weapon is called a 'rifle', you should remember that." He was quoting regulations at me. I though that if I puked a 'turkey on whole wheat' on him, he might get the message. I put my disgusting cigar in a cigarette butt filled ashtray on the night stand.

"Okay, let's get this veteran under ground," Pape said, breaking the seal on the bleach bottle and anointing Harvey Singleton generously with it.

Pape handed me another pair of latex gloves. He apparently had a box of them somewhere inside his jacket. "I'll go down and get the stretcher and body bag. Unless you want to go?" He smiled at me.

"No, I don't mind going for it." I felt green. "Anything to get this over with." And maybe get a breath of fresh air, I thought.

"Don't let it get to you, Hop. Old Harvey here is in bad shape I'll admit, but I've handled worse. When we had that plane crash out at O'Hare, that was real bad. All the heads were burned off the bodies..." I went for the stretcher and body bag, trying not to hear the rest of the nightmare I was going to have tonight. I heard Mike laughing at me as I hurried down the hall trying to get a breath of fresher air.

2410, Sergeant Andrews, was sitting out in front of the building when I got down there. He was parked behind the wagon, driver's side window down, smoke rising up through the opening. I didn't bend down to speak to him, I was trying to take breaths of fresh air before I vomited.

"You need any help?" he asked, after I gave him a brief description of what the situation was in 1208. It wasn't really a question. Andrews wasn't going up to the apartment to help with a stinker. He was usually the desk sergeant and was out of his element tonight, as I was.

"And what kind of help would be available if I needed it?" I had to ask.

"I...don't know really. They're talking about not transporting bodies in the wagons anymore, but that's just talk." He blew a cloud of smoke thoughtfully at the windshield. "What do you need?" When you don't know, answer with a question. They teach that technique on the first day of Sergeant's School, then it takes years of practice to perfect.

"I need to have a week off," I said, going over to the wagon to get the bag and stretcher. "Last week!"

Pape grinned at my green enthusiasm when I got back with the stretcher, but he stopped kidding me. I told him about the sergeant being downstairs and his offer of 'help', he just shrugged and started laying out the bag next to the bed. I went around to the far side of the bed, the side that didn't have the body fluid balloon on it.

I wasn't sure, besides blood, what was in that dark fluid, but it wasn't bursting all over me if I could help it. There were several pictures on the dresser next to the bed. I looked at them, not to reminisce with Pape, but to give my eyes something else to look at. And my stomach too.

There was indeed a picture that reminded me of Viet Nam. Five kids, crowding together in front of some jungle background. Fatigues, short hair cuts, all smiles for the folks back home. '147th ORD. DIV.', was written across the bottom of the photo, with a silver tipped pen. Three white boys and two blacks. Viet Nam was the first war where they figured out how to get the black soldiers killed alongside everybody else, but at a higher rate.

From the pictures on the dresser, I figured out which one was Harvey. In his present condition, Harvey Singleton didn't look much like himself. His face was swollen and purple. His hair, much like a dolls hair, stuck straight out from his skull like straw. He was naked, except for a pair of brief's that were sunken into the bloated mottled flesh. I didn't know if we had to remove the brief's before they would take him at the morgue, but it didn't matter, because I wasn't doing it. Period. My face must have reflected my feelings.

"Don't worry, Hop. No problem." Pape said laughing when he looked at my face. "We just roll him off the mattress, right into the body bag. One, two, three."

Where had I heard words like that before? They sounded something like, 'don't worry, Sonny, this won't hurt. It's just a little needle'.

I checked my gloves, to make sure that they were intact, took a big breath and decided to get on with it. We both grabbed a corner of the mattress on my side and lifted it up, struggling to get a handhold where there was none. Harvey didn't roll, as much as slide off the bed, hitting the floor with a sickening squishy thud. When I got a whiff of the underside of the body, I had to turn away to the little bedroom window Pape had opened, for a few breaths of fresher air.

Pape got the bag up around the huge body after flipping the mattress back onto the bed. The bleach fumes had easily been overcome by the renewed stench from the underside of the decaying body. It apparently didn't affect Pape, I tried not to puke.   By the time I had settled my stomach enough to go and help him, he had Harvey half zipped into the bag.

I had to pull the ends of the bag together, sort of stuffing the slimy flesh into it while Pape finished zipping it up.   I wanted to wash my hands immediately, with the gloves on, then throw the gloves away and wash again.   I didn't really know what to do next.   I hoped that Pape, who was the brains of this operation, had a plan, because the bag was leaking and we were on the twelfth floor.

We rolled the bag onto the stretcher.   Pape said that if we had tried to dump him into the bag, while it was on the metal poles of the stretcher, the body would have busted for sure.   I didn't know why I needed to know that information, I was never doing this again.

"Now bend your knees, don't lift with your back," Pape said, having done this countless times.   I was trying to figure out how I was going to pick up the thing without getting any of the smutz on me.   We bent out backs, flexed our knees and Harvey came creaking off the floor.

Pape had the heavy end, and stood for a moment, steadying himself like an Olympic weight lifter.   We faced each other with the stretcher between us, Mike's face was reddening with strain, I felt it too.   I had the feet again and tried not to trip over my own when Pape backed out of the room.   In the living room he stopped and I came around, like we were moving furniture.   Then I ended up walking backwards, out the door and down the long hallway.   I guessed because I had the lighter end, or because I was the dummy.

At the elevator, Mike expected me to hold the stretcher with one hand and open the manual door with the other.   Harvey was every bit of 240 pounds and I realized what he was driving at, if we put Harvey down we might not get him back up again. Leaning the edge of the stretcher on my knee, I grunted mightily and got the door to open.   The elevator wasn't big enough.

It wasn't wide enough to lay the stretcher down in it and close the door.   We finally had to stand poor Harvey almost on his head and wedge him in diagonally, which also ended up trapping me behind the body in the elevator. Pape waved good-bye, pushed the button for the first floor and closed the door on us, smiling wickedly.

"Mike! You better run down those damn stairs and meet me at the bottom or..." I quit threatening, he probably couldn't hear me now as the elevator passed eleven. Either I had gotten used to the smell, or I was just too busy trying to keep out of the slime that was leaking out of the bag, because I didn't vomit on the way down.

When it finally stopped and the door started to open, I was surprised that Pape had made it down so quickly. It wasn't him. The little woman who opened the door got the next surprise. She was about 5 feet tall, maybe a hundred pounds, seventy if she was a day, with silver blue hair. I couldn't believe that anyone that small could scream so loudly.

First, she'd looked at the stretcher with the pear shaped bag strapped to it, propped up and blocking the entrance to the car, then at me. Then she got a whiff of Harvey and figured what was in the bag. It took Pape awhile to walk down, but she was still screaming when he got there.

Harvey and I waited patiently behind the scissors gate for him to handle the disturbance. We must have been a sight. Pape didn't laugh at me when he finally got the woman calmed down and in the custody of the manager. I also didn't laugh or comment when a whole bunch of Harvey Singleton sloshed onto Pape's arm and jacket. It wasn't funny at all. The stretcher and the outside of the bag were all juicy now, we had a hell of a time getting the body out of the elevator. The only thing good about it was that it wasn't me.

We left Harvey laying there in the lobby while we commandeered the manager's bathroom and washed up as best we could. Pape produced two more pair of latex gloves from his endless supply and we got back to work. The manager was happy to see the back of us. I hoped that we didn't have to come back later for the little old lady.

"Don't tip this son-of-a-bitch," Mike ordered, while I strained to pick up the stretcher. Apparently he wasn't considering this guy an old Army buddy any longer. I had the feet again and therefore had to walk backwards into the street. We had propped open all the doors, to make it easier to get him out of the building, and to get some fresh air in the lobby.

It was hard to get the stretcher in the back of the wagon, we could have used some help carrying the body, but there were no volunteers. Once we had Harvey in the back of the truck, Pape threw his gloves in the street, I took mine off and put them on the body bag before I closed the door. This was the only funeral procession Harvey Singleton was ever going to have. We'd found out from the manager that he had no family, and we called the station to send someone out with a Coroner's Seal to close the apartment.

We didn't lock the back of the wagon, nobody was coming within fifty feet of us. The ride to the morgue was slow and airy. We kept the windows open the whole way, even though a light rain started to fall.

Once we got to Harrison Street, and backed up to the dock at the morgue, Pape produced more gloves and went to get a wheeled cart. I figured that he knew the attendants pretty well, because all we did was wheel the body into the receiving area and then we left.

"When I have a bad one like this, I give those guys a 'fin' and they take care of the body. I think it's worth it." Pape said.

"Five bucks. I wonder how much they would have charged to make a house call?" I said, laughing with relief. "I would have been willing to pay, whatever the cost." I offered to split the five dollar expense with Pape, but he refused, saying that I shouldn't have had to do a dirty job like that in the first place. I wondered how he figured that.

Mike asked me if I would mind if he went home and changed his clothes. They were still rank with decayed body fluids. "Would I mind if you changed clothes? Mike, I wouldn't even mind if you took a shower." We both laughed. Pape lived on the west end of our district. I knew which block he lived on but had never been to his house. He directed me down a dark street lined with similar bungalows and had me park in front of his neighbor's driveway.

I agreed to wait for Pape in the nice warm wagon. It was raining steadily now, and getting colder. I figured it wasn't too late to take a little nap. I'd sure earned it. After a few minutes, just as I was getting comfortable, headlights came down the quiet street and a car pulled up into Pape's driveway.

All the doors sprang open and a bunch of wild kids poured out of the little compact car. Book bags swinging and coat tails flying as they ran to the house. Pape's wife, I couldn't remember her name, popped the trunk and I could see that it was loaded with groceries and packages. She sort of half-waved at the wagon, not asking for assistance, but I was already getting out to give her a hand.

"Oh, I thought you were Bruce Sapper," she said when I ran up to the car, trying to stuff my hair under my hat so it wouldn't get too wet. I could tell she hadn't expected Sapper to get out of the wagon, in the rain, and help her carry her groceries.

I looked down at myself and smiled back up at her. "You thought I was Bruce Sapper?"

She laughed an apology at me and we grabbed the bags and sprinted for the house. Inside the nice little cottage, a tornado was blowing. The kids were going at 200 MPH. "I did a 'triple axle' today, Daddy!" A pretty little girl exclaimed proudly. She was maybe twelve years old, though she seemed tall for her age. I realized that most Westerners expected Asians to be short people.

The other girl, she had a rounder face and I thought that she must have been the one that they had adopted in China, Susan, was displaying a water colored painting of flowers. She showed it to me and watched my face when I told her it was very nice. It was. If I had seen it framed in the Impressionist section of the Art Institute, I wouldn't have thought it out of place. She looked

William J. O'Shea

to be about ten years old, though not as pretty as her sister, the figure skater.

"Daddy!" A little brown haired boy begged for his chance to be heard. "Listen to me play my new piece." Pape just stood there in the middle of the chaos watching me struggle with the bags of groceries. He was drying himself with a towel, biceps bulging out of a clean T-shirt, I could just make out a faded US Army tattoo on his forearm. Finally, he woke up and took two of the bags from my strained fingers. I found a place on the counter to put the others.

The little artist, apparently satisfied with my critique, put her painting back into a large folder, and started to put the groceries away. Pape's wife, I thought her name was maybe Lori, came into the kitchen and it seemed to be too crowded for me all of a sudden.

"I'll wait outside, Mike," I said, thinking of the quiet warmth that awaited me in the wagon.

"Yeah, thanks, Hop. Believe me, I wish I could get out of here too." He smiled, I didn't believe him. He loved these wild Indians. "I'll be out as soon as I get them calmed down." Lori smiled at that, I think she did most of the calming down around here.

He left the kitchen in one direction and I started for the front door. Before I made it to the door, I was accosted by two of the children. Karen, I think was the Korean girl's name, pointed to one of the many pictures on the walls of the dining room. "I won the National Figure Skating title for my age group last year," she said proudly.

I looked at the picture she was pointing to and saw her standing next to a trophy that was almost as big as she was. I commented on how nice she looked and how proud she must have been to win such a big trophy. I didn't add that it was obvious that she would grow up to be a classic Korean beauty, with the almond shaped eyes that a man can drown in.

"Do you want to hear me play my new piece?" The little boy was standing next to me with a little violin sticking out from under his chin. He had puppy dog eyes with inch long lashes. Silky light brown hair and the fair skin of the Caucasus gave the lad a definite European look. I had to hand it to Mike and his wife, they had taken on a lot of responsibility adopting the world's orphans. The little boy didn't wait for me to answer and started sawing on the tiny instrument.

I hardly heard the screechy music because my attention had become riveted to the photos on the wall. There were dozens of framed pictures of the children at different ages, each at a different competition or recital.

"Micky!" The boy stopped playing when Pape hollered at him from the kitchen door. I almost jumped out of my shoes. "Go down in the basement and practice!" Little Micky was apparently prohibited from torturing visitors with his violin. That was fine with me. He started to put out a lower lip then smiled at me and ran into the other room. Other than a few hollow threats, I didn't think that these children received much punishment.

"I'll be right out, Hop," Pape said to me again. I had to consciously order my feet to start walking. Once out in the wagon I just sat there behind the wheel, my thoughts racing faster than the idling engine could ever go. My mind asked questions and went to places that it didn't want to go.

Chapter 36

When Pape finally came out of the house and got into the cab of the wagon, I glanced over at him peripherally and put the shift lever in gear. Did he look different to me, or was it just my imagination? I almost hit a parked car pulling away from the curb and had to abandon my question to concentrate on driving, fumbling with the wiper switch to clear the windshield.

"That envelope that you brought over to the old man earlier wasn't tax returns, was it, Hop?" Pape spoke first after we had gone half-way back to the station. We were eastbound on Devon, passing the Indian Sari Palaces where they sold the expensive cloth used in their fashions. People scurried to get out of the rain, it was after ten but Devon Avenue worked late hours, many of the businesses were still open.

"Why do you say that, Mike?" I wanted to act like nothing was bothering me, but my stupid mouth had to ask the question. I wasn't really asking him a question though, I was demanding an explanation. Anger was boiling over in me, viciously ripping apart all the smart things that I should have been thinking of doing.

Common sense went right out the window with compassion, hope, fear and everything else, except rage. "Is that why you broke into my locker?" I asked foolishly.

"Broke into your locker?" First he asks a question, opening the door, and now he was going to act dumb. "I only mentioned it because I saw you take something out of that kid's jacket the other night, when he was laying there on the hood of the squad car. I figured that it had something to do with that Chung guy. He was related to those people who were killed, wasn't he?" He was trying to draw me out, I went.

"You seem to know a lot, Mike." My knuckles were white on the black steering wheel where I gripped it at 2 and 10 o'clock. I was surprised that it wasn't bending. It was pouring rain now. I could hear thunder and see flashes of lightning in the clouds.

"Well, it's no big deal. I won't say anything. Whatever it was, is your business," he said, quoting the old police veteran's unwritten law. I'd kept my mouth shut about a lot of things over the last three decades as a Chicago Police Officer. I had rolled with the punches, kept my nose relatively clean, and made it through to today. Today was a whole new day though.

"It is a big deal, Mike. As big a deal as I can think of." We were stopped at the light on Ridge Avenue, just a few blocks from the station. When the light changed all I would have to do was top this little ridge, cruise down the hill a little ways, left turn into the back of the parking lot and I'd be okay.

"What are you talking about, Hop?" His voice changed again, a little more serious now. I should have kept my mouth shut. I should have been smart enough to curb my anger and think intelligently. Thirty years of experience to draw from, and here I go; it was snapping time in the city again.

"I'm talking about pictures, Mike. Pictures of children. I'd like to know why Master Chung has a picture of your kid on his shelf!" When I thought about the packet of photos in my jacket pocket, and the pictures that Ah had taped to his cash register, I remembered. I remembered a picture of a Korean girl, smiling happily, tall and beautiful, with those dark almond eyes. I remembered the same photo had been on the wall behind Sung's work bench. My voice had risen until I was shouting at the top of my lungs in the cluttered little space.

"Answer that one for me, will ya?" I tried to lower my voice, he just sat there looking at the dashboard.

"Tell me why an old Korean man has a picture that looks like your daughter, Karen, on his shelf? Tell me why the guy in the liquor has the same picture taped to his cash register? Tell me what happened to the picture of a Korean girl which was taped to the wall behind Park's work bench? Tell me why the girl in those pictures is a dead ringer for your daughter?" I was a raging madman.

Somebody got up the nerve to beep their horn behind us, causing me to realize that the light had been green for awhile. I lurched into motion going eastbound. I started driving faster, concentrating on getting to the station. Trying to shake the fury that clouded my mind.

"Go straight," was all Pape said. It was just a whisper. But there was authority in it. I looked over to where he sat on the other side of the boxes of papers and junk. In the passing street lights and a brief flash of lightning, I could see the barrel of the weapon that was pointed at my side. The part of me that wasn't covered by the bullet proof vest.

He was obviously holding the object of his authoritative demand. The thing looked like a cannon, resting there on the edge of the cardboard box. The barrel looked big enough for me to put my finger all the way into it. I recognized it then. It was the .50 caliber Army six shooter that had belonged to Colonel Sung Park, South Korean War hero.

Pape may have had the authority, but I was fully unsnapped. I slammed on the brakes, stopping in the middle of the street, eastbound on Devon. The station just a half block to the left. Safety and sanity were just a short block away.

Too bad, because I was past caring. "Shoot! Go ahead and shoot me! Because this ends here!" I was really nuts now, begging a killer to do it again. "Go on and shoot, you son of a bitch, and then go over there and turn your ass in." I pointed north at the corner of the gray brick police station that we could see from where we sat.

"Drive." Was all he said, calmly.

"Drive this!" I pointed down. "I'm not helping you commit another murder. If you're going to shoot me, shoot!" I wasn't getting any saner.

In a flash he transferred the gun to his left hand and grabbed me by the throat, under my jaw. His fingers clamped down hard, shutting off the flow of blood. Before I realized what was happening, I started seeing stars. I grabbed his arm, frantically trying to pull his hand away. It was as hard as steel. I tore at his vice-grip fingers, unable to breathe. The twinkles started to join together into black clouds. I tried to strike out at him. He easily blocked the blows with the barrel of the gun, hurting me more than I was able to hurt him.

When I finally remembered that I also had a pistol, I popped the snap and tried to pull it from my holster. He put the cannon down, and relieved me of my service revolver with frightening ease. All the while, he continued choking the life out of me with an iron grip.

When I tried, desperately, to grab for the door handle and lock, he shook me like a rag doll and slammed my head into the glass behind the seat a few times. I stopped struggling, not voluntarily. He released the pressure on my throat but still held my head against the back window. I realized that I had nearly passed out. My deprived lungs immediately took in a gasp of air.

"Drive. Or I'll just keep squeezing until you're unconscious and drive myself. And don't try any of your cute driving." He squeezed my throat again to emphasize his control of the situation. I took my foot off the brake and started rolling the wagon east on Devon.

He took his hand away from my neck, but kept leaning close to me. "Is that how you killed Brian White?" I said squeakily, rubbing my throat. Getting a taste of what must have happened to White should have smartened me up, but the lack of oxygen didn't do anything for my self-preservation instinct.

"I knew you were too smart for me, Cassidy." I didn't feel very smart. "Too smart for your own good." That, I might have agreed with. "Just like Brian White thought he was. Yeah, the woman did ask for me when he answered the phone that day, before she asked him to leave a message for you to call. He thought he was going to squeeze me. But he was the one that got squeezed instead." He snorted at the irony.

"...When he passed out, I just took his weapon and put his finger on the trigger and...pow, then I went in the bathroom stall. When you ran by, I ran out after you. He deserved it. Piece of shit." He really believed that Brian White deserved to be murdered.

"That didn't give you the right to kill him." I said without thinking again. Stupid is as stupid does.

"The right! The right!" He screamed into my ear. Just what I needed to do, piss this maniac off some more. He jabbed the gun barrel into my arm pit, grating it along my ribs. I tensed, thinking he was going to pull the trigger. "What about my rights? What about my family's rights?" His voice cracked. Apparently oxygen started getting back into my brain, because I managed not to say anything stupid.

"Okay, what gave you the right? What about your family?" If I was going to die, I wanted to die knowing what happened.

We were half way to the lake now. I thought about when I'd been taken for ride a few days ago, by Inon Moon, and wondered if I could use the same trick to get out of this situation. I didn't think I could get the truck into the lake before Pape shot me. I figured I would have to go along for now, he had the barrel of the .50 caliber in my arm pit, and I didn't want to feel his fingers on my throat again. I had to keep him talking and pray for a break. I prayed, he talked.

"When I saw you looking at those pictures of Karen, I knew that you'd figured it out. It all started with that fucking Bruce Sapper. He had a loose stone on that goddamn ring of his, and I went in to the jewelry store with him to get it tightened. You were right when you suggested that he took some 'old gold' and had Sung Park make a ring for him." His voice was shaky, but I could tell that he wanted to get a mountain off his chest. I was willing to listen, but there was no absolution coming from me.

"I noticed the picture on the wall behind the workbench, and foolishly commented on it. Then Sapper said that the girl in the picture looked just like my little adopted daughter, Karen. The Korean said it was an old picture of his own daughter, but only in passing. It was the wife, Sui, who suspected something. I knew that I'd made a mistake when I saw the look on her face." He sighed heavily at his 'mistake'.

When we got to Sheridan Road, Pape poked me with the gun and made me turn left, north. Then he continued his confession, I wasn't a priest, but in a sense, I had the right to hear it. The radio was quiet, I prayed for a job, anything.

"A couple of days later I thought I saw her and the husband driving past my house. They must have followed me home from work or something. They were trying to get a look at Karen, and last week they did. On Thursday afternoon, when I picked her up from school, Karen told me that a man and a woman had spoken to her at recess, and asked her name. She said that they looked like her, like Koreans. I knew it was the Parks then."

The sheeting rain had cleared the streets of all but the most desperate venturers, I risked a glance over at Pape. He had a wild look. His eyes were wide as he recalled the events, sweat running down his face. The gun wasn't pointed at me now, he gripped it tightly in his right hand, using it for emphasis as he told the story that must have been burning inside him. I tried to swallow and got a sharp pain in my throat. Now I knew what a damaged trachea was, and how it felt.

"I didn't know then that the woman had called the station. I went right over to the jewelry store and confronted them that afternoon. I told them to stay away from my daughter, that they had no right to talk to her. I threatened to arrest them...Then the woman said that Karen was their grand-daughter, the child of their own daughter."

Even though I was shocked, I kept my mouth shut, looking around for some kind of escape, the more he talked the more I realized how dangerous the situation was. I was living minute to minute. The door lock on my door was down, I would have to reach back to unlock it. Every vehicle was different, the one I was riding in was very secure. It was a dumb thought anyway, if I managed to jump out of the moving wagon, and he didn't put a bullet in me before I hit the pavement, he had three guns and I had none. I prayed for a plan.

Meanwhile, Pape was getting to the point of his confession. "I didn't mean to hurt anyone, Hop," nobody does, "the woman started screaming at me, saying that Karen was her daughter's child, and that she would give blood for a test. I couldn't get her to shut-up. She was screaming at her husband, too. Apparently he had disowned his daughter when she'd gotten pregnant. Then the woman went in the back of the store and came out with this."

He waved the barrel of the hog-leg around to show me what he meant, as though I wasn't getting it. I tried to picture the huge black revolver in Sui Park's little ivory hands. "I could see that she was straining to pull the trigger. She was pointing it right at me. When I saw the hammer going back, I grabbed the gun from her and it went off. The bullet went past my shoulder and she started screaming even louder. Then I hit her...to make her stop screaming."

He was looking down at the floor now, the gun hanging down between his knees, I almost made a jump for it but he looked up at me, crying. I don't know why it took so long, but it wasn't until I saw the tears that I really started to get scared.

"I didn't intend to hit her so hard. I had gone there upset, and she had just made it worse. She tried to kill me..." He made a self justifying statement that wasn't going to fly anywhere. "When I hit her, she flew back through the little doorway and landed on the sofa...I could see from the way her head was turned that she was dead. But I swear it was an accident...When I turned to look for the husband, I saw what she had been screaming about. The bullet had missed me and hit him in the side of the head. They were both dead...Oh God, I didn't mean for anything like that to happen. I'm so sorry." He sobbed. He was right about one thing, he was a sorry-son-of-a-bitch. He had better keep praying to God for forgiveness, because he wasn't getting any from me.

"I believe you Mike, it was just an accident. Let's go to the station, I'll get some help for you. Don't worry. It won't be too bad. Please, Mike." Where had I heard this bullshit speech before?

I didn't care what I was saying, I was willing to say anything at this point to keep this nut from shooting me.

"No. I can't. My kids, they need me. You know how they are about adoptions these days. They would have taken my Karen away from me. They might even take Micky and Susan too. Having Karen was what made it possible to adopt the other two...my wife...she had to have a baby. You've got to understand, Hop. She was going crazy, we'd tried everything but she just couldn't get pregnant, and she was getting older. Then when I had the opportunity..."

I wasn't going to understand, at least not to the point where I could justify his actions. I was having trouble figuring out just what his motivations were though, then I got a clear picture. "It was in that very same building, where we just had the 'stinker', that I found Karen." He said between sobs, trying to get his voice under control.

"Found her? I thought you went to Korea and adopted her." I didn't know why I was bothering to ask these questions. The need to know was jeopardizing my immediate future.

"I took a week off, then got some phony papers made up, birth certificate and stuff." His face was pasty white in the dark interior of the cab, shining where the light reflected the tears. "If only I had never gone in that jewelry store with Sapper. He doesn't know any of this, all he cares about is collecting junk and eating. I was working with Tim O'Leary back then, that was when I got Karen."

"You found her, you got her? How did you get the baby?" I must have been a little crazy to ask.

"One night we got a call of a woman screaming at the Pratt Arms. When we got up there, Timmy and I found a Korean girl alone, and having a baby. We tried to save her but she never opened her eyes. The baby was born and we wrapped it in sheets. We couldn't find anyone who knew her. There was no identification anywhere in the apartment, just a cockroach infested dump. So we brought the dead girl to the morgue as a Jane Doe...and I took the baby home to my wife."

I had thought I was getting rational again. I thought I was finished snapping. Not a chance. I went all the way nuts with that revelation. "What! You what! You stole a fucking baby! Are you crazy? I knew an old traffic man who took a live chicken because the violator didn't have any money. I've heard of coppers stealing everything under the sun, doing crazy things. But this is unbelievable. You took a newborn baby from a dead woman and brought it home!"

"That was twelve years ago." He said it as though there was a Statute of Limitations on stealing babies. If you got away with it for 'X' amount of time, the kid was yours to keep.

"You know how DCFS (Illinois Department of Children and Family Services) was back then. Karen would have grown up in a foster home or an orphanage. We've given her everything, she's going to be a great figure skater some day. She's my daughter, I love her. I love them all." He sniffed and wiped his nose with the back of his hand.

"That's why I have to keep going," he said sadly, "for my kids. I can't stop. They'll never make it without me...I have to keep going, for them."

"By 'keep going', you mean that your going to keep killing people until this problem goes away? Forget it, Mike! They already know that Brian White was murdered. It's only a matter of time before they get around to you. Especially if anything happens to me." I added futilely.

"Did you set the Puerto Rican kid up, too?" I had to ask.

"That junkie was another piece of shit that was better off dead. He rang the bell at the jewelry store when I was arguing with Karen's grandparents, and the old man waved him off. He saw me in there though." He said 'grandparents' as though he wished that the child really could have had real grandparents.

"That's why I left that gang scarf in there. I knew that the Homicide dicks would go for it. But it didn't fool you, Hop." More correctly, it didn't fool Jurkov. I wished he would magically appear to help me out of this jam I was in.

"When I put Rodriquez in the wagon after that fight, he whispered in my ear. He wanted to squeeze me too. He didn't care about my kids either. So, I reduced the charges, gave him bond money and fixed up a bag of dope as the first payment. We find a lot of dope on prisoners that guys don't search good enough, and I had a bunch of heroin and stuff in my locker. I mixed it all together and flavored it with some powder I found in the janitors closet. I knew the junkie would shoot it up first chance he got. He's better off dead."

"Who made you God!!" I was seesawing from stupid to nuts. "I saw the picture that was on Singleton's dresser. The guy who was 'in the same unit as you were'. '147th. ORD. DIV. That's short for 'Ordinance Division', isn't it? Your specialty was blowing things up, wasn't it Mike?" It was all so obvious, now that I had blundered into the answer. Pape was a Major in the Army Reserves and had access to munitions. He was the one that was seen going into my house. Pape was the person who put the bomb under my bed. This bastard had already tried to kill me. I was getting real tired of that.

"Are my landlord, his wife, and his four children pieces of shit, Mike? Are they garbage who are better off dead? Are your kids more important that his?" I was screaming at him.

"I said I was sorry. They didn't get hurt." He sniffed himself sober. "Turn here," he said and I realized that I'd just argued myself out of more time.

We were at Morse Street and Sheridan Road, one block east was Lake Michigan. Pape didn't have to choke me or poke me with the gun barrel, I just turned right. My mind raced with the overload of information. This man had been my friend, he had saved my neck back there on Clark Street. But he'd also blown up my house. I knew he regretted what he had done and what he was about to do. It didn't make me any wiser to understand it, as I thought it would. The knowledge that I'd searched for had been provided. It wasn't going to do me, or anyone else, any good.

Morse Avenue is wider than most of the other streets up north that dead end at the lake. It was well lighted and lined with buildings. The numerous trees were just budding out so the rain was the only thing that distorted vision. It was coming down so hard that the wipers had trouble handling it. Down at the end of the block all I could see was an eerie blackness. The only thing at the end of this street was a narrow strip of grass and two hundred miles of ice cold water. Lightning flashed out over the lake momentarily, not reflecting anything but the nothingness that was out there.

"Drive up into the park." Pape gave me more directions when we reached the turnaround at the end of the street.

There were no people on the street, dogs would have to wait until the rain eased up. The only cars were parked, crammed into every conceivable space. At the end of the street the sidewalks came together behind the turnaround and led up into Loyola Park. I could just see, when the wipers cleared the window for a second, the ornamental lamps that dimly marked out the pavement as it wound its way through the grass. Not more that a few hundred feet wide at any point the little strip of park ran from Pratt, north to the city limits, with access at each street.

The wagon hesitated when the front tire came up against the curb. I had to give it more gas to force the wheels up onto the sidewalk. The entrance to the park was guarded by a little berm or hill, that the sidewalk cut through. The sides of the opening in the hill, with ten feet of space in between, were fortified by cement walls.

There was enough room between the walls to drive a car or a police wagon through. Even though it was supposed to be for foot or bike traffic only, squad cars or ambulances had to have enough clearance to get to the lake in case of an emergency. Or in case someone wanted to drive up in here and take a nap, as I had planned to do earlier. There were no police cars or people of any sort, in sight. All the headlights showed me was the rain blowing horizontally from left to right.

I had to give it a little more gas again to pull the rear end up over the curb. Once they came up onto the sidewalk, we were rolling steadily toward the berm. Even though there was enough room to fit the wagon through the berm, I ended up close to the left side of the path. Instead of following the pavement, the left front tire started to ride up the edge of the concrete wall. All I had to do was turn the wheel to the right to get the tire off the edge of the berm wall and back on level ground. I wish I could say that I was clever enough to think of it myself, but it was probably because I wasn't a very good driver.

I also don't know what made me give it more gas, it wasn't a plan. My feet and hands were doing things before I could think about them. The left side of the wagon started to rise as the wheel rode up the edge of the wall. "What are you doing?" Pape cried out. It was his turn not to react quickly enough.

Pape was screaming something that I wasn't listening to. I was trying to drive the wagon with the left side off the ground, balancing on the right wheels. The headlight on my side illuminated only the dark sky and the sheeting rain.

The blue and white van cleared the berm, wobbling. I was falling toward Pape holding onto the steering wheel, more for support than to drive with. Through the windshield I could see the wet world begin to turn, tilting sideways, spinning oddly. The wagon turned onto the grass, the left side going higher and higher. It went in an ever tightening circle, like a dog looking for a place to lay down.

When the circle got small enough, or I pulled on the wheel enough, the huge prisoner van squealed and fell over on it's right side with a wet thud. The wheels continued to turn, with no road under them, the engine coughed, then she stopped and just laid there like a dead elephant.

I was still holding onto the steering wheel, though I was standing on the box of forms, fire extinguisher, handcuffs and other junk. Under all that was Mike Pape. "Cassidy! You're dead!"

I heard a muffled cry from under the pile.

"Oh, 'no' I'm not!" In fact, I felt like dancing. I tried to stomp the son-of-a-bitch to death. I was holding the wheel and jumping up and down. He cried out in pain, which only gave me more determination to mash Pape into a little red puddle.

William J. O'Shea

Just as I thought that I'd at least knocked him cold, it was dark and I couldn't tell where he was under all the junk, he grabbed my foot. When he twisted it, pain shot up my leg, and my escape instinct renewed itself. I stopped jumping, trying desperately now to climb back to my side of the cab, which was 'up' at the moment. I couldn't free my leg, it felt like he had my foot in a vise.

The door was there, right over my head. I could reach the lock and work the handle, but I knew I wouldn't be able to push it up and open. Not with my foot held so firmly. I tried to stomp his hands off my ankle with my right foot, but he wouldn't let go. He just kept wrenching my left ankle, I imagined tendons tearing and bones breaking. The pain was intense now, blinding me for a second. Frantically, I looked for another way out.

I let go of the wheel with one hand, afraid to completely let go and maybe fall down, giving Pape something else to twist into a pretzel. Reaching for the window crank, I tried to turn it so I could open the window.

It took me a second to figure out which way to turn it, all the while Pape was twisting my leg off. It hurt all the way up to my hip now, the window was more than halfway open, I could feel the rain on my face. Letting go of the steering wheel I quickly reached up and grabbed both sides of the window frame, and kicked as hard as I could. The effort multiplied the pains that were shooting from my ankle to my back, but he let go.

My right foot found a purchase on something and I got my head through the window. The rain immediately obscured my vision. When I tried to lift myself out of the cab using my left leg for support, it gave way and I almost fell back in. Using only my right leg and arms, I managed to crawl up onto the side of the wagon. It was a long way to the ground from here.

I slipped, or fell, off the door just as a flash and a loud boom came up through the open window. I knew that a .50 caliber slug had followed that flash. When I hit the grass, it was soggy but I still wanted to just lay there and rest for awhile. Then I heard Pape trying to climb out of the wagon. Struggling to my

feet I ran, it was more like a fast limp. Where could I go? Pape
had the radio, and the guns. The rain was coming down so hard
that I couldn't see where I was going. I just limped away from
the lights of the wagon, trying to find a hole to crawl into.

Knowing he would catch me if I ran back up Morse, and
already having been in the lake once this week, I headed south
through the park. I wasn't able to move very quickly, my left leg
was barely holding me up. I couldn't see anything, the rain
washed into my eyes, so I just ran. Suddenly I found that I was
surrounded by a huge clump of bushes. Somehow I had gotten
myself trapped. The bushes were thick, no way to get between
or around them. The only way out was to retrace my steps, back
in the direction of what I was running away from.

When I turned, I saw Pape standing there, ten feet away from
me. One hand was held up to his eyes, shielding them from the
rain, the other was pointing at me. I didn't see the gun, but I saw
the flash when he fired it at me. I was in the air, when I heard
the shot. I didn't realize that I had been shot until I landed in the
bushes. I couldn't breathe, I thought that I had felt my ribs
crack, but these realizations also told me that I wasn't dead. Yet.

I just laid there, unable to move, thinking about dying. Then
I heard Pape's voice. "2472! 2472! We're pursuing gang
offenders north..." His voice transmitted a false panic and he
started clicking the button on the microphone to simulate being
cut out by other units.

"The rain...click...separated from my partner...click...heard
shots fired...click, click..." Pape was setting up the scene for
explaining how I had gotten shot with the gun that had killed
Sung Park. I heard the usual confusion on the air. Units asking
for more information and the dispatcher trying to quiet
everybody down so she could do her job. Who? What? Where?
They wanted to know. I was the only one who knew why.

And I was dying. Actually, now that I thought about it I
wasn't that dead. I realized that I was breathing shallowly now.
I took stock of my situation. I was trapped in the bushes. It

would only be a matter of time before Pape found me and put a few more slugs into me. I prayed for a way out.

'Please, God, don't let me die here in these bushes, I know I'm not your greatest servant, but I'm doing the best I can.' 'By the way, you don't happen to know Claire's grandmother, she had this dream, and I was wondering'...I was losing it.

When I didn't get an immediate answer, I never had before, I felt around my body to see where I had gotten hit. There seemed to be a hole in my shirt, but with all the rain I couldn't tell if any of the wetness around it was blood. I tried to look but I couldn't see anything, then I realized that I was on my back and the rain was blinding me. Rolling over on my side sent pains all through my body, sharp branches and thorns cut into my face and hands. When I managed to wipe the water from my eyes, there was a flash of lightning, and I saw it right there in front of me.

It wasn't a path exactly, or a trail, it was more like a little tunnel in the dense bushes. I didn't know how it had been formed, maybe some animals used it regularly enough to keep it open. Light glistened off the puddle of rain in the bottom of the narrow space. At least it was somewhere to go. I dragged myself through the mud, into the little tunnel and down the path until I found myself in an alley.

My left leg wasn't responding, but I got my right foot under me and stood up. I was in the alley between two of the streets. The backs of the three storied buildings towered over me, lighted only by occasional lamp posts and lightning. It was hard to breathe, it felt like there was a metal band tightening around my chest. My lungs were on fire, burning more with every labored breath.

I looked down at my chest and saw a black hole in my shirt, on the left side. I probed the hole with my fingers, trying to see if it went all the way through my vest, not thinking that if it had gone through the slug would be in my heart. I was rewarded by a marble sized bullet dropping into my hand. The vest had stopped a .50 caliber slug.

"Cassidy? Where are you? Come on, Hop." I heard Pape call out from behind the bushes. He sounded like someone trying to coax a cat out of a tree. He was past crazy. He was desperate, and there's nothing more dangerous in the world than a desperate man. Except when there's two desperate men.

The walls of the brick canyon that surrounded me were high and secure. All entries to the alley had long since been barred and locked. I could hear Pape thrashing around in the bushes, which only left me one way to go.

Stumbling and lurching, I started up the alley. Thunder boomed all around me, magnified as it echoed off the buildings. It motivated me as much as the threat of Pape finding me. Every step was agonizing. Each breath brought stabbing pain, I thought that I might have a broken rib. Holding my ribs and dragging my leg as I limped along, I fought against the current of a small river that ran down the middle of the alley on its way to the lake.

Suddenly I was at Sheridan Road. A busy street with lights, people and safety. I lurched into the street. There was a car going north and I tried to flag it down. I must have looked like the hunchbacked bell ringer. The car almost ran me over trying to go around me. I wiped rain from my eyes with a muddy hand, trying to see. There wasn't a soul in sight. The rain continued to pour down, the storm more furious than ever.

Looking all around me, I was in the middle of the street, I saw a figure silhouetted in the mouth of the alleyway I had just come out of. It was Pape. I turned and fled across the street and into the darkness of the residential streets west of Sheridan Road. I heard Pape shouting and then another loud boom, but I didn't get hit, so I just kept moving as fast as I could drag myself.

I didn't know what street I was on. I thought about going up to one of the apartment buildings to beg for sanctuary, but didn't want to risk getting caught in a hallway by Pape if no one would buzz me in. What citizen would invite a soaking wet, shot, one legged man, who could hardly breathe let alone talk, into their house. I kept going, frantic, pain aflame in my mind.

The darkness was deepened by the rain and the numerous trees that lined the parkway. I still couldn't tell where I was. The street wasn't Morse though, it was too narrow. I could hardly look up because the rain totally obscured my vision then, so I just plodded along grunting with every step and praying nonsense in between breaths. Beaten down by the rain and cowering with fright each time lightning struck, I begged God for help. I prayed for a car to come down the street. If a car came by, I had decided to throw myself in front of it. It was better than the alternative, to stop here and wait for Pape to catch up.

Step, drag, breathe. I couldn't breathe. I had to stop, I couldn't go any farther. I thought about trying to squeeze under a parked car like a wounded dog. Then I realized that I was going uphill. I knew that Clark Street would be at the top of this hill. Maybe another half block. I tried to focus farther ahead, it seemed to be lighter there in the distance. It looked like Clark Street was a mile away. The way I felt, it may as well have been. I followed the parked cars on my left and the buildings on my right toward the light.

Drag, step, drag, then I just stopped. I didn't want to, but my body wouldn't move. I remembered Pape telling me that strength and stamina were what I needed. He had them. Well, he had the strength that's for sure. My strength was gone, did I have stamina? Did I have that thread of human life, that wouldn't break, in me?

The light, that was Clark street, neared as I managed to stumble towards it, then I stopped again. I couldn't breathe and I was getting dizzy. I forced my legs to move, I couldn't feel the pain in my left leg any longer, but it wasn't responding well. I stumbled a few steps and started to fall. Something loomed up before me. When I slammed into it, I realized that I had hit a tree growing in the parkway. I slid down the rough trunk and laid in the mud.

Grabbing the bark where it had split from age, I pulled myself up the huge bole, trying to crawl around the other side of the trunk and maybe hide behind it. Wiping my eyes ineffectively I tried to peek around tree in the direction that I had come from. There he was, coming slowly toward me. He was in no hurry. I wasn't going anywhere.

My whole body, except my head, was concealed behind the tree. I didn't know if he had seen me, but I was going to find out in a few moments. I couldn't stand, even though I tore at the bark trying to pull myself up. Finally, I just let go, slid into sort of a kneeling position and waited. Knowing about when he should arrive, when what I thought was too much time had passed, I risked a look around the back of the gigantic trunk.

Pape was only a few feet from the tree now, but he was staggering. He looked like I must have when I was trying to make it to the top of the hill. He was dragging his left leg, just like I had. I could see him clearly now, Park's .50 caliber in his right hand.

When he was close enough to see me behind the tree, I tried to move, but couldn't. I just watched him come toward me. When he finally looked down and saw me there next to the tree, and our eyes met, I could tell that he was in trouble. He dropped the gun and reached up to the back of his head, with his right hand. I hadn't noticed until now, that not only was he dragging his left leg, his left arm also hung lifelessly at his side.

He didn't fall like I had, stumbling. Pape just collapsed. He hit the cracked and broken pavement next to the tree, falling so hard that he actually bounced. I didn't need to have ambulance '41 here to tell me that Mike Pape was dead. Apoplexy, the old people called it. Stroke, aneurysm, I'm not a doctor, but I knew that no CPR was going to bring Pape back. I dragged myself across the short distance between us.

His face was frozen in a grimace of agony. I managed to sit up next to him, leaning my back against the tree, and took his head in my hands. His terror filled eyes stared up into the rain, no reflex to close them when the drops fell. Putting his head on my lap, I closed his eyes with my middle and index fingers. His

William J. O'Shea

face seemed to relax. There was nothing in this world for him to be afraid of any longer. His case had gone to a higher court.

Figures came running out of the dark towards us. Two men dressed in civilian clothes. I clutched Mike to me as if they were going to harm us. They just stopped and looked down at us. It was the two Russians from the Bagel Nook. The dark red-haired one and the darker bear-like one. They didn't look like ignorant immigrants now.

"Jurkov, sends us." The bear pronounced it 'Yer-cov', the way it was supposed to be pronounced, not the way Jurkov liked to say it. "How can we help you? Are you injured?" The red one said in perfect English. The question was directed at me, it was obvious to them also that Pape was dead.

When I didn't say anything, they started to bend down to check my condition. I waved them off. The red one had a radio and spoke into it. I remembered Jurkov saying that someone would 'be around' and that sometimes deep cover agents ended up 'working for us'.

Not for 'us', I didn't work here any longer. "The gang-bangers," I managed to say, "they went that-a-way." I pointed over my shoulder at nothing and no one.

When they rushed off after my imaginary killers, I looked up from where I sat to try and figure out where I was. There was a tall wire gate across from me. I looked over my shoulder at the tree that I had hid behind, realizing which tree it was. It was the giant Red Oak that I had tried to question last week, the tree that was on Farwell just around the corner from Clark. I was outside the rear gate of Sung Park's jewelry store.

The tree that had given me shelter was the same one that had been growing here for hundreds of years. A sapling when Clark Street was just an Indian trail. It cared not one bit for the actions of men. It wouldn't tell me what had happened last week, but it was willing to give me sanctuary when nothing else would.

We just stayed there, Mike and I. I looked up the length of the huge trunk, its tree sized limbs sprouting reddish new leaves, drops splashing off my face. The rain was just a drizzle now, but it was just enough. As it washed the events of the last week out of me, I just sat there rocking Mike, gently, until someone came and took him from me. I hadn't noticed the lights and sirens, just the soft rain and the easing of the pain.

William J. O'Shea

EPILOGUE

Well, that's the story, Stanley, my account of it anyway. On the other hand, the scuttlebutt and the official account are pretty close for a change. It goes like this: When I spotted the gang-bangers, I jumped out of the wagon and Pape rolled it trying to keep me from being hurt. Then he saved my life again when the gang-bangers shot me. He's received the Medal of Valor, posthumously, and his family will get a full pension.

The reason that I'm sending this, or telling you anything at all, is that the Army is dragging its feet on Pape's government pension. I need you to cut the red tape for me on that. Lori Pape is very grateful for the fund raising benefits that we've had for her family, but it's not enough to raise three kids on. Don't worry, I'll be keeping an eye on them, even though I might be going to St. Croix soon for a little honeymoon.

Let me know as soon as you can get the ball rolling out there in Washington, and thanks for everything.

Yours truly,
Basil (Hop) Cassidy

P.S. All those things I said about you being able to scare the wax off the floor and looking like a big black wolf, are true and I meant every word of it.